THE
BUCHAREST
LEGACY

ALSO BY WILLIAM MAZ

The Bucharest Dossier

THE
BUCHAREST LEGACY

THE RISE OF THE OLIGARCHS

WILLIAM MAZ

OCEANVIEW (PUBLISHING
SARASOTA, FLORIDA

ISBN 978-1-60809-619-0

Published in the United States of America by Oceanview Publishing

Sarasota, Florida

www.oceanviewpub.com

10 9 8 7 6 5 4 3 2

To my parents

THE
BUCHAREST LEGACY

CHAPTER ONE

Bucharest, Romania
April 1993

IT WAS A night like any other night he had known in Bucharest, only
more so. Three years after the revolution that was supposed to have
brought relief to the millions of poor wretches, the city still resembled a celestial black hole rather than a European capital. Other than
the central area of the city, the streets still stood in darkness, due
partly to lack of fuel and partly to the broken bulbs and smashed
lampposts that still awaited replacement or repair. Not much had
changed in the past three years. Cousin Irina, the diva actress, had
been right. It would take a generation.

So much for revolutions.

But this night the darkness acted as a friend to Bill Hefflin. Even
though Romania now classified itself as a democracy and the streets
no longer crawled with Securitate, former dictator Ceausescu's secret
police, Bucharest had become a cauldron of foreign security forces,
racketeers, thieves, and roaming gangs that vied for territory. He had
been warned. Still, the days of Cold War espionage were over. Romania was now a U.S. ally, and Russia was beginning to shed its own
communist history with the election of Boris Yeltsin.

The defector he was to meet was supposedly KGB, but this was no
classic exfiltration. All Hefflin had to do was drive him to the American embassy, babysit him for a few hours, then place him on one of

the American military airplanes, which the friendly Romanian government now allowed to land—and depart—on a regular basis. The Agency had asked him for this favor since he had already planned on returning to Bucharest—his first time back since the revolution—to check on his charitable organizations. They were run by his own teams of American personnel. He didn't trust the government to manage the money without their skimming off the top.

Why had he accepted this assignment? After all, he was no longer part of the Agency, not since he had become a billionaire overnight thanks to Boris's recovery of Ceausescu's offshore bank accounts. Boris, his KGB asset, his mentor, practically his second father. He was amused at how he considered Tanti Bobo, the old Romanian gypsy, his second mother and Boris his second father. How many people were blessed with two sets of parents?

Perhaps he just wanted to replay those days again, for nostalgia's sake. This was actually the second assignment off the books for the Agency since his resignation. The first one had been a simple pickup of a package from a train station locker in Berlin. He suspected that the Agency was trying to lure him back, to appeal to his nostalgia, which they knew was his weak spot. His life was full of nostalgia, though it had been partially cured by his finding his sweet Pusha.

Truth be told, the Agency was strapped for manpower. Bucharest Station had been downsized since the dissolution of the Soviet Empire, an outpost with few risks and fewer rewards, or so he'd been assured. After the Gulf War, Langley's eyes were now focused on the Middle East. Postponing his plans for a few days was no big sacrifice, especially since it allowed him to recapture memories of his clandestine work, which, he had to admit, he missed.

This night promised no such intrigue, however, as he sat in an old Dacia on a cold, gloomy April evening in Bucharest. It began to drizzle. Even though there were no adversaries to elude, he didn't turn on the wipers or the engine, preferring to pretend this was a real operation and thus follow procedure to not divulge his presence. The odds were that the heater of the Dacia wouldn't work anyway. It was the first thing to go, usually within the first month out of the factory, and had to be repeatedly repaired. He had "borrowed" the car from among those parked on a side street and planned on returning it at the end of the night. No one would miss it. Gas was still scarce and expensive.

He spotted a shadow at the end of the street, created not by streetlamps, which were dark, but by the light of the full moon. He glanced at his watch, and it read exactly 3:00 a.m.

The defector is punctual. A good sign.

At first the figure was too far away for its footsteps to match the echoes they created, but as the man drew nearer, they began to sync. He wore a dark raincoat and fedora, as if he had copied an old spy movie. Hefflin had seen the phenomenon before: Mafia leaders spoke like Don Corleone, policemen mimicked New York cops seen on TV series, and lovers emulated seduction scenes from classic movies.

Life copies art.

Hefflin flashed his headlights once to announce his presence. The man quickened his pace. It was just as the man approached his car that Hefflin spotted the headlights entering the end of the street.

What the hell?

His body stiffened; his instincts suddenly stirred by the rush of adrenaline that made his fingertips tingle.

Could they have followed the defector? Or me?

He turned on the engine just as the man got in. He intended to back up out of the narrow street, but another car now turned into the other end.

A trap? What the hell?

He sat paralyzed for a moment, unsure of his next move, or the rules of this new game. Did the old rules still apply? Was he now expected to act like an Agency field operative? Did he have that authority? He needed to make a decision.

"Get out!" he barked at the defector.

"Why?"

"They followed you. Get out!"

"What are you going to do?" The defector sat frozen, his face contorted in horror.

Hefflin jumped out of the car just as he heard the gunshot, the bullet bursting the car windshield.

These guys are serious.

His passenger half fell out of the Dacia, and Hefflin pushed him into the doorway of a building, then turned back and plunged his handkerchief into the opening of the gas tank. As he lit the handkerchief with his lighter, a second shot rang out, this time the bullet hitting the side of the building. He scrambled into the doorway, grabbed the defector, still partly paralyzed with fear, and pulled him inside the building.

The hallway was pitch black; the light bulbs broken. With the aid of his lighter, Hefflin was able to drag the man down the hallway until he found the steps to the basement. At the bottom of the stairs, he pushed through a metal door that led to an alleyway. As they reached the adjacent side street, he heard the explosion. The building windows burst, shards sprayed both Hefflin and the defector and crackled on the cobblestones like fine sleet. A ball of fire hurtled high above the buildings, followed by the cries of men.

He pulled the defector toward a main street where he knew a pay phone stood.

No backup needed, they said. Just a routine pickup, they said. Christ!

He held onto the man's collar for fear he would panic and flee, then dialed the number he had been given.

"Control," a man's voice answered.

Hefflin spoke his numbered code.

"Confirmed," Control said. "What is your status?"

"Pickup compromised."

"Your location?"

Hefflin gave it to him.

A moment of silence, then, "Go to location Alpha 5."

He tried to remember what that meant. He had previously memorized the prearranged pickup spots throughout the city, but that had been three years before, and they were now just a jumble in his brain. Had they even kept the same codes all this time?

"Where is Alpha 5?"

"You are on a non-secure line," Control said.

"Look, the operation was blown. Enemy agents are swarming in the area. Now tell me the fucking rendezvous point!"

There was silence, then Control gave him the intersection of two streets.

Hefflin hung up and dragged the defector onward at a clip.

"Where are you taking me?" the man gasped. Though he was tall and slim, the man now hunched down, his clean-shaven face twisted in fear, like a WWII prisoner being dragged to some Nazi camp.

"A pickup point," Hefflin said. "The embassy entrance will be crawling with KGB, if that's what these guys were. We'll never make it inside."

They picked up their pace. The defector seemed calmer now and was able to keep up, his understanding of the situation having probably eased his fears. Blaring sirens rose to a pitch, followed by fire trucks passing by the main boulevard, then faded again.

"How much farther?" the defector asked. He was beginning to pant.

"A few more blocks that way." Hefflin pointed with his chin, one of the Romanian gestures he automatically reacquired after arriving in his country of birth. The truth was he wasn't sure of the location. He hadn't been in Bucharest in over three years and then only for a few weeks. But the streets sounded familiar from his childhood.

A few minutes later, they reached their destination, a small square where several streets converged. He checked the street signs to make sure. This was the spot. Now where the hell was the Agency team? Then he spotted two cars, idling on different side streets, each with four men inside.

How the hell do they know this pickup location? Were they listening on the phone line?

Another car now approached the square, two men inside. The license plates were of the special format reserved for embassy vehicles. It slowed down to a crawl, the men searching every street corner.

"Is that our car?" the defector asked, the pitch of his voice raised in fear.

The other two cars turned on their headlights and burst toward them.

"It's too late. It's been spotted."

"What are you saying? The car is right there. What are we waiting for?"

"You want to come out of this alive? Then do as I say." He grabbed the defector and pushed him down the dark street away from the square.

"Where are you taking me?"

"Look, the pickup is blown. This has now turned into an exfiltration. I have to get you off the streets." He didn't know any of the Agency safe houses in Bucharest, but he thought of one apartment, if it was still available. A long shot. He dragged the defector along like a parent pulling his child toward the doctor's office.

"We had a perfectly good car in front of us and you refused to take it," the defector complained. Hefflin remained silent and just kept tugging him along.

They reached their destination twenty minutes later. The building felt familiar, though Hefflin had only been there once, in '89. All the windows were dark, as expected in the middle of the night. The front door was locked. Hefflin removed two pieces of metal from the lining of his jacket collar—a remnant from his old days—inserted them into the keyhole, and gently worked them. A moment later he heard the click.

Inside it was pitch black. With his lighter he found the stairs and they slowly climbed to the second floor. He wondered if someone else was living in that apartment now. It had been three years, after all.

Hefflin knelt and used the same instruments to pick the lock to the apartment. As he silently pushed open the door, the smell of stale cigarettes engendered a warm, familiar feeling. By the moonlight he could make out the piano, the Tiffany-style lamps, the red Persian rug. The place had survived unchanged.

He signaled the defector to remain silent, then quietly made his way through the apartment. He hadn't realized how large it was. Besides the living room there were three bedrooms, one of which had been turned into a study, a large kitchen, and a formal dining room where his family's mahogany dining set still stood.

No one seemed to be living in the apartment. A thick layer of dust covered the tables and windowsills. The authorities had forgotten about this place. Many dossiers had been pilfered and burned during the revolution and, apparently, so had the government listing of Boris's apartment.

When he returned to the living room, he found the defector sitting on the couch, smoking a cigarette.

"You lit a cigarette? There might have been someone in here." Hefflin seethed.

"Whose place is this?" the defector asked. "A high-ranking official, by the looks of it."

"An old friend." Hefflin picked up the phone receiver but found no dial tone. At least the telephone department realized no one had paid the bill.

"We'll spend a few hours here, until I decide how to bring you in," Hefflin said. "Hopefully, the KGB will give up searching for you, if that's who they were."

"This exfiltration is becoming a catastrophe." The defector raised his voice. "You don't understand. I have vital information, critical to the survival of your agency. You cannot treat me like this."

"Critical to the Agency's survival? Does the Agency know this?"

"I told them, but seeing how things are turning out, they apparently did not take me seriously. They sent an amateur."

The defector put out his cigarette in the ashtray and stood. "I hope this bungled operation is not typical of the CIA. And you should use the proper term. The KGB no longer exists. The foreign intelligence service is now the SVR." He stomped into one of the bedrooms and slammed the door.

It will always be the KGB for me.

Hefflin lit a cigarette as his eyes drifted to the antique dining room set that Hefflin had grown up with and that his father had sold to Boris when the family had emigrated from Romania. It still stood in Boris's old apartment, shrouded by memories of his childhood that hung like cobwebs.

CHAPTER TWO

Bucharest
1966

HE HID UNDER the table, the embroidered tablecloth that hung down almost to the floor making him practically invisible. There he would play with his toys until he heard the footsteps, the women's voices, and saw the painted toenails that would pass by his hideout—red, pink, orange, like lollipops. The women would enter the last room, his father's office, and the moans would soon begin, low and deep, quickly followed by high-pitched screams. His mother told him not to pay any attention to them, that the women were sick and his father was making them well. He hummed to himself so he wouldn't hear those agonizing cries, while continuing to play with his toys.

After some time had passed, the doors would open and his mother would come out pushing a metal cart on wheels. On top of it lay a shiny basin from which protruded several long, metal instruments. She'd roll the basin to the kitchen then return to his father's office and accompany the woman out. Sometimes his mother made coffee for the woman and they'd sit at the table under which he hid, the painted toenails almost touching him.

But this one particular afternoon, a few minutes after the woman left their apartment, he heard a pounding at the door. For a brief moment his parents stood frozen, silent, as if they could pretend no one was home. Then his mother raced to close the kitchen door where she'd rolled the metal cart with the shiny basin.

When his father opened the front door, he saw three policemen in uniform.

His parents stood aside while the policemen walked directly to his father's office as if they knew exactly where to go. When they opened the door, he could see bloody sheets on the floor. Another policeman rolled out the shiny basin from the kitchen, then lifted one of the long instruments, its tip red with blood.

"Doctor, I have to inform you that you are under arrest," the policeman said.

His mother burst into tears. His father kissed her, hugged him, then put on his jacket and walked out with the policemen. After a while his mother stopped crying and started cleaning the office and washing all the instruments.

His father returned two hours later and said they just had him fill out some forms, then told him to return in three days for a hearing. His mother said they needed a lawyer. How about Trent, the lawyer who lived downstairs? His father shrugged. What was Trent going to do? The evidence was all there.

Three days later his father put on his coat, kissed him and his mother, and walked out. Several hours later his father returned wearing a big smile.

"A most extraordinary thing happened," his father said. "Trent and I are standing before the judge, the prosecutor is ready to present his case, when a man I've never seen before walks into the courtroom. He has the bearing of someone important. He goes straight up to the judge, whispers something in his ear, and the judge's face grows pale. The man then just turns around and walks out. The next moment the judge pounds the gavel and says, 'Case dismissed due to insufficient evidence.' The prosecutor stands up to object that he hasn't even presented his case yet, but the judge is already walking back to his chambers. And that was it."

His mother dropped into a chair and crossed herself three times. "Miracles can happen even in communist Romania."

CHAPTER THREE

Bucharest
April 1993

THE MEMORY HAD come as a flash, a mote of time. His father was never bothered by the police again. No one ever spoke of that incident, as if it had never happened. From the intel that later passed his desk, he learned that all forms of contraception had been outlawed in Romania during Ceausescu's reign. The dictator had wanted to increase the Romanian population, but birth rates continued to plummet. No one wanted to bring up children in that cauldron of hell. Abortion, though illegal, had become the only option, a routine in every woman's life. He remembered that his cousin Irina had once told him that she had had twenty-two abortions that she could remember. Twenty-two, and she was still in the prime of life. He wondered what the faithful in America would say to that.

Hefflin placed the gun on the night table of the second bedroom and stretched out on the bed. He needed to concentrate on the mess he was in, and figure out how to get this insolent defector out of the country. How had everything gone so wrong? The KGB knew the location of the pickup as well as the alternate rendezvous points. The Agency had preset rescue sites throughout Bucharest, the choice based on proximity. Whoever blew this operation, it wasn't an accident.

He slept for a couple of hours like a baby, meaning that he woke up every few minutes, his nightmares replaying the events of that night. When he woke up for the last time, he heard movement in the apartment. He picked up his gun and slowly opened the door. The noise emanated from the kitchen—footsteps and sounds of clanging china. When he reached the door, gun in hand, he found the defector sitting at the kitchen table sipping from a cup.

"I found some Russian tea, old, but drinkable," the defector said. He was fully dressed in a wrinkled, oversized gray suit and gray tie—the uniform of the communist apparatchiks.

Hefflin reinserted his gun in the small of his back, sprinkled some tea in a cup from the open can, and poured some hot water from the steaming kettle.

"What plans have you come up with?" the defector asked. "There will be SVR at the airports, train stations, and borders. I do not look forward to a jab of ricin from an umbrella."

The Russian was referring to Georgi Ivanov Markov, a Bulgarian dissident who had been murdered by the Bulgarian Secret Service with an umbrella that shot a pellet containing ricin, a deadly poison.

"No airports or train stations," Hefflin said. "I'm betting they expect us to drive to Hungary."

The defector smirked. "With what car? You blew up the nice one we had."

Hefflin felt the urge to smack the arrogant little prick across the mouth, but elected to finish his tea.

"I'll be back in a few minutes," Hefflin said. "Just be ready to hop into the car."

The defector spread his arms. "As you can see, I am ready now."

"Clean up the place before you go, including the kitchen." He said goodbye to Boris's prized apartment and the years of memories hiding in its shadows, which Hefflin wished he could garner for himself. "Wait inside the doorway downstairs. When you see me pull up, jump in."

"*Da, da,* I know the routine."

Hefflin returned forty minutes later sitting in the back seat of a white Skoda, two men in front. The defector opened the back door and got in.

"Who are these men?" the defector asked, as if insulted that strangers had been involved in the operation without his approval.

"Friends of ours," Hefflin said. "Hungarians."

"Balzary?" The defector's voice rose.

"You know Balzary?"

"The Hungarian chief of station? Everyone knows him. A wonderful man. Too good for this shithole of a country."

Hefflin bit his lip. *This is* my *shithole of a country, you KGB scum.*

"At least you found a newer car this time," the Russian added. "Please do not blow it up again."

"So this is your package." The driver smirked. He had a Romanian accent. "You should teach him some manners."

"I'm just the babysitter," Hefflin said. "Just get us to your embassy in one piece."

"No problem." The driver chuckled.

Hefflin had called Balzary, his friend from the days of the revolution and a fellow Harvard alum. He had decided to avoid the American embassy now that the operation had been compromised, and the KGB was on the alert for them. They would probably be watching it, maybe even with snipers.

"I'm in the middle of a blown operation," Hefflin had told Balzary from a pay phone. "Need immediate pickup."

Balzary hadn't asked any questions. A team met Hefflin a half hour later and drove back to Boris's apartment to pick up the defector. Balzary's immediate reaction didn't surprise Hefflin, for the Hungarian had proven his friendship during the revolution, even saving his life from a Middle Eastern sniper.

They now drove mostly via side streets, avoiding traffic, which was beginning to pick up now that the sun was rising. The Hungarian embassy was about twenty minutes away, and he worried that they would be intercepted. He didn't know how many personnel the KGB had devoted to stopping this defector, or if they had paid off the local police to be on the lookout for them.

When they turned onto Strada Georges Clemenceau and passed by the Romanian Athenaeum, a warmth spread over him. He remembered his parents bringing him to the famed concert hall as a child, when he had been so captivated by the beauty of the building that he hardly heard the orchestra. Opened in 1888, the neoclassical structure was designed by the French architect Albert Galleron. Ionic columns guarded the entrance, a circular dome hovered above the hall like a halo, frescos depicting important events in Romanian history covered its internal walls, and an expanse of marble, upon which he would slide, formed the floors. The building radiated an image of a Greek temple.

As they sped down Strada Rosetti, his memory already fading, they passed a car with two men parked on the side of the road, then, an instant, in which Hefflin made eye contact with the driver. The car screeched and followed. Within minutes a second car burst out of a side street and blocked the road. Balzary's man veered onto the sidewalk, then took a sudden turn into another side street. The two cars followed.

"Don't worry. I'm a native of this city," the driver yelled.

Ahead, Hefflin now saw a boulevard with traffic going in both directions—the early morning commute. Their driver stepped on the gas.

"What are you doing—are you crazy?" the defector cried.

Their car plunged through the traffic, over the divider, and into the oncoming lanes. Automobiles screeched to a halt, some sliding into each other, others crashing into parked cars.

"Ha! Our car has steel-belted tires," the driver yelled, "and a supercharged engine."

Hefflin saw the two cars following them try the same maneuver. One crashed into an oncoming car and the other stopped before it reached the boulevard. They now took another turn the wrong way down a one-way street, but another car appeared at the other end. Balzary's man flashed his lights. The oncoming car accelerated toward them.

"Where the fuck did he come from?" the driver cursed. "Put your heads down. The body is bulletproof, but the windows are not."

He accelerated toward the oncoming car, a game of chicken. At the last moment they veered onto the sidewalk. As the two cars passed each other, the driver and his sidekick slouched down into their seats. Hefflin pushed the defector flat in the back seat and covered him with his own body. Three shots rang out. The side windows burst; shards sprinkled Hefflin's back.

"We're a block away," the driver called out. "Hold on. It'll be a short landing."

Hefflin raised his head enough to see the gates of the embassy held open by Hungarian security men. Then Hefflin spotted it, another car speeding perpendicular to theirs, aiming to T-bone them. Balzary's man accelerated, heading straight for the open gate. The other car barreled toward them, ten feet away now. Just as their car entered the gate, the other car swished by them and pulled off their rear bumper. The tires shrieked, their car twisted, slid sideways, and came to a stop a few inches from a wall.

"I told you it would be a short landing," the driver said with a chuckle. "All in one piece?"

*   *   *

Aberjan Balzary awaited with open arms and a bottle of *tsuika*, the traditional plum brandy of Romanians and Hungarians.

"I don't want to know how you fucked up your operation or even what kind of operation it was," Balzary declared. "And I certainly don't want to know if it had anything to do with that explosion, which woke up half of Bucharest a couple of hours ago and sent two KGB operatives to the hospital."

"Good, because I couldn't tell you anyway," Hefflin said. "How the hell are you going to get us to the airport is the question."

"Easy. Nobody messes with official embassy cars, especially those carrying military brass. Your people should have thought of that."

"I was told it was a babysitting operation," Hefflin smirked.

"No such thing in this country, even if it's an ally now," Balzary said. "And your Bucharest station is barely able to keep up. They're depending more than ever on our service, but that's another story. We'll need another time to catch up."

Balzary ordered two military uniforms and two diplomatic passports to be created. Within a couple of hours Hefflin and the defector were sporting the uniforms of Hungarian colonels while riding in an official Hungarian embassy limousine with flags flaring, being driven to Otopeni Airport. Hefflin had decided to return to Langley with the defector to figure out how this operation had been so badly blown. They were waved through passport check and boarded the American military plane without further incident. As the plane took off, Hefflin had to admit that he owed Balzary yet another favor.

CHAPTER FOUR

New York
April 1993

THE BURNING WOOD in the fireplace crackled like distant fireworks. Although it was early April, a late-season cold spell had settled over New York. They had fallen asleep on the floor after making love the night before upon Boris's mink coat, their traditional love nest. The fire still warmed Hefflin's skin, almost burning it. Or maybe it was his own internal embers that always blazed in Catherine's presence.

Catherine had let her dark hair grow longer now, unlike when he had first met her at Harvard, though she still wore her eyeliner in the Cleopatra style whenever she desired to make love. Her body glistened in the light of the fire, her skin smooth as velvet, hairless except for that one triangle below her bikini line that she left un-shaved—her signature, she called it. As Hefflin gazed at Catherine's serene face, he wondered how someone could be so beautiful and interesting. How did she feel to be admired and lusted-after wherever she went, to have such power over men, and to know it from a young age? Why hadn't it created a narcissist or a hedonist? All right, perhaps she was a bit of a hedonist, but he loved that about her.

Her lips now widened into a smile. "I can feel your eyes on me even in my sleep."

"You're awake. How sneaky of you."

"I'm still a spy, you know—just taking an extended maternity leave." She opened her eyes and pulled him on top of her. She gave him a long kiss then, as he tried to caress her breasts, pushed him aside.

"It's morning." She stretched, then let out a high-pitched cry. "If we start again, we'll be playing on Uncle's mink all day."

He smiled at her little French accent. "So? We have nowhere to go."

"You may not, *chéri*, but I have a young boy to take care of."

"Jack will be fine with Yvette."

"*Jacques* needs his mother, not a nanny." She kissed him again. "I hope he doesn't want to be a spy. I couldn't go through life worrying, like I did with you for the past two days."

He lay back down next to her. "That sure was a botched operation."

"From what you tell me, you acted marvelously. It's when the *merde* hits the fan that you recognize the great field agents."

"Maybe I spiced up the story to make myself look good in your eyes," he said.

"No, you're too honest, at least with me, and too ready to take the blame. There was a security breach. They were waiting for you at the pickup point."

"That will set the Agency's hair on fire. I'm glad I'm no longer part of it."

She rested her jaw in her palm, her eyes focused on his. "I know you don't mean that. You miss it. Last night you made love like you had been rejuvenated."

She was right. The exfiltration, despite its having been blown by some security breach, or because of it, had ignited his craving to re-engage with the Agency. It had been his only spiritual home before Catherine. Maybe it still was.

"So, I gather you didn't have a chance to look around Bucharest, no other fact-finding?" she asked.

"The plan was to place the defector on the plane and then spend a few days in the city. But fate had other things in store for me."

"It was a silly idea, anyway," she said. "Your father and mother were your real parents. I saw how much they loved you, how they doted on you, spoiled you." She let out a laugh. "Your crazy notion that Tanti Bobo was your real mother is, well . . . crazy."

"No crazier than finding my little Pusha at Harvard," he said. "No crazier than Boris, my KGB asset, being her 'uncle.'"

His little Pusha, the love of his childhood whom he had left behind when he and his parents had emigrated from Romania, now lay beside him in the form of Catherine, a mondaine who had grown up in Parisian high society. It never failed to amaze him.

"You have a fixation, a neurosis." She nuzzled him.

"The story is a bit strange, don't you think? Tanti Bobo gets pregnant at the same time as my mother, then she's ostracized by her clan because her lover is a non-gypsy, a *gadjo*. They burn all her clothes, her name can't be spoken in the clan, any memory of her is erased among her people, and then her father steals the baby. It doesn't figure."

"He grew sentimental."

"No, not a man who declares his daughter dead to him."

She laid her head back down. "You'll never let this go until you find out for sure. Sooner or later, you'll have to go back and find that gypsy clan."

"The *Mandale* clan, in the *Kaldaresh* tribe. It can't be that difficult."

"They're nomads. Who knows where they are now."

"If I set my mind to it, I'll find them," he said.

"If you set your mind to it, you can do anything," Catherine said. "But you're afraid."

He remained silent, considering.

"Well, I always think it's better to know, good or bad, than to wonder for the rest of your life who your true parents were," she said, then turned over and pinched his arm tenderly. "Now let's get up and do our workout before we play with Jacques."

But he couldn't take his mind off Tanti Bobo, the gypsy seer who had foretold the eventual reconnection of Fili, his childhood self, with Pusha, his vernal love who had later metamorphosed into the wondrous Catherine.

CHAPTER FIVE

Bucharest, Romania
1970

THEY WERE SITTING around a small table under the apple tree—his mother, Tanti Bobo, and Mrs. Babescu. Mrs. Babescu, a thin woman with a mustache, drank the last of her coffee, swirled the grounds on the inside wall of the cup, then set it facedown on the saucer to dry. His mother did the same.

As Tanti Bobo picked up Mrs. Babescu's cup and turned it to the light, Fili caught a glimpse of the dark pattern made by the dried coffee grounds on the inside wall.

"I see prospects for a marriage," Tanti Bobo said. "Is one of your daughters being courted?"

Mrs. Babescu smiled proudly and nodded. "The older one, Lula, she has a suitor. He hasn't proposed yet, though."

"Don't worry, he will," Tanti Bobo said. "And he won't ask for a dowry, either."

"What dowry? We have nothing." Mrs. Babescu shrugged. "Those days are over."

Tanti Bobo twirled the cup and bent her head to the side to see by the light of the lamp. "I see a long life for you, with many grandchildren, a lot of happiness. You have a good cup, a happy cup. I haven't seen a cup this good in a long time."

"May God be merciful." Mrs. Babescu crossed herself.

"Now, Fili, let's see what your mama's cup shows." She held his mother's cup up to the light. "You'll receive two letters. One is a sad one. The envelope has a black band around it. A death. Someone dear to you."

His mother let out a gasp. "Who is it? Can you see?"

"No, but it will be painful to you. Your cup is dark except for one area here." Tanti Bobo pointed with a crooked finger. "A second letter will bring you good news. You've been waiting for this letter for a long time. That's all I see."

"It's in God's hands. May he be merciful." His mother crossed herself three times.

"Now, Fili, let's see what your palm shows."

Tanti Bobo opened his palm and held it for a long time, her dark eyes glistening.

"Your life line splits, here." She pointed. "If you take the right path, you will have a happy life. But there will be dangers, not from without but from within. You have experienced love very early, maybe too early. You will experience its loss. Years later you will have a chance to find your love again. If you do, you will be saved." She closed his palm. He didn't understand a word she had said. He suddenly grew afraid and ran after the chickens, whose wild cackling could always be counted on to take away his fear.

Two days later, he found an envelope sitting in the mailbox, a black band around one corner. The stamps on it had pictures of warriors wearing strange helmets and brandishing swords. From Greece. He handed the envelope to his mother who put it on the table and looked at it for a long while without opening it. When she finally read it, she went into the bedroom and cried. His father told him that her cousin in Greece had died.

Three days later he saw Mr. Ciorba, the postman, hobble up the stairs to their house. He was a big man with a limp. He walked the

streets all day delivering letters with a limp. Fili's father said it was
from the war. Mr. Ciorba rang their doorbell and handed his mother
a large envelope.

"I think this is what you've been waiting for, Madame Doctor."

That evening they ate his favorite dinner: schnitzel with mashed
potatoes. He figured the dinner was because of the good news in the
letter, for he knew how hard it was for his mother to find beef, or
meat of any kind. But then why were his parents so quiet? His mother
had a strange look on her face, a faint smile she got whenever she was
sitting on some surprise. His father's face remained calm,
thoughtful.

"We received good news today, Fili," his mother said.

"What kind of news?"

"You remember we've been talking for many years about wanting
to go back to Greece?"

It had been a story repeated in the family for as long as he could
remember. His parents had applied to return to Greece years ago. By
now it had become a running joke. No one expected the government
to ever let them go.

"Well, we were finally granted the visas," his mother declared.

He felt a sense of doom. "We're moving to Greece?"

"Yes, darling, isn't it wonderful?" His mother smiled. His father
ate calmly, his eyes on his plate.

"Can Pusha come with us?"

"No. Pusha is Romanian. Her home is here."

They would leave without Pusha? "When are we going?"

"Our visas expire in a month," his father said, not meeting his
eyes.

"How long will we be gone?"

"We'll be starting a new life, darling, a beautiful new life in a
gorgeous country full of sunshine," his mother said. "And there's the

sea, clear, blue, and warm, with long, sandy beaches where you can play and build castles all day."

Fili felt his schnitzel form a big knot in his chest. "I don't want to go without Pusha."

His father looked up at him with his usual calm. "Now, Fili, I know you love Pusha. But if you still love her when you grow up, you can come back, like a knight in shining armor on a white horse, and sweep her off her feet."

"When I grow up?" He tried to imagine the picture his father had formed in his mind, returning as a knight in shining armor on a white horse, rescuing Pusha from the evil communists, then riding back to Greece to spend the rest of their lives on the beach making sand castles. But no. No! He would have to live all those years without Pusha.

"I don't want to go," he declared.

"It's the best thing for you," his father said. "You'll realize that when you're older."

Tanti Bobo's words came back to him then, and he began to understand. "You have experienced love very early, maybe too early. You will experience its loss. Years later you will have a chance to find your love again. If you do, you will be saved."

CHAPTER SIX

New York
April 1993

AND HE HAD been saved. As he now gazed upon Catherine, he once more thanked Boris in that great spy ring in the sky for helping to fulfill Tanti Bobo's prophesy. He had found his love again—Pusha, Catherine—and he felt blessed.

He marveled at the sight of Catherine as she began the slow-motion movements of the short Tai Chi routine, seeming to feel the Chi energy course through her arms and legs with each flowing motion. Then she repeated the same movements at a whirlwind pace, a fluid frenzy of blows and sweeping parries against a shadow opponent.

Back in her basic stance, she eyed her targets: twelve burning candles, the only source of light, positioned on various objects around the room. She clicked on her stopwatch, then sprang into action. As her body twirled through the air, her bare feet extinguished each flame without disturbing the candle. Coming to rest, she clicked off the stopwatch and stood in complete darkness, staring at the fluorescent dial. Nine seconds.

"I bettered my time by one second."

"Your Tai Chi is impressive, if I needed to put out candles," Hefflin said as he flicked on the light.

"Tai Chi is superior to your vulgar Krav Maga, *cheri*. And it has style." Catherine threw him a kiss.

While most people were aware of the health benefits of Tai Chi, they knew little of Tai Chi's status as one of the most powerful martial art forms.

"The Israeli defense force created Krav Maga for street fighting," Hefflin said, "not style points."

"Krav Maga is an unnatural amalgam of disparate styles, a mongrel," she teased.

"It simply takes the best moves of each form to create the deadliest fighting system of all," Hefflin retorted. "Most of the moves are too violent for sparring, which places me at a disadvantage."

"In more ways than one." She threw him a smile. "You are also forgetting Dim Mak." She had taught him some of the moves of this lethal form of combat, considered off limits even to the most advanced martial arts masters. It relied on blows to precise pressure points, based on Chi meridians, which supposedly rendered an enemy incapacitated or dead. She had learned Tai Chi, and later Dim Mak, from a master who had escaped from China through India with the aid of her father, a State Department attaché at the time. The master later immigrated to France where he established his own following in Paris, with Catherine as his first student and the only one to whom he had divulged the secrets of Dim Mak.

"Are we going to spar or will you keep making speeches?" he dared. "You lost three out of the last five sessions."

"I won seven out of the last ten, but who's counting?"

They were both barefoot and wore shorts and T-shirts. Hefflin raised his arms casually, faked a punch to her face, then swept a foot at her ankles, which she avoided by a quick jump.

"I know all your moves." She grinned. "You can't surprise me."

"Yeah? Do you know this one?" He faked a jab to the right, then followed with a punch to her ribs, which she avoided with a gentle twist of her body, followed by a quick slap to his head.

"Point." She beamed.

He retreated. "Lucky blow."

She stepped toward him, faked a kick, then thrust the heel of her palm toward his chest. He stepped to one side, grabbed her arm with one hand, then pushed her face backward with the other, forcing her onto the mat.

"Two points for a takedown."

"You smudged my eyeliner," she groaned as she looked at herself in the mirrors that lined the walls. "Minus two points."

"Your eyeliner? Is that a new rule?"

"Ladies' privilege."

"Oh, the same ladies' privilege you used when you wore a corset and opera gloves for our strip chess match?"

"Which you lost—may I remind you."

"Only because I was dazzled by your beauty. I still am."

She stood shaking her head in disapproval, then lit the candles once more and switched off the lights.

"I think we should do something different today," she said.

She pulled off her T-shirt, then unclasped her bra and flung if off. A moment later she stood stark naked before him, her skin glistening, the flickering of the candles transforming her into an apparition, a goddess.

"You lost that chess match, even though I used a move that your father taught both of us," she said.

"The hidden bishop. Like I said, I was distracted by your wiles."

"You were a young student then, naïve. My wiles only cost you a chess match. But now you're no longer that student. If you have to confront a beautiful assailant, it could cost you your life." She motioned for him to attack.

He couldn't take his eyes off her sleek, lustrous skin, like that of a seal. He felt his desire for her overwhelm him.

"I can't."

"Then defend yourself."

She swung toward him with her fluid movements—a flickering, swaying shadow—feigned a kick to his groin, then landed a hard blow to his sternum with the heel of her palm. He barely saw it coming, unable to take his eyes off the feline motions of her naked limbs, those pearly breasts that always seemed to smile at him, the alluring darkness below that single triangle of hair. He landed hard on his back, the jolt awakening him from his reverie.

"Get up," she said. "Stop looking at my body as an object of desire. It is lying to you."

As he rose, she swung her foot at his head, which he avoided, then twirled and landed a slap to his face.

"I could have killed you then," she said. "You were still ogling my breasts."

"How can I not?"

She feigned a blow to his ribs, then swung her foot through both of his, which dropped him to the floor. She then straddled his chest, brought her knees on either side of his head, and squeezed.

"Do you want this again?" she dared, fondling the glistening pinkness between her thighs. "This time it will kill you."

She rolled off him, then took her stance once more.

"You must dehumanize your enemy." Her face now all stone. "It is a deadly weapon, a ruthless, soulless machine."

He tried to wipe that alluring form from his eyesight, to see it as an inert object, but his gaze kept dancing all over it. Then he focused on her eyes as a way of avoiding every other part of her.

"Not the eyes," she said. "They will remind you of their humanity. See my body as a stick figure, a computer simulation. Focus on the trajectory of the arms, the legs."

They danced around each other, she with her gentle motions that seemed to make her float through the air, he with the more rugged stance of the deadly Krav Maga. His mind now tried to reduce the movements of her body to those of an inert figure, to distill her limbs into lines, inanimate weapons. She swung her left arm to fake a blow, then turned to deliver another with her right. He read the moves correctly and placed one leg behind her, then swung his arm against her chest to thrust her to the floor.

She lay out of breath, smiling. "That's better."

He lay down beside her, their hands touching. Who was this woman? He had never seen this side of her, the lethal operative. But then he reminded himself that she had taught him how to be a spy while at Harvard. She was now teaching him how to dehumanize an enemy.

She pulled him to her, then showered his face with kisses until he could barely breathe.

"Maybe we should forget Krav Maga and Tai Chi and just suffocate our enemies with kisses." She giggled.

"The guys would beat the crap out of me."

"A bit sexist, aren't we?" She rose. "Same training tomorrow. Time to say hello to Jacques."

* * *

He watched her kiss the boy's cheeks, his eyelids, all the while her own face exploding with pride of ownership, as if having a baby were a rare accomplishment. All organisms reproduce, he wanted to say. It was the one and only imperative that evolution, and God, had imposed on mankind. Go and procreate. Neither God nor Mother Nature seemed to care whether we wrote great poetry or built beautiful cities, only that we passed on our genes to the next generation.

The boy had his lips, thick and pouting, his strong chin with that little dimple, and his dark hair. But the eyes were all hers, dark, large, with long eyelashes. They only needed that Cleopatra eyeliner to complete the transformation.

What hubris! People create reproductions of themselves as if they believe the world needs more copies.

It was clear that he and Catherine viewed the world from different angles, through disparate lenses. Catherine felt an identification with the child, a oneness that he hadn't yet experienced. Even the boy's name was a topic of gentle disagreement. Whereas he referred to the boy by the American Jack, she preferred her French *Jacques,* conjuring images of Proustian Faubourg Saint-Germain soirées. The boy would have an identity crisis—that was one topic he *did* understand. His own veils of personae—the Romanian of his early childhood, the Greek of his parents, and his adopted American one—had created a palimpsest of sometimes contradictory individuals.

His own name was no better. He had been baptized Vasili, an old, proud name that meant "king" in Greek. But when as a child he had tried to pronounce his name, it came out as Fili, so that's what his family called him. In America Vasili translated into William, then Bill. Before going away to college, he had changed his family name of Argyris to Hefflin to avoid being labeled an immigrant. Now he used the alias James Blake for part of his public life. So he responded to Fili, Vasili, William, Bill and James, as well as Argyris, Hefflin, and Blake. Though all this was meant to protect his privacy, it further eroded the core of his identity.

That's how children inherit their parents' baggage.

"What are you thinking?" Catherine asked as she snuggled little Jacques.

"I just love watching you with the baby," he lied.

She placed the boy down on the thick carpet. "He's a happy child, sleeps through the night and wakes up smiling. But you're jealous at all the attention I give him. That's natural. All men feel neglected when a baby arrives."

"It's not just jealousy," he said. "I just . . . don't get it."

"How could you? You can't be a father if you're still a child."

Her words cut through him and he gasped.

Still a child? Can she be right?

For years he had yearned for his lost childhood, and his sweetheart, Pusha, whom he had left behind in Bucharest. But when he had discovered that Pusha and Catherine, his Harvard love, were one and the same, he thought he lived an enchanted life in which he got both loves in one. But Catherine's words had now awakened something that had remained hidden to him. He realized that the little boy in him felt cheated. Little Fili still hadn't found his childhood Pusha, only the adult Catherine with painful memories of the death of her parents and her time in the orphanage.

"How can you say I'm a child?" he objected, though without conviction. "I've had to fight for my life in Bucharest, to kill. Those aren't the acts of a child."

"I didn't say you were psychotic," she said. "The adult you deals with reality just fine. But little Fili feels abandoned."

Yes, she is right. But how will I ever let Fili go?

CHAPTER SEVEN

Virginia
April 1993

THROUGH THE ONE-WAY mirror, Sam Watertown, the chief interrogator, assessed the defector being questioned inside the soundproof room—the deep tenor of his voice; the blank, bureaucratic face; the nonchalant crossing of the legs; the languid dangling of the cigarette, allowing the ashes to fall to the floor rather than into the ashtray on the table. They all alluded to arrogance, even contempt. This initial, soft questioning was only the first step in determining what the man knew, what he offered, how much he was willing to give up, how much he held back and for what price.

He came bearing gifts—microfilm containing the detailed plans of Desert Storm, the operation conducted by the U.S. and allied forces to expel Saddam Hussein's military from Kuwait. According to him, the Russians had possessed this intel before the operation had even begun, and had shared some of it with the Iraqis. Considering the overwhelming victory by allied forces, that information did little to improve the Iraqi military response. While this revelation produced high interest at Langley, the defector dangled allusions to other intel he was not yet ready to discuss. It would be a negotiation, not a seduction with this one. And it would be tedious, like a slow dance to the tune of a third-rate band in some Eastern European underground café.

Watertown was about to turn off the microphone and return to his office when he stopped in mid-motion. *What did the guy just say?* The interrogator, a man in his thirties with only mid-level clearance, had missed it. He was now turning to other questions. Watertown listened more intently. The defector answered the next question, then, in passing, dropped the bomb a second time.

The cup of coffee slipped from Watertown's hand as he sank into a chair. It took him a moment before he ordered the team to stop the interrogation.

CHAPTER EIGHT

New York
April 1993

WHAT WAS IT about mornings that so elevated the spirits of beings, human and otherwise? Even Bentley, Catherine's Vizsla puppy, which she had bought for Jack, pulled on his leash and jumped for joy, as if surprised that a new day had suddenly dawned and it was still alive to enjoy it. Hefflin was aware of the myth—that a dog believes that every time you leave you have left forever and is ecstatic when you magically reappear. Perhaps Bentley thought the same about mornings. But he had recently gained new respect for a dog's intellect after observing Bentley steal a cracker covered with pâté from a party tray on an end table, then seeming to rearrange the remaining pieces to hide the theft.

Catherine appeared to be thinking similar thoughts as she walked beside him on their usual path in Central Park wearing a broad smile.

"Don't you just love mornings?" she marveled. "It feels like the world is washed clean."

It's just a mirage, darling. It's the same world, the same people, good and bad.

He didn't believe in the washing of sins or the redemption of souls with deathbed conversions, a lesson that Luca Soryn, the Securitate sniper, had taught him. But he also didn't want to spoil Catherine's ebullience.

"It's a beautiful morning," he said, "especially since I'm so in love." He kissed her lips.

"Easy, now. Bentley will see us, and he's only a puppy," Catherine said straight-faced.

Central Park buzzed with the usual frenetic activity—young people in business attire hurrying to their jobs, joggers on their way to the running track around the reservoir, nannies pushing strollers while conversing in patois, French, German, or a dozen other languages.

It was their usual morning walk, a time to be alone together, away from Jack, or *Jacques*, who was now with Yvette. After Hefflin's experience in Bucharest, he felt relieved to be in Central Park, an oasis where he felt that nothing and no one could reach him. After landing the day before at Langley Air Force Base and handing over the defector to two Agency men, he felt relieved that he had washed his hands of the whole deal.

Part of their walk took them past the old tree on which a chalk mark used to appear several times a year, the sign that Boris, Hefflin's Kremlin asset, had left a message in the dead drop, a hollow spike planted in the earth. They paid homage to that tree every morning in memory of Boris who had died over a year before, the victim of his dearest companions: cigarettes and vodka. No day went by without Hefflin fondly remembering the last months of Boris's life, spent in their new penthouse facing Central Park, Boris's wedding present, paid for by Ceausescu's offshore accounts. It still left a bitter taste in Hefflin's mouth to accept that money, but Boris had convinced him that he could do better things with it than return it to the thieves that still ran Romania.

Boris's half-serious words of wisdom still made him smile.

"Life is like borscht," Boris would say. "Eat sour cream and just taste everything else."

Or, while playing one of their many chess matches during the long months of Boris's illness: "Beware of the hidden bishop. In life as in chess, it is one unexpected figure that can spell your doom." The hidden bishop was a chess move that both Hefflin and Catherine had learned from Hefflin's father. But knowing that his father and Boris had played chess together in Bucharest, who had taught the move to whom was up for dispute.

"Do you think Uncle is watching us go by his dead drop every day?" Catherine asked. "He probably uses one of those space-time portals to see everything we do."

Her use of the word *Uncle* to refer to Boris, even though she and Boris weren't related, harkened back to old European conventions, where close friends of the family were given the honorific of uncle, aunt, or cousin as a show of love and long-standing friendship.

"I hope he doesn't see *everything* we do," Hefflin said with a smirk, then felt a jab to his ribs.

He didn't know who spotted it first, for they both stopped simultaneously. A black cat standing on the grass suddenly decided to run across their path. He remembered the last time a similar or, perhaps, the same black cat had graced him with an omen. It had been in December of 1989, right before he spotted the chalk mark on the tree announcing a message from Boris demanding that he come to Bucharest to *create* history. Tanti Bobo had brought up both him and Catherine believing in such magical missives, and they both now stared at each other.

"It's just a cat," she said, though they both rushed toward Boris's tree, dragging Bentley along.

The infamous tree now had a diagonal chalk mark from top right to bottom left. They both stared at the line, neither speaking. Bentley pulled on his leash, demanding to know why they insisted on standing still.

"What's it mean?" Catherine asked.

He felt the nausea well up, tasted the bile. She squeezed his arm as she sensed his distress. Was it a joke? An adolescent's vandalism? The mark hadn't been there the day before, he was sure of it. They both nodded at that tree every time they passed it in memory of Boris. They would have noticed.

Boris was dead. No one, other than a few top people in the Agency, knew about Boris's dead drop, and Hefflin hadn't been a part of the Agency for the past two years. The possibilities surged through his mind. Had Boris divulged the dead drop to someone else? That wasn't something Boris would do. Had Boris written down the code to the chalk marks to remember them, which someone had later found? That, too, didn't sound like Boris.

They could just ignore the whole thing, but neither he nor Catherine could overcome their curiosity. He had to see if the spike was there, embedded, waiting to be opened. And, if so, what it contained.

He counted four benches on the right, then three trees beyond, under which the spike would be buried. He knelt beside the tree and started digging with his pen. A moment later he struck metal. He removed the metal spike, about five inches long, cleaned off the dirt, and placed it in his pocket.

Back in their apartment, they stared at the spike lying on the coffee table as if it were a sinister projectile, neither yet ready to open it. He felt their lives were about to change irrevocably, that the smartest thing would be to throw it away, pretend they had never seen the damned chalk mark. But someone knew about their dead drop, about their daily walk along the same path, about their paying homage to Boris's tree. They had been kept under surveillance—not something easily done to two experienced agents.

Catherine finally grabbed the spike and pulled off the top. When she turned it over, a piece of paper dropped out, folded multiple times to fit inside the spike. It now lay on the table like a dead bird, its wings mangled, its body crunched and brittle.

"Go ahead," Catherine said. "I opened it; you unfold the paper."

He tried to swallow, but his throat felt parched. He gently pulled the paper apart and laid it flat on the table. They stared at it—at first not comprehending—then not believing.

Greetings, Vasili,

I am back from my little vacation and I am ready to restart our previous arrangement. I am glad our usual dead drop is still functioning. Send packages when ready.

Boris

They both stared at the note in horror.

"What can this mean?" Catherine whispered, as if fearing the walls to their apartment had ears.

"Whoever did this obviously doesn't know Boris is dead," Hefflin said. "And he's got it backwards, as if *I* had been sending Boris intel."

"But who would even know the code name Boris—which you gave him?" Catherine's face and voice betrayed fear.

Hefflin's soul sank. "Only a few higher-ups in the Agency. Unless . . . Boris told someone."

"That's not something he'd ever do. Your relationship was sacred to him."

Then, who?

"Why do I feel like I'm being set up?"

The world had suddenly flipped overnight. The morning had brought not a bright new beginning but a return to an older, more dangerous epoch.

CHAPTER NINE

Virginia
April 1993

THE HELICOPTER SWAYED gently across the Virginia fields as the vibration of the rotors echoed throughout Hefflin's body, rattling his bones, his nerves. The two men sitting across from him in granite silence had arrived at his apartment at nine in the morning requesting his presence at Langley.

"Who requested it, exactly?" Hefflin had asked.

"The director of operations, sir," one of the men answered.

He hadn't bothered to ask for the reason, for they probably didn't know. He simply kissed Catherine, hugged Jack, and donned a black blazer over his polo shirt and jeans. Whatever the reason, he feared it was somehow connected to the defector.

The helicopter began to descend as they approached a secluded brick house surrounded by an expanse of lawn and, beyond that, acres of woodland.

"I thought we were going to Langley," he said.

"Change of plans, sir," one of the men answered.

As the helicopter landed on the grassy field, he spotted snipers on the rooftop and men in dark suits carrying submachine guns patrolling the perimeter.

He was greeted by the DO's assistant, who escorted him into the library. The large room evoked images of old-world splendor, with floor-to-ceiling bookcases laden with leather-bound volumes, a Persian rug covering a parquet floor, leather couches and club chairs, and a monstrous mahogany desk behind which Elliot Ingram, the CIA director of operations, sat sipping coffee. As Hefflin walked in Ingram stood and extended his hand.

"Thanks for coming, Bill," Ingram said, a broad smile materializing too easily. "Sorry for the inconvenience."

Ingram was a tall, thin man in his fifties with a full head of graying hair, the rugged face of an outdoorsman, and the mannerisms of a patrician. Old Yale pedigree, Hefflin knew, and the man made the most of it. He had been with the Agency all his adult life, the third generation in his family.

"Your boys didn't sound like I had much of a choice," Hefflin said, returning a fake smile.

"Those fellows watch too many spy thrillers. Come, sit down. I need to explain the situation."

Ingram escorted Hefflin to a leather chair. The door opened and two other men joined them.

"These are two of my deputies, Johnson and Benedict. They'll be sitting in on the conversation. Coffee? Tea?"

"Since I left before breakfast, coffee, please—a lot of it."

A pot of coffee and four cups appeared a moment later without Ingram having to order it, so Hefflin assumed the room had ears. The two other men sat on the couch while Ingram took the chair across from Hefflin.

"So, we have a bit of a hot potato on our hands with which we thought you might be able to help us."

"If I can," Hefflin said.

"The defector you exfiltrated from Bucharest," Ingram began.

"You mean the babysitting operation?" Hefflin smiled.

"Yes, we'll get to that. This defector is a Romanian who claims he was part of the old Securitate. He says he was recruited by the KGB while working in an ultra-secret unit created by Ceausescu. The unit was called U0920. Have you heard of it?"

The defector is Romanian? And he called his own country a shithole?

"I'm aware of the unit," Hefflin said. "Ceausescu formed it in the early seventies to spy on his party officials and generals. He was afraid of a coup, so he had any of his underlings removed, or arrested, if they had any contact with outside intelligence services, especially the KGB. Ceausescu's main fear was the Soviets, with whom he openly disagreed when it suited him. He cultivated an image of independence from Moscow that garnered him Western economic help and angered the Soviets."

"Your memory is accurate, Bill, as always. I have to say that we've missed you around here. The Eastern European desk has not been the same without you. After Bush and Yeltsin declared the Cold War to be over, the focus has shifted away from the Russians to the Middle East. I think that's a grave mistake, but that's neither here nor there." Ingram poured a cup of coffee and handed it to Hefflin, then poured another one for himself.

"The defector's name is Rodovan Coianu. A few weeks ago, he walked up to one of our agents in Bucharest who was having his breakfast at a local café and said he wanted to defect. He immediately told our man that he was KGB and had important intel."

"And you decided to bring him to the States without first hearing what he had to offer?" Hefflin asked.

The sting of the implied criticism produced a crease on Ingram's cheek, which disappeared in an instant.

"It's not often we get a KGB walk-in, Bill, especially now that our focus is on the Middle East. And our active recruitment has gone down as our personnel in the former Soviet bloc has dwindled. In fact, we're quite shorthanded, especially in Romania. That's why we asked you to bring him in. We figured it was a low-risk operation, and we had little to lose. If he turns out to be a plant, we can always drop him off at the nearest Romanian embassy."

"It shouldn't have been so complicated," Hefflin said. "Romania is an ally, now."

"It's an ally to a degree. Iliescu still harbors warm feelings toward Russia. He was dragged kicking and screaming into creating a democratic Romania. As you know, he was a classmate of Gorbachev and supports the same ideas of a gentler socialism."

The CIA put an end to that, Elliot, by creating a bloody revolution, ensuring that the people would have nothing to do with socialism. But you don't want to talk about that, do you?

"So you thought this would be a cakewalk? I'm not even in the Agency anymore. And without backup?"

"We thought he was overstating his importance, as defectors often do," Ingram muttered.

"That's obviously not what happened."

"No. And it gets us to what Coianu said in the initial briefing this morning."

"I'm all ears."

"He dropped the name *Boris*."

Hefflin stared at Ingram, unable to breathe. He could feel the eyes of the three men on him, watching to see how he reacted.

"Did he say any more?"

"The chief interrogator stopped the debriefing at that point," Ingram said. "He thought he needed my input first, before he went on. I thought we needed yours."

My input? What are they looking for?

"We don't even know what he was referring to," Hefflin said, glancing at the two deputies.

"It's all right, they've been read in on Boris," Ingram said. "We're all well aware of the incredible run you had with Boris over the years and the valuable intel he provided. Boris, the KGB asset who has never been wrong." Ingram raised an eyebrow. "We all still speak with admiration of your actions in Romania. But, as we all know, Boris disappeared right after the revolution."

He died of cancer in my apartment, Elliot. Leave him in peace.

"He never made contact again, as I have reported to the Agency on numerous occasions," Hefflin said. "I assume that, with the convulsions taking place in Russia, either he's no longer in a position to help us, or he's dead. As you know, I have no way of contacting him."

"Yes, that was the problem all along, wasn't it?" Ingram mused. "He insisted on dealing only with you and on keeping his identity secret. Did you ever find out why?"

An old debt to my father. But that's nothing I will discuss with the Agency.

"No, he wouldn't tell me. It's all in my report."

"And you never found out his identity while in Bucharest?"

"He wore disguises the couple of times that I met with him—false beards, sunglasses, hats."

"Yes, so you stated. And the code name Boris was one you gave him, right?"

"He, or someone acting in his name, first made contact during an opera I attended at the Met. While I was in my seat, someone stuck a piece of tape on the back of my neck containing a microdot. I never saw who did it. The opera was *Boris Godunov*, so, I just gave him that operational name."

"So Boris was only a code name used internally by us?" Ingram clarified.

"Yes. Only the people at the Agency who had access to my file knew that name."

"Our former DO was one of them. He died of a heart attack in your apartment."

Fucking Avery. I poisoned him, Elliot. He threatened to kill me because I discovered he had murdered Professor Pincus, my beloved CIA mentor.

"An arrhythmia, they called it," Hefflin said. "A tragedy. He was a capable man."

He was a murderer.

"But others knew about Boris," Ingram said. "Stanton, the Bucharest Chief of Station, for one."

"We believed Stanton was assassinated during the revolution by the Securitate," Hefflin said.

Stanton was terminated by Avery because Stanton had discovered Avery murdered Pincus and started a bloody revolution in Romania.

"It seems that Boris left quite a few bodies in his wake," Ingram said.

"I don't think we can ascribe any of that to Boris," Hefflin said. "A lot of old debts were collected during that chaos in Bucharest. Stanton must have made a few enemies."

"So, as far as you know, Avery, Stanton, perhaps the director, and maybe the deputy director, were the only ones who knew about Boris," Ingram said. "And you, of course."

"I'm sure there were others in the Agency with top clearance who had access to my file."

"And Boris has been silent ever since you returned from Bucharest in '89?" Ingram asked again.

Should I tell him about the message in the dead drop? Not yet. He's already trying to paint me into some kind of corner.

"I never heard from him again," Hefflin said. He'd repeated it so many times that it now sounded like the truth.

Ingram thought for a moment, then his face blossomed into a smile. "And you got married to a Ms. Catherine Nash, the daughter of a former American ambassador. How is married life?"

"Great, thanks. We have a one-year-old son."

"Congratulations. And you now live in a 5th Avenue penthouse."

Is he hinting he knows something? Why is he tiptoeing around all this?

"My mother-in-law comes from old French aristocracy," Hefflin said. "It's all in my file." Boris had assured him that the false trail of funds he had created from his mother-in-law's estate to Hefflin to pay for that apartment would withstand the Agency's scrutiny.

"Yes, you certainly married well. How did you two meet, again?"

He knows all this.

"We first met as undergraduates at Harvard, then we lost track of each other for some years. We met again in Bucharest, during the revolution. She was there covering the events for *Le Monde*. At least, that was her cover. I later found out she worked for the DGSE."

"Yes, very romantic. You've led quite a charmed life." Ingram nodded, letting the idea float. "Well, to return to our immediate problem, we have a defector who drops the name Boris in our laps—a name which, for argument's sake, only a few in the Agency knew. Now the defector knows that code name, too. We have to find out how. I'd like you to conduct the next round of interrogations."

"Me?" Hefflin jumped up. "I'm no interrogator. You have professionals for that."

"You're the man who knows Boris, who knows all the details. You were his handler, after all."

"I handled nothing," Hefflin snapped. "I was only the recipient of his intel."

"You went to Bucharest to meet him. You're the only one who has actually spoken to him," Ingram insisted. "Look, Bill, just talk to this Coianu fellow, see what he has to say. You may even want to speak in Romanian and perhaps pick up any inflections or mannerism that only a native can. You won't be alone in this. It will all be videotaped and analyzed by our shrinks."

Hefflin remained silent. He knew that they would also be analyzing his own behavior in those videotapes.

"I can't force you to do this, of course," Ingram said. "But I thought you would have personal interest in finding out what this man knows."

"Fine, Elliot, I'll talk to him," Hefflin relented. "But don't expect a professional interrogation." He knew the conversation would reflect as much on him as on the defector.

CHAPTER TEN

Virginia
April 1993

THE DEFECTOR SAT on the living room couch with two Agency men across from him, sipping tea, trading jokes. Even when he laughed his lips barely showed teeth, his gray eyes cold as diamonds. He still wore the same crumpled gray suit and tie, and smelled as if he hadn't yet been allowed to take a shower. When he saw Hefflin, he opened his arms wide in a histrionic welcoming.

"Ah, my good friend who saved my life," Coianu said in English. "Have I tired out the first debriefer?"

"We'll be taking turns," Hefflin said. "It's going to be a long process."

"No problem. I have all the time in the world."

The two Agency men left the room. Hefflin sat in the chair at an angle to Coianu, not wanting to create an adversarial stance so early in the process. A carafe of tea and one of coffee stood on the side table, along with several cups. Hefflin poured a cup of coffee for himself and settled back in his chair.

"So, why don't we pick up where we left off," Hefflin said casually.

"We left off quite abruptly," Coianu said. "It is when I mentioned the name Boris. I must have struck a nerve."

"So, you say you were a KGB plant inside U0920," Hefflin said, ignoring the remark.

"I worked in the unit for the last five years before the revolution, at which point it was disbanded. The KGB recruited Securitate agents—me being one of them—to infiltrate this unit because it interfered with the KGB's attempts to approach members of Ceausescu's nomenklatura. As you know, U0920 was created by Ceausescu to keep an eye on his underlings for fear they would conspire against him. For once he was right."

"What have you been doing since the unit was disbanded?"

"I have been on other KGB assignments in Bucharest, mostly overseeing recruitment of new assets. I had high clearance. That is how I obtained the document about Desert Storm."

"Why did you wait so long to defect?"

"Well, with the collapse of communism in Russia, I figured I might as well cash in on the intel I possessed, before it got stale." Coianu let a smile twist his lips.

"Tell me about unit U0920 during the Ceausescu years."

"The unit had personnel trained in human surveillance, the insertion of listening devices in homes, telephones, automobiles, the usual. My work was a little different than the rest. Since I had two masters, I not only surveilled Ceausescu's underlings for the Securitate, but the KGB tasked me to surveil their own agents."

"How's that?"

"Ceausescu was not the only one who was paranoid," Coianu said. "The KGB was well aware of the CIA's efforts to recruit its agents and was always keeping an eye on its own. The problem was that Bucharest was crawling with KGB agents during Ceausescu's time. Even now, Iliescu turns a blind eye to their activities. He wants to be on good terms with everybody." He chuckled. "So, you can imagine how much manpower would be required to keep an eye on all those KGB agents. What we did instead was bug certain phones we knew these agents used to pass on messages—public phones in certain areas of the city that are not bugged by the Securitate."

"You just used the present tense," Hefflin noted. "Is the new Securitate still bugging phones?"

Coianu shrugged. "Nothing has changed. The old system is still in place. All the phones in private homes still come with microphones installed at the factory, and nobody dismantled those public phones—mostly in the heart of the city—that were hardwired by the Securitate. Whether or not they are still monitoring them is academic. They can if they want to."

"Go on."

The defector leaned back with a cold stare and crossed his arms. "Before I proceed further, I want assurances. Written assurances."

Hefflin bristled at the man's pomposity and felt like slapping him. "What kind of assurances?"

"First, a house, perhaps the size and quality of this one." Coianu looked around the room. "In the U.S. location of my choosing. Second, one million dollars in a Swiss numbered account. Third, ten thousand dollars a month for life. And fourth, a new BMW seven series every three years."

Hefflin could barely control himself. "The little you've given us until now isn't worth anything near that. What happened to the critical information about the Agency that you bragged to me about?"

"I gave you the plans for Desert Storm, which the Russians have had since the beginning. And you have been intentionally ignoring Boris. When I receive these legal assurances, I will give you the rest. And believe me, it will be worth it."

The defector leaned back on the couch and crossed his legs, foot dangling. "I think it is a very reasonable offer, no?"

Hefflin felt his temples throb. "You think you can just walk up to one of our agents, bullshit us into bringing you here, then drop some Russian name just to whet our appetite?"

The defector lit a cigarette and blew out smoke rings. "Ingram seemed to be interested. He stopped the interrogation the moment I mentioned the name."

"He is the director of operations. He doesn't concern himself with names. I think you're just here to start a little brushfire, Mr. Coianu, or whatever your name is. You want us to waste our time digging back years in our archives to find some obscure asset with the ridiculous name of Boris whom no one has heard of."

"I never said Boris was a CIA asset," the defector said.

Hefflin sat silent for a moment, focusing on not letting the mistake he had just made show on his face. He had assumed that during the initial interrogation, when he wasn't present, the defector had named Boris as an asset. It was a natural assumption, but a trap, nevertheless, into which he had just blindly stumbled.

"So, you confirm that Boris was a CIA asset?" The defector smiled, his teeth now showing. "That is why your men stopped the debriefing. And you must be the Agency's Boris expert. What were you, his handler?"

The question cut through Hefflin's gut. He turned away to hide his reaction.

"The reason they brought me here, Mr. Coianu, is that I speak your language," Hefflin said in Romanian. "But your English is perfect. I think we're done here."

Hefflin turned to go.

"Now, now, let us not get emotional," the defector said in Romanian. "It is a chess game, pure intellect. The best game in the world. That is why the Russians excel at it. Let us talk like intelligent men."

"We can drop you back into the hands of the KGB," Hefflin snapped back in English.

"Yes, you can, and you would be doing the KGB a big favor. It will be a long time before another defector knocks at your door."

"A small price to pay. At least we won't have to deal with bullshit artists."

The defector rose. "Come, come, let's take a walk in the garden and cool off. It is too nice a day to stay indoors."

Coianu walked out of the room and Hefflin reluctantly followed. As Coianu reached the door to the garden, one of the deputies rushed out of the library and threw Hefflin a small coin, which Hefflin caught. It was a listening device. He slipped it into his pocket and turned toward the defector, who was waiting for him at the open door to the garden.

"We still have some sun, and it's still warm outside," Coianu called to him.

Hefflin followed the man into the garden, which was just beginning to bloom.

"You do live well in America, there is no denying it," the defector remarked. "I want to have a taste of this life before I'm too old to enjoy it. So, where did you learn Romanian?"

"I studied it in school," Hefflin said.

"No, your accent is flawless. You were born there."

"I have an ear for languages."

"No, you can't fool me. No one can learn a new language as an adult and have no accent. Even though I know English well, I will always have my cursed accent. I started learning it in high school. To not have an accent, you have to learn a language before the age of eight or ten, at the latest, from natives."

"My parents spoke it in the house. I learned it from them."

"Oh? Immigrants from Romania? Now it gets interesting. Where do they live?"

"They both passed away some time ago," Hefflin said.

"My belated condolences." The older man nodded respectfully, then walked on through the garden, Hefflin beside him.

"I think I need to pull up my skirt a little higher, to show some leg," Coianu said. "The truth is, I do not require any written contracts. You can always tear them up later." He shrugged. "I just wanted to see whom I was dealing with."

"We'll give you what you deserve depending on the intel," Hefflin said.

"All right, then." The man looked directly into Hefflin's eyes. "I am here to tell you that you have a KGB mole inside the CIA."

Hefflin felt a frigid wave pass through him. A mole in the CIA was what everyone always worried about. To have a mole inside the opposite camp was the Holy Grail of any intelligence service.

"How do you know this?"

"First of all, I am higher up in the KGB than my position at U0920 would imply. As I began to tell you, U0920 had listening devices in some of the public phones in the outskirts of Bucharest that the KGB agents used to communicate. One day, I intercepted a conversation. Two men. The one in Bucharest identified himself as Boris, and asked when the next parcel would be delivered. The other man said he had it ready and that it would arrive in two days at the usual place. The man then asked if the customary sum had been transferred to his account, and Boris said yes."

"How do you know the asset was CIA?" Hefflin asked.

"Because the other man's final remark was that this would probably be the last parcel for a while because, and I quote, 'Avery is getting suspicious.'"

Avery! The previous director of operations.

The defector's words felt like a body blow.

"When did this take place?"

"A week before Ceausescu's execution."

When I was there, and the entire country was going up in flames.

Hefflin couldn't breathe. It felt as if the dead weight of Boris had just dropped on his chest.

"Do you have anything to corroborate what you're telling me?"

Coianu reached for his left shoe, pushed on the heel, and slid it open. From inside he removed a rolled-up piece of paper.

"This is a copy of a wire from Moscow, intended for the KGB chief of station in Bucharest. It is dated March 2, 1993, a little over a month ago."

Hefflin unrolled the paper, then unfolded it. It was written in Russian.

"I can translate it for you." Coianu looked down at the paper. "It says: 'Our agent, whom the Americans know as Boris, reports that his asset is getting nervous. Prepare exfiltration plans in case asset requests it.'"

Coianu reached into Hefflin's jacket pocket, removed the listening device, then squeezed it tightly in his hand to block the sound of their voices. Switching to Romanian, he said, "If Boris was a CIA asset, as you admitted, then he was a triple agent, and his handler is the prime suspect as the mole inside the CIA. If I were him, I would disappear, if it is still possible." He opened his hand and let the listening device drop back into Hefflin's pocket.

CHAPTER ELEVEN

INGRAM STOOD FACING the window of his office, searching the Virginia fields beyond for God knows what. He had been smoking one cigarette after another for the past ten minutes, pacing, then stopping before the window again. Hefflin and Ingram were now alone, the assistants excluded from this meeting, an ominous sign. They had been driven to Agency headquarters in separate cars, the interrogation of the defector apparently over, at least for the moment.

"An intelligence service—any of them, take your pick—is rife with rumors," Ingram said, still looking out the window. "The most common one is that they have a mole inside their ranks. Understandable. After the debacle in MI6 with the Philby gang, everyone became paranoid. It's the one thing an intelligence service fears the most. It exposes all the operations, assets, everything. In the CIA, it actually goes way back to Angleton, who became obsessed by the idea of a mole. He almost destroyed the Agency searching for one." Ingram was referring to James Jesus Angleton who had served as the chief of counterintelligence from 1954 to 1974, a time of great upheaval for the CIA.

Ingram took a drag from his cigarette, then dropped it in an ashtray and lit another.

"What I'm going to tell you has to remain between us," Ingram said. "Only a few people in the Agency know about it, for obvious reasons. Over the past few months, we've received intel from several assets confirming that the KGB has obtained some of our most sensitive documents. Most of it is technical material—specifications of weapons systems, strategic plans, Navy operations in the Middle East, and now, from our Mr. Coianu, our military plans in the Gulf War. So, we've suspected for months that we have a mole, and the defector has now confirmed it."

Ingram ground his cigarette in the ashtray as if crushing a bug, then turned to Hefflin. "On top of it, Mr. Coianu now tells us that the Russians not only know the name Boris, but that Boris is the handler of that mole inside the Agency."

"I don't believe it," Hefflin said. "Boris gave us superb intelligence, which has never been proven false. Besides, Boris is a common name."

"There are no coincidences in our business, Bill. There can't be two KGB agents with the code name Boris. As far as the intel Boris gave us, yes, we could verify much of it through other means, but much of it we could never verify because we didn't have any other asset with Boris's unique access—minutes of Politburo meetings, Gorbachev's personal notes, secret meetings between Gorbachev and Middle Eastern leaders—the list is long."

"What, exactly, are you saying, Elliot?"

"I'm saying that the defector's cable, if real, is forcing us to reexamine the entire history of Boris."

"No, Elliot. You can't believe that Boris was a double agent."

"A triple agent, actually. A KGB agent who we thought was spying for us but was actually working for the KGB all along, and handling a mole in the CIA to boot. Maybe he was feeding us some true intelligence, which we could verify, buried among a slew of false intel, which he knew we could never verify."

The two men remained silent; their eyes locked.

"That reasoning makes me the prime suspect as the mole," Hefflin said.

"I'm afraid it does."

Hefflin did not break eye contact. "I'm not the mole, Elliot."

Ingram turned back to the window. "I know you're not, Bill." A definitive statement.

Hefflin hesitated, suspicious. "Why are you so sure?"

"Because Avery was not the only one who had a friend in the National Security Counsel."

Hefflin felt his heart pounding in his temples. "How's that?"

"I saw the fax you sent to the National Security Advisor when you returned from Bucharest at the end of the revolution, before Avery destroyed it. In it you implicated Avery in the murder of Professor Pincus and of the Bucharest chief of station, Stanton."

Hefflin, still a Boy Scout at the time, had thought that he could force an investigation by faxing intelligence to both Avery and the president's national security advisor incriminating Avery in the murder of Pincus and Stanton

"You know about that?"

"And then I assume Avery appeared at your apartment to silence you, maybe even kill you. I don't know how you did it, but I know Avery didn't conveniently die of a cardiac arrhythmia." Ingram chuckled.

On a gut instinct, a whim, Hefflin decided he had to trust somebody. "A poison, a present from Boris."

Ingram nodded. "I'm not surprised. The Russians have elevated poisoning to a fine art. You were an analyst, thrown into the role of a field agent against your will. And you uncovered things about the revolution in Romania that the Agency needs to keep secret. Avery's killing Professor Pincus, your recruiter and mentor, to egg on the president to instigate a bloody revolution, and then killing Stanton because he uncovered Avery's actions, went beyond the limits, even for us. I'm sure he also threatened to kill you. You had no choice. He got what he deserved." Ingram kept his gaze out the window. "I still can't stop admiring you, Bill. Most agents would have folded."

Hefflin sat silent, not quite believing what he was hearing. A heavy weight lifted off his chest. He could breathe again.

Ingram put out his cigarette and poured himself some coffee. "You know what I like about you, Bill? You don't want anything—not wealth, which you already have; not status; not power. After your years of running Boris and your tour in Bucharest, you could have had your pick of positions in the Agency. Instead, you just walked away. As far as I'm concerned, you've proven your loyalty to this Agency and this country."

"Thank you."

"Don't thank me until you hear what else I have to say. The Agency is in a difficult spot. We have a mole with high clearance, able to steal vital strategic national secrets. So, what are the possibilities? A) The defector is telling the truth: he heard Boris's name in a phone conversation talking to the mole and the cable he showed us is real. Conclusion: Boris was feeding us bullshit all along while running a mole inside the Agency. B) The mole found your operation with Boris in our files and informed the KGB, which then sent this de-fector to make us doubt everything that Boris ever sent us and to implicate you as the mole, thus deflecting away from the real one. C) Boris was caught, tortured, and spilled everything, then the KGB sent the defector to do as in B. Options B and C mean the defector is a KGB plant, sent here to set our house on fire."

Ingram brushed back his hair, as if clearing the cobwebs from his brain. "So, now we have to narrow down our suspects from the list of our Agency personnel with high enough clearance to have had access to the Boris files. Unfortunately, in an organization as large as ours, that's more people than the short list we spoke about before—on last count, over six hundred."

"What?" Hefflin gasped. "How the hell does the Agency keep any secrets?"

"Like the Brits before us, we've become too complacent and too large. We also lack imagination. We don't believe anyone, especially someone in the Agency, could possibly prefer communism over democracy. After all, communism is what we've all been working to combat all these years. But money, well, that's something else. Money can corrupt any of us, especially those that have a grievance or a personal problem. So, we've recently created a special unit that is trying to narrow that figure down." Ingram sipped his coffee, momentarily lost in thought. "And besides the damage, we also have the added problem of knowing whom to trust. That's the destructive consequence of suspecting there's a mole. Everyone with that level of clearance becomes a suspect. It rots the Agency from within. That's what happened during Angleton's day, which finally drove him out of office."

Ingram hesitated for a moment, then seemed to make a decision. "Which brings us to your botched exfiltration. The NSA detected a telephone call from a pay phone in Washington, D.C. to a number in Bucharest two days before you flew there to pick up the defector. I believe our mole made that call to inform the Russians about the exfiltration. The mole probably didn't know the defector's identity or the KGB would have arrested our Mr. Coianu before he even got to you."

"That explains it," Hefflin said. "The KGB even knew the emergency rendezvous locations the Agency uses. How much does that narrow down our search?"

"A bit," Ingram said. "But that kind of information is available to most of the senior staff, not to speak of some NSA personnel."

Ingram pulled out a bottle of Johnnie Walker Black from his desk and poured himself a glass. His face twisted as he gulped down his drink.

"I need someone I can trust, Bill, someone beyond reproach. The irony is that that person is also the number one suspect."

Hefflin felt the walls closing in on him.

"Bill, you have a talent for field work. You proved it numerous times in Bucharest and with Avery. I need you. The Agency needs you . . . the country needs you. We have to rid ourselves of this vermin before he destroys us all."

"What are you asking me?"

"We have to find Boris. He's been silent for three years. Your mission, should you choose to accept it"—Ingram let out a low chuckle—"is to return to Bucharest, find out about unit U0920, and check out the defector's story. Then find Boris."

Boris has been dead for over a year.

"And if I find him?"

"Bring him in, if possible. If not, eliminate him."

Do I tell him? It would open up a Pandora's box—my father's saving Boris's life at Stalingrad, the many ways Boris tried to repay his debt, his reuniting me with Catherine, finding and then giving me Ceausescu's billions, and his staying in my apartment during his last months on earth. Most importantly, they'd know that I've been lying to them all these years. They'd never trust me again.

"Bucharest is still the center of this whole mess, Bill," Ingram said, seeing the dejection on his face. "The defector is from Bucharest, U0920 is in Bucharest, and Boris was last seen in Bucharest. From what you've told us, Boris spent decades in Bucharest, off and on. That's where you have to pick up the trail. There have to be people there who know him, under whatever alias he uses. You're the only one who met him, who could recognize his facial features, how he walks and talks, despite his disguises. You're the only one who can do this, Bill."

"If the mole told the KGB about Boris, then they might also know I was his handler," Hefflin said. "They'd want to find out what Boris gave me and tell them his identity. Since I never knew it, the mole doesn't know it, so the KGB doesn't know it either. But they may think I do. I may be walking into a trap."

"Going after his handler is beyond the pale, even for the KGB," Ingram said. "The KGB knows how the Agency works. It works the same as theirs. The handlers don't analyze the intel, and the analysts don't know the identity of the handler's assets. They wouldn't expect you to know anything about Boris's intel."

Hefflin tried one last appeal, to Ingram's heart, if the man had one.

"Elliot, I have a family now, a beautiful wife whom I love and a young boy. My life is no longer just my own to use as I see fit."

"You may not have a life at all if you don't find Boris and our mole," Ingram said. "Look, Bill, I may trust you, but the wolves in the Agency want blood. If we don't find the real mole, you're the obvious suspect, we both agreed on that. As I see it, you have no choice."

Bucharest. Boris. I thought that part of my life was over.

Ingram settled behind his desk and began writing with his fountain pen on official Agency stationary, after which he stamped his seal. When he finished, he looked up at Hefflin.

"This is a letter signed by me stating that you are acting on my orders and directs anyone in the Agency to follow your instructions. You may remember Cardinal Richelieu in *The Three Musketeers* writing a similar letter, a *carte blanche,* for Milady, his agent." He chuckled. "It will open all doors to any corner of the Agency." He handed the paper to Hefflin. "By tonight you'll have everything you need in a safety deposit box at this bank in New York—a Beretta, in case you don't have one, a diplomatic passport, money in various currencies, and instructions on deposit boxes in banks around the world with similar items." He handed Hefflin a card with the name of a bank in Manhattan and a safety deposit number with a code. "Welcome back to the fight. This time I know our side will win."

Hefflin acknowledged the line from *Casablanca* with a smile.

"By the way, there's an international business conference starting in Bucharest tomorrow. That may be a way for James Blake to rub some elbows and introduce himself as an American businessman. I'll sign you up before you get there." Ingram stood. "Now, I want you to meet the head of the special task force." He pressed the button on his desk phone. "Ask Reggie to come in."

A moment later the door opened and in stepped a figure Hefflin knew.

"Tyler?"

Reginald Tyler, the head of *The Three Musketeers*, his Fly Club friends at Harvard whom Pincus had also recruited into the Agency.

CHAPTER TWELVE

Langley
April 1993

"GOOD TO SEE you, Hefflin," Tyler said as he shook Hefflin's hand enthusiastically.

"You're leading the task force?"

"They couldn't find anyone else stupid enough to take the job," Tyler said, then looked up at the DO.

"You two get reacquainted outside," Ingram said. "I'm sure you have a lot to catch up on."

As they left Ingram's office, Hefflin focused on the face of the young man he'd known at Harvard who, along with Pincus, had recruited him into the Agency. It now had some new wrinkles, and his body movements had a certain gravitas. Unlike Hefflin's analyst path, Tyler had chosen to be a field agent from the start, and Hefflin felt a little jealous. Everyone knew that the way to acquire power in the CIA was to join the operations directorate. No analyst had ever been promoted to a top-level position.

As they walked down the corridor, Tyler gave Hefflin a quick summary of his life during the past few years. He had spent considerable time in the field offices in Rome, Athens, and Mexico City, until he was promoted to be the deputy chief of counterintelligence. He was married twice and divorced twice, no children, with a home in Virginia.

"I met my second wife in Mexico City," Tyler said, "where I was posted for two years. Her father is a wealthy businessman. I thought I lucked out, but she didn't see it that way." He gave an apologetic smile. "I guess it's the job. No woman likes her man to keep secrets from her. You?"

"Married, one boy," Hefflin said.

"Congrats. Where did you meet her?"

"Harvard. Her name is Catherine . . . Nash."

Tyler stopped in his tracks. "No. Really? But I thought she dumped you when she graduated."

"We met again later," Hefflin said. "It's a long story, for another time."

"That's great, Hefflin. You two were quite an item. Thought you'd never get over her, and I guess you never did."

They started walking again.

"Listen, why don't we have lunch and discuss this whole project I'm supposedly heading," Tyler said. He suggested the Agency Dining Room, which only served lunch for top-level staff.

It resembled a trendy café, complete with tablecloths, wicker chairs, and waiters with security clearances. The chef had been "borrowed" part-time from one of the top restaurants in D.C. in order to create a cultivated oasis inside the secretive walls of Langley. Since Hefflin had been stationed in New York, he had never taken advantage of the culinary benefits of CIA headquarters.

"The food is quite good here," Tyler said. "Try the soft-shell crabs. They have this incredible sauce."

Hefflin once more felt like an outcast, a former analyst from the New York outpost being feted by an insider at the company dining room.

"You must have luxuriated in great restaurants all over the world," Hefflin said.

"Oh, sure. I was fattened for two years in Mexico City by my wife's family. Gained twenty pounds and hated to leave. But in our line of business, eating at a public restaurant isn't that much fun. You always think someone's watching you, and most of the time you're right." Tyler laughed.

There was something about Tyler that didn't seem quite right to Hefflin, a nervousness, a constant shifting in his seat and waving of his arms, which Hefflin attributed to Tyler having spent time abroad in places where they spoke with their hands, and to the constant anxiety that came with a field job.

After they ordered, Tyler cleared his throat and adopted a more serious demeanor.

"I've been trying to get a handle on this molehunt, which, I don't have to tell you, isn't going to be a trivial matter."

"How are you going about it?" Hefflin asked.

"Our first task was to catalogue our losses," Tyler said. "And there have been plenty. Then we started to figure out who in the Agency had access to that information. We began with over six hundred personnel, but we've recently been able to narrow it down to about two hundred and twenty."

"I see your problem," Hefflin said. "This sounds like it will take months."

"More like years, in my opinion," Tyler said. "And now there's this defector. From what I've been told, he mentioned Boris, the asset you ran."

He knows about Boris? Of course he does. He has reviewed everyone's files, part of his job.

"It's a code name I gave him," Hefflin said. "I never found out his real name."

Tyler nodded. "Strange, isn't it? Where is Boris now?"

He is dead, poor fellow. Let him rest in peace.

"He never made contact again after I returned from Bucharest. Then I left the Agency, and that was that. I assume he either left the KGB or . . . was caught and executed."

Tyler rubbed his chin. "And the defector claims that Boris was somehow involved with the mole we're hunting for?"

"You were listening to my interview with him, I gather," Hefflin said.

"No, I was just quickly briefed on it. So how the hell do you explain it?"

"I can't," Hefflin said. "All I know is that Boris always gave us great intel. He has never been wrong."

The food arrived, and they ate in a silence pregnant with Tyler's unspoken insinuations. When they were finished and the table cleared, Tyler leaned toward him.

"You see how this puts you in a peculiar position, don't you, Hefflin? Besides having access to all the intel, you were Boris's handler."

"You know analysts don't have access to the names of assets or operations," Hefflin said. "The intel we get is scrubbed. As for being Boris's handler, I handled nothing. He just delivered intel whenever he chose."

"True." Tyler nodded again. "Still, until the real mole is found, you have to be considered the prime suspect."

"Well, then, you'd better find the mole real fast."

"Trying to, believe me. But, like I said, it may take a while. In the meantime, they may want you to take a polygraph."

A polygraph! I'll never pass it, not with everything I've hidden from the Agency. And who is they? Would Tyler ask for one?

"If they do, then I'll take it. I have nothing to hide," Hefflin said.

Tyler let out a satisfied sigh. "Well, good, then. I'm sure you'll pass with flying colors. This may all be a fool's errand in the end."

Hefflin let the silence settle.

"I mean, there may be no mole," Tyler said. "The KGB probably heard the name Boris somewhere else—foreign assets are notorious liars and often play a double or even triple game. I've seen plenty in my time. And the KGB constantly intercepts our communications, like we do theirs. Then they sent this defector to screw with our heads."

Hefflin nodded, ostensibly agreeing. But Tyler was dancing from one extreme possibility to another, practically accusing him of being the mole and then suggesting that the mole did not exist. Hefflin's head was spinning. He needed to end this conversation.

"Thanks for the lunch, Tyler. And good luck in your molehunt." He stood.

"Where are you off to?"

"I have a wife and child waiting for me. Let me know what you find."

With that Hefflin left the dining room, then the building, relieved that he was no longer a part of it, just a part-time field agent brought in for special operations, if that. But he knew his relief was temporary. Both Ingram and Tyler were right. For the time being, he was the obvious suspect.

CHAPTER THIRTEEN

Langley
April 1993

Elliot Ingram sat at his desk, pondering everything Hefflin had told him. He trusted the man and liked him, and he had faith in his own instincts. But his belief in Hefflin had to be kept secret, even from his most immediate people. And he had to test his own prejudices. If he was wrong, he didn't want any misguided loyalty to come back and bite him.

A knock on the door, then Tyler walked in.

"So, how was lunch?" Ingram asked.

Tyler sat facing him, a look of discomfort on his face. "He seemed fine, at ease, confident. I pressed him several times about Boris's identity, that being his handler made him the prime suspect, and he seemed to take it all in stride."

"Did you talk about his wife?"

"I asked him how he met her again after she left him in college, and he just said it was a long story."

"No mention of her money?"

"No, we didn't get into that."

"Did you ask him about a polygraph?"

"I brought it up, and he said he had no problem taking one. I really think we're barking up the wrong tree."

"Why? Because he almost got killed bringing in the defector? We only have his word for what happened."

"The car blast was heard throughout Bucharest," Tyler said, raising his voice. "And we have the report from Balzary's men. Everything Hefflin told us was accurate. He's not the mole. I've known the guy for years. He's got a stellar record. The intel from Boris is massive and has never been false. If you suspect him, why did you bring him in to interview the defector?"

"To see how he would handle it. It's all on film. The shrinks are analyzing it as we speak—body language, facial tics, the works. In the meantime, I want you to familiarize yourself with everything in his file. Concentrate on Boris, especially regarding the operation in Bucharest." Ingram gestured to the file on his desk.

Tyler stared at the file, a bitter scowl on his face. "I've already done that."

"Look, I know you guys were friends at Harvard, that you and Pincus recruited him. You have to put all that aside. If you can't, I'll get someone else."

"No, no, it's not a problem," Tyler said. "It's just that having been Boris's handler immediately makes him the prime suspect. It's too obvious."

"Sometimes the obvious answer is the right one."

Tyler touched the file as if it were a holy document. "Where is he going now?"

"I sent him to Bucharest to look into this unit U0920 the defector mentioned and verify his story. And to search for Boris."

"And if he finds him?"

"Bring him in—or eliminate him."

Tyler fiddled with a paper clip. "The thing is, we don't have proof that any of Hefflin's story with Boris is true, going back years."

"That has always been the problem," Ingram said. "As long as great intel kept coming in, we took his word about Boris."

Tyler's face twisted in conflicting emotions. "In Bucharest he may just disappear."

"No. His wife and child are in New York. As long as they're here, he's not going anywhere."

As Tyler left the room, Ingram sat back and tinkered with his fountain pen. He was taking a big chance on Hefflin. Tyler was right. No one could confirm anything Hefflin had told the Agency about Boris. As far as anyone knew, Hefflin and Boris could still be in contact. Although Hefflin hadn't been officially in the Agency for the past two years, he had been allowed to keep his security clearance in the hope that he would return to the Agency. Good field agents fluent in an Eastern European language were not easy to find.

I want to trust my instincts, Bill. Don't prove them wrong.

CHAPTER FOURTEEN

Flight, New York to Bucharest
April 1993

FIND UNIT *U0920, then find Boris, Elliot Ingram said. Bring him in, if possible. If not, eliminate him. But Boris is already dead. And despite Elliot's assurances, I am still the prime suspect as the mole.*

He swirled his Johnnie Walker Black, then sipped some more of it. Through the window of the plane, he could see only mountains of cumulous clouds below—primordial creations of Biblical proportions, a frightening sight, one to which he had never quite grown accustomed.

He had decided to fly Delta, which was now offering service to Bucharest. He didn't cherish another experience with TAROM, the Romanian airline, though he assumed that their cabin crew were no longer members of the Securitate. But who knew? The Securitate still existed, though it had since been split up into several discreet units and renamed. Among them was the SRI, the counterespionage unit, and the SIE, the foreign intelligence service. He knew he would never get used to the new names. To him, it would always remain the Securitate, and the new Russian SVR would always be the KGB. He realized that Ingram felt the same, for Ingram had also used the term KGB in their discussions.

His diplomatic passport was under the name of James Blake, a wealthy American businessman who had established a foundation to help Romanian orphans, now part of the State Department's effort to improve economic relations. He sported a three-day-old beard and had dyed his hair a dark blond. Together with his tortoiseshell glasses, he hoped these changes would be enough to avoid being recognized as the former diplomatic attaché who had visited Bucharest in '89.

His mind returned to the abysmal orphanages, some of which had been rehabilitated by his foundation, though most were still left untouched. Catherine had spent several months in one of them after her parents' death, the thought of which always made him cringe. But the problem was too widespread and the new Iliescu government too strapped for money and too disinterested to tackle the broader issues of poverty and social disruption that capitalism had brought.

His efforts now also included convincing Western countries to adopt some of those children, an effort that had only been partially successful. Romanian orphans had acquired a reputation for being damaged by their atrocious treatment. Some children had even been returned because of their unruly behavior or inability to adapt. He wondered how prepared those generations of damaged Romanian children were for the new capitalist system.

He landed at Otopeni Airport late in the afternoon. When he had arrived a few days before to babysit the defector, it had been in the middle of the night, the airport empty, the streets dark. Under daylight, he could now view the airport properly. It was the same structure but a very different scene than the one he had experienced under the communist regime. Instead of the single Russian Aeroflot plane parked on the tarmac, the airport now bustled with planes from all over the world. Gone were the military guards carrying submachine guns. Gone were the soldiers standing like caryatids at each corner.

After picking up his luggage, which contained several expensive suits that would bolster his cover as a wealthy businessman, he proceeded to the passport check. In '89 a smug soldier had demanded a pack of Kents. This time he was just waved on with a cursory glance at his diplomatic passport. The Romanian economy needed foreigners to spend precious dollars, and the orders had obviously come down to make the process pain free.

He passed through the crowd in the arrivals terminal with his rolling valise and exited the building. The bright sunshine of an April afternoon did not diminish his disappointment. The parking lot was still filled with the same domestic automobiles, a sea of Dacias, in black and white, the only colors available, with an occasional Czech Skoda and Russian Pobeda. He had obviously expected too much to change too quickly.

There was no embassy car waiting for him this time. The Agency did not want Bucharest station to treat Hefflin as a member of its staff. James Blake was simply a wealthy businessman working with the State Department to increase trade and investment in Romania, which explained his diplomatic passport. He, thus, boarded a taxi and told the driver in intentionally broken Romanian to take him to the Athénée Palace, where he had stayed in '89. He wanted to see what, if anything, had changed in that once regal hotel that had been so besmirched by the communists.

"How is Bucharest after the revolution?" he asked the driver.

"Ah, worse than ever," the driver answered. "Now we have plenty of food and clothes imported from Europe, but no money to buy it. One big tease. The crooks in the government are getting rich while half the population is unemployed. At least everyone had a job before. So much for capitalism."

"Still crooks in the government?" Hefflin asked.

"Always crooks. That never changes. They just wear different hats." The driver lit a cigarette. "At least now I can smoke a Kent without being afraid that the Securitate will ask me where I got it."

Hefflin leaned back in the seat and decided to just watch the city go by. His original visit had been in the middle of December, and he now felt fortunate to return in April. The air was redolent with the smell of grass and trees. The men on the streets wore short-sleeved shirts and the women, summer dresses.

"Don't get me wrong," the driver went on. "For some people—the educated, the new entrepreneurs, the taxi drivers like me, life is definitely better. I can deal in dollars from tourists, for example—illegal before. With dollars you can have a decent life here. But the rest of the people, ah." He waved his cigarette, which dropped its ashes in the car. "The pensioners have it the worst."

Hefflin felt a pall of depression spread over him. He had hoped for a faster transition to a new economy, a new life. But it had barely been three years, he reminded himself.

"Take me through the old sector," he told the driver.

"Why? You want to see the underbelly of our city?" The driver sounded insulted.

Within a few minutes they found themselves in the historic section of town surrounding Strada Lipscani. The streets were mobbed. Electric wires hung across dilapidated buildings, obviously illegally patched together by whoever thought himself an electrician. Neon lights advertised a bar, a tattoo parlor, a gambling joint, a strip club.

"Don't come here at night by yourself," the driver said. "Thieves everywhere, and worse. The area is run by gangs. They saw American gangster movies, and now they mimic them. You American?"

"Yes."

"Well, then, maybe you're used to it."

On several street corners Hefflin spotted women wearing bikini tops and thongs that left little to the imagination. The ladies of pleasure were out in the open now, selling their wares without compunction.

"This is just what you see on the streets," the driver said. "Inside there's sex, drugs, perversions of all kinds." He spat out the window. "Bucharest has become what they call a 'destination city' for sex, like Bangkok. The government does nothing because it improves the economy." He threw the cigarette out the window in disgust. "Now let's get to your hotel. Unless you're one of those perverted Westerners, in which case you can get out now. Don't bother paying me."

"I'm sad to hear all this," Hefflin said. "Let's hope it's just a transition to something better."

"A transition." The driver laughed. "During communism, they always told us we were in a transition toward a utopia of egalitarianism. It never happened. Now we're in a transition toward democracy and capitalism. No, I think we've arrived. This is what it looks like."

As they were about to turn onto Calea Victoriei, a policeman on motorcycle blocked the traffic. All cars came to a stop. A moment later a string of black Mercedes limousines sped by, then the policeman took off and the traffic started up again.

"What were those cars?" Hefflin asked.

"The oligarchs." The driver spat out the window. "They appeared out of nowhere a year or two after the revolution. Don't ask me anything more."

The taxi pulled up to the entrance of the Athénée Palace. He handed the driver a fifty-dollar bill without figuring out the conversion from the local *lei* displayed on the meter.

The driver gave him a toothless grin. "I know this means nothing to you, but I thank you just the same. You're a good man."

Hefflin rolled his bag into the hotel, looking forward to washing off the miasma that had settled over him.

CHAPTER FIFTEEN

Bucharest
April 1993

HE DIDN'T KNOW what he had expected—the removal of the worn
red carpet, perhaps, the replacement of the rickety furniture, maybe
a new reception desk. But everything seemed to be just as he had left
it in '89. If anything, it looked even more pathetic, perhaps because
of his dashed expectations. At least now there was a young woman
receptionist wearing a uniform consisting of a white shirt and black
pants that looked relatively new. She smiled as she asked him for his
passport.

"Your reservation is for five days," she said in good English. "Is
that right, Mr. Blake?"

"It depends on how my business goes," he said.

"A businessman. There are many of you here. Welcome to Bucharest." She typed on what appeared to be a new computer. At least she
wasn't a Securitate informant, as in the days of Ceausescu, though
the hotel was still government-owned. No Western hotel chain had
yet decided to invest in the Athénée.

"The place looks empty," he said.

"The hotel is fully booked, sir, with businessmen like yourself.
They are all at the conference at the InterContinental. I assumed you
were also here to attend it."

She handed him the key to his room and pointed to the elevator. "Second floor. I hope the room will be satisfactory."

He thanked her and rolled his bag to the elevator, all the time expecting to be accosted by the ladies who used to pounce on Westerners for a "good time" in exchange for a couple of packs of Kents or a bag of real coffee. To his surprise, there were none. Despite his original dismay at those flagrant approaches, he now felt a tinge of disappointment. Then it occurred to him that the vultures must have followed their prey to the conference.

The room was what he remembered except that now there was a small minibar with miniature liquor bottles. He immediately looked into the bathroom to make sure there was toilet paper, something that had been scarce in the past. Two welcome improvements. Perhaps there would be others.

He left the hotel as the evening settled over the city. He hailed a taxi and told the driver to take him to the InterContinental hotel. Ingram had suggested he attend the conference to rub elbows with the upper echelon of Bucharest. Besides, he had an evening to kill, and he was curious to see what kind of business conferences they now conducted in this struggling new capitalist democracy.

CHAPTER SIXTEEN

Bucharest
April 1993

As WITH THE writing of a fictional plot, one cannot accept coincidences in the business of espionage, his Agency mentors had taught him. If there has to be a coincidence, there can only be one. More than that and you lose the reader, or your life. The rule was supposed to hold even though life inflicted dozens of coincidences on a weekly basis. Ergo, the rules of the Agency and of fiction were held to a higher standard than those of real life.

These thoughts flashed through Hefflin's mind as he entered the conference room and spotted a familiar face hobnobbing with other middle-aged Westerners in gray suits. Harold Mayfield, the Chicago businessman who had come to his hotel room before the revolution seeking a leg up, a business advantage in the form of America's plans for deposing Ceausescu. He had even offered Hefflin a job with a sizable signing bonus if he could just hint at CIA plots. Mayfield had had visions of great profits in bringing Romania into the 20th century, plans that, three years later, had not even begun to materialize.

He doubted Mayfield would remember him after three years, especially with his new disguise, which he itched to try out. He worried that the three-day-old beard was darker than his newly dyed dirty blond hair, but hell, there were men who had naturally brown hair and red beards.

He approached Mayfield backward, allowing himself to be jostled toward him. After a few minutes of this dancing about, talking gibberish in English to a businessman from Bonn, he stood a few feet away from Mayfield, his back still to him. When the German moved on, Hefflin turned and faced the men behind him, among them Mayfield.

"Hello." Hefflin smiled broadly. "I'm James Blake, from New York."

The men introduced themselves—one was from Munich, another from Paris, and a third from Tel Aviv. When it was Mayfield's turn, he smiled and extended his hand.

"Harold Mayfield, from Chicago." Mayfield kept his smile, showing no sign of recognizing Hefflin.

"Another American. What field are you in?" Hefflin asked.

"Automated manufacturing," Mayfield answered. "Everything from engines to conveyor belts. You?"

The Graduate suddenly popped into his mind.

"Plastics."

"Wonderful. Plastics are used in all sorts of equipment. Any company in particular?"

"I represent several of them," Hefflin said. "Here to get the lay of the land. They need to rebuild the whole country, it looks like."

The other three men all represented companies dealing with military equipment, from fighter jets to tanks to small arms—the military industrial complex.

A bell rang, the signal to return to the conference room for the next speaker.

"I guess they want us back in," Mayfield said. "You staying in this hotel also?"

"No, at the Athénée," Hefflin said. "I'll be inside in a minute. I need a drink to be able to sit through another presentation."

"Perhaps we can have a drink afterward, both being Americans and all," Mayfield said. "They say they'll be done by seven. Let's say seven fifteen at the bar?"

"Fine," Hefflin said and walked off.

The crowd, consisting mostly of men, slowly filed into the conference room as Hefflin stood in a corner and watched them go by. He recognized several government officials, among them the deputy defense minister, several generals in full uniform, and the deputy foreign minister. The Romanians were going all out.

Who the hell are you, Mayfield? Why do I always bump into you in Bucharest? And now at a conference dealing in military equipment.

Having nothing better to do, and some time to do it in, and craving to use his old skills again, he walked over to the reception desk and asked for a piece of paper and an envelope. After scribbling gibberish, he folded the paper, placed it in the envelope, and sealed the flap. On the face of the envelope, he wrote *Mr. Harold Mayfield* and handed it to the receptionist.

"Can you send this up to Mr. Mayfield's room immediately, please?"

"Right away, sir," the receptionist said, then rang a bell.

Hefflin lingered in the lobby holding a copy of the *International Herald Tribune* while a bellboy approached the receptionist and took the envelope. Hefflin followed him to the elevators and got in after him, along with other guests. On the third floor the boy exited, and Hefflin followed. The boy stopped in front of room 307 and knocked. Hefflin walked past him and saw him insert the envelope under the door.

Hefflin waited a few minutes after the boy left, then returned to room 307, used the two small metal strips he carried to unlock the door, and walked in. After determining there was no one in the room, he picked his envelope off the floor and placed it in his pocket.

He then turned on a bed lamp and began rummaging through the drawers. Finding nothing of interest, he next tried the closet, where a gray pinstripe suit, several dress shirts, and a pair of dress shoes were neatly stowed. In the top shelf of the closet, under two extra blankets, he found a leather briefcase. He brought it close to the lamp and, using the same tools, unlocked it.

He first noticed several passports from different countries. They bore Mayfield's picture, but with different names. Beside the passports were wads of Romanian *lei*, American dollars, and German deutschmarks. In the accordion file section he found a Walther PPK, fully loaded.

What kind of a salesman are you, Harold? And why are you so sure your briefcase won't be stolen by the chambermaid? They must know you; perhaps they even fear you.

He wiped the gun clean before putting it back in the case, placed the case on the top shelf under the blankets, and returned to the bar.

CHAPTER SEVENTEEN

Bucharest
April 1993

As THE LECTURE came to a close, the bar began to fill with business-men lining up to order their drinks. They spoke mainly English, the universal language, with an occasional dive into French. Hefflin could usually tell their country of origin by their accents, but not always. Belgian, French, Swiss French, and Canadian French had similar accents in English, at least to Hefflin's ear. Some Eastern European languages also produced accents between which Hefflin couldn't distinguish.

"Sorry to be late," he heard a voice behind him.

Hefflin turned to find Mayfield's cheery face.

"I had to go up to my room and drop off all the paraphernalia they hand out. Been waiting long?"

"Just got here myself," Hefflin said.

"But where are those pamphlets we all got?"

"Oh, I don't keep any of that stuff," Hefflin said. "I find I never read them anyway. So, what will it be?"

"A dry martini for me," Mayfield said and caught the eye of the bartender to order. "What are you having?"

"I'm trying the local drink," Hefflin said. "Plum brandy. *Tsuika*, they call it. It's not bad, really."

"I tried that when I first got here," Mayfield said. "Couldn't quite get into it. So I decided to stick to what I know."

"This your first time here?"

"No, I've been an occasional visitor for years," Mayfield said. "I always think there's money to be made here, but I've been repeatedly disappointed. Things always move more slowly than we anticipate."

"Yes, the more things change, the more they stay the same." Hefflin tried to bore the man with triteness. "So, what do you think of the place?"

"It's comfortable enough as hotels go on this side of the world."

"I meant the country," Hefflin said.

"Oh, well, it's pretty backward. So many things they have to change first—patent rights, tax laws, judicial system—all of it. But you must know all that."

"On top of which they have no money," Hefflin said.

"It's the usual game we play." Mayfield chuckled. "The U.S. government lends them money to buy from American firms. In the end, the American taxpayer subsidizes American business. A great deal, no?"

A great scheme, of which few taxpayers are aware.

"We've done it over and over again, all over the world," Hefflin said.

Mayfield sipped his martini while looking around the room, eyeing the ladies of the night who had appeared out of nowhere.

"Great party scene here, isn't it?" Mayfield beamed. "These women. Makes me wish I was ten years younger and twenty years freer." He laughed, then took off his wedding ring and slipped it in his pocket.

"They don't care about that," Hefflin said. "They just want the dollars."

"Yes, I know. It's just for my benefit. It allows me to fantasize about being free."

It occurred to Hefflin that there were so many levels of freedom, not just the one related to politics. It reminded him of the conversation he and Gabor had had the last time he was here. The famed Romanian actor had made the point that Western freedom was illusory. Money dictated most forms of freedom—the freedom to make your voice heard, to pick up the phone and ask your senator for a favor, to travel wherever you wished, and to have as many lovers as you could handle. Although Hefflin now had all the money he could ever want, he still only desired Catherine, the love of his life.

"I would stay away from these women," Hefflin said. "AIDS is rampant here."

"We do have protection, no? Still . . ."—he replaced the ring on his finger—"you're right. A few minutes of pleasure isn't worth the risk, not to speak of the guilt. I've never gone through with it. I find that just taking off the ring for a bit is enough. So, Mr. Hefflin, what are you doing back in Bucharest?"

Hefflin froze, his pulse bounding in his temples.

"I didn't recognize you at first, what with the changes you made since our last meeting," Mayfield said. "But I'm a poker player, Mr. Hefflin. I've spent many nights honing my skills in the casino of Monte Carlo, among others. And I've learned to notice small ticks or movements that define a person—what we call 'tells.' You have two: a way of looking directly into someone's eyes when you're lying, and an intense effort to appear at ease, which you work hard to cultivate."

Hefflin winced. That's what Catherine had told him when they had first met, that he had a studied gentleman's style, as if copied from old movies.

"What do you say we go up to my room and discuss matters in private?" Mayfield suggested.

"I didn't know we had any matters to discuss," Hefflin said. "But as you wish."

They paid for their drinks and took the elevator up to the third floor.

Once inside the room, Mayfield casually removed the Walther PPK from his inside jacket pocket, pointed it at Hefflin, and motioned for him to sit down.

He must have retrieved his gun from his room before our meeting at the bar.

Hefflin sat in a chair across from him. "Why the gun?"

"I find it gives me reassurance," Mayfield said. "Bucharest is not the same as you might remember it, I'm afraid. Besides the usual organized crime, which has rules, we now have these gangs that roam the streets, unruly youngsters with a penchant for kidnapping Westerners with money. And compared to these poor wretches, all Westerners have money."

"It can't be a great place to do business," Hefflin said.

"No, but if you wait until they clean it up, you'll be too late to the dinner table. So, Mr. Hefflin, the last time we met you were a cultural attaché—another name for a spy. You arrived just before the revolution and left right after. A coincidence, no doubt." He chuckled. "Now, that's a story I'd like to hear."

"I'm a private citizen now, Mr. Mayfield, or whoever you are, which is a story *I'd* like to hear."

"Fair enough, but since I'm holding the gun, you can go first."

Hefflin eyed the gun, then shrugged. "That toy is of no consequence. I can take it from you whenever I wish."

"Let's not try. I'd hate to shoot you for no reason."

"I don't like people pointing guns at me." Hefflin moved his foot, causing Mayfield to turn his eyes, then reached across and lifted the gun out of Mayfield's hand.

Mayfield stared at the gun for a moment, then his eyes settled into a look of resignation.

"I guess you haven't lost your tricks since you left the Agency. I underestimated you, Mr. Hefflin. I won't do it again."

Mayfield stood and casually opened the minibar from which he removed two small bottles of vodka. He poured two glasses and handed one to Hefflin.

"I find that a discussion such as ours goes down better with a drink, don't you?" Mayfield took a sip and settled back into his chair. "Very well, since you now have the gun, I'll go first. I'm an independent contractor, you might say."

"Don't tell me about conveyor belts," Hefflin said.

"No, not conveyor belts. Armament."

"Like everyone else here."

"Yes, but they are here to sell. I am here to buy."

Hefflin remained silent.

"Romania, along with all the other former Soviet satellite countries, will join NATO at some point. It will take a few years but they're already preparing for it. The major American and European defense companies are here to sign contracts to replace all the Soviet systems with NATO-approved hardware, from jets to tanks to small arms and everything in between. So, did you ask yourself what the Romanians and the other former Soviet satellites will do with all the Russian systems?"

"They'll sell them to Third World countries," Hefflin said.

"Bingo. That's where I come in. I'm what they call the middleman. I find the markets, procure the suppliers, and join the two parties. I guess I do function like a conveyor belt of sorts." Mayfield preened. "In the process, I get a hefty commission, of course."

"You're an arms dealer."

"That's such a negative word. Arms are like any other commodity. If I were selling clothing to European fashion houses made with Bangladeshi child labor, you wouldn't have the same reaction."

"Were you an arms dealer before—when we first met?"

Mayfield waved his hand. "I naively thought there would be a sudden rush to Westernize after the revolution, so I figured to get in on the ground floor in all types of Western goods. Silly me. But, yes, I've been dealing in arms for decades. It's kept me in bespoke suits and Rolexes, not to mention houses all over the world."

"You just said you wouldn't mention the houses." Hefflin kept a straight face.

Mayfield let out a chuckle. "And I won't mention the yacht moored in Monte Carlo."

"Please don't."

"Before the fall of communism, I dealt mainly in the Far East, in casinos, arms, and other things. But this historic change in world alliances promises to be a veritable bonanza. All these former Soviet allies have military equipment up to their gills, and they need to get rid of it." He shifted in his seat. "I am telling you all this because I could use a man like you. I made you an offer the last time, and you turned it down."

"I didn't know you were dealing in arms the last time."

"Yes, twenty percent commissions on deals in the hundreds of millions does put a different face on it, doesn't it? I'll even offer you a hefty signing bonus."

Hefflin took a long sip of the vodka. "I have to admit, it sounds intriguing. But in your line of business, you must deal with all sorts of nasty characters."

"That is an unfortunate aspect of my profession. Ergo, the need for a gun. And a bodyguard, but I let him carouse in the bar tonight. I didn't think I needed him." He let out a laugh. "But these things are nothing you can't handle, from what you've shown me." Mayfield leaned forward, his face suddenly sober. "That's why I need a man like you."

"Perhaps you can first help me a bit in my present line of work," Hefflin said.

"I still don't know what that is." Mayfield leaned back.

"Let's call it information."

"Espionage? Industrial, I assume, now that you're out of the Agency. Wonderful. We can be of great help to each other."

"Partly industrial. I need to find out about a unit in the old Securitate called U0920. Since you deal in arms, I figure you must have contacts in the Securitate."

Mayfield thought for a moment. "That is not exactly industrial espionage, is it? I'm afraid I haven't heard of that unit. I do have friends in that arena, but they don't talk to me about their secrets. That's how I stay alive."

Hefflin hesitated. *Should I risk it? What risk is there? Boris is dead. And the Russians already know about him.*

"Then maybe you might have heard the name Boris somewhere in your travels," Hefflin said.

Mayfield rubbed his chin. "Boris is such a common Russian name, and there are still many Russians in Romania. You hear it everywhere. What business is he involved in?"

"Same as me, information."

After thinking some more, Mayfield's face suddenly lit up, as if the sun had just risen. "I know who you need to see. This man knows everyone. He is the undisputed king of the underworld."

Hefflin felt an ominous sensation ripple through him. Dealing with the underworld was not something he'd envisioned.

"He goes by the name of The Owl." Mayfield peered into his eyes. "What's the matter?"

"A strange name, isn't it?"

"They copy everything American." Mayfield chuckled. "We have Carmine 'The Cigar' Galante and Thomas 'The Toupée' Bilotti and they have 'The Owl.' And now that I come to think of it, the password to get in to see him is 'Boris.' Another wild coincidence."

Hefflin felt his pulse skip a beat. "The world is full of them." He removed his gold cigarette case and offered Mayfield a Dunhill, which Mayfield accepted. As Hefflin brought his gold lighter up to light Mayfield's cigarette, he pressed one of its sides. There was no audible click, just a silent opening of a miniature lens—his latest spy gadget. The miniature camera had been originally created in 1938 by Walter Zapp, a Latvian engineer, who called it the Minox. The Japanese developed the first Echo 8 cigarette lighter camera in 1951. Several variations had since been developed for the Agency.

"This man you're looking for, Boris, is he KGB by any chance?" Mayfield asked.

Hefflin said nothing, surprised at the man's sudden guess. Was a guess similar to a coincidence?

"Not that I care," Mayfield said airily. "I deal with all sorts. But if he is, The Owl may not be the right person to ask. He deals mostly in the underworld—practically owns the black market. He also supplies manpower to various gangs throughout Romania for some of their more . . . sensitive operations. Since the revolution, he's found that dealing in spycraft isn't as profitable as his other dealings. Still, he'll steer you to the right person if he decides to help."

Hefflin stubbed out his cigarette in the ashtray and rose. "I'll think about your offer." He placed the gun on the table.

"Do me a favor," Mayfield said, "don't mention my name to The Owl. Tell him you were referred by someone else."

CHAPTER EIGHTEEN

Bucharest
April 1993

THE ATHÉNÉE BAR buzzed with activity. The businessmen had returned from the conference with seemingly unquenchable thirst, and the female vultures had followed. The quiet bar Hefflin had left now bustled with women wearing colorful dresses with bare midriffs, strapless tops, miniskirts, and stiletto heels.

Hefflin squeezed his way to the bar and ordered a Johnnie Walker Black, straight up, a double. He watched the bartender pour it, praying that it hadn't been watered down. Satisfied that it was the real deal after tasting, he turned to face the tightly packed crowd.

The businessmen stood with drinks in hand, discussing the political situation, Romania's economy, the need for former Soviet satellites to rearm—in other words, their business concerns. Among them filtered the women. Some men seemed receptive, inviting them for a drink, while others tried to ignore them. But these carnivores were not easily ignored, for they were all young—some very young—and beautiful. They clung to the men's sides, sometimes stroking their derrieres, sometimes clutching them. At one point a Frenchman raised his arms in a gesture of "enough is enough," bursting out, *"C'est pas le Pigalle!"*

But it is, mon ami, even raunchier than the Pigalle. Whom do you think they learned it from?

A woman squeezed in beside him at the bar and ordered a vodka martini, dry, with a twist. She looked to be in her late twenties or early thirties. She wore her long black hair in a tight bun, and her red lipstick matched her nails. The tasteful black skirt, an inch above the knee, and the tailored black jacket over a white blouse marked her as apart from the vultures. Besides, she paid for her own drink.

"Hi. Where are you from?" he asked.

She gave him a casual smile. "D.C. now. Before that, Minnesota." She spoke English fluently with what, on first hearing, was an American accent. But then he thought he heard another faint accent that was neither mid-Atlantic nor Minnesotan. What the hell was it?

"What do you do?" he asked.

"I'm the executive secretary of one of those moguls over there." She pointed to a tall sixtyish man with silver hair. "The president of Nordam Industries. You?"

"Oh, sorry, I'm James Blake. Investor . . . in all sorts of industries, arms being one of them."

"Amanda Thayer." She extended her hand. "So, you're here to see what deals are made, then choose in which company to invest. We call you vultures, hovering over the winners to share in the spoils."

He smiled at the word, which he had just used to describe the prostitutes. There was a lesson in there, somewhere.

"Your company needs investors to thrive," he said. "I'm here to do due diligence. You can't blame me for that."

"Well, I can tell you that our company is certainly thriving," she said. "And now, with all the new military equipment these former Soviet satellites will need, it's going to be quite a profitable ten or more years." She scowled, then finished her martini and ordered another.

"You don't look all that happy about it," he said.

She waited for her drink to arrive before answering. She took a deep swallow, then turned to him.

"I attended a Swiss boarding school, then got a degree in art history from Vassar, with a minor in English Lit. I wanted to be an educated, cultured person. I envisioned working for Christie's or Sotheby's. Instead, I'm the secretary of an arms manufacturer." She shook her head.

That explains the faint accent.

"Life takes many wild turns," he said. "Look at me. I always wanted to be a spy. Now I'm running an investment firm." He chuckled.

"You're still here to spy. For profit, not country."

"I never thought of it that way."

"Don't patronize me. You're obviously good at it. Is that a Brioni suit?"

He was surprised she had recognized the Brioni. Few people did. It had been Catherine's idea, part of her lessons in the finer things money could buy. He still enjoyed feeling the soft material every so often, though he couldn't justify the exorbitant price tag.

"You have a good eye," he said.

"Art history is not just old paintings," she said. "You look good in it. But you have the body for it."

A backhanded compliment.

"Thank you. Yours isn't bad either."

She frowned histrionically. "That's the clumsiest come-on I've ever heard."

"It wasn't a come-on," he said. "But yours was."

She laughed. "All right, maybe it was. What of it? Can't a woman come on to a man?"

"They have for millennia," he said, "just not so obviously."

She shrugged. "We're two Americans in a backward Eastern European country. And we're both single." She eyed his ring finger. Agency regulations were adamant about not wearing a wedding ring. No agent wanted to declare that he or she had a family that could be harmed or used for blackmail, though he had slipped one on the last time he was here to scare off the vultures before realizing they didn't care.

"We've both had a few," she continued, "and we're both good looking."

"Is that all you need to go to bed with someone?"

"That's more than I need for good sex," she said. "I would have stopped at the Brioni. Maybe not even the Brioni."

"I'm afraid I need to know you a little better," he said.

"Now, that's unusual." She slurred her speech a bit. "I've never met a man who wanted to know me better before sleeping with me. What are you . . . married, gay?"

"Careful."

"There's such a thing as being too careful." She brought her lips closer to his. He could smell her perfume, a subtle expensive one.

He remembered the agreement at which he and Catherine had arrived: If they had to engage in sexual acts as part of their mission, they wouldn't consider it infidelity. They wouldn't even have to report it to the other. Such was the trust between them. But, alluring as this woman was, he could not imagine how sleeping with her could be considered an essential part of his mission.

She received a third drink, paid the bill, and raised her glass. "I'm taking my drink up to my room. Number 404. You're welcome to join me if you're in the mood."

He followed her with his gaze as she made her way through the crowd trying to hold her martini glass above her head without spilling. Having reached the elevator, she took a gulp, then entered.

He had no interest in casual sex, though part of him found that disinterest disturbing. Didn't he owe it to the males of the species to sleep with as many women as he could? Surely James Bond would never have these misgivings, and Casanova had less interest in quality than in quantity, another conquest to add to his list. Many men followed that same formula without ever feeling the emptiness, not knowing anything else.

He dismissed those puerile tactics as symptoms of male insecurity, an affliction from which he did not suffer. Casanova and James Bond were stunted teenagers. The truth was that Catherine was the only woman he ever thought about, his childhood love that could transform herself on a dime into a French ingenue or coquette or slut, depending on her mood, and his. How much more blessed could a man be?

He paid the bill and finished his scotch. As he jostled his way to the elevator, he spotted a young man waiving at him from across the room. He was dressed in official-looking attire, meaning a cheap gray suit that hung on him like he had slept in it. Hefflin changed his direction and made his way, after several apologies, to the young man.

"Excuse me, Mr. Blake, sir," the young man began in heavily accented English. "I am from Ministry of Commerce. There seems to have been oversight for which Ministry apologizes." He handed Hefflin a square envelope. "It is official invitation to gala day after tomorrow in honor of participants of conference."

Hefflin recognized this as Ingram's doing, getting his name on the official roster of conference attendees at the last minute.

"Where is it held?" he asked.

"At *Casa Poporului*," the young man said.

Ceausescu's palace, Ceausescu's monstrosity.

"The President is expected to be there," the man added.

Iliescu. Well, well.

"Thank you. You can assure the Ministry that I'll be attending."

The young man bowed and left.

CHAPTER NINETEEN

Bucharest
April 1993

Stan Vogel, the Bucharest chief of station, was in his late forties, clean-shaven, of middle height, with a wiry frame over which a gray suit hung as on a wire hanger. His desk in the Operations room of the embassy was clear of any files or papers, unlike that of Jack Stanton, his predecessor, which had had stalagmites of files growing on it.

Hefflin had arrived at the embassy first thing in the morning to present his credentials. Vogel studied the piece of paper Hefflin had just handed him. "I've heard the CIA has used such a document in the past, a so-called carte blanche, but have never seen one before." He held it up to the light. "Rare, old-fashioned, and a bit dramatic, isn't it? Still, the concept has a long history, dating back to the Roman Empire. I'm wondering why the DO felt the need to write such a letter and to grant you such powers, Mr. Blake."

"I'm afraid that's on a need-to-know basis, Mr. Vogel," Hefflin said.

"Are you part of the Agency?"

"That's also on a need-to-know basis. But you're welcome to get Ingram on the phone and confirm the letter if you doubt its authenticity."

Vogel rubbed his chin, then his left eye twitched.

"No, it's got his seal on it, and the paper has the watermark. And I know his signature. So, I'm at your disposal, to the limits of my ability. Our outpost here has shrunk since the downfall of the Soviet Union. It seems the dons at Langley believe the Cold War is over. I'm not so starry-eyed. Russia has always had imperialistic tendencies, whether under the czars or the communists. So, what can I do for you?"

"You can give me a general idea of the local situation, for starters," Hefflin said.

"Oh, the Romanian nomenklatura is the same as it's always been," Vogel said. "Intelligent, corrupt, venal, petty, conniving. They've had a long history of occupation during which to hone those skills. The people are as miserable as ever. Almost half the population is unemployed now, unlike during the communist days. The birth rate is still dropping. The young intelligentsia is leaving the country in droves seeking better jobs in Western Europe. A real brain drain."

"Have things improved at all since the revolution?"

"Not as much as we expected," Vogel said. "Iliescu says the right things, but drags his feet on real reform. The truth is that many from the old guard are still in power, just wearing Western hats."

"And the Securitate?"

Vogel gave him a cultivated smile, as in, "Are you kidding?"

"They broke up the old Securitate into several departments, but some of the same people are still running it," Vogel said.

"What do you know about unit U0920?"

Vogel shrugged. "It used to be a unit inside the Securitate devoted to spying on Ceausescu's own underlings. Disbanded after the revolution."

Hefflin was disappointed. He had hoped that the local Agency office would know something more than what was included in official reports.

"One more thing," Hefflin said. "I'd like a photograph developed."
He handed Vogel his lighter.

"Sure. It'll be ready within the hour," Vogel said.

Hefflin stood. "I'll also need access to your computers."

"No problem. I'll get you a temporary password. You can use any
one in the Operations room."

A memory had resurfaced overnight that had remained dormant
for two years. At some point during their meetings in '89, Boris had
said that he had been the KGB chief of station in Bucharest earlier
in his career. Why hadn't he followed up on this vital clue sooner?
Had he repressed it because he really didn't want to find Boris's real
identity?

He sat before a computer screen in the Operations room and tapped
in his temporary password. When the screen opened up, he typed the
search phrase "KGB chief of station, Bucharest, 1950–present."

A list of names appeared on the screen, along with photographs.
He recognized many of the names from his analyst days. The photographs had been taken clandestinely, most of them on the streets of
Bucharest. They were black and white and of varying degrees of
quality.

He scrolled down to the earlier years, beginning with the '50s.
These photos were of an even poorer quality, taken with more prim-
itive cameras. He marveled at the clothes people wore in those days,
the restored pre-war cars, the classic French-style buildings of the
old quarter, many of which had later been razed by Ceausescu to
make room for his palace.

From his wallet he removed the picture that Tanti Bobo had given
him. It depicted three men in short sleeves: his father, Professor Pincus, and Boris. The date was stamped on the back: 1947.

He focused on the pictures in the computer file and tried to match
them to the young face of Boris. Some chiefs of station had remained

on the job for years, others for shorter periods. If Boris had been in his late twenties or early thirties when that picture with his father was taken, he wouldn't have been made chief of station for at least a decade, at the earliest. Most of the men in the photographs looked to be in their forties and fifties, though it was difficult to gauge age in those grainy pictures.

As he continued to scroll down, his heart began to sink. None of the pictures even remotely resembled Boris. Most men were relatively short, stocky, some obese. None even came close to Boris's six-foot-two build.

When he reached the end of the 1980s, he scrolled back and looked at the pictures one more time. Boris had to be there somewhere, perhaps in some disguise. But most men were clean-shaven and none even wore sunglasses to obscure their faces.

As he closed the file and signed out, the thought began to dawn on him: Boris had lied. He had never been the KGB Bucharest chief of station. What else had Boris lied about?

He decided to put that aside for now. He had another date with his past that morning.

CHAPTER TWENTY

Bucharest
April 1993

HE NEEDED TO see it all again—the old house, the *maidan* where his family kept chickens, the apple tree—though he dreaded the degradation and decay he knew he would find, a patient on his deathbed. He no longer harbored the cloying nostalgia that had previously gnawed at his insides, despite Catherine's psychological assessment. He had found Pusha, his childhood love, who had blossomed into the sophisticated Catherine, so he didn't have to depend on his memories or on those crumbling buildings as monuments to his lost childhood.

And yet, as he approached his former house, he felt the strings of lost days and years tug at his heart. It was sad to admit, but his childhood in Bucharest, those innocent days with Pusha that seemed to go on forever, had been the happiest time in his life. He remembered reading somewhere that when you start looking backward at your life rather than forward you know you're getting old. By that measure, he had become an old man at the age of eight when he had been forced to leave Pusha behind.

His house, and the entire compound of smaller houses, which had been his mother's dowry, now stood empty, with only memories hanging about like Christmas decorations. The original house was a two-story stucco structure in which his parents had lived before the war, with the other one-story houses being rental properties. But when the communists took power after the war and nationalized all private property, they decided that such a large house was too decadent for only one family and placed another couple, Mr. Trent, the lawyer, and his wife, in the first floor. After some modifications, their one-family house was transformed into a two-family structure. But as the years passed by without anyone caring enough to maintain the buildings, since no one but the government owned them, the houses became uninhabitable and were scheduled to be demolished under the Ceausescu regime. Then the revolution occurred, and all plans were suspended. The houses remained empty, in limbo.

But as he now approached, he thought he saw children running in the yard. He could now make out laundry hanging on lines strung between the buildings, the windows no longer boarded up. A moment later, two children ran to the front door of his house and entered. Life had returned to his old home.

As he opened the wrought iron gate he saw a middle-aged man in a dirty sleeveless shirt sitting on the steps, smoking a cigarette and watching him. Two young men, tall and muscled, stepped out of the house. They were all dark-skinned.

Gypsies.

"Good morning," Hefflin said in Romanian. He pasted a smile on his face. "How are you this fine morning?"

"Who is asking?"

"The owner of the house you are illegally occupying," Hefflin answered, though that was not strictly true since Hefflin had not yet convinced the new democratic government to return the previously nationalized property to its rightful owner.

The two young men stepped back, unsure of themselves. The older man stood.

"You are here to kick us out?"

"It depends. Why are you living in my old house?"

"We saw it was empty, boarded up. We thought it was abandoned."

"Don't you have a place of your own?"

"We did, a miserable one-room apartment in the Ferentari district, for my wife and four children. Now the new government threw us out even from that one. They told us to leave the city. Where can we go?"

Hefflin approached the man and offered him a Kent. The man nodded and took one. Hefflin took one for himself and lit them both.

The man looked him up and down. "You from America?"

"Yes. I was born in this house," Hefflin said.

"Ah." The man nodded. "So you must have many memories. It must be difficult to see strangers living in it, and gypsies no less."

"So, is the government only mistreating you or all Roma?"

The man's features softened. "Thank you for using our rightful name." He dragged on his cigarette, smoking it down to a stub. "Years ago the communist government created what they now call the gypsy ghetto in the Ferentari district to isolate us from the rest of the city. Miserable, small apartments, four to six people to a room, but at least they were ours. We thought the new government would be better. Instead, they now see their chance to drive us out entirely." He dropped the cigarette butt and stamped it out with his foot. "Treat us like human beings, that's all we ask. But old hatreds die hard. Many Roma have ignored the edicts to evacuate, and the government hasn't yet taken any action. We saw our chance to move here, and we took it."

Hefflin looked up at the windows of his childhood home, now filled with the fearful faces of two children and a middle-aged woman. They were now creating their own memories in his old house.

"You have nothing to worry about from me," Hefflin said. "At least my old house is being put to good use."

The man's face brightened with outright joy. "So we can stay?"

"For as long as the government lets you," Hefflin said.

"Ah, they're so disorganized. It will take them months, maybe years, to figure out who is living here."

The man turned to one of his sons and spoke in their dialect. A moment later the son reappeared with a bottle of clear liquid and two shot glasses.

"Let me offer you some *tsuika* for your kindness," the man said as he poured.

Though it was still morning, Hefflin accepted. It would have been an insult to refuse. Both men downed their shots.

"So, what tribe are you?" Hefflin asked.

"*Kaldaresh*, the *Mandale* clan."

Hefflin's gut turned. "*Mandale?* I knew an old woman who was part of your clan. She used to live in that house there." He pointed.

"Yes, since you lived here you must have known her," the man said.

"She was practically my second mother. She died during the revolution, right before Ceausescu fell."

The man grimaced. "You shouldn't say things like that, not out loud, at least."

"Why?"

"You sleep with dogs, you get fleas," the man said. "Calling her your second mother makes you a gypsy-lover."

"She was a dear friend. She told me a story once, when I returned to find her, right before the revolution," Hefflin continued. He needed to proceed cautiously. "She had a child, by a *gadjo*, a lieutenant in the Romanian military."

The man's eyebrows tightened; his face dropped all amity. "She told you about that? She shouldn't have."

"She said two men from your clan came in the middle of the night and took her baby."

"Nonsense. Why would they? The clan wanted nothing to do with her. She ran away with a *gadjo*. Her name was erased from our memory. I can't even remember it if I try." The man shook his head. "The *voivode*, her father, wanted nothing to do with her little bastard."

Hefflin felt his anger rise up into his throat. "Do you know what happened to the baby?"

The man shrugged. "We forgot about her, I tell you."

"But you didn't quite forget, did you?" Hefflin said coldly. "It's not by accident that you showed up here. You knew where she lived."

The man stood. His two sons took two steps forward.

"I think you should go, before I lose my temper," the man said.

"I don't give a damn about your temper," Hefflin said. "I want to know about the old woman and her son."

"I warned you." The man nodded to his two sons. They approached Hefflin with clenched fists. When Hefflin didn't back away, one of them took a swing. Hefflin avoided the clumsy attempt, then followed with a blow to the ribs, which brought the man down. The second son was about to deliver a right hook when Hefflin stepped into the punch and struck the man's solar plexus with the heel of his palm. The man crumpled to the ground. Hefflin grabbed the older man's shirt collar. "Tell me what you know about her."

"Yes, all right. I heard that she was l-living alone in this c-courtyard of empty houses," the man stammered. "But I found her house empty. I didn't know she died until you just told me." The man looked down, avoiding Hefflin's eyes. "When a man has no options, he will swallow his pride."

Hefflin let go of his collar. "I want to talk to the *voivode*."

"Her father? He's dead. His brother's son is *voivode* now."

"Where can I find him?"

"In the Ferentari district. Just ask anyone." The man stared at Hefflin. "Where did you learn to fight like that?"

"I watched a lot of Kung Fu movies," Hefflin answered. "I was going to let you stay here indefinitely, but seeing how you treated me, I'm going to give you a month to find another home. When I return, I want to see my house in the condition you found it."

The man stared at Hefflin with fear in his eyes. "What are you doing back in Bucharest? Nothing has changed here. It's the same miserable place it's always been."

"Just looking for someone from the past."

The man looked up at him, a glimmer of hope in his eyes. "I can do you a favor, if you let me stay here for two months."

"What favor?"

"There is a man, a Roma from our clan. I used to work for him, but not anymore. He can find anyone in Bucharest."

"Is that right? What's his name?"

"He's known as The Owl."

Hefflin's face froze.

"What's the matter?" the man asked.

"Nothing. It's just that you're the second man who mentioned that name."

"Everybody knows The Owl, at least everybody in a certain class of people."

"Does he have a real name?"

"That's the only name I am allowed to say. He owns a strip club on Strada Lipscani. Tell the bartender that Boris sent you."

Boris. So Mayfield was right.

"What's your name?"

"Django. But my name won't get you in. It might even get you thrown out." The man let out a sad chuckle.

Hefflin left the man with the promise that he could stay two months and walked to the back of the compound of houses to visit an old friend, the apple tree under which he and Pusha would sit and tell each other their dreams. The stool upon which Tanti Bobo sat now stood empty, forever waiting for a partner who would never return.

As the old memories suffused his mind, he realized Catherine had been right. A part of him had never left this place, would never leave it. The little boy named Fili would always crave to relive those happiest of days. If there were a heaven, he would choose it to be a replica of this courtyard, with the apple tree in whose shade he and Pusha and Tanti Bobo basked in each other's presence.

CHAPTER TWENTY-ONE

Bucharest
April 1993

HEFFLIN FOUND VOGEL in his office, the picture he had taken with his lighter on Vogel's desk.

"That's Harold Mayfield," Vogel said as he handed the picture to Hefflin, "an American businessman. He's been around Bucharest for years. Why the interest?"

"He was at the conference, and he carries a gun."

Vogel shrugged, the common Romanian bodily expression having apparently rubbed off on him. "That's not surprising. He's in the import/export business, which he's been doing off and on for years in Romania. During Ceausescu's time, he brought in Western goods for the Party stores where the apparatchiks used to shop. Small time. As for the gun, well, things have gotten a little rough in Bucharest. Many people carry. I suggest you wear one, too, if you know how to use it."

"He says he's also in the armament business," Hefflin said. "He wants to market the old Russian systems from the former Soviet satellites to the Third World."

"You spoke to him, then." Vogel eyed him disapprovingly. "Yes, we know about his scheme, too. He doesn't exactly keep it a secret. Someone has to unload those old systems, so I guess he figures why not him. That's not illegal. But he's too small time for that. He inflates his own importance. We haven't found any real dirt on him, although you can't do any business around here with totally clean hands. The bottom line is that we lost interest in him some time ago. Was there anything else?"

Hefflin thought it peculiar how casually Vogel had dismissed Mayfield's importance, but let it go.

"I need to send a secure fax, then I'd like to make a call to the States."

"Sure. You can use this office. It's a secure line. The fax machine is right there." Vogel pointed to a corner.

"And I'll take your advice about a gun. A Beretta and two clips."

"Right. I'll be right back." Vogel returned a few minutes later with the Beretta and the clips, which he set on his desk.

After Vogel left the room, Hefflin faxed Mayfield's picture to Catherine with the request for her to use her DGSE contacts to find out anything she could about him. He waited a few minutes for the fax to go through, then called her.

CHAPTER TWENTY-TWO

New York
April 1993

CATHERINE STARED AT the photograph, a face unfamiliar at first glance, but then reconsidered. The eyes, perhaps, touched a possible distant memory, but it could be just déjà vu.

The phone rang. The voice on the line was tinny and crackly.

"Catherine?"

Her heart leapt. "Yes, it's me, *chéri*. How are you?"

She let him rattle on that he was fine, that Bucharest hadn't changed much, that he missed her. All she wanted was to hear his voice, distorted as it was, and imagine being there with him.

"Everything okay over there?" he asked. "How is Jack?"

"Jacques is fine, growing a few inches every day, it seems. Everything is fine."

Then he switched to the picture he had faxed.

"See if the DGSE has anything on this guy, Harold Mayfield. He's an American businessman who seems to hang around Bucharest a lot. He was also there in '89. Fax anything you find to Balzary. It may be nothing."

"Yes, of course, I'll find out what we have on him," she said, realizing that she had referred to the DGSE as *we*. She hadn't left the French security service, not in her heart.

"I miss you terribly," she heard him say.

"I miss you, too. It's the first time we've been apart for this long since our wedding."

"I promise not to make it a habit," he said.

She suspected they would eventually have to get used to it, that they would return to their previous lives as field agents, though for different agencies.

She wanted to tell him about the men she had noticed following her—once in Bloomingdale's, a man in a dark coat looking at women's lingerie, and another time while she was walking down 5th Avenue where two men with crew cuts wearing Red Sox hats and identical shorts walked behind her on the other side of the street. They were obviously not New Yorkers, nor Americans, probably, since they didn't know how incendiary Red Sox hats were in Yankees territory. But she decided he had enough to worry about in Bucharest. He didn't need her problems to add to his. Besides, she was a trained DGSE field agent. She could take care of matters until he got back.

And then the call wound down with mutual declarations of love and it was over. She held on to the receiver as the feeling of abandonment swept over her, accompanied by a flash of fear. She brushed away the thought, tucked the photograph into her purse, and told Yvette she would return in an hour. She jumped into a taxi and asked for the French consulate where she personally knew the DGSE chief of station.

CHAPTER TWENTY-THREE

Bucharest
April 1993

HEFFLIN RETURNED TO the Athénée and stopped at the bar for a drink. He wasn't in the mood to be alone. It was early, so the place was not yet crowded. He decided he wanted something different, so he ordered vodka on the rocks with a lime. He was pleasantly surprised to find that, three years after the advent of capitalism, limes had finally arrived in Bucharest. He sipped his drink and turned to watch the people. The usual ladies had appeared, though they seemed less interested in accosting him. Perhaps it was because they no longer worked for the Securitate, though he reminded himself that there still was a Securitate, albeit under a different name. The ladies had probably just awakened, their day just beginning—breakfast time, requiring a pot of coffee, perhaps. But no, they were welcoming the new day with cocktails. It reminded him of tales of his grandfather who apparently began each morning with a shot of Greek coffee and one of cognac.

Several men sat at one table, Westerners wearing well-tailored suits. A tall, dark-haired man in a gray suit—not well-tailored—walked in and ordered a vodka, straight up, in broken Romanian. When the drink arrived, he downed it then turned to Hefflin.

"I hear you ask about Boris," the man said in English.

Hefflin stared at the man with a blank expression, as if insulted at being addressed without a proper introduction—a trick he had learned from Catherine. "Who are you?"

The man removed a photograph from his inside jacket pocket and slid it toward him. It was a black-and-white image of Brezhnev standing on the podium of Lenin's tomb overlooking a military parade in Moscow—the usual picture of Soviet leaders seen the world over. Standing next to him were several ministers and generals. Behind him was the leader of the KGB, Semichastny, along with other men he didn't recognize. Hovering almost a foot above them was a face he *did* recognize. He tried to hide the sudden rush of adrenaline.

"Where did you get this?"

"It is gift from Balzary. He sends greetings."

Balzary. He already knows I'm in town. What a spy.

"How is Balzary?"

"He invites you to dinner tonight at eight at *Caru Cu Bere* to—and I quote—'shoot the bull.' May I tell him you will attend?"

Hefflin nodded, and the man left. He hadn't thanked Balzary properly for helping him with the defector and was glad to have that opportunity tonight.

Hefflin focused on the picture. The tall man was Boris—no doubt about it—standing right behind Brezhnev. Boris must have been high in the KGB, since only the most important and trusted men in the hierarchy were allowed on that podium. How had Balzary come across this picture? How did Balzary even know the code name Boris?

As he picked up the photograph to place in his pocket, he glanced at the back: a name and a date written in black ink: *Vladimir Dovrosky, 1962.*

So he now had a name attached to that face. Boris had more disguises than Sherlock Holmes, Hefflin had told him once, an observation that had caused Boris to burst into laughter, afterward declaring he had read all the stories, that he loved Holmes. That scene had taken place in the car on their way to the helicopter that would take them to the trial and execution of the Ceausescus—the first time he had seen Boris's real face. He wished he had taken a picture, either then or during the year Boris had spent in their penthouse in New York, though he was sure Boris would not have allowed it. All Hefflin had now was a picture of a younger version— Boris standing on the podium behind Brezhnev—and an even younger one—Boris next to Pincus and his father.

CHAPTER TWENTY-FOUR

Bucharest
April 1993

CARU CU BERE was located in the old town near Strada Lipscani, a short walk from the American embassy. The restaurant dated back to 1899 when it quickly became the center of Romanian society. The exterior of the massive building was impressive, built in the neo-Gothic style, with spires, pinnacles, arches, and small verandas. But it was the interior that made Hefflin's heart ache. Even the decades of communist neglect couldn't hide the beauty of the restaurant. The main dining room was a vast space with a vaulted ceiling, skylights, ornate wooden archways, and stained-glass windows. The walls and ceiling were painted with bucolic scenes and colorful patterns. A curving wooden staircase led up to the second floor from which diners could gaze down onto the circular bar of the main room. Alcoves off the main hall formed dark corners for more private tête-à-têtes.

He tried to imagine how the place had once been, with the high society of pre-war Europe whispering of secret liaisons and furtive trysts while deciding the fate of the world. The establishment had endured, though faded and worn now, with a bureaucratic neatness that disinfected and sterilized it. Nevertheless, it was still the most popular restaurant in town, especially with the apparatchiks.

Even though he had arrived early, the bar was already crowded. At one table spread with Romanian delicacies, he heard American English spoken, the diners' voices rising with laughter. Based on their discussion, they seemed to be embassy personnel. One young man was looking forward to having a gourmet dinner with his new wife in New York City. A woman was frustrated at not being able to find any clothes in Bucharest worth buying. Two people were taking turns describing their last Caribbean vacations.

Hefflin felt out of place, not an uncommon feeling for him. He was ashamed at the gaiety of his American colleagues, seemingly insensitive to the suffering of the locals around them. But he felt equally ashamed of the Romanians, who had endured the yoke of dictatorship for over forty years with hardly a peep until snipers started shooting at them and began the bloodiest revolution of the former Soviet bloc. And now, the promises of the revolution had yet to be fulfilled.

The restaurant had already begun to fill with mostly gray-suited apparatchiks, the only locals who could afford the prices or who would dare attract attention to themselves. Unlike the animated Americans, these faces were somber, swollen, their heads leaning toward each other, used to speaking in hushed voices to elude the listening devices that had been scattered all around them during the Ceausescu days . . . and probably still functioning. These same corpulent bureaucrats who had once run the communist government now seemed even fatter and more sinister than before.

Who were these men—for they were all men—who had decided to be minor spokes in a grand wheel with a tyrant at the hub? What had they told themselves, their wives, their children? They had all known what life was like in the West. They had certainly seen pictures, films, intelligence reports. Had it been a stubborn refusal to admit that they had chosen the wrong system or simply fear that had kept them in line? And why were they still in power?

Under Ceausescu, arrest, incarceration into psychiatric wards, and summary execution had all been real consequences of resistance or, as the government labeled it, counter-revolutionary activities. But why hadn't they joined hands and said, "No more, we're done"? The answer came to him quickly: because no one trusted the person next to him. One moment you thought you were part of a united group and the next you were the odd man out, the others being either informants or too scared to opt for a better future over a momentary advantage. One study estimated that one out of four Romanians was either a member of the Securitate or an informant. A more sober analysis by the CIA had the number at one out of twenty. Either way, it was impossible to know whether the informant was your uncle, your friend, or the lady next door.

He found Balzary sitting at a table for two in a private alcove, away from peering eyes and the blaring gypsy band, which had just begun with their traditional *lautereasca* music. Balzary stood as Hefflin approached and extended his hand.

"This meeting place is better than the last time I saw you," Balzary said as they sat.

"The last time you saw me, I was one step ahead of a bullet," Hefflin said. "Thank you, by the way."

"I think we need a few drinks before we get serious." Balzary signaled the waiter for two Johnnie Walker Blacks.

"So, I hear you're going to be a big shot now, head of the Hungarian external security," Hefflin said.

"Not for a few months," Balzary said. "All that means is that I'll have more headaches and a slightly higher salary. But it doesn't compare with you. You married well, I hear."

"By well I assume you mean the woman I love."

"That, too. But you know what I mean: above your social position." Balzary smirked. "And don't give me any crap about America not having a caste system—all based on money, of course, not pedigree."

"I married above my level in all respects," Hefflin said. He remembered that Balzary had seen him walking arm in arm with Catherine while at Harvard, but didn't bother telling him the story of how they had found each other again.

"I hear you have a 5th Avenue apartment facing Central Park," Balzary went on, "all paid for by your wife's fortune."

"You've been checking up on me."

"Just curious to know how one of my Harvard classmates is doing. Speaking of fortunes, you know, they never found Ceausescu's offshore accounts. They say he never had any. That's the official version, anyway."

"And the unofficial one?"

"Just guesswork on my part. I figure somebody got to it before the Romanian government did. Lucky guy." Balzary avoided his eyes.

The drinks arrived—doubles—the glasses almost filled to the brim with Johnnie Walker Black.

"To the lucky guy," Balzary toasted.

They clinked glasses, the whiskey spilling. Hefflin swallowed without echoing the toast.

"So, what's the story with that picture?" Hefflin asked.

"It's in our files—probably in yours, too, if you know where to look," Balzary said.

"Why did you have your man deliver it to me?"

"I heard you were looking for Boris," Balzary said casually.

"How?"

Balzary removed a piece of paper from his pocket, unfolded it, then handed it to Hefflin.

—*Eyes Only*—

James Blake, aka Bill Hefflin, is in Bucharest to ascertain identity and location of CIA asset code-named Boris who may have been compromised. Would appreciate any assistance. Bypass usual channels.

Elliot Ingram
Director of Operations

Hefflin stared at the message, unsure of what to make of it. "Why would Ingram divulge the code name Boris to you?"

"In the two years you've been away, your agency and mine have grown pretty close," Balzary said. "Hungary is a democracy now, and an indispensable intelligence ally. Your Bucharest staff has been reduced and Langley doesn't trust the new Romanian government. We've become Langley's eyes and ears in this region."

Hefflin tried to gauge Balzary's demeanor, this Harvard alum who returned to his country of birth while it was still communist to become a top spy, and now a Western ally. How much did he know?

"Who is Vladimir Dovrosky to you?" Hefflin asked.

"Vladimir Dovrosky was part of the KGB 1st Directorate, the external intelligence service, stationed in Bucharest, when my agency first took notice of him in the late '40s. In the late '50s he was promoted to be the head of Brezhnev's personal KGB detail as part of the 9th Directorate. That's what he's doing on that podium in '62. Sometime after that, Dovrosky was moved back to the 1st Directorate, where we lost track of him. He was rumored to have been spotted in several locations over the years—Paris, Bucharest, Beirut, Athens, even New York—but definitive identification was never made. We think he was wearing disguises and traveling under various aliases."

That sounds like Boris.

"How were you able to track him, then?" Hefflin asked.

"He had lovers all over the world. Their description of him all matched."

"What did they describe, exactly?"

"His naked body, to put it bluntly," Balzary smiled. "Tall—about six foot two or three—with a Russian military tattoo on his right shoulder . . ."

"Many Russians have that tattoo."

". . . and two scars, one on his right thigh and another on the right side of his chest."

Hefflin knew the causes of those scars. The thigh wound was due to shrapnel, for which his father had applied a tourniquet when he found Boris bleeding to death outside Stalingrad. The second scar was the result of the large needle his father inserted to treat his tension pneumothorax, followed by the larger chest tube inserted by the Russian doctors when Boris was eventually found.

"He certainly got around," Hefflin said.

"Yes, he's quite an incredible man," Balzary said.

"But I still don't understand how you know this man is the Boris I'm looking for."

"My man spotted you during the revolution with a tall man wearing a white beard. That was the first time."

"There was another?"

"At Ceausescu's trial."

"What?" A shiver suddenly ran down Hefflin's spine.

"You were dressed as a Romanian soldier and were standing next to Dovrosky behind the camera so you wouldn't be filmed." Balzary raised his eyebrows. "Am I right?"

"How do you know that?"

"General Stanculescu. He recognized Dovrosky, of course, because he was not wearing any disguises at the time. But he didn't know you. He forgot about it during the revolution, but later he remembered and tried to find out who you were. By then both you and Dovrosky had left Bucharest. So, on a whim, he went to the Securitate files and, lo and behold, he found pictures of you entering and leaving the American embassy during the time of the revolution—the new State Department attaché."

I should have foreseen that, and so should have Boris.

"And then he came to you," Hefflin said, "his buddy, the head of station of the Hungarian secret service and accomplice in the revolution, to ask why Dovrosky had brought an American cultural attaché to Ceausescu's trial and execution."

"Something like that."

"And you said?"

"That I didn't know you."

"No, you said more than that, I think. You said I was there to patch things up with Dovrosky and Gorbachev for the CIA having thwarted the quiet coup that Gorbachev had planned. You also assured Stanculescu that despite Iliescu, Gorbachev's classmate, becoming head of the new government, he shouldn't worry because Bush was now in charge, not Gorbachev. Iliescu was now a capitalist."

Balzary's face grew dour. "Something like that."

"Was it worth it, those thousands of civilian deaths?"

"How did you find out?" Balzary asked.

"My good friend Avery told me," Hefflin said, referring to the previous director of operations. "The same Avery who murdered my old Harvard professor."

"Pincus?" Balzary stared up at him. "Avery murdered Pincus? Why?"

"Pincus was a prominent member of a White House committee on Romania. By blaming his murder on the Securitate, Avery hoped to push President Bush to intervene in Romania, the last Soviet bloc holdout. And then I sent Langley Boris's message from Gorbachev to not interfere with the Russians' coup. That pushed Bush over the edge. He gave Avery the go-ahead to start the revolution with the snipers, which you provided, with General Stanculescu directing parts of the military. Avery then murdered Stanton who found out about Pincus and the snipers."

"He murdered his own chief of station? Christ. I had no idea. That's two murders." Balzary raised his voice. "But I didn't provide the snipers. I just let them come through Hungary. So, what did you do?"

Hefflin recounted how he had sent anonymous faxes describing Avery's actions to both Avery and the national security advisor and threatened to go public if nothing was done. Avery intercepted the message to the national security advisor and came to Hefflin's apartment to make him an offer he thought Hefflin couldn't refuse.

"He threatened to have me take the rap for everything if I didn't forget what I knew and become his protégé."

"Good God! You'd have been under his thumb for the rest of your life."

"When he saw that I resisted, he threatened to have me killed."

"What did you do?"

"Fate intervened. While having a glass of Johnnie Walker Black, Avery had a fatal cardiac arrhythmia."

Balzary nodded. "That was your final refusal, I gather." He chuckled. "Poison?"

Hefflin allowed a slight curling of his lips.

Balzary lit a cigarette and watched the flame burn down the match. "You certainly learned to be a field agent quickly. I knew you weren't a part of the plan when we first met in my car."

"And you shot the sniper before he could tell me," Hefflin said.

"It was necessary. I wanted to keep you out of it. You were a naive analyst, and I preferred you remain that way."

"I suppose I should thank you," Hefflin said. "But now I have another soul on my conscience."

Balzary waved his cigarette. "If you're going to count souls, you're in the wrong business."

Hefflin let Balzary's words linger. He had the death of several souls on his conscience.

"Have you told Ingram that Dovrosky is Boris?" Hefflin asked.

"Not yet. I wanted to pass it by you first."

"Thank you. Let's keep it to ourselves for the time being."

"As you wish." Balzary leaned back in his chair. "I'm going to go out on a limb, since you're being so coy. In my position, I've had access to all the files, including those under the previous communist regime. Apparently the KGB has suspected for some time that they have a mole inside their agency, going back a couple of years before the Romanian revolution. They asked Hungary, a Soviet ally at the time, to assist in finding this mole. The KGB got close to identifying him in Bucharest during the revolution, but their agent died of an apparent heart attack before he could report, another peculiar coincidence."

The fat man, whom Boris killed with the poison.

"On his body was found evidence pointing to the deputy ambassador to Romania as the mole," Balzary continued. "The intel consisted of offshore accounts, photos with a Romanian singer who was suspected of being a CIA asset, and so on. Well, that sent the KGB into a frenzy." Balzary chuckled. "They found the offshore accounts and recalled the deputy ambassador to Moscow where he has been rotting in Lubyanka ever since. The only reason they haven't executed him yet is that they're not convinced he is the mole."

"Why not?"

"They realize he didn't have access to much of the intel they know has been compromised. He stole money, yes, but stealing . . . well, that's par for the course in this part of the world."

"What then?"

"They're back at searching for the mole." Balzary picked up his menu. "Let's order. I can't think on an empty stomach."

CHAPTER TWENTY-FIVE

Bucharest
April 1993

THEY CONSUMED THE eggplant salad and skinless *mititei* sausage—dishes Hefflin craved from his childhood—along with a mediocre local wine, in relative silence. Their dinner plates cleared, they turned to a brandy of dubious origin.

"It's been three years since this country has supposedly had a free-market system, and they still can't import good brandy," Balzary said. He plunked his glass on the table in disgust. "So, where was I?"

"You were about to finish telling me how you assess the situation," Hefflin said.

"I've made a few more deductions," Balzary began. "If Dovrosky was your Boris, a mole inside the KGB, and you came to Bucharest to meet him in '89, then I'm guessing you must have been his handler or at least the analyst most involved in assessing the intel he provided."

Hefflin felt the time had come when he had to decide on how much to tell Balzary, a man who had proven his loyalty on several occasions.

"I was both," Hefflin said.

"That's better." Balzary smiled. "How did you recruit him, if I may ask?"

"I didn't. He just started sending me intel."

"You personally?"

Hefflin recounted the tale of his father who had treated the critically wounded Boris outside of Stalingrad, then Boris's lifelong effort to repay that debt.

"That's a wonderful story," Balzary said when Hefflin had finished. "Dovrosky has always been a very loyal man, with incredible ethics, for a spy, anyway. This is all beginning to make sense now."

"I thought you said you don't know him," Hefflin said.

Balzary raised his finger. "I never said that. You just assumed."

"You know Boris?" Hefflin almost jumped out of his seat.

"Not as Boris, of course," Balzary said. "I know him as Vladimir Dovrosky. Remember that when I returned to Hungary and joined their intelligence service, Hungary was still a loyal Soviet ally. Dovrosky was KGB, so he came and went as he pleased."

"So, how did you meet him?"

"He sought me out, actually," Balzary said. "I was a mid-level agent then, in Budapest, slowly working my way up the ranks. He just appeared at my apartment one night, at one in the morning. I was terrified when he identified himself as KGB. I thought I was in trouble."

"What did he want?"

"He sat in a chair, removed a bottle of Stoli from some pocket, and we started drinking."

"That sounds like him," Hefflin said.

"We spoke in English. He seemed to know everything about me—when my parents and I had emigrated from Hungary to America, when I had been a student at Harvard, when I had returned to Hungary. Everything."

"That sounds like him, too."

"We talked and drank all night. I had to call in sick the next day because I was still drunk." Balzary burst into laughter.

"What did you talk about?"

"He wanted to know why I returned to Hungary. At first, I gave him the party line—that I believed in the socialist cause, and I had returned to offer my services. He just laughed and told me to cut the crap. He then started telling me point by point how communism would never work, how corrupt the system was, how it was going to fall any day, and how I needed to prepare for that eventuality."

"He trusted you enough to tell you all that?"

"He was KGB. If I were stupid enough to tell somebody what he told me, he could bury me. But I didn't need any convincing. By that time, I'd been in the country long enough to see everything for myself. I knew communism's days were numbered. What I didn't know was whether this KGB guy was for real or just there to trap me into saying something stupid and arrest me."

"How did you go about figuring that out?" Hefflin asked.

"I didn't have to. He foresaw that, too. He said, and I quote, 'Aberjan, I know you think this is KGB trap. But I make deal with you, to prove it is not. Okay?'"

"Deal?"

"Yeah. He offered to provide me intel about the West that he received from other sources. He would create for me a plausible explanation of how I had recruited an asset and then have me deliver the intel to my masters."

"Western intel? In return for what?"

"In return I would provide him intel about the Hungarian secret service—agents we had in the West, ongoing operations, Western assets, and so on."

Hefflin remembered all kinds of intel about Hungarian assets and operations that had crossed his desk.

"Did he tell you what he intended to do with the intel you pro-vided him?"

"Not at first," Balzary said. "And I didn't ask. But what else would he do with it but pass it along to some Western agency?"

"And you were okay with that?"

"I told you, I already saw the writing on the wall. And I was am-bitious. I knew that I needed to rise up the ranks of the service before the government changed. The higher up I was, the more leverage I would have with the new government that took over."

"You'd know where all the bodies were buried," Hefflin said.

Balzary nodded. "I knew that power lies in information. And I knew that the officials that would take over in a new democratic regime would be some of the same ones that were in the old commu-nist one. And they all had secrets to hide."

"Apparently it worked," Hefflin said. "Boris made you into a star. You became the Bucharest chief of station and soon you'll be head of the entire external service."

"That was the strange thing about Dovrosky. He seemed to want to share intel with both sides, as if he wanted everyone to know ev-eryone else's secrets." Balzary shook his head. "Funny, isn't it? Now I realize where all the intel I gave him went: to you!"

Hefflin couldn't help but smile. "The more I learn about Boris, the more amazed I become." But then, another thought occurred to him. "The intel about the West that he gave you, how good was it?"

"Good enough to impress my higher-ups, but nothing like what I gave him," Balzary said. "He made sure that what he gave me didn't place any Western assets or agents in danger, if that's what you mean. Most of it was technical stuff—the specifications of a new West German radar system, a new French fighter—things that the KGB already knew but which the Hungarians didn't."

They both sat in silence, staring into the distance.

How much more complicated will Boris's story get?

"So, how has Boris suddenly become a problem for the CIA?" Balzary asked.

In for a penny, in for a pound.

"The KGB is not the only one that has a mole," Hefflin said.

Balzary nodded with a look of dejection. "I've suspected as much. But how is that related to Boris?"

"This KGB defector that I was asked to bring in a few days ago—"

"—When you woke up half of Bucharest." Balzary laughed.

"During his debriefing, the defector confirmed that the Russians have a mole inside the CIA. Then he dropped the name Boris." Hefflin described the intercepted call and the wire message implying that Boris had been working for the KGB all along.

Balzary leaned back, considering. "Boris was KGB, after all. Although he hated the communists, he still had to deliver intel to his masters to protect his position. But managing a mole inside the CIA? He'd never do that. The intel would be too damaging to the U.S. Besides, that would be a betrayal of you and your father."

"It's even more ridiculous than that," Hefflin said. "The mole is continuing to operate up to the present. Recent intel, like the plans for Desert Storm, and my own blown operation with the defector, are two examples, but there have been others."

"So? I don't get it," Balzary said.

I have to tell him. I need an ally.

"Boris died over a year ago."

Balzary's eyes widened. "Are you sure?"

"I was with him. He died of cancer."

Balzary nodded. "Doesn't the CIA know this?"

"No. I want to keep it quiet from the Agency, and thus the mole, since the KGB thinks Boris is still alive. Besides, I haven't told the Agency anything about Boris's relation to my father. If I tell them now, they'll never trust me again."

Balzary leaned back and lit a cigarette. "You think the KGB knows Boris was your asset?"

"I have to assume the mole told them. From the kind of intel that's been compromised, Ingram thinks the mole must have a high security clearance, and thus access to Boris's files."

"So, as it stands, both the CIA and the KGB think Boris is still alive," Balzary said. "If you don't find the real mole, you're the obvious suspect until proven otherwise."

Hefflin nodded. "That's why I'm here. I have to find out about unit U0920 where the defector supposedly worked. And if what the defector told us is true, I need to know who is setting me up."

"Yes, I remember the unit: Ceausescu's mechanism for spying on his own underlings. But it was dissolved when the Securitate was dismantled after the revolution." Balzary shook his head. "This is a major problem. All the intel Boris provided you over the years is now suspect. Langley must be going nuts trying to recheck it all."

"Some of it was confirmed from other sources after we received it, but not all of it," Hefflin said. "Much of it was too sensitive. That's what made Boris the most valuable Kremlin asset we've ever had."

They finished their drinks, then Hefflin asked to be dropped off at the American embassy. As Balzary's black limo pulled up in front of the embassy entrance, Hefflin drew a photograph from his jacket pocket. "Do you know this guy by any chance?"

Balzary glanced at the photograph. "Mayfield? He's been coming to Bucharest for many years, off and on. An American businessman. Why do you ask?"

"It's just that he came to see me once back in '89, to ask about American plans regarding Ceausescu. He wanted a leg up in business deals. I ran into him again, this time at the InterContinental bar."

"I'd stay away from him," Balzary said. "He's not as nice a guy as he seems on first meeting."

"Oh?"

"Just an impression," Balzary demurred.

In the Operations room of the embassy Hefflin looked up Vladimir Dovrosky in the computer files. He found a sparse report, along with the identical picture Balzary had shown him. The report contained the same information that Balzary had recounted except for one new item:

"Dovrosky is believed to have fathered an illegitimate child while in Bucharest, though this has never been confirmed. Present identity and location of the child unknown."

CHAPTER TWENTY-SIX

New York
April 1993

CATHERINE'S HANDS TREMBLED as she read the report she had just received, then she glanced once more at the new photographs the DGSE had supplied. One picture showed Mayfield and Nicu Ceausescu, the former tyrant's debauched son, standing side by side posing for the camera, their arms on each other's shoulders, smiling. In another they stood on a yacht, one holding up a large fish, the other pointing to it with an expression of awe. Two buddies, years earlier, without a care in the world. She now realized where she had seen Mayfield's face before.

It had occurred such a long time ago, but the images were still seared in her memory. The disgust rode up into her chest, her throat. They had to pay. Somehow they had to pay. But what could she do? She had Jacques to think of, and men were still following her. She had noticed others now. A black van had been parked on her side of the street for several days, and a black sedan always trailed a few cars behind whenever she took a taxi. She noticed the same woman at Bloomingdale's on two different occasions, and an older man with a cane passed by her building regularly. There seemed to be so many of them all of a sudden. Too many for just one agency. She was sure it was related to what her husband was doing in Bucharest.

Her husband. She still hadn't grown used to that word or to the notion of being married. But they had a boy now, and she had better get used to it. She needed to keep him safe. She needed to up her game.

She gathered the report and the photographs and faxed them to Balzary's office in Bucharest as Hefflin had requested. That done, she sank into the couch and let the memories slowly sweep over her. She had kept them from her husband, thinking that she could just bury them in a corner of her mind and forget. But deep inside she always knew this moment would come.

She saw them in her mind, the two men dressed in jeans and leather jackets who appeared at the orphanage in the middle of the night and ordered the lone female guardian on duty to line up all the girls under sixteen years old. The girls stood barefoot in their skimpy nightgowns while the two men inspected and judged, whispered and smiled. She was told to take a step forward, then was led back to her bunk to get dressed. The woman told her she had been chosen to go to a better place where the prettiest girls go. They put her in the back seat of a black car where another man sat, who she now knew had been Mayfield. He told her to roll up her sleeve. Just a vaccination, he said. The needle hurt but she did not complain. She soon felt her body melt into the soft seat. As she sank into a dark slumber, she was just happy to be out of that horrible place.

CHAPTER TWENTY-SEVEN

Bucharest
April 1993

THE NEXT MORNING Hefflin sat in Balzary's office and focused on the faxed documents from Catherine. Balzary's assistant had called him to pick them up, since Balzary was back in Hungary for a few days. As he rifled through the new photographs, he realized Harold Mayfield and Nicu Ceausescu had known each other for many years. During Hefflin's stint in Bucharest during the revolution, Mayfield had portrayed himself as a businessman who had arrived in Romania to take advantage of the expected change in the communist regime. But now it was obvious that Mayfield and the dictator's son Nicu had been friends for at least a decade before. Nicu seemed to be in his early twenties in one picture, while Mayfield looked slightly older. The DGSE reported that Mayfield had been seen with Nicu on multiple occasions in Bucharest and Monte Carlo during the '80s.

Monte Carlo, where Mayfield said his yacht was moored.

Nicu Ceausescu, a cocaine-sniffing drunk and sexual pervert, was known to have lost vast sums on gambling around the world while the people of his country starved. Originally sentenced to twenty years for ordering the troops to fire on civilians during the revolution, he was released after two years by the new government because of his supposed terminal alcoholic liver cirrhosis.

The other pictures were even more disturbing. One, obviously taken with a telephoto lens, showed Mayfield with Yasser Arafat entering a hotel. In the other, Mayfield and Arafat sat together at a table, along with several other men, having dinner. On the bottom of each, in pen, was written *Beirut, 1979.* The report stated that Mayfield was known to have contacts with other Middle Eastern leaders, including Muammar Gaddafi.

The more Hefflin read, the more intriguing the story became. Mayfield had attended Yale University on a scholarship and then earned an engineering degree at MIT. His first job was with Nordam Industries, a defense and aerospace company.

Nordam Industries. Where have I heard that name before?

Several years later, he quit to form his own firm, the International Investment Group, based in Chicago. At that point he began traveling widely, to Romania and other Eastern European countries, as well as to Asia, Turkey, and the Middle East. The group invested in several industries but became very successful in one area in particular: Asian casinos.

He dropped the report on the desk then let the information sink in. Mayfield was more interesting than he had imagined. Certain questions sprang up immediately. What kind of relationship did Mayfield have with Nicu Ceausescu? And what the hell was he doing with Arafat? Or Gaddafi, for that matter? Mayfield had suddenly become more complicated.

As he started to replace the report in the envelope, he noticed a footnote at the bottom of one page. It listed a Bucharest address, along with the words: "Mayfield's house in Bucharest, but he often stays at the InterContinental Hotel for business purposes."

* * *

He awoke in the middle of the night with the remnants of a dream, an allusion to an answer in symbolic form—much like the German chemist August Kekulé who had dreamed of a snake swallowing its tail, which gave him the solution to the structure of benzene. The dream was now fleeing faster than he could grab it, like trying to catch a scampering rabbit. He caught an image: a man with a white beard holding a gun to an Asian man's head. They seemed to be in Harvard Yard and the bearded man was pointing to the "statue of three lies." The famous statue depicts a handsome young man sitting in a chair with a book in his lap. Underneath it the inscription reads, "John Harvard, Founder, 1638." The problem is that John Harvard was not the founder of Harvard College, the date of its founding is actually 1636, and that is not a depiction of John Harvard in any event, but of a model. So what was the dream telling him? Who was the Asian man the bearded man was threatening? What did any of it mean?

The hint of a hypothesis began to germinate. If the dream were symbolic, perhaps the man with the white beard represented Boris, who had worn such a disguise before. And perhaps Boris was not pointing a gun at an Asian man, but a man who was somehow connected to Asia. Mayfield had invested in Asian casinos, and his life must certainly be replete with lies and secrets. Still, that felt damn flimsy.

A plan now formed in Hefflin's mind. The business conference was supposed to last several more days. Mayfield was probably going to remain at the InterContinental Hotel for that period, which meant his house would be vacant—unless someone else lived with him, which was unlikely, since he supposedly lived in Chicago. Perhaps the dream was telling him he would find something incriminating in Mayfield's house—a proverbial gun to his head.

The entire idea sounded preposterous, even crazy. Still, as Boris had once told him, the crazy ideas were sometimes the best. But he felt more meaning was embedded in the dream, something even more profound and ancient, which he couldn't decipher. The dream took place in Harvard Yard, the birthplace of his manhood and his eventual path to the Agency . . . and the beginning of his saga with Boris.

CHAPTER TWENTY-EIGHT

Bucharest
April 1993

IN THE MORNING he stopped by the CIA's Operations room to call Catherine on a secure line to discuss the intel she had sent him and perhaps solve the riddle of his dream.

The moment she answered the phone, he knew something was amiss. Her voice sounded harried, focused yet absent.

"Jacques is crying a lot, sees shadows everywhere. I've spent most of my time going over the books of our NGOs." Catherine's voice sounded crackly, but not from the quality of the phone line. Her words also spelled danger. Afraid of her phone line being monitored, she spoke in their code words. Jack's seeing shadows meant she was being shadowed. And the reference to NGOs meant she felt danger.

"Listen." Her voice again, distant, suddenly too calm. "I think I'm going to take Jacques and Yvette to the Hamptons. It's become much too hot in the city."

The Hamptons! That was their fail-safe word. It meant she needed to clear out immediately, to go underground, because the situation was becoming too dangerous.

"Are you sure?" he asked.

"It would be good to let Jacques romp on the beach. How's the weather in Bucharest?"

"The weather's fine here," he said, meaning he had not encountered any danger.

"Great. Please stay safe where you are. I love you always." She was telling him to stay put where he was, that he didn't need to return home. She would take care of everything.

He told her he loved her, then heard the click. He put down the phone and sat back to think. The plan was for her to drive to a spot she chose at random, without letting him know the location, in case he was compromised, or the phone was tapped. She was to avoid commercial airlines or trains.

Why was Catherine in danger? Was she being paranoid, or was someone really following her? He had never known her to be anything but calm and self-assured, especially under duress. And he knew she was an excellent field agent. Her training certainly taught her how to lose someone following her. And after he had seen the strength of her bond with Jack, her love of her son would drive her to do anything needed to keep him safe.

Was the KGB following her? The CIA? Why? He felt helpless. He knew there was nothing he could do. If he returned to New York he wouldn't find anyone at home and wouldn't be able to figure out where they had fled. The only logical action was to continue his mission in Bucharest, whatever that turned out to be.

Sweet, clever Catherine, I hope you know what you're doing.

CHAPTER TWENTY-NINE

New York
April 1993

CATHERINE KNEW THE original plan had to be scrapped and a new one devised. Driving somewhere at random, alone with Jacques and Yvette, was no longer a viable option. Too many personnel were following her. She needed somewhere more secure.

She picked up the phone and dialed.

A woman's voice answered. "World Aviation."

"Mr. Grant, please."

Clicking, then another voice: "Grant speaking."

"This is Mrs. Blake."

"Mrs. Blake, so nice to hear from you. I was actually going to give you a call. The item you and your husband were looking at—"

"Yes?"

"Another party expressed interest. I was wondering whether you have made a decision."

"We have," she said. "That's why I'm calling. We'll take it."

"Wonderful," Grant said. "I'll draw up the papers. You won't be sorry. It's the best on the market."

"I'm planning to fly to St. Barthes today," she said. "Can it be ready by this afternoon?"

"It can be ready in an hour, Mrs. Blake. We will need full payment, of course."

"And the pilots?"

"They're available on a twenty-four-hour basis, as we discussed. They'll be at Teterboro waiting for you."

"I'll wire the funds immediately. I'll see you in three hours. Have the papers at the airport for me to sign."

"Splendid. I'm glad you chose our company, Mrs. Blake."

She hung up and immediately sought Yvette. "We're going on a trip. Get Jacques ready. You won't need any clothes other than what you'll be wearing. We'll buy everything when we arrive."

"But where are we going, *Madame?*" Yvette asked, a bit flustered.

"It's a surprise you'll like, I promise," Catherine said as she sat down to make more calls.

* * *

Their pre-war building on Fifth Avenue, like most pre-war buildings in New York City, had no underground garage. But it did have an arrangement with the adjoining newer building to rent garage space. And, as is the case between many New York buildings, there was a basement connection.

Catherine held Jacques while Yvette rolled the one carry-on down the corridor into the garage of the adjacent building. Three identical black Lincoln Continental limousines awaited, all with tinted windows, making it impossible to see inside. They climbed into the back seat of one and settled in.

The three limousines drove off at five-minute intervals. The first limo took the West Side Highway south toward the West 30th Street heliport, where one could catch a flight for the Hamptons. The other two drove north on the West Side Highway. At the George Washington Bridge entrance, one veered right toward Route 95 North to the Throgs Neck Bridge, then onto 495 East to the Hamptons. The

third limo, which held the three of them, took the bridge into New
Jersey toward Teterboro Airport. Catherine didn't notice anyone following them. Whoever was trailing her would have had a hard time
dealing with three limousines, not even knowing whether she was
inside any of them.

A mere twelve miles from Manhattan, Teterboro served as the
closest airport for corporate jets and private aircraft for New York's
wealthy residents. It allowed no commercial flights and its services
were geared toward making air travel for the privileged as efficient
and discreet as possible. The highway traffic was no heavier than
usual, and they arrived twenty-five minutes later.

After passing through passport check, they walked onto the tarmac where dozens of private airplanes were parked. A middle-aged
man stood before a Dassault Falcon 50 three-engine jet designed
specifically for private transatlantic flight. Two male pilots in uniform stood next to it.

"Welcome, Mrs. Blake. The crew is ready and the plane is fully
fueled. We have received the transfer of funds, thank you." The man
handed her several papers, which she signed without even glancing
at them.

"We'll be taking off right away," she told the pilots as she carried
Jacques onto the plane, followed by Yvette.

The cabin had a capacity of three crew and eight passengers. The
only crew on this flight were the pilot and copilot. They took off
within minutes. As soon as they reached initial cruising altitude,
Catherine pressed the call button, and a moment later the captain
walked out of the cockpit. He was a tall man in his fifties, she estimated, a former Navy pilot with twenty years' experience flying big
jets for commercial airlines.

Catherine led him to the back of the plane.

"There is a change of plans," she said.

"Oh?"

"The new destination is Nice, France."

The captain nodded. "I'll file the new flight plans with the tower."

"No, you won't."

"Excuse me?" The man stared at her, his mind obviously working.

"There are people after me and my child. We have intel they're planning to kidnap us."

"Intel?" The former Navy man caught her word choice. "You mean . . ."

"My husband is in the Agency. Now overseas."

"Then the Agency should be taking care of you," he said.

"There's no time for that."

The captain looked down at his shoes. "I could lose my license."

She handed him a piece of paper.

"These are two numbered accounts in a Cayman bank, along with their codes. One for you and the other for the copilot. Each has three hundred thousand dollars in it."

The captain stepped back, his face gaunt. His gaze drifted beyond her, then refocused. He took the piece of paper and placed it in his pocket.

"I'll file the new flight plan a half hour after we land," he said. "An oversight. Is that enough time?"

"It will have to do."

*   *   *

The captain returned to his cabin and closed the door. As he settled in his seat, the copilot turned to him.

"What did she want?"

"A change of destination. Nice, France."

"Nice. These people know how to live."

"That's the rich for you," the captain said. "They think they're different from us mortals."

He pressed the button and reported his new destination to the tower. He didn't mention the paper in his pocket to his copilot.

CHAPTER THIRTY

Bucharest
April 1993

THE BUILDING'S LIGHTS lit the skies of Bucharest like a mammoth bonfire. *Casa Poporului*—the People's House—changed from *Casa Republicii* after the revolution, was also known as Ceausescu's palace or, more commonly, Ceausescu's monstrosity. Larger than the Pentagon, it boasted 1,100 rooms, numerous conference halls, living quarters for high officials, and a radiation-resistant bunker in case of nuclear war. The building had cost 1.3 billion euros, all while the people stood in line for food.

In the end it had not protected Ceausescu from the popular uprising, which had ended with the Ceausescus' pathetic attempt to escape via helicopter from the rooftop of the Central Committee building, followed by a kangaroo trial and hurried execution.

Perhaps if Ceausescu had spent that money on his people he would still be alive, Hefflin thought, as he parked his rented Opel along the serpentine driveway.

He followed the guests inside the building where they congregated to gaze at the crystal chandeliers, the gold leaf on the ceilings, and the purple curtains embroidered with real silver and gold. Waiters dressed in tuxedos served champagne cocktails. He spotted a bar set up in a corner and ordered a Johnnie Walker Black, then walked with it to mingle. He despised conferences and had avoided them over the years. He wasn't quite sure what he was doing among those pillars of industry. Most of them peddled armaments, the last thing the Romanian people needed.

"A penny for your thoughts," came a voice behind him.

When he turned around, he saw Amanda Thayer, the executive secretary, brandishing a martini. She wore a strapless white cocktail dress with matching white heels. Her hair was up again, not in a bun this time but in a serpentine intertwinement that left two sexy tendrils on either side of her face.

"My thoughts are worth more than that," he said. "Been here long?"

"My second martini," she said. "I figure I need at least five to get me through this evening."

"Nice to see you pace yourself," he drawled. "I don't think I can take any more speeches or lectures."

"Oh, there won't be any of that tonight," she said as she edged closer. "Tonight's for striking deals."

"Here? While everyone's drinking?"

"That's how business deals are made. What kind of businessman are you?"

"Not a very good one, I guess," he said. "I like to be sober when I negotiate."

She stepped away and gave him the once-over. "That's a different Brioni you're wearing. And a Patek Philippe." She held his wrist. "Whatever you're selling, you must be good at it."

"A trust baby," he said. "So, where are these deals supposed to be made?"

"They're going to have a few drinks first, then the food will be rolled out, then they'll slowly retire, a few at a time, into private rooms."

"You've been to some of these already," he said.

"They're all the same." She waved her hand, then sipped her martini.

"So, where are these private rooms?"

"All over the place. Didn't you get the literature?" She pointed. "Down that corridor there's a whole bunch. This place is crawling with rooms. They'll just hobble in there with their bourbons and cigars and start talking numbers. A total bore, if you ask me."

"You're the executive secretary. Don't you go with them?"

"No, only the principals, and only men, in my experience. But hey, what are you doing here if not to make deals?"

"I've already made my deals," he said. "I'm just here to drink."

"Then we can drink together, like two outcasts on our own little island." She stepped in closer. He smelled the same perfume again, a bit overwhelming.

A quiet descended over the room. An entire cadre of men had entered the hall, at the head of which sauntered President Iliescu. He was a short man in his early sixties, with graying hair and a receding hairline. As he ambled in dressed in a dark gray suit, he received outstretched hands, which he shook with a patrician smile. Soft applause began somewhere in the back of the room, then spread throughout the hall until everyone tried to at least make a clapping motion while balancing their drinks.

"This is where I get nauseated," he murmured to Amanda.

"Don't worry. He won't be here long. Just showing his face."

Iliescu made the rounds, shaking hands and spitting pleasantries, until he reached the middle of the room where he raised his hands to quiet the applause, which had already died down by then. After welcoming the Western business leaders who would "return Romania to its rightful place among the nations of Europe," he expressed the hope that this evening was the first step in the long process of the integration of Romania into NATO. Another faint applause followed, after which Iliescu and his cohorts proceeded to the tables at the back of the room and settled around bottles of wine.

A bell rang, the signal for everyone to choose his table and take his seat. An army of waiters appeared carrying trays of *mititei*, stuffed cabbage, *mamaliga*—the Romanian polenta, various local carp dishes, grilled lamb and pork, and stuffed eggplant—delicacies the Romanian people hadn't seen in decades. The waiters placed the trays in the middle of the tables and proceeded to serve. Local wines were poured until everyone had a full glass, at which point Iliescu rose again to propose a toast.

"To a free and resurgent Romania!"

The guests acknowledged him by gulping their wine and returning to their conversations.

Amanda pulled Hefflin by his sleeve toward a corner table. "Let's grab a couple of seats where we don't have to listen to the babble."

"Don't you have to be with your boss?"

"Whatever deals he strikes, he'll tell us tomorrow," she said, dismissing the idea with a wave of the empty martini glass. "For the underlings, tonight's for playing."

Three men were already seated at the round table, engaged in a discussion that didn't seem to allow for intruders. Amanda ordered another martini from the hovering waiter.

"No *vino* for you?" Hefflin asked.

"Too slow," she responded. "I've been guzzling wine since my stint in a Catholic boarding school. We used to steal it from the church. It has little effect on me."

As Hefflin was about to sit, something caught his eye. Now that most guests had taken their seats, it was easier to view their faces. Yes, it was Gabor at a distant table. He had met the famed Romanian actor in '89 at a party in Gabor's apartment. And sitting next to him was Irina, Hefflin's cousin, a well-known stage actress.

Well, well, she does get invited to the best parties.

He noticed Irina speaking to another man sitting on the other side of her, even placing her hand familiarly on his arm. The man looked to be in his late forties or early fifties with a head of black hair. He wore a powder gray suit that, even at that distance, looked expensive. They seemed at ease together, laughing at each other's jokes and tilting their heads for a whisper.

An item.

Hefflin sat, and the waiter poured him a glass of wine. He was sure Irina would recognize him even at that distance, and even with the scruffy beard, blond hair, and fake glasses. He had hoped he could avoid having to explain why he had not notified her that he would be in Bucharest. He decided he would feast on the authentic Romanian food, which he never could find in the States, even though a couple of mediocre Romanian restaurants had sprung up in Queens.

As the evening wore on and the food and wine were consumed, he noticed some of the businessmen leave their tables, one by one. At some point he realized that the government officials had also disappeared, along with President Iliescu.

He was about to excuse himself from the fair Amanda, who had heroically held up the conversation all by herself, when he spotted a familiar figure walking toward a side door leading to the private rooms: Harold Mayfield.

Just as Mayfield passed out of the hall, Hefflin hurried to the door. As he peered around the corner he spotted Mayfield open another door and walk inside. Apparently, he was there to make a deal. When Hefflin returned to his table, Amanda asked, "Who is he?"

"Who?"

"The man you followed."

"Oh, him. I thought I knew him, but I was mistaken. So, what happens now?"

"Nothing much. This isn't exactly the Met Gala." She sipped her drink. "When the meetings are over, they'll all trickle back to their tables, do some more drinking, and go back to their hotels. Some decide to leave directly without returning."

"And Iliescu? Is he in one of those rooms?"

"No. He doesn't make any deals himself. He's probably back home already, snuggling up to his little babushka with a glass of *tsuika*. He's known to hate these gatherings."

"At least that's one thing we have in common," Hefflin said as he rose.

"You're not leaving me alone here, are you?" She pouted; the little girl afraid of being stranded.

"I'm sure you won't be alone for long."

"Can we get together later?" Her eyes pleaded like a lost child. "At the Athénée bar, perhaps?"

"I'll be sleeping. And I think you've had enough martinis for one night. I'd hate to be you in the morning."

"Oh, I don't get them, hangovers, I mean. My metabolism is such that they just go right through me, the martinis."

"You've been blessed by the gods, then. Don't dare them."

He walked out of the ballroom with one last glance at Irina, who was still in prime form, entertaining both Gabor and her man. He hoped she hadn't seen him.

Outside he found several groups of businessmen standing around smoking cigarettes and whispering. Some of the deal rooms must have let out already.

He found his Opel and climbed inside, then slid down in his seat, motor off, and waited.

He didn't have to wait long. As guests began to trickle out, he spotted Mayfield trotting down the steps and hurrying to his car, a white Mercedes parked a few cars ahead of Hefflin's. The Mercedes drove off and Hefflin followed at a discreet distance.

It was past eleven in the evening, yet the streets still rumbled with traffic. Not only were there more cars on the road compared to three years ago, but they drove faster now, more like the Italians. Apparently, the new democracy had unleashed an inherent bravado and recklessness, which the communists had managed to suppress for forty years. The traffic enabled Hefflin to follow with less chance of being spotted.

The white Mercedes stopped on a side street in front of a nondescript hotel and Mayfield walked inside. Hefflin pulled up a few feet with the lights off, shut off the motor, and slid down in his seat. Through the windows of the hotel, he observed Mayfield speak to the receptionist, then emerge alone and walk to a dark corner of an alley where he lit a cigarette. A moment later two men emerged from the hotel wearing light gray suits and white shirts opened at the neck. They were dark-haired, Middle Eastern looking.

They walked toward where Mayfield was waiting, then the three of them continued down the dark street. At the first street corner, they turned around and walked back, all the time engaged in a discussion. When they reached the hotel entrance again, the two men shook hands with Mayfield and reentered the building.

Who the hell are these Middle Eastern men and why is Mayfield talking to them right after discussions with Romanian government officials?

Hefflin followed Mayfield to the InterContinental where Mayfield was staying, but he knew the interesting part of the evening was over.

CHAPTER THIRTY-ONE

Bucharest
April 1993

THE LAST TIME he had seen the house was during the frigid, violent winter of 1989. It was now a little past noon on a warm April day, and lilac trees blossomed in the small garden. He had called ahead that morning, unlike the previous time when he had shown up unannounced after twenty years of silence.

When the door opened, Irina greeted him with a stage smile and the pose of a diva. She stared at him for a moment, not seeming able to fit his new look into her old image of him.

"Cousin? Welcome back to our little swamp!" she exclaimed in Romanian. "You changed your hair. And what's with the beard and glasses?" She embraced him, then took the bouquet of red roses he had brought and showed him inside.

"If women can change their look, why can't men?" he asked.

"You should be an actor," she said. "You seem to like disguises. Or maybe you're still a spy."

While she searched for a vase, he took in the view of his beautiful cousin, a stage actress who had succeeded in reaching the pinnacle of her profession even during the misery of communism. She wore a green strapless dress that looked as if it had been painted on her. Italian, he guessed. The black high-heeled shoes flashed red soles, which matched her red nails. She noticed him studying her.

"What? You don't approve?" she asked, her eyes wary of a Western critic. "The dress is Ferragamo and the shoes are Louboutin. They opened a new outlet here selling odds and ends of various Western designers. They had only two pairs. One of them happened to fit me."

"They're beautiful," Hefflin said. "Your entire outfit is gorgeous. I was just wondering why you dressed up?"

But they don't sell Ferragamo dresses or Louboutin shoes in any outlet, Irina, and certainly not one in Bucharest.

"I wanted to show off my new riches to my American cousin, if you must know."

She winked, then sashayed to the kitchen to fill the vase. In a moment she returned and placed the vase of roses on the dining table.

"It took a month to have the dress taken in," she embellished the lie. She settled into the couch he knew from his childhood on which she had shown him a book containing Bosch's painting *The Garden of Earthly Delights*. The naked figures in unnatural poses and the grotesque animals had made him vomit at the time. "I have a seamstress who works miracles. But I had to lose a little fat first." She giggled. "I have a trainer now. He comes here three times a week to torture me."

The living room had a few additions—new purple velvet drapes, a brand-new German TV set, a copy of a Brancusi bust, its oval eyes seeming to follow his every move.

"I can afford a few more things now," she said as she noticed him peruse the room. "I get paid extra, per performance, and I do more television work. It's slowly opening up, for us actors at least."

She poured from an open bottle of French champagne.

"It's the bottle you brought me the last time you were here," she said. "I saved it as a plea to the gods for your return."

She kept rambling on, as if trying to delay the explanation that he awaited.

"What is that silky suit you're wearing?" she asked suddenly. "Armani?"

"Brioni," he said, a little embarrassed.

Her eyes opened wide. "I bet *you* didn't get it from an outlet store. You came into money."

"I married well."

"Who is she? Tell me everything."

He told her about Catherine, his Harvard love, the heiress to a French fortune. He skipped the part about her being Pusha, his childhood sweetheart, and how Boris had arranged for them to meet again at Harvard.

"You were born under a lucky star," she said in wonder. "And you said she comes from money?"

"An old French family," he said.

"Aristocracy. I'm proud of you. You're not still a spy, God forbid?"

"No, retired," he lied.

"Of course. What would you be doing spying when you have all this money?"

"That's not quite fair," he objected, more as a way of livening up the conversation. "If you had accepted all those millions that Victor left for you, you'd still be acting."

Victor Vulcan, her previous lover, Ceausescu's moneyman, had left her an offshore account worth twenty million dollars. She'd refused it then, but would she refuse it now?

"Of course I'd still be acting, but that's my passion. You can't compare my art with your spying."

He marveled at her vanity. The nightly applause had given her a sense of being worthy of that spotlight whether on or off stage. He said nothing, though he suspected that the comparison was closer than she imagined.

"How is your love life these days?" he asked, inching toward the subject.

She returned her gaze to her glass of champagne, lifted it to her lips, and sipped. "You always know everything. Why torture me?"

"I'm no longer a spy, remember?"

"He's a businessman now," she declared. "We all have a past that we want to forget. It's a new world, at least in Romania."

It's the same world, Irina, with the same players. Some of them are just wearing better suits.

"He sounds interesting," he said. "Tell me about him."

"Oh, there isn't much to tell." She brushed back her long brown hair, now with tasteful blond streaks. "He runs a couple of private security firms. After all, that's what he knows, so what else could he do? Quite successful at it, apparently."

"So he was in the security services before?"

She looked down. "You know he was Securitate, so why do you make me say it? He was never involved in any atrocities or in field work, however, just a desk job."

Christ! How does she pick them? First Ceausescu's moneyman, now a Securitate apparatchik.

"How did you meet?"

"Gabor introduced me to him, at a party. He's divorced, with two children that live with his wife. What else do you want to know?" She looked at him with piercing eyes, daring him.

"I'd love to meet him."

"Why?"

He shrugged. "No particular reason. He sounds interesting."

She leaned back in the couch. "Now, Cousin, I know you. You don't just do something for no reason. You sound like the old spy."

"No, Irina. I left all that behind. I'm just a businessman now. And in business, the more friends you make, the more opportunities you find. Simple as that. Besides, what's so unusual about my wanting to meet my cousin's new boyfriend?"

"Well, if that's the case"—she shifted in her seat—"we can have dinner together. He's coming over tomorrow night. I'm supposed to be cooking for him. We're celebrating our one-year anniversary together."

"Wonderful. I'll bring the champagne. If I won't be imposing, that is."

"No, he'll want to meet you. He loves America and Americans. And, as you say, you're both businessmen. He may want to pick your brain. Capitalism is a new concept here. The rules are all different. Everyone is trying to figure them out. It's quite dizzying." She placed her hand to her temple. "They want me to star in a French film, you know, for more money than I made in my entire life from that miserable salary they still give me. I don't know how I survived."

You survived by having your previous lover bring delicacies from the Party stores, and by bribing the butcher to save meat for you. But let all that dwell in the past.

"There is one thing, though," he said, "a minor issue. In my new life, I go by the name of James Blake."

"Another alias? You said you weren't still a spy."

"I'm not. That's why I needed a new identity, and a new look. I wanted to rid myself of my old life."

She nodded. "I can understand that. You made some enemies, no doubt. I still have no idea what you did in your previous life."

Nor I in yours.

"Let's call it a clean break for both of us, then," she declared with a stage smile. "And good riddance to the old life."

They spent the afternoon talking about her, as was usually the case with Irina, the diva. The new roles she had played, a new television series in which she was starring, the planned French film in which she would have a nude scene.

"I lied," she declared. "I didn't lose weight to fit into the dress. The French director told me I'd have to lose five kilos. The camera adds a couple to start with, and a nude scene . . . well, that's going to be another new experience. You have to promise never to see the film." She giggled, the champagne getting to her.

"I deserve more credit than that," he said. "I am capable of separating my cousin from a character in a film, and I can certainly look at a nude as a form of art."

"Oh, don't give me that." She laughed. "I saw the way you looked at me when you walked in. Men are all the same."

"I was eyeing your outfit, actually. You didn't get a Ferragamo dress and Louboutin shoes from any outlet. Nor that Brancusi reproduction."

"All right, they were gifts, what of it? And it's not a reproduction. It's an original, or so he says." She stared into his eyes to see his expression.

"An original Brancusi? Your new lover must have real money."

"He says he bought it from the government at a bargain. It was just sitting in a warehouse, along with works by other Romanian artists. At least now you, and I, can take pleasure in it. Is that so bad? People have private collections all over the world. Why can't I have a little Brancusi?"

Who is this woman before me? I don't recognize her.

"What happened to your concern for the people who can now hardly afford the jacked-up food prices?"

"Yes." She looked away. "Their miserable lives haven't changed. But that is our new system, isn't it? How many poor people do you have in America? Communist equality didn't work. In the jungle there is no equality. The strong or the smart dominate; the rest try to survive as best they can."

"We've left the jungle hundreds of thousands of years ago," Hefflin said.

"Have we? What is American capitalism but a jungle?"

He remembered a man from Ghana selling fake Rolex watches on 5th Avenue who had told him something similar: "New York is more of a jungle than the one surrounding my African village."

"'A rising tide raises all boats.' Isn't that what one of your presidents said?" Irina continued. "Hopefully, capitalism will eventually do the same to this country. In the meantime, I don't have to be one of those miserable poor. There are enough of them. They don't need one more."

She disappeared into the kitchen, only to return a moment later with a bowl of black caviar and a plate of toasted bread. "It's Sevruga, from Iran. Let's enjoy it without this agonizing guilt you're laying on me. We have only one life."

We don't know that, Irina, but that's another topic.

Her admonition cut deeply into his own guilt over his newfound wealth. He knew he had to either get rid of the guilt or the money.

The conversation turned to politics, a new topic for Romanians, who had lived all their lives under one-party rule.

"We have more political parties now than I can count, with names that change every few months," she rattled on. "They form alliances, only to dissolve them a week later. I can't keep track of any of it."

"The messiness of democracy," Hefflin said. "It is the worst form of government, except for all the other ones, as Churchill said."

"I never thought of politics before. Now we are bombarded with it every day, wasting our time and emotions. Besides, they all lie, so what's the point of even listening to them? A benevolent prince would be my choice. But there is no such being."

"What do you think of Iliescu?"

"Oh, he says the right things, but nothing gets done. It's as if he's slowing down our transition on purpose." She waived her hand. "But what do I know? If you want to find out what's really happening, you should talk to some of my journalist friends. Radu Milan, for instance. He knows everything."

"Where can I find him?"

"He's always running around after one story or another. The best way is to go to the bar at *La Premiera*, a new restaurant behind the National Theater. You can find him there every evening pumping his friends for information."

He left late in the afternoon, dizzy with champagne and the inner turmoil that Irina had caused to resurface. The irony did not escape him. Communism had corrupted everyone by forcing them to bribe and scrounge even for the basics of survival. Capitalism now corrupted by bringing out greed and egotism, not for survival anymore, but for luxury.

Where were the angels of the world?

CHAPTER THIRTY-TWO

Bucharest
April 1993

IT WAS ONLY a little before five in the afternoon, but Strada Lipscani already pulsated with activity. A red neon sign blinked "Girls" on the front of the building where a line of men had formed. Two large men dressed in black stood guard, deciding whom to let inside, as if it were a disco club in New York. From what Hefflin could see, the decision depended on how the men in line were dressed.

Hefflin wore a black Brioni suit with faint blue pinstripes and an Yves Saint Laurent silk tie. He stepped up to the two men and handed each a fifty-dollar bill. After eyeing the bills incredulously, then staring at Hefflin's suit, they opened the door and waved him inside.

The Stones' "Satisfaction" blared at ear-piercing decibels. The crowd of men whistled and shouted at the strippers performing on the stage, which lined the wall beyond the long wooden bar. One woman hung upside down on a trapeze, another coiled around a brass pole. Other women dressed in black corsets, fishnet stockings, and black stilettos mingled among the men, offering more immediate satisfaction.

Hefflin shouldered his way to the bar and caught the eye of the bartender, a tall man in his thirties wearing a black vest and bow tie over a white shirt.

"I need to see The Owl," Hefflin yelled above the music in broken Romanian.

"Who is asking?"

"Boris."

The bartender stiffened, then motioned him around the bar to a black door. It led into a dark corridor lit by red bulbs hanging from the ceiling. At the far end two large men stood on either side of a green door. They signaled for Hefflin to lift his arms, then patted him down. Satisfied, they told him to wait while one of them knocked, then entered the room. A moment later the man reappeared and nodded for him to go inside.

Hefflin stepped into a large office that became eerily quiet the moment the door closed behind him. The paneled walls were lined with books. Red leather chairs and a plush, Persian-style rug completed the allusion to an Ivy League library. Behind an ornate antique desk sat a man who looked to be in his early sixties, with gray hair that sprang up like a crazed Einstein. On the desk before him stood a chess set, its figures frozen in positions of attack and counterattack. The man stared at the board, rubbing his chin.

"It is not easy to play against yourself," the man said in English with what sounded like a Russian accent. "You always know your opponent's moves ahead of time." He let out a chuckle, then looked up. "This game holds me prisoner all my life. I cannot escape it. Sit, sit."

Hefflin settled into a chair before the desk. "You read me as an American when I walked into your office?"

"A Westerner, certainly, the moment you walked into my club." The man pointed with his chin to the five television screens lined up on the far wall, which displayed the inside of the club from various angles. "Your suit is too fine even for stinking millionaires that have sprung up in our country. So, what can I do for you, Mr. Blake?"

Hefflin was taken aback. "How do you know my name?"

"I like to keep track of rich Westerners who visit city. I know everyone on convention list, and their companies. You were late addition, and mystery." The Owl broke into a smile. "I, for one, love mysteries. My library is full of them. From Edgar Allan Poe to Agatha Christie to Arthur Conan Doyle to John Le Carré, and everyone in between." He waved his arm at the walls lined with books. "I especially like *Spy Who Run in from Cold.*"

"Close enough."

"So, why are you here, Mr. Blake?"

"I'm an investor here to seek new opportunities," Hefflin said, "and to promote more American investment in Romania."

"May I see your passport?" The Owl extended his hand.

"Why?"

"In this country people say many words. Most of time they mean nothing. Documents are harder to forge."

Hefflin handed him his passport.

The Owl studied it for a moment. "Why diplomatic passport?"

"Like I said, I'm here to promote economic relations between our two countries. The State Department thought a diplomatic passport would give me more credibility."

"And it protects you from arrest." The Owl chuckled. "Are you CIA?"

Hefflin hesitated. "Used to be. Now I'm a private businessman."

"Ha! Just like in our country. Former Securitate now businessmen. Funny, no?"

"I married well," Hefflin said.

"Marrying well is an old tradition. So, who sent you to me?"

"Django. He said he used to work for you."

"Ah, yes, loyal man, but weak-minded. I had to let him go." The Owl's mouth pursed slightly. "What can I do for you?"

"He said you are the man to see if I need information."

"He has big mouth. That was another problem. What kind of information?"

"I need to know about unit U0920."

The Owl sized Hefflin up for a moment, seemingly unsure of what to say. "CIA should know something about it."

"Like I said, I'm not with the CIA anymore."

"Then why do you need to know about secret Securitate unit?"

Hefflin shifted in his seat. "It has to do with a friend of mine whom I'm also looking for. A man I knew only as Boris."

"Boris?" The Owl chuckled. "That is like saying John or Bill in English."

"I knew him in '89, before the revolution. Boris is the name I gave him."

"Ah." The Owl nodded. "A code name, when you were CIA. Now coin drops, as you say." The Owl pressed a button under his desk and a moment later the same bodyguard entered.

"A bottle of our best cognac and two glasses," The Owl ordered in Russian-accented Romanian. Then, turning to Hefflin, he said in English, "A good discussion always goes better with drink, no?" He opened a silver case on his desk that was filled with cigarettes. "In communist days we used to import Kents in black market." He shrugged. "What did we know? That was what people wanted. These days I have graduated to Dunhills. They kill you just as fast, so I might as well enjoy higher quality."

Hefflin took one and The Owl used an ornate gold lighter to light Hefflin's cigarette, followed by his own. A waiter appeared with a silver tray bearing a bottle of cognac and two snifters. The waiter poured three fingers into each glass then quietly left the room.

"To Boris," The Owl toasted as he lifted his snifter.

Hefflin echoed the toast and they clinked glasses.

"You are not first man to ask me about Boris," The Owl said, "but somehow I get feeling name means more to you."

"Someone is trying to incriminate him," Hefflin said. "I want to help him clear his name."

"Very noble of you. He is lucky to have such good friend." The Owl stood and pondered the chessboard once more. "What would you do if you were playing black, Mr. Blake?"

Hefflin stood and peered down at the board. He studied it for a long moment, then his mind lit up. "Black wins in four moves."

"Show me, please."

Hefflin moved the pieces, then the last forced move by a white knight to protect his king, which exposed the path of the black bishop that lay hiding on the other side of the board.

"Checkmate."

"Bravo!" The Owl beamed. "How do you know that move?"

"The hidden bishop. I learned it from my father."

"And who did he learn it from?"

Hefflin hesitated. "From Boris."

"Ha! And he learned it from me!" The Owl cried.

Hefflin stood frozen, unable to catch up to the old man. "Are we speaking of the same person?"

"Of course we are, James. Or should I say, *Vasili*?" The Owl grinned. "Close your mouth. There is good explanation for everything. Life for individual is linear, but for group, or society, it is fractal, as in Chaos Theory—in physics terminology." The Owl removed a photograph from a desk drawer and handed it to Hefflin. It showed Hefflin standing at the Gala holding a glass of scotch.

"I recognized you moment I saw photograph," The Owl said, "despite your new look."

"How do you know me?"

"Two operations in '89: your meeting at *Red Barrel* with man you call Boris, and extraction of certain minister of agriculture."

Vulcan, Ceausescu's moneyman and Irina's lover, who was caught in Constanta trying to flee.

"You were involved in both operations?"

"They were all my men: waiters in *Red Barrel*, cook, even clients. Remember how they stood to block Securitate men from seeing you when they walked in? And how you were whisked out by back door?" The Owl's eyes beamed with pride. "You think it all happened by accident? I was sitting at table to oversee operation. And extraction of minister went as planned by my men, without any problems, until his wife turned him in to Securitate."

"There was a girl helping with the extraction," Hefflin said. *Catherine.*

"Yes, Boris brought her in to put minister at ease. He liked pretty women. But then it was woman who betrayed him, after all. His own wife." The Owl slapped his thigh again. "Ironic, no? Man's greatest weaknesses: money and sex."

"The minister only spent a year in jail, I believe," Hefflin said.

"Yes, like all criminals after revolution, they were condemned to twenty years and released in one or two. But they never found Ceausescu's money. I do not think Vulcan has it either, though he has his own little nest egg in Switzerland, which he is enjoying now in the South of France." The Owl shook his head. "Another corrupt apparatchik. At least I am honest about being thief."

"The man I met, and whom I call Boris," Hefflin said. "What is his real name?"

The Owl grew wistful. "His real name? I do not think even he remembered it. His KGB name was Vladimir Dovrosky, but I originally knew him as Yuri Garogin from old days. He had so many aliases. I never saw his real face, either. He always wore some beard or mustache, or he dyed his hair or wore rags and hobbled like crip-ple. Still, I loved him. He used to come here and read all my books. He loved Sherlock Holmes best." He shook his head again. "Games you people play. I used to deal with all security agencies, since one time or other they all needed my services. I have known man you call Boris for long time, and we did many operations together."

"How did you decide to use the name Boris as your passcode?"

"Funny story. One day, in mid-'80s, we were discussing changing name I used for my passcode. Too many people had heard it and it was becoming security problem. Out of blue, Yuri suggested I use Boris. I thought it was joke. He jokes a lot, as you must know."

"Yes, he does." Hefflin almost used the past tense, but caught him-self in time.

"It is just simple name, but I soon got to like it. But now I think I have to change it again."

"Why?"

"Name has become strangely common in my circles," The Owl said. "During end of eighties, name grew to be used by many people in underworld, in all sorts of ways. Some used it as synonym for any clandestine operation, as in 'Let's do a Boris,' while others used it to refer to any sly or witty trick, as in 'He pulled a Boris on me.' Over past few years name has taken on life of its own, becoming almost mythical. I always suspected it was he who spread name around, as way of protecting himself, somehow. Now I think I know why."

"To obscure the significance of the code name in case it was com-promised?" Hefflin asked.

"Precisely. Like I said when you asked just now, you are not first man to be interested in that name. Within past year KGB asked me about it, then, recently, nice young man from CIA."

"What did you tell them?"

"I told them truth: that I do not know anyone by that name." The Owl looked older all of a sudden. "I lost track of Yuri over past three years. I hope all is well."

I hope so, too, in that great spy ring in the sky.

"I, also, have lost track of him," Hefflin said.

"He was full of life, that man. And stories."

"Stories?"

"Yes, many colorful stories, one in particular," The Owl began as he sipped his cognac. "He had obsession, a debt to pay."

"A debt?" Hefflin's heart pounded in his throat.

"He always talked about it, to me, at least, like maniac—Greek doctor serving in Romanian Army who had saved his life at Battle of Stalingrad. He never told me who doctor was, but he said he had holy oath to repay that kindness for rest of his life. He did so in many ways: by helping doctor when he got caught performing abortions . . ."

It was Boris who helped my father with the abortion trial!

". . . helping family emigrate to Greece, paying for doctor's son to attend college, even creating fantastic circumstances for son to meet girl he had not seen in over twenty years."

Catherine!

"Incredible as stories were, I believe every word. That is who he is—loyal to core. But somehow, I get feeling you have heard story before."

Hefflin turned his face away to hide his emotions, then drank some cognac to steady himself. *This can't be a coincidence. There are no coincidences in our business.*

"He helped many people, and not because he expected they would pay him back," The Owl continued. "I remember his helping a Jewish professor and his wife escape Romania, for instance. He was friend of that doctor. He used my men to do it. We dressed them up as gypsies and brought them through Bulgaria to Turkey in one of our horse-drawn wagons."

Pincus!

"Yes, he traveled everywhere with his job, cultivated many friends," The Owl went on. "Women, too. But none for long. They came and went. 'Women are like trollies,' he used to say. 'If you miss one, you can always catch another.'" The man chuckled. "Except for one woman. He loved her deeply, though he could never settle down. He never told me her name, as if he was protecting her. The man has way of making you feel he is opening his heart to you without actually telling you anything specifically." The Owl smiled. "I guess it is his KGB training. Did he ever mention any of these stories to you?"

"I never knew him that well," Hefflin demurred.

"Yes, he helped many people escape—Jews, Greeks, Armenians, even gypsies who had been festering in jail for some minor theft."

"So, how do you know the name Vasili?"

"Yuri spoke about you, and those stories I told you. Let us be frank. You are son of doctor, are you not?"

Hefflin nodded.

"Do not worry. Yuri never told me your real identity or what business he had with you. Even if he had, I know how to forget."

From the bottom drawer of his desk The Owl removed a metal box, then searched its interior with his fingers. He finally retrieved an envelope, which he brought back to the table and handed to Hefflin. Inside was a letter in English, written in pen, dated February 3, 1991.

"*Spending my last months on earth with Vasili, true son of mine. Be happy for me.*"

There was no signature. Hefflin's eyes watered.

"You know, Vasili, you should learn who your true friends are," The Owl said. "I am one of them. I know Yuri has passed on.

He loved you very much, and I loved him. So, why are you in Bucharest?"

Hefflin hesitated. How much could he trust this leader of the underworld? But The Owl was Boris's longtime friend, a man Boris had trusted with his life.

"Boris used to be my asset," Hefflin said. "Someone is now saying that the intel he gave me was false."

"Who says this?"

"A defector who claims he was a KGB plant in unit U0920. He calls himself Rodovan Coianu. I need to find out if his story is true, to begin with."

The Owl rose and started pacing, thinking. He was a thin, relatively short man, but full of energy. "Unit was used by Ceausescu to spy on his own. As far as I know it was disbanded after revolution, together with rest of Securitate. To find out if this defector of yours worked there will be difficult, and costly."

Hefflin pulled a wad of hundred-dollar bills from his jacket pocket and dropped it on the table. "Will a thousand dollars be enough?"

"This money is for bribes, not for me. And things are more expensive now. Two thousand should do it."

Hefflin dropped another wad of cash. "If you don't mind my asking, are you Roma?"

The old man looked at him with misty eyes. "Thank you for using proper term. Yes, I am Roma, gypsy, but I do not advertise it. Bad for business." He poured himself some more cognac. "But in my heart, I do not know what I am. I was born in Ukraine, and lived in the fields in one of those horse wagons with my family and clan. There is nothing like five people—me, my parents, and two brothers—squeezing together under a fur quilt every night. Definition of intimacy." He laughed. "We always moved on one step ahead of authorities. Then one year, when I was fifteen, we crossed border into Romania. My clan decided we would have easier time here. Once we arrived in Bucharest, I got together with right people— wrong people from your point of view—and learned ways of underworld."

Another unanchored spirit.

"That explains your Russian accent," Hefflin said.

"Yes, I cannot get rid of it. It is same in Romanian."

"There is another matter, a personal one. The *Mandale* clan."

The old man's eyes grew wide. "Part of *Kalderash*. Of course."

"I'd like to speak to the *voivode*."

"*Voivode!*" The Owl thought for a time. "Old *voivode* died some years ago. Since he had no children, mantle passed to his brother's son, old man himself now."

"Didn't the old *voivode* have a daughter?"

The Owl shook his head. "They do not speak of her. It is as if she never existed. These are unfortunate laws of our people, which we must change. You see, wherever Roma go, they are treated as aliens, considered nomads, even if they live in one place for generations and try to adapt. Only way we can retain identity is by ossifying old traditions to not forget them."

Just like the immigrants I grew up with in Worcester.

"She fell in love with young *gadjo*, non-gypsy, and they disowned her," The Owl added. "I have moved past those old traditions, but they have not."

"I heard she had a child," Hefflin said.

"Yes." The old man nodded. "Boy. He was banned also, of course. But I do not know what happened to him or her. It has been so long. You know her?"

"I met her once, briefly," Hefflin lied. "I heard she was killed during the revolution."

"Strange," the old man said. "Roma do not usually get involved in demonstrations."

"Where can I find the clan in case I want to talk to them?"

"They live in Ferentari neighborhood, where most Roma live," The Owl said. "But I would not go there. It is ghetto. If you do, go in daytime, and mention my name. That will save you from being mugged . . . or worse."

As Hefflin rose to go, he asked, "By the way, why do they call you The Owl?"

"Because I am smarter than rest of them, and wiser." The Owl winked. "But that is not saying much."

CHAPTER THIRTY-THREE

Bucharest
April 1993

LA PREMIERA WAS located behind the National Theatre, as Irina had said. It reminded Hefflin of Rick's Café, with a busy bar and terrace where the nomenklatura could hobnob with journalists, actors, and "intellectuals."

It was past seven in the evening and the place was busy. Irina had said that Radu Milan could be found there on a daily basis, his watering hole where he could discuss politics with his journalist colleagues and perhaps pick up some fresh bit of news from his apparatchik contacts.

Hefflin shouldered his way to the bar and ordered a Johnnie Walker Black, neat. When the bartender returned with the drink, Hefflin asked him in broken Romanian if Milan was around.

"Where are you from?" the bartender asked.

"America. A journalist." Hefflin pulled out an American passport—not his diplomatic one—just enough for the bartender to be convinced.

"Ah, in that case, he is over there, the guy in the white shirt and black jacket." He pointed with his chin.

Milan stood next to several men, all of whom held glasses of beer. After downing his scotch, Hefflin ordered a glass of beer and waited until Milan turned from the group and proceeded toward the bar with his empty glass.

Hefflin put on his friendly American smile and introduced himself. Milan faced him with a stern look.

"*New York Times*, you say?"

Hefflin showed him his passport and a fake press card, part of the package Ingram had provided.

"A mutual friend suggested I talk to you, to get a feel for the situation in the country," Hefflin said.

The man raised his hand for Hefflin to say no more, then nodded. "Let's take a walk."

Milan left his empty glass on the counter and walked out of the restaurant. After a minute, Hefflin followed. He saw the young journalist turn into the first side street, which was practically pitch black, the only light coming from the half moon and the surrounding buildings. In a moment Milan appeared out of a doorway and started walking beside Hefflin.

"Who is this mutual friend?" Milan asked.

"Irina Argyris."

"Ah, a great actress and a lovely woman. How do you know her?"

"Her cousin in New York is a good friend of mine," Hefflin said.

The man nodded. "So, what do you want to know?"

"You can tell me what you think of the government, to start with," Hefflin said.

Milan waived his hand. "They are corrupt, but that's nothing new in this country. They are all remnants of the old nomenklatura, the old thinking. They can't let go of central control."

"And Iliescu? Where does he stand?"

"With one foot in the West and the other in the East. He's a socialist in his heart, now forced to pretend that he loves democracy.

He was a friend of Gorbachev from their student days, but now that Gorbachev is gone, he doesn't know what to do."

"He declared that he wants to join NATO," Hefflin said.

"Yes, while at the same time he negotiated a secret friendship treaty with Moscow."

"Are you sure of that?"

"I have it on good authority. But Iliescu is afraid to present it to the parliament to pass it. The people would rise up in arms."

"But why is he doing this? Surely Romania's future lies with the West."

Milan smiled wryly. "Iliescu is like a pretty girl with two suitors. He plays one against the other. Yes, he wants the West's money, but he also knows he needs to be friends with the sleeping bear to his east in case the bear wakes up one day. Russia won't stay down forever. So, Iliescu is always vague about reforms, playing coy. That's what small countries do."

"He has begun to privatize state companies," Hefflin said.

"Very slowly, one at a time. And they all go to his friends."

"You mean, the new oligarchs?" Hefflin asked.

Milan nodded, but remained silent.

"What is the connection between the oligarchs and the government?" Hefflin pushed on.

The man stopped walking and turned to Hefflin. "I am sorry, but that is not a topic for our discussion."

Hefflin removed two hundred-dollar bills from his pocket and attempted to hand them to Milan.

"Put that away," Milan snapped in English. "I don't take money. But I can get killed talking to you about such matters."

"Does the Securitate still do that kind of thing to journalists?"

The man started walking again. "The new Securitate is the same as the old one, with the same people, except that now they are fighting for personal wealth, which is a bigger incentive than ideology."

"How?"

"Look, you cannot write this. This is—how you say?—background information. Do not even write that you got it from a local journalist. Is that clear?"

"Crystal."

The man looked behind him, then at the buildings on either side of the street.

"Everyone in the West thinks we had a popular revolution, but few here believe that. It was a coup d'état by the old guard. I don't know if they started the revolution or joined it afterward once they saw it would be successful, but the result is the same. Outside forces were probably involved, most likely the Russians."

It was the Americans, Milan, but I can't tell you that.

"Iliescu's original plan was to create a kinder socialism, Gorbachev style," Milan went on, "but then he saw that the people would not allow it, that the carnage had radicalized the population. So, he changed his tune, declaring democracy and a free-market system. But he and his friends quickly discovered that this was a golden opportunity. They realized they could privatize government industries and take possession of them, one at a time, before anyone else could."

"How?"

"I don't know exactly, but suddenly we have all these newly privatized companies and no one can figure out who the true owners are. Then we started seeing millionaires being driven around in black Mercedes and building mansions in the outskirts of Bucharest."

"Christ. How many industries are we talking about?"

"Before the last election in '92, one of my Securitate contacts told me that if Iliescu won, they would then have all the time they need to complete their task. After that, it wouldn't matter who won future elections. Well, Iliescu won, so it's all over. They are slowly absorbing Romania's top industries."

"Can you give me the names of some of these oligarchs?"

"No. I've said too much already."

"Give me a hint. Something."

Milan hesitated. "Think of the Securitate, their dossiers on millions of private citizens, which fill dozens of warehouses."

"So, you're saying the politicians in the government are using the Securitate dossiers? How?"

Milan shook his head. "It's the other way around, my friend. The Securitate owns the politicians. Their dossiers are full of compromising material on all of them. And if they don't have any, they manufacture it, like they did during Ceausescu's time. The country is run by them."

Hefflin tried to wrap his mind around what Milan was saying. "Have you published any of this?"

"I tried to, a piece of it, but was immediately fired from my job. I think that my newspaper was owned by one of the oligarchs. The oligarchs now own many of the large media outlets. These days I write for small, independent presses, but they, too, are afraid."

As Milan was about to turn away, Hefflin caught his arm.

"One more thing: Do you know this man by any chance?" Hefflin showed him the picture of Mayfield.

Milan glanced at the picture, then pushed it away. "You want to get yourself killed? Put that away, and don't show it around." Milan extended his hand. "Tell Irina I said hello, and I wish her the best. And tell her to let her better angels guide her. Whatever you write, I haven't spoken to you. You don't know me. *Noroc.*"

With that Milan disappeared down the street, and Hefflin turned around to walk back the way he came.

CHAPTER THIRTY-FOUR

Bucharest
April 1993

THE TWO-STORY STUCCO house stood in the heart of an exclusive neighborhood of pre-war French-style villas that reminded Romanians of better times. A wrought iron fence surrounded the property, and a small garden bordered a brick path that led to the entrance. The windows were dark, silent. Hefflin's watch read a little past ten. Milan's reaction to Mayfield's photograph had finally convinced Hefflin to examine Mayfield's home.

After surveilling for an hour, Hefflin exited the rental car and donned a wide fedora he had bought at a local store to hide his face from the peering eyes of any neighbors. Finding the gate unlocked, he walked up the path to the front door, then stopped and listened. Hearing no sounds, he pressed the doorbell and heard the chime. No response. If someone else resided in that house, he or she was a heavy sleeper. He removed the two metal strips from the lining of his jacket collar, picked the lock, and entered.

He eased into a dark hallway holding his Beretta with both hands. The faint moonlight allowed him to make out paintings on the walls, a Persian rug, a mirror. He silently made his way through the living room, then the dining room, both furnished with old-style heavy mahogany pieces from pre-war days.

He ascended the stairs, stopped midway when one of the steps creaked, then continued to the second floor. He found the master bedroom, a guest bedroom, then a third room converted into an office, all unoccupied. Mayfield lived alone. An ornate desk stood on one side of the spacious office. Two leather chairs faced it, with a leather couch and a coffee table on the other side of the room. A mahogany credenza stood against one wall and an Aubusson rug covered the parquet floor.

Mayfield knows how to live.

He quickly moved behind the desk and lit his miniature flashlight. Three drawers formed the right side of the desk. Inside the first one he found the usual items—stationary, a box of envelopes, pens. The second contained bills—all marked as paid—announcements of business conferences, receipts from restaurants in Bucharest and Athens, and used airline tickets. He noticed that Mayfield had traveled to Athens six times in the past six months, a few times to Paris with a further connection to Nice, and twice to Beirut. Some of the flights had layovers in Istanbul. There were no recent tickets either to or from the U.S.

In the bottom drawer, below business ledgers, he found a leather monthly planner.

A peculiar place to keep a planner.

Holding the flashlight in his mouth, he used his Minox miniature camera to photograph the pages going back a year.

After replacing the planner below the ledgers, he moved on to the credenza, which contained three drawers. The top drawer contained only one item: a humidor filled with Montecristo cigars. The sec-ond drawer comprised of what looked like mementoes. A miniature Palestinian flag was draped on top of a piece of yellowed paper with English writing: "To my good friend and ally in our eternal strug-gle." It was signed by a single initial "A."

Arafat!

Next to it lay two boxes containing medals of some sort, an Arabic-style 19th-century pistol, and an old map depicting a large country in place of Israel, labeled "Palestine." He photographed the items, then proceeded to the bottom drawer.

When he opened it he let out a slight gasp. More than a dozen expensive men's watches lay scattered about haphazardly. Among them he noted several Rolexes, a Cartier, two Omegas, a Patek Philippe, a Baume & Mercier, and several brands he didn't recognize.

Why are these expensive watches thrown in the drawer like discarded toys? And why so many?

He lined them up facing him and took several pictures. He then scrambled them into the random pattern in which he'd found them and moved on to the bedrooms. After going through the closets and drawers and finding nothing but expensive clothing, he exited the house, relocked the door, and drove to the Hungarian embassy.

*   *   *

Hefflin and Balzary hovered over the enlarged black-and-white photographs spread across the table. Hefflin had decided to take the film to Balzary to develop in the Hungarian embassy laboratory rather than to the CIA chief of station. He knew he couldn't operate solo for much longer, that he needed an ally, and Vogel just didn't seem the type.

"The airline tickets match the entries in his planner," Balzary said. "Athens on this date, then Beirut, then Athens again a month later."

"He's been to Athens every month for the past year," Hefflin observed, "each time on the same date."

"Maybe he has a Greek lover," Balzary suggested.

"But he stays only one day, then either returns back to Bucharest, or flies to Beirut on this date, or to Nice here," Hefflin said. "A long distance to travel for a quickie."

They focused on the photographs of the watches, strewn in the drawer like worthless relics.

"What kind of man treats beautiful watches like that?" Balzary shook his head. "They're worth thousands of dollars each. What condition was his apartment in?"

"Neat, clean, expensive furnishings. Everything in its place. No, Mayfield is not a sloppy guy, if that's what you mean."

Balzary reread the report Catherine had sent, then reviewed the photographs. "He's got friends in all the wrong places—Arafat, Gaddafi."

"Why didn't *we* have that intel?"

"The French have a long history in that area—old friendships, long-term assets. And they don't always like to share."

"How well do you know Mayfield?" Hefflin asked.

"A bit. He always came across as a playboy, a joker. I quickly lost interest."

"The report says he had connections to the prince. In the photo they look like buddies."

"I saw them together a couple of times, playing tennis at the Party tennis club once, in a restaurant another." Balzary hesitated, his eyes grazing the floor. "They used to go together to Nicu's houses in the outskirts of the city where he kept girls at his beck and call, his version of a harem."

"I heard rumors about that. Was it really true?"

"Unfortunately. They even invited me one time, but I refused, of course. Like I told you before, Mayfield isn't such a nice guy. But he and Nicu are birds of a feather. Nicu is a maniac. Whenever I saw him he was drunk—I mean violently drunk. And a cocaine user. Once I saw him stand on a restaurant table, dead drunk, and piss on the food of the other guests. Another time I heard he punched the waiter because he got the order wrong. Of course, the waiter hadn't."

Nicu just forgot what he had ordered. Nobody dared object to any of it. He was the prince who could do no wrong. He was convicted and sentenced to twenty years but he's out now, for health reasons."

"And he was supposed to be the heir? Why didn't you tell me he and Mayfield were buddies when I asked before?"

"Truth is, I was a bit embarrassed. I considered Mayfield a buffoon, a pervert, like Nicu. But now, with the new intel about Arafat and Gaddafi that Catherine has provided, I have to reassess my opinion of him."

They stared at the pictures of the watches again, turning them one way, then another, trying to guess at a puzzle they suspected was hidden somewhere inside them.

Hefflin looked at the photo of the planner. "He's due to fly to Athens again this month. I need to find out more about him, to decide if he's worth my trouble. Can you get me in to see Nicu?"

Balzary hesitated. "I can put out some feelers. I don't know how sick he is. He may be bedridden for all I know."

CHAPTER THIRTY-FIVE

Bucharest
April 1993

THEY SAT AROUND the old dining table that Irina had inherited from her parents, a heavy Gothic revival piece that had been in style before the War. Irina had gone all out to create an atmosphere of elegance and celebration. The table was set with the fine, paper-thin china that reflected the relative wealth of her family during the time before the communists, when her father had been a restaurateur. Lit candles in silver candlesticks and crystal wineglasses, all new, accompanied the old silverware, laid out upon one of her mother's embroidered white tablecloths. Hefflin had arrived with a cold bottle of Veuve Clicquot a little past five—an early dinner—which he had bought from one of the new stores in the city.

Irina's lover, Constantin Gorga, was a handsome man, tall, with dark hair and strong but refined facial features. He spoke softly, with subtle gestures of the hand and a tilting of his head as if whispering secrets for only the chosen few, which he had probably studied from the mannerisms of the old moneyed class of Europe.

Irina had introduced Hefflin as James Blake, a Romanian friend of her cousin in New York and a businessman interested in investing in the burgeoning democracies of Eastern Europe. Hefflin had whispered this introduction to Irina as he walked in because he needed a reasonable excuse for being able to speak Romanian well, since Irina knew no English.

After finishing a lavish dinner of homemade Greek moussaka and the ubiquitous *mamaliga*, they sat around enjoying glasses of the French cognac that Gorga had brought.

"I thought I recognized your name, and I just remembered," Gorga said softly, pondering. "I believe you are the head of a nonprofit organization working to benefit the orphans here in Romania."

Hefflin was surprised. His name did not appear on any documents or ledgers of his NGOs.

"Two of them, actually," Hefflin said. "The other is for pensioners, who seem to have been left behind in the drive to democracy."

"Galant endeavors and much needed," Gorga said. "We have lived for hundreds of years under one occupation or another and know nothing about true democracy. On top of which we have evolved certain features to survive. One of them is corruption."

"Oh, darling, let's not go into those morose subjects," Irina jumped in. "We're here to celebrate our anniversary."

"But America is in no position to judge us," Gorga went on. "Old man Kennedy made much of his money in bootlegging during the American Prohibition. Rockefeller colluded with the railroads to drive his competitors out of business. Today, corporations bribe politicians to pass favorable tax laws."

Hefflin was impressed by the man's knowledge of the U.S.

"It's the pettiness and pervasiveness that bothers us," Hefflin said.

"A remnant from the communists, God curse them. In America, the people are spared such indignities, and that's a blessing. Until they try to figure out where all their tax dollars have gone." Gorga leaned back in his seat, aware that he had spoken too long. "I'm not condoning corruption, James. I'd love to live in a country where it doesn't exist. I believe I would be successful there, also. But there is no such place. We are all fallen angels, my friend."

The same exact expression Boris once used.

"Well, now that we've analyzed all the problems of the world, let's have some desert," Irina declared. "I bought some *savarina*."

Hefflin remembered the fluffy cake soaked in rum, stuffed with whipped cream and topped with raspberry jam. He felt his resistance weakening. He couldn't simultaneously battle both Gorga's arguments and Irina's *savarina*.

"So, James, how did you enjoy our gala?" Gorga asked. "I'm sure it doesn't compare to what you're used to in New York, but you must give them good marks for trying."

He saw me at the gala.

Hefflin eyed Irina who frowned, but remained silent.

"I'd just arrived in town and only attended as a curiosity," Hefflin said. "I usually try to avoid such events. I'm surprised you saw me."

"I have the curse of remembering faces," Gorga said, "especially new ones."

So, he didn't just remember my name in relation to my nonprofit. He probably looked me up on the list of attendees after he saw me at the gala—the only name he didn't know.

"What line of business are you in?" Gorga asked.

"I'm an investor, like Irina said."

"The conference focused on military equipment," Gorga pushed on, "so that must be your interest."

"I go wherever there is money to be made. In Bucharest, it now seems to be in arms sales."

"A pity, isn't it?" Gorga said. "The last thing this country needs is more arms. But they have this ambition of joining NATO. I think it will be years before that happens."

"You attended the gala also," Hefflin pointed out.

"Irina insisted on going. I have no interest in arms, or galas, for that matter, but I like to please her." He squeezed Irina's hand.

"What do you want me to do, stay in this house all day?" Irina objected. "I have to see people, *be* seen. My art demands it."

Gorga offered her an indulgent smile. "So, James, how long will you be staying in Bucharest?"

"It depends," Hefflin said.

"On what?"

"The opportunities I find. I understand that some government industries are being privatized, although they seem to be immediately purchased by a select few."

Gorga's face twitched. "Don't believe everything you hear. Privatization is proceeding slowly, too slowly in my point of view, but it is done transparently. Every worker is given stock in the company, which is fair and follows European guidelines."

"The funny thing is, the stock all ends up in a few hands in the end," Hefflin said.

"Workers are free to do with their stock as they please."

"Yes, they are free to sell it for pennies because they are poor or are threatened. I understand the concept."

"I don't know whom you have been talking to, James, but I suggest you do not embroil yourself in local politics. The government is still young, and there are forces who would like nothing better than to topple it and inject a fascist one. Then we'd be back in the dark ages."

"Oh, you men and your politics," Irina interrupted. She escaped into the kitchen and returned with one of the rum-soaked tortes his mother used to bake, in which was embedded a lone, lit candle. "Happy one-year anniversary, darling."

Irina and Gorga embraced.

"Congratulations," Hefflin said as he stood. "It is time for me to say good night and let you two celebrate privately."

The evening ended with embraces from both Irina and Gorga, for Romanians love to hug. As he headed back to the hotel, Hefflin felt disturbed by what the former Securitate man had said that evening; he had made sense in the same way that Boris had. They both viewed man as flawed, an assessment with which no one could argue. It was their conclusion that bothered Hefflin: Man should just accept that fact and stop agonizing. We are what we are. Let's move on. Irina seemed to have adopted the same attitude—enjoy the good things in life if you're lucky enough to have them. Stop ruminating about everyone else.

The irony was that every criminal arrived at that same conclusion sooner or later, as a self-defense mechanism: *God made me what I am. It's his fault.*

Realpolitik, the principle of dealing in diplomacy on purely practical rather than moral or ideological grounds, formed a larger variation on the theme. Bismarck, and later Kissinger, were its more famous proponents. But Hefflin sensed something else between the lines of Gorga's little speech, a certain melancholy that the world was as it was, and a reluctant capitulation to its corrupting force. It lacked the optimism—or just the humor, perhaps—of Boris.

As Hefflin left Irina's house, he realized he was collecting interesting characters—Mayfield, The Owl, and now Gorga—none of whom had anything to do with his mission.

CHAPTER THIRTY-SIX

Bucharest
April 1993

A COLD WIND blew from the north, though it had the smell of spring in it. Following Irina's dinner, Hefflin spent an hour walking the streets of that once magnificent city that had been strangled by Ceausescu's iron grip. To his surprise, it now showed signs of life. New restaurants had sprung up, as well as a few stores that sold Western goods. The kiosks displayed a dozen new newspapers and magazines and the music stores blared American music. Long gone were the lines for food. The markets in the central part of the city displayed fresh meat and vegetables, but the jacked-up prices were mostly aimed at the nomenklatura, who had raised their own salaries but had forgotten about the common workers still mired in the obsolete, government-run factories and the communist-era wages. These wages that had once sufficed to purchase the stale food and poorly made clothing now barely bought bread and local *telemea* cheese.

During his forays through the city over the past few days, he thought he had spotted men following him—twice on foot, another time in a black Dacia. He was easily able to lose them by going in one entrance of a building and exiting another. Were they the local gangs looking for an easy target, the new Securitate, or the KGB? Whoever they were, he had come up on their radar.

He brushed his concerns aside, for his mind was still alive with thoughts of Catherine. He had promised himself he wouldn't agonize about her, that she was a better field agent than he would ever be. Yet, not knowing where she and Jack were now hiding, or what dangers they were facing, gnawed at his guts. He tried to concentrate on Mayfield, Nicu Ceausescu's buddy, who seemed to have his fingers in a lot of pies, from Asian casinos to Middle Eastern leaders to armaments. The visit to his house had produced some peculiar intel, but none of it made much sense.

He found himself on a dark, menacing street, lit only by the dim lights from a restaurant. As he passed by the adjacent alleyway, he saw two old men and an old woman rummaging through the restaurant's garbage cans. The woman had gray hair covered by a bandana. An old shawl covered her faded dress. He asked her why she was searching the garbage.

"What else can I do on my meager pension?" She held up a half-eaten pork chop. "Still, I eat better quality food now than I ever ate under Ceausescu, may God curse him, even though it's the remains of others' meals."

He handed her and the two old men each a fifty-dollar bill and walked on.

Shaken by the memories and the abysmal conditions that still plagued the Romanians, he passed by a side street, where he spotted colored lights strung between several buildings. Below them a row of women lingered, lined up against the walls as in old French movies. Lone men strode down the middle of the street assessing each in turn, while the women struck poses and beckoned with *"Mon cheri, love awaits you."* Some pulled down their colorful tops for a more direct approach.

He thought of Times Square and certain parts of the Lower East Side where he had encountered similar scenes, though not as gaudy.

Under the communists, the prostitutes sold their wares inside hotels catering to Westerners. Now they had gone public, adopting the worst examples of Western cities.

He had had enough and decided to return to his hotel. He craved a more civilized society, at least on its surface, with a Johnnie Walker Black in his hand and a female face to talk to.

As he neared the Athénée he passed by an alleyway from where he heard some commotion. The alley was narrow and dark, but he could make out several men who seemed to be fighting. As he approached, he realized two men were holding up a third man, while another punched him in the abdomen. Then he realized the man being punched was actually a boy, a teenager.

A high-pitched scream, then a woman lunged out of the shadows at the man throwing the punches. As she tried to scratch his face, the man slapped her and she crumpled to the ground. Two children ran out of the shadows crying "Mama!" and knelt down to help her as she lay on the ground, sobbing.

Hefflin sauntered up to the larger man with both hands in his pocket, an unthreatening stance.

"Excuse me, old chap, but should you really be beating a boy like that?" he asked in an exaggerated British accent.

The men stopped and stared at him, no doubt shocked that someone would be stupid enough to intervene. The large man took a step toward him, muscles bulging in his thick neck.

"Private business," he said in ragged English. "Move along before you get same."

"Beating a helpless boy is not very sporting, you know." Hefflin feared he had pushed the caricature too far. "What is your business with him?"

The man stood dumbfounded, then his body straightened.

"Come here, and I will show you my business."

The man took a step toward Hefflin while the other two men dropped the boy and slowly encircled him.

Bring down the leader first.

The man, who wore one of those baggy gray suits of the old Securitate, loomed several inches above Hefflin.

"You tourists should mind your business," the man growled. "They are *tsigani*, gypsies. Not belong in this part of city. Maybe you are gypsy lover."

"What are you, Securitate?"

"Securitate no longer exists, you stupid American. Run away before I get angry."

American? Is the man such an imbecile that he doesn't recognize a British accent?

Without removing his hands from his pockets, Hefflin stepped to one side then jabbed his heel hard into the side of the man's knee. The man howled, toppled over like an old oak, then hit the ground hard, his face breaking the fall.

One of the other men took two steps toward him. He was shorter and stockier, all muscle. Hefflin feigned a kick to the groin, which caused the man to instinctively protect it with his hands, then delivered a knuckle punch to the ridge of the man's nose. The man dropped to his knees, stunned. Hefflin kicked the side of his head with his heel, which thrust the man to the ground. When Hefflin looked up he saw the gypsies disappear down the alley. The third man stood facing him, his gaze focused on something behind Hefflin.

It was then that he felt the blow. It landed on his back, then a second glanced off the side of his head. He knew, even in that instant, that if it had been a direct blow, it would have cracked his skull open. He went down on all fours but did not lose consciousness. A kick to his stomach lifted him off the ground and stole his breath, then a punch to the kidney spun him and sprawled him on the pavement. He lay flat on his back, choking for breath, the pain rising up to his chest. Half conscious, he saw shadows hovering over him.

Where the hell did they come from?

"Don't kill him. Puiu gave specific orders to just scare him," a voice said in Romanian.

A figure knelt next to him and lifted his head by his hair.

"You listen to me, American. You get on plane and fly back home. You stick your nose any more, and it will be cut off. Understand?"

They know me. They were waiting for me to approach the Athénée. This whole thing was a setup.

A deeper voice suddenly yelled from the end of the street, in Russian.

The Romanians stood silent, unsure of themselves, then slowly retreated, walking backward, as if afraid to turn. They lifted their two wounded comrades and dragged them away to waiting cars.

How many different groups are there?

More voices now, all speaking Russian. He felt himself lifted and carried to a car, then pushed into the back seat. He lay sprawled on his back, two men in the front. He heard the doors to several cars closing, then the revving of engines. As the car started moving, he fought to stay conscious, but gave up and allowed himself to drift off.

CHAPTER THIRTY-SEVEN

Bucharest
April 1993

HE AWOKE JUST as he was being dropped into a soft chair. Everything looked out of focus. As his vision slowly began to clear, he saw a man sitting on a couch across from him. Several men walked around. One of them handed him a glass of water, which he gulped down.

"Mr. Blake, or should I say, Mr. Hefflin, it is pleasure to meet you," the seated man said in English with a heavy Russian accent. "You call me Stefan, okay?" He was obese, with sparse gray hair and a belly that bounced every time he growled his words. He reminded Hefflin of Sydney Greenstreet, the portly actor in *The Maltese Falcon* and *Casablanca*.

So much for my disguises.

"We have long memory, unlike you Americans," Stefan said, perhaps detecting Hefflin's surprise. "And we have photographs."

Stefan lifted a file from a battered leather briefcase lying on the floor next to him. He removed two large black-and-white photographs. One showed Hefflin exiting the American embassy in Bucharest, the other caught him yawning while sitting in a trolley car. On the back of each, written in English in black ink riddled with ink drops, was a date: "December 1989."

"Beautiful handwriting is mine," Stefan said. "Pen was British brand, which I have since discarded. It always leaked, like everything else made in West."

Hefflin tuned out the propaganda while he tried to figure out when that picture in the trolley had been taken. As far as he could remember, in 1989 he had only been in a trolley once, for a rendezvous with Boris, after which Boris took him to his apartment. A few moments later a KGB agent arrived whom Hefflin had dubbed "the fat man" at the time. Now he realized that was no way to distinguish one KGB agent from another.

So, it must have been the fat man who took those pictures. But how did he get them to his masters before being poisoned by Boris?

But then he remembered that when Boris had returned the body to the KGB, planted with evidence incriminating the Soviet deputy ambassador to Romania, he had never searched the body, and had thus allowed the camera to return to Moscow. Another instance wherein Boris had not been perfect.

"Well, Stefan, what is so important that we can't discuss over a scotch?" Hefflin groused, his mind still groggy.

"I love scotch, do not get me wrong," Stefan said, "but it does not compare to Russian vodka." He signaled his men with a raising of his chin, and a bottle of Stoli appeared with two glasses. The Russian poured, handed one to Hefflin, then raised his own. "To our new friendship."

"Are we friends already? We've just met."

"I just saved your life," Stefan said. "That makes us automatic friends. Besides, comrade Yeltsin is friendly man. All Western newspapers love him. How can we not be friends?"

"I thank you for getting me out of trouble," Hefflin said. "Who were those guys, anyway?"

Stefan shrugged. "Who knows? Bucharest full of gangs now. That is what you get with capitalism. You must be used to it, no?"

"To our new friendship, then." Hefflin raised his glass, then emptied it into his mouth.

"First time you come to Bucharest was just before revolution, as cultural attaché," Stefan went on.

"Of etiquette."

"Yes, of etiquette," Stefan echoed with a harsh laugh. "Since then, you have become wealthy."

"My wife's side of the family," Hefflin said.

"Ms. Deveraux, aka Nash, now Hefflin, or Drake. A good catch, if I may say."

He fucking knows all about my private life.

"You may."

"A good catch. You make little stir in certain parts of Bucharest by returning."

"Oh?"

"Do not be so humble, Mr. Hefflin. You are well known in my circles. You helped foil Gorbachev's plans. An honor for you."

I had nothing to do with foiling Gorbachev's plans, damn it! It was all Avery.

"I don't know what you're talking about, Stefan." Hefflin rubbed his head and felt some coagulated blood matting his hair.

"You were last American to arrive before revolution. After which, all hell broke loose, as you Americans say, first in Timisoara, then in rest of country."

"I came to observe. Romania was the last Soviet satellite left. It was on its last legs."

"It could have evolved more peacefully." Stefan raised his voice. "Calm, civilized transition to benevolent, socialist country. Gorbachev's vision. But no, you Americans wanted blood, like in all your gangster movies."

The man is right. The Agency did all that, and more. The blood of thousands is on its hands.

"I think you were involved in revolution, Mr. Hefflin. You and your station chief, Stanton."

No, Stefan, we had nothing to do with it. Avery killed Stanton because he found out.

"You have a great imagination, Stefan. The popular uprising was the result of forty years of Ceausescu's cruelty. The people had enough."

"Did the people hire snipers from Middle East to fire on women and children?" Stefan burst out.

The snipers. They shot civilians and military alike, to rile the people and confuse the military to fire indiscriminately, even on each other, to start the revolution. Avery's plan.

"You have it all wrong."

"A lot of coincidences, Mr. Hefflin."

"The world is full of them."

"Perhaps. But not *our* world. And now you return to Bucharest. Why?"

"I run a couple of nonprofit organizations," Hefflin said. "I'm here to see how they're doing."

"A very noble thing, to help poor now that capitalism has left them in dirt," Stefan said. "That was never case under communism."

They were all starving, Stefan, except for the nomenklatura.

"I think you are also searching for friend of yours," Stefan said.

"What friend?"

"A man named Boris."

Ah, here it comes.

"Boris is a very common Russian name, I don't have to tell you, Stefan. Along with Natasha. We even have a cartoon about them."

Stefan bristled. "It is code name."

"Ah. I have had friendships like those. Most end tragically."

"This one might also if you are not careful." Stefan gulped his drink and set the glass on the table. "I will put my cards on table, Mr. Hefflin. I am also interested in finding Boris."

"So now he is your friend, too? What a coincidence. Why do you want to find him?"

Stefan shifted in his seat, his face flushed, probably from several previous vodkas.

"Why, why, why—" Stefan waived his hand, then removed his handkerchief and wiped the sweat off his brow. "You know we cannot deal with *why* here."

"You have been searching for Boris for some time," Hefflin said. "You suspect he is a CIA asset."

Stefan stared at him. "How do you know this?"

"How, how, how—" Hefflin waived his arm. "You know we can't deal with *how* here, Stefan."

"Of course. I am sorry." Stefan dragged on his cigarette, then put it out. "I will tell you what I think, Mr. Hefflin. I think you are in trouble. I think CIA believed Boris was mole inside KGB working for you, but now they realize he was working for us all along and that you were *his* mole passing intel to *him*. I believe you are in Bucharest on personal mission to find Boris and eliminate him before your masters find him, or, at very least, to strike deal with him, perhaps share some of that wealth you suddenly found."

"You should know if I am your mole or not, Stefan," Hefflin said.

Stefan shifted in his seat, his face showing embarrassment. "Agents are peculiar breed, I do not have to tell you. They are very jealous of their assets. Many of our agents do not share identity of sources even with their masters. In some cases, as you are aware, they do not even know real identity of asset."

Hefflin tried to wrap his mind around what this Russian was saying. Stefan had just admitted that the KGB had a mole inside the CIA from whom they had learned all about Hefflin's arrangement with Boris. From their mole they also knew the CIA was conducting a molehunt. The big revelation was that Stefan also admitted that the KGB didn't know the identity of their own asset inside the CIA.

And what about the defector? The KGB obviously knew from their mole that a defector would be meeting Hefflin, since they had been waiting for him, but did they know the defector's identity or what he had told Langley?

The Russian's body melted into the cushions. "I think we are very well suited for each other, my friend. As I see it, our goals converge."

"How so?"

"We both want to bring Boris in from cold—you to protect your own life and me to find out whether he was hero or traitor. We should combine forces."

Boris can't be brought in from the cold, Stefan. He's already dead cold. But you obviously don't know that. And you're not sure who Boris was really working for.

Hefflin saw the humor in it all. Both the CIA and the KGB knew they had a mole inside their agencies, and they both thought Boris was at the center of it, a man who had been dead for over a year.

Stefan leaned forward. "Deal is this." Stefan's spittle sprinkled Hefflin's face. "At some point in near future, we will allow certain information to be found by CIA pointing to someone else as mole. That will let you off hook with your agency, and it will allow you to continue your activities for us. In return, you forget about killing or bribing Boris. Instead, you find him and present him to us. In addition, you will wire five million U.S. dollars to this account in

Luxembourg from your wife's fortune." Stefan handed him a piece of crumpled paper with wiring instructions. "My retirement fund. A good deal, no?"

Hefflin studied the Russian's porcine face, which no longer displayed a smile.

"And if I refuse?"

"Why would you refuse? You have been working for us all these years. Admit it, and let us go on. You do not have to remain anonymous. We know how to protect our sources. But—" Stefan searched for his cigarettes—"if you are foolish enough to insist on your anonymity, you will have CIA after you."

"The CIA?"

"They already have eye on you. You are obvious suspect. If you do not confirm you are our asset, we will not be able to use countermeasures to divert CIA's attention to someone else. Then they will arrest you, and we both lose."

Does he really think I'm their mole, or is this just a setup?

Stefan poured two more glasses of Stoli and left them on the table.

"These drinks are to toast our new arrangement." Stefan beamed.

Hefflin picked up his glass and drank it.

"We don't have an arrangement yet," Hefflin said as he stood. "I'll have to think about it."

"What is there to think about? You are worried about my five million dollars? Okay, I will make it three, to show goodwill. Is that better?"

"Give me a little time, Stefan."

"Time is short. Events are moving rapidly. Here is my private number at embassy." Stefan handed him a card with only a telephone number written in pen. "I will await your call."

CHAPTER THIRTY-EIGHT

Bucharest
April 1993

THE FERENTARI DISTRICT was located several kilometers south of the center of the city. Hefflin arrived midmorning using a rented Skoda. Few taxi drivers agreed to drive him there, and those who did told him they wouldn't wait for him and warned that he'd never find another taxi to return him to the city.

He now saw why. Piles of open garbage surrounded the row of five-story buildings on Aleea Livezilor, filthy water ran along the cobblestone streets, and barefoot children played with the stray dogs scouring the refuse. The area smelled of open sewers and rotting detritus. A horse-drawn wagon piled high with scrap metal creaked by. The sound of *lautereasca* gypsy music emanated from an open window.

Several men appeared from behind a building and strode toward him. As they approached, he realized they were young, in their late teens or early twenties. They wore baggy dark pants, some torn, and dirty white shirts that hung open to reveal their bare chests. Two of them wore knives tucked inside their belts. One brandished an empty bottle.

They came stalking toward him and surrounded him. The older one said in English, "Take off clothes."

Hefflin realized how stupid it had been for him to wear his Brioni suit in this neighborhood.

"Why? Do you need it for a soirée this evening?"

"Yeah, we have soirée here every evening." The young man laughed, spreading his arms to show the garbage strewn around him. The other men joined in the laughter.

Hefflin took out his wallet and lifted two hundred-dollar bills. "Here, you can buy your own suit."

"I will take money, too, together with your suit," the young man said.

"No, you can't have my suit. What will I wear to the soirée?" Hefflin smiled.

"You can wear your skin, if I decide to leave it on you." The man took out a knife and held it high.

"That's not very friendly."

"You want friendly? I give you friendly." The man signaled with his chin to the younger man with the bottle, who now sprang at Hefflin from the side.

Hefflin stepped into the raised arm, delivered an elbow to the man's chest, then grabbed the bottle as the man crumpled to the ground. Two others lunged at him with swinging fists. He kicked one in the groin, then caught the other's swinging arm with his free hand, twisted his fingers, a move that Krav Maga had borrowed from Aikido, and brought him down screaming. The two remaining men now brandished knives. As one thrust his knife toward Hefflin's chest, Hefflin stepped to one side and struck the man's head with the bottle. The man sprawled to the ground, bleeding. Hefflin swung around to face the last man, the leader, who now stared at him, his knife trembling, his face betraying fear. The man suddenly turned and ran into the building, the others scurrying after him.

A moment later two other men came out of the same building. They both wore oversized suits and dark, wide-brimmed fedoras. They were tall, potbellied, middle-aged, and strode toward him with authority. Hefflin dropped the bottle and inserted his hand into the side pocket of his jacket and gripped his Beretta. When they reached him, they stopped and blocked his way.

"*Taves Bahtalo!*" one man said.

Hefflin recognized this greeting to be the Roma equivalent of "good luck to you," similar to the Romanian *Noroc!* He repeated back the phrase then, in fluent Romanian, asked to see the *voivode.*

"Who are you?" the same man asked. "What is your business here?"

"It's a personal matter. I just want to talk to him," Hefflin said.

The man looked him up and down, not to assess but to intimidate. "Your Romanian is native, but you are dressed like an American. I suggest you go while the going is good." The man opened his jacket to reveal a gun tucked under his belt.

"The Owl sent me," Hefflin said. "He asked that you show me common courtesy."

The man took a step back. "The Owl? Why didn't you say so? You could have spared our boys the agony."

"They didn't give me a chance."

"Yes, they are hotheaded at times. Where did you learn to fight like that?"

"Part of my job."

The man nodded, sensing authority.

"And you want to see the *voivode,* you say?"

"We may have some common friends from the old days," Hefflin said.

"Well, then, come with me. He doesn't live in these apartments. He has his own house down a few blocks. I suggest we take your car. You don't want to leave it here."

They drove for a few blocks, and during the short trip he saw similar piles of refuse strewn between buildings and down alleyways. Two women wearing colorful dresses and bandanas washed clothes outdoors in large tubs, while several men stripped to their waists cooked some sort of barbecued meat over an open fire.

"Why is all this garbage here?" Hefflin dared ask.

"The city doesn't collect the garbage, that's why," the man said. "They say the area is too dangerous."

"Based on my own reception, you can't blame them."

"We have to protect ourselves. Nobody else will. During the *Mineriad*, the miners destroyed our homes, beat our men, and attacked our women."

The man was referring to the attacks by miners brought into Bucharest in 1990 and '91 by President Iliescu to put down anti-government demonstrations.

"They don't consider us human. We are animals to them." The man spat out the window. "The sewers haven't worked in years. For a while, we had no electricity, but a few months ago they fixed that, at least."

The man motioned for him to stop in front of a red, one-story house made of cinderblocks. The place was neatly kept, with trees and shrubbery surrounding the property. Laundry hung on a line to dry. On the tin roof he spotted a television antenna.

The men led him through a side alley to a door where he was told to wait. One man entered, and a moment later the door opened and an elderly woman appeared. She smiled and asked him to come in.

Old, simple furniture crowded the small living room, probably handed down over generations. Beds lined two walls, and an old television stood on a rickety table against the third. In the middle of the room an old man sat at a square wooden table. His bronzed face bore deep crevices and one of his earlobes was missing. He wore a clean white shirt and black pants, and projected the confidence that comes from respect and authority. One of the men introduced him as the *voivode*.

"My name is James Blake, a Romanian American," Hefflin said. "The Owl thought you might be able to help me with a small matter."

"You were born here by your lack of accent, so you must have changed your name," the old man said.

"Yes, it's one of the things some of us choose to do to get along in America," Hefflin said. "Thank you for inviting me into your home."

"We have done the same over the years. We adopt the names of the country we find ourselves in, hoping to be accepted. A losing proposition." The old man grunted. "This is the best house in the neighborhood, Mr. Blake. I have two rooms for six people: myself, my wife, two of my sons, and their wives. The poor souls living in those apartment buildings have one room for their entire families, sometimes six or eight people. The natives in the deepest African jungles have better living conditions."

Hefflin didn't know how to respond except to nod.

"Sit down, and tell me what I can help you with," the *voivode* said.

Hefflin pulled a chair and sat. The other men did the same.

"I knew a Roma woman in my childhood," Hefflin began. "She was very dear to me, practically my second mother."

The men shifted in their seats. Hefflin knew this was not something one said in Romania, even if true.

"She died in '89, during the revolution. But before she died she told me her story—of falling in love with a *gadjo* years ago, of having his baby, and of being ostracized from the clan. I think you know whom I'm talking about."

The *voivode* remained stone-faced.

"I want to find out what happened to her child," Hefflin went on. "She told me that her father, the *voivode* at the time, took him from her."

The hard slap on the table startled him. The *voivode's* face now trembled; his black eyes cold as coal.

"That person is not to be spoken of in my presence. She does not exist. Now please go."

Hefflin leaned back in his chair to calm his own nerves, for he wanted to smash that old man's face onto the table. This was his life the old fool was toying with, and he wasn't going to leave without finding out all the old man knew. He fished in his pocket and removed a wad of hundred-dollar bills, which he placed on the table. The old man stared at it, his eyes growing wider.

"You should not walk around with such money, especially in this neighborhood," the old man said. "Men would kill for a tenth of that."

Hefflin removed his Beretta and placed it on the table next to the money. The two men jumped up and took a few steps back.

"Other men have tried," Hefflin said. "There's a thousand dollars here. Which will it be, the carrot or the stick?"

The old man did not hesitate. He swept up the money and thrust it into his pocket.

"When her father, the *voivode*, found out she had soiled herself with a *gadjo*, and that she was now carrying his bastard, he did the correct thing and brought it before the *Kris*, the Roma court," the old man said. "Of course we decided she had broken our law and was no longer Roma. She was told to leave with what she could carry and the clothes on her back. We then burned all her other possessions. We later heard that she took poison—at least she still had some dignity—but that some cursed doctor saved her life. That is all I know."

"That cursed doctor happened to be my father." Hefflin seethed, his hand itching to clutch the gun.

The *voivode* pushed back his chair, his hands trembling. "I am sorry. I didn't mean . . ."

"What happened to the baby?"

"I don't know. We wanted nothing to do with it. It was not Roma."

"She told me your men came in the middle of the night and stole it."

"Then she lied to you. She was an outcast, as was her bastard. Her name was no longer even allowed to be spoken."

Hefflin picked up the Beretta. "I know you people keep track of members of your own clan, even if you disown them. Especially the daughter and grandson of the *voivode*. You know what happened to that baby."

The old man stared at the barrel of the gun, his brittle face trembling. "He ended up in America. That's all I know. I swear."

"America! How? When?"

"I heard through the grapevine, from another clan. I don't know how or when."

America. Well, well.

"You'll be happy to know that she died a violent death during the revolution," Hefflin said.

The *voivode's* face grew stern. "Yes, I know, but I am not happy. Not because she is dead, but because she fell at the hands of those murderers."

Hefflin took a long breath to let his anger seep out of his chest and eased his fingers, which begged to pull the trigger. But what good would it do? What could he even say to this stubborn old man who held on to old customs that had long ago outlived their usefulness?

"I want you to know that she was the kindest and wisest woman I've ever known." Hefflin's voice trembled. "I'm going to find that baby, whom you call a bastard, and when I do, I'll make him a very wealthy man, if he isn't already. He can then come back and thank you for freeing him from your moronic traditions. But if I find out you're lying, I'll be back, and I won't be alone."

"I don't doubt it," the *voivode* said.

As Hefflin drove out of the ghetto, he felt his suspicions had been partly vindicated. Tanti Bobo's baby boy had not been stolen by her father as she had said; it had somehow ended up in America. Did that prove that she had given her baby to the Greek doctor and his wife to bring up as their own? No, but it brought him one step closer. The real possibility that he may be that half-gypsy boy began to dawn on him. His entire Greek identity now seemed ephemeral, the image of his beloved parents growing transparent, phantasmal. He may not be Greek at all, but half gypsy, half Romanian. Part of him felt joy that his instincts might actually be confirmed, but part was also filled with grief at the thought that his adoptive Greek parents may have sacrificed themselves by leaving Romania in order to make sure their adopted gypsy boy grew up in America. They had loved him, there was no question, but if his instincts proved accurate, they had also kept a crucial truth from him. Another crime, besides taking him away from his Pusha, for which he would have to forgive them posthumously.

CHAPTER THIRTY-NINE

BY THE TIME Hefflin arrived at the Athénée, it was already late afternoon, and he was looking forward to a hot shower to wash off the miasma from the gypsy ghetto. He didn't know how to think of those poor people. Did he have a right to judge them? It was always easy to blame the victim. Why didn't they clean out the garbage themselves and deliver it to the municipal dump? Why did they continue to live in those cramped apartments, more like jail cells, rather than leave the country and find more welcoming arms, as his parents had? He knew the Romanians treated them as subhuman, calling them *tsigani*, a term that encompassed not only gypsy but beggar, thief, and criminal. The Romanians blamed them for whatever crimes, diseases, or catastrophes plagued the nation. The gypsies who had managed to leave the ghetto and integrate into Romanian society often prospered, mostly by denying their gypsy roots and passing for native Romanians. The process hit home for Hefflin, for it bore an obvious resemblance to his own turning of his back on the cauldron of immigrants in Worcester to become a "true American."

He knew he had lost a great deal by abandoning his own kind, as had The Owl. The suffocating closeness of such a community, the worn traditions and mannerisms, the fact that everyone knew your life and you knew theirs, were the reasons he had left. And yet they were the very things that he missed, that had given him a sense of belonging.

His reverie dissolved the moment he opened the door to his hotel room and smelled the strong aroma of gardenias. He expected a naked woman to be lying in his bed, as he had once found in '89, but when he turned on the lights, he saw a man dressed in a fine gray suit, with hands folded across his chest as if lying in a coffin, sleeping in his bed. Startled by the light, the man suddenly sat up, dazed. Upon seeing Hefflin, he smiled weakly.

"I do apologize. I must have dozed off." The man spoke in English with an accent Hefflin couldn't place. He jumped out of bed and rushed to the mirror on the wall to fix his hair and pink tie. He was a short, thin man in his thirties, clean-shaven, with slicked-back black hair and a pink handkerchief in his breast pocket, which he now used to gently pat his face. After returning the handkerchief to his pocket, he played with it for a moment so that it protruded just the right amount. He then turned to Hefflin and said, "I have been waiting a long time. So what does one do in such a case? The bed was the obvious solution."

"Who are you?"

"Oh, my name is not important. I sometimes forget it myself." The man sat in a chair and crossed his legs. "I am here to discuss a certain person of mutual interest—a man you call Boris and I know as Janus."

Hefflin pulled up a chair and sat across from him. "Janus. Now that's a fancy name."

The man shrugged. "He liked ancient mythology. As I am sure you know, Janus was the Roman god depicted as having two faces, one facing the past, the other the future. In his case, I think one faced the East, the other the West. Anyway, that is neither here nor there. I have been told you know his whereabouts or at least something to help locate him."

"Who told you that?"

"I am afraid I am not at liberty to say."

"Why do you want to find him?"

"I am not at liberty to say that, either. This is a delicate matter. You understand."

"I don't know if I do," Hefflin said. "What *are* you at liberty to say?"

"I am willing to pay a great deal of money for such information. Let us say, ten thousand U.S. now and ten more upon locating him."

Hefflin laughed. "I spend more in a week. You'll have to do better than that."

"My masters are not wealthy, Mr. Blake. And, I dare say, we can be of service to each other."

"How so?"

"We can combine our efforts to locate him, for one. There are other, less benevolent forces searching for him. And I have more interesting information I can bring to your attention."

"How do we even know we're talking about the same fellow?"

"We do not, for sure, but I have reason to believe that we are."

Hefflin rose. "I'm afraid I'm going to have to know more about you and your masters before I jump into bed with you. I'm old-fashioned that way."

"I am sorry to hear that." The man stood, casually inserted his hand inside his suit jacket, and removed a small pistol. "Kindly raise your hands behind your head and turn around. I intend to search your pockets."

Hefflin stared at the man, surprised at the sudden turn of events "With that little thing? Does it even fire bullets?"

"Do not think that I am not willing to shoot you. Kindly raise your hands and turn around."

Hefflin did as ordered. As the man started to pat him down, Hefflin stepped on the man's foot, causing him to cry out, then swung his hand and grabbed the gun. He then landed a gentle punch to the jaw. The man slumped unconscious into his arms. Hefflin gently placed him into a chair and went through his pockets. He found a passport, Lebanese, bearing the name Amir Baghdadi. The wallet contained a couple hundred U.S. dollars, some local notes, and credit cards with the same name. In a side jacket pocket, he found a piece of paper with a note written in longhand: "James Blake, Athénée Palace Hotel."

Hefflin returned the items to the man's pockets, then slapped his face to awaken him.

Baghdadi sat up, dazed, and perused the room, then sprang up and hurried to the mirror.

"You drew blood, and my collar is stained," he cried, then wiped the blood from the corner of his mouth. "This is a Battistoni shirt, I'll have you know."

"Sorry, but you were wielding a gun," Hefflin said as he picked up the pistol from the floor.

"Only as a form of persuasion. If I knew you were such a brute, I would have brought some local gorillas with me."

"Why don't you stop prancing around and tell me who you are and why you're here, Mr. Baghdadi," Hefflin said.

The man hesitated, then sat back in the chair.

"I am a member of the Lebanese secret service. Janus has been a contact of mine for many years, but has been inexplicably silent for some time. I am simply trying to find him."

"How did you hear of Boris?"

"The Russians have put out the word that they are searching for him. They offered quite a bounty."

"How much?"

Baghdadi hesitated. "One hundred thousand for information leading to his capture."

"And you offered me ten?"

"That was only my initial negotiating position," Baghdadi protested.

"And this Janus, tell me about him."

"He is KGB. For years we have been exchanging intel, never for money, just one piece of intel for another. Some of it he obtained from the West, some from the East. He didn't seem to care which side received the intel. That is why I said Janus faced East and West. From what I have heard, the Russians have been searching for a mole inside their ranks for some time. Now they float the name Boris. So, I concluded that Janus and Boris could be one and the same man."

"Is this a State interest or personal?"

Baghdadi blanched. "I calculated that if he is worth a lot to the Russians, he is probably worth a lot more to the Americans. You are CIA, are you not?"

"Certainly not," Hefflin snapped. "All right, Mr. Baghdadi, maybe we are looking for the same man, I don't know. But if we are, I'll double what the Russians are offering. How does that sound?"

Baghdadi's face bloomed. "That will be quite satisfactory. But, as I alluded to before, I have other intelligence I believe you may also be interested in."

"Oh?"

"You have shown a certain photograph around town, I believe."

Mayfield? How does he know? I only showed it to Balzary and Milan.

"What of it?" Hefflin asked.

"May I see it, please?"

Hefflin removed Mayfield's picture from his pocket and handed it to Baghdadi.

"Yes, I know this gentleman. Mr. Harold Mayfield has been involved in arms dealings for many years in the Middle East and other places."

"Who has he been selling arms to, and from whom?"

"During the communist days, he sold to everyone—PLO, Syrians, Libyans, Lebanese, and African countries in the subcontinent. They were all Soviet-made arms. His source was the Soviet satellite states."

"What about since the fall of communism?"

Baghdadi's face grew weary. "There is no scarcity of wars, Mr. Blake. That is the unfortunate human condition. The weapons are coming from the same Middle Eastern countries Mayfield sold to before, which are awash with arms. There are rumors that he is involved in a large shipment about to pass through Lebanon in the very near future. Janus, himself, was very interested in Mr. Mayfield's activities. In fact, he was the initial source of my intel on him."

"Oh?"

Baghdadi leaned back, considering. "Janus is a strange fellow. The more I got to know him, the more I liked him. He despises arms dealers. The promoters of death, he calls them. Janus is an idealist at heart, Mr. Blake. He once told me that a spy's aim should be to make the military of all sides obsolete. I do not know exactly what he meant by that, and I did not dare ask."

"A strange thing to say."

"Yes, but Janus is a strange fellow in many ways. He has always appeared to me wearing a disguise. And they were very imaginative. One time he sat next to me at a bar in Lebanon dressed as a Viennese aristocrat, with a black goatee beard and a monocle. Another time he showed up in Bucharest dressed as an old coal miner, wearing a ragged white beard and white hair. He even had coal dust smudged on his face and hands. Both times I did not recognize him until he introduced himself." Baghdadi let out a gentle laugh. "He should have been an actor. I told him he missed his calling." He stood. "I think we can do business, Mr. Blake. You will find my terms quite reasonable."

With that, Baghdadi opened the door and quietly shut it behind him.

CHAPTER FORTY

Bucharest
April 1993

ALONE IN HIS hotel room, Hefflin mulled over what Baghdadi had told him. As The Owl had said, Boris had had many friends throughout the world, among them apparently this Baghdadi character, a Lebanese security operative, if he could be believed. Baghdadi knew Boris as Janus, the two-faced god who, as Baghdadi had said, looked both East and West, a sharer of intel. So the Russians had put out a bounty on Boris, offering a hundred thousand dollars, along with a suggestion that Hefflin was a man with some knowledge of Boris. Now everyone would be searching for Boris, and Hefflin.

Fucking Stefan. He knows how to squeeze.

As he was about to pull out a Johnnie Walker Black from his minibar, he noticed the envelope that had apparently been slipped under the door. It had no postage markings. Hand delivered. On its face his name was written in fine calligraphy. Inside was a handwritten invitation for that evening at eight p.m. at "The Business Roundtable." Underneath, it stated that a car would pick him up in front of his hotel at seven thirty. There was no telephone number or address for him to RSVP.

They're assuming I will accept.

* * *

The car was a black Mercedes. A liveried driver opened the back door without uttering a word.

"Where are we going?" Hefflin asked.

The man did not respond, but simply touched his cap respectfully and drove off.

The house was a three-story stone neoclassical building located in the Popa Soare quarter, along with other pre-war estates that had survived Ceausescu's days. The building had been recently renovated, for many of the other beautiful homes stood in sad disrepair.

He was greeted at the entrance by a stately white-haired man wearing a tuxedo. He was about to extend his hand and introduce himself when the man turned and led him into a large living room, and Hefflin realized the man was the butler. The room contained a pastiche of heavy antique furniture, modern red leather couches, and walls lined with paintings of English fox hunting scenes—an interior designer's nightmare.

About a dozen or so men stood holding flute glasses containing a reddish drink. Some seemed to be in their sixties or older, others in their thirties or forties, all dressed in well-tailored suits. An elderly man approached him wearing a broad smile, which caused a chill to run down Hefflin's spine. It reminded him of how the Mafia greeted a colleague they were about to eliminate. The man introduced himself as Ion Popescu, the equivalent of John Smith, then introduced him to the group. The men all mumbled words of welcome but did not introduce themselves.

"It is good of you to accept our invitation," Popescu said in Romanian.

The man knows I speak Romanian. Should I use my broken version or my native tongue?

He decided these men knew more about him than he imagined, so he decided to be the native-born friend of Irina's cousin, the story he had given Gorga.

"I'm honored to be here, though I'm not clear who you are or why you invited me," Hefflin said in native Romanian.

"And still you came." Another smile. "That is the kind of man we are looking for—daring, willing to take manageable risks. Please enjoy some Kir Royale."

A liveried waiter appeared with a silver tray upon which stood a glass, which Hefflin picked up.

"We are a group of businessmen, like yourself, who are interested in developing this sad country of ours, which has remained mired in misery for decades," Popescu said. "I understand you were born here and that you have been quite a successful investor in America."

"I am at a disadvantage," Hefflin said. "You obviously know more about me than I about you."

"Only for the time being," Popescu said as he formed a slight smile. "We prefer to remain discreet until we know that we are dealing among friends."

The conversation continued with questions from the men regarding his business investments, whether he had partners, and had access to Western capital. He responded in general terms: his investments varied widely, both in the U.S. and across the world; he had many friends on Wall Street but no partners, thank God; and he had access to relatively unlimited capital, if needed. The men murmured among themselves, seemingly impressed, perhaps envious. The image Hefflin wanted to portray was of a man of immense wealth who did not need them. They needed him.

At the sound of a chime, the men ambled into a large dining room in which stood a long, rectangular dining table, which did not fit the name of The Business Roundtable. He was shown to a seat in the middle, with the older men arranging themselves across from him, the younger ones gathering themselves on his side. At the head of the table sat Popescu.

An army of servants appeared through a side door bearing silver platters of delicacies: black caviar, European cheeses, prosciutto, domestic salami from Sibiu, and *mititei*. Hefflin now noticed the waiters serving from bottles of Fleur Petrus. The conversation suddenly grew livelier.

"So, how old were you when you left Romania?" one of the elderly men asked.

"I was eight when my family left," Hefflin answered.

"And yet you speak the language so well."

"We spoke it in the house. My parents wanted me to keep our traditions and language."

"Very commendable," another man said. "You are a friend of Irina Argyris, I believe."

The question took Hefflin by surprise.

"I am a friend of her cousin in New York."

"And you have created some NGOs to help the children, I understand," Popescu said.

"A rush to capitalism often leaves some behind, children and pensioners being the most vulnerable," Hefflin said. "But it seems that much of the population is struggling."

"That is why we need Western investment," Popescu said, bringing the discussion around. "We cannot do it alone."

"To attract investors the government needs to make some necessary changes," Hefflin said. "Patent protection, a legal code to match Western ones, an honest judiciary, and honest politicians."

The men's focus returned to their meals, as if Hefflin had hit a sore spot.

"All of these changes are happening as we speak," Popescu said. "But things always move more slowly than we desire. In the meantime, privatization of State companies is proceeding on track. Unlike during the communist days, these companies are now becoming efficient and profitable."

"A good first step," Hefflin said to inject some positivity.

"That is the reason we asked you here, Mr. Blake," Popescu said. He now seemed to have gained a more authoritative bearing, his back stiff, like a military man's, his voice commanding. "There are companies being privatized regularly these days, and they can be bought at a considerable discount. We can get you in on the ground floor. For a man of your resources, the investment would be minimal, though not insignificant by local standards. You would receive a substantial stake in the company with a very high upside potential. And you would be helping your country of birth. Does such an arrangement interest you?"

"It depends," Hefflin said. "I would have to know the particulars of the company, the potential of turning it around, the markets, and the realistic upside."

"Of course, all of that is understood," Popescu said. "As for the upside, we can safely say that, if managed properly, we can guarantee at least a tenfold return on your investment over the next five years."

Hefflin sat silent, focusing on not letting his surprise show on his face.

"How can you guarantee such a return?"

"These companies were run badly under the old regime," Popescu said. "They produced poor quality products, were severely overstaffed to provide a job for everyone, as the communists always bragged, and never upgraded their equipment to produce anything the West wanted to buy. With new investment and management, and the low wages in Romania, they can compete in the West and become quite profitable."

"I see. And how can you get me in on the ground floor, as you say? Aren't the employees given shares in the newly privatized companies?"

"Yes, that is true," Popescu said. "But shares can be bought from them for a minimal amount. A piece of paper with a vague promise cannot compete with cash in hand."

Hefflin leaned back, trying to suppress the nausea rising up in his chest. Milan had told him about the dealings of such men.

Are these men the oligarchs?

"Thank you very much for your generous offer, gentlemen," Hefflin said. "I will seriously consider it."

Popescu's face grew gaunt. "I was hoping you could give us a more positive answer tonight. We don't make this kind of offer to just anyone."

"Then why make it to me?"

Popescu shifted in his seat. "You are obviously a successful businessman, and we were hoping you could help us expand our markets to the West, perhaps bring in other investors."

"The city is full of Western businessmen attending the conference," Hefflin said.

"They deal mainly in armaments. We need investments in a variety of industries—chemical plants, manufacturing, banking, new media. Romania has become what you call 'the Wild West' of investing. It is all for the taking, if you have the right connections. We have those connections, Mr. Blake. In fact, we *are* those connections. And you are Romanian, after all. We like to keep it in the family, as it were." The man let out a forced chuckle.

"As a Romanian, I have to tell you that I do not like to take from the poor in order to become even wealthier than I am," Hefflin said. "Honestly, I have no need for more money. I am only here in the hope of helping my country of birth get on its feet. And I don't usually accept such generous offers from people who insist on anonymity. Nevertheless, I said I will consider your proposal." Hefflin stood.

"Thank you for an illuminating evening, gentlemen. Please have your man drive me back to my hotel."

"The offer will be on the table for the next forty-eight hours, Mr. Blake." Popescu handed him a card with an embossed telephone number. "If I don't hear from you in that time, I will assume you are not interested. In which case, we will go down another path."

Hefflin chose to ignore what sounded like a warning, but simply nodded and left the room.

CHAPTER FORTY-ONE

Bucharest
April 1993

THE FIRST THING he did the next morning was shave off his beard and get rid of his glasses. There was no point to retaining them. The Russians had already identified him. Obviously, he couldn't pull off disguises as well as Boris. Besides, he hated facial hair, and so did Catherine.

The weather was sunny and warm, so he decided to take his breakfast at one of the cafés that had sprung up since the revolution. He had not heard from Catherine, and his anxiety was growing. He found a café a few streets down on Calea Victoriei and sat at an indoor table in the back of the room, well away from the windows. On the way he had bought a couple of the new newspapers that had sprung up in the past three years, and he now settled down to peruse them. He quickly discovered that they were filled mostly with political propaganda, exaggerated analysis of the government's progress in creating a free-market system, and reporting of the growing nationalist/fascist movement, spurred on by one political party in particular to cleanse the nation of its impure elements—read as gypsies, Hungarians, Jews, Greeks, and anyone else they decided fit that category.

He set the papers aside with disgust. The propaganda wasn't that much different than during Ceausescu's days. These newspapers were controlled by the government, perhaps the oligarchs. As he took his first sip from the cup the waiter set down, he had a pleasant surprise: it was real coffee. A vast improvement over nechezol—the concoction of barley, oats, chickpeas, and chestnuts that the Ceausescu regime had substituted during its waning years. Hefflin had avoided coffee ever since he'd arrived for just that reason.

He sensed a figure hovering over him. When he looked up, he saw the face of Baghdadi, the man he had found sleeping in his hotel bed. Baghdadi bowed and said, "May I please join you? I have not yet had my coffee."

"Please do," Hefflin said.

Baghdadi caught the eye of the waiter and ordered. He sat silent as the waiter set his cup of coffee on the table. When the waiter was gone, he said, "You are a man of great means, it is obvious, and knowledgeable of the ways of the world."

"Which ways are we talking about?"

Baghdadi leaned forward. "As I mentioned before, I possess intel that is quite valuable, and may I say, dangerous, for its possessors. You are aware, of course, of the tragic situation in Yugoslavia."

Hefflin was well aware of it. Since the fall of communism, various states making up Yugoslavia had demanded independence. The Serbs, under Slobodan Milosevic, objected to the secession of any state. This led to the Yugoslav Wars and the ongoing atrocities, especially against Muslim populations. As a result, the United Nations Security Council had imposed an arms embargo on Yugoslavia.

"What about it?" Hefflin asked.

"What if I were to tell you that various countries and independent actors are violating the embargo?" Baghdadi fiddled with his tie.

"I've heard of illegal arms getting into Yugoslavia on all sides, but it's difficult to prove," Hefflin said.

"What would intelligence about a major provider of such illegal arms be worth to you or your country?"

Hefflin regarded the little man who oozed the cloying scent of gardenias.

"It might be worth a lot."

Baghdadi removed a piece of paper from his jacket pocket and passed it to Hefflin.

The paper was a cargo manifest of the *Magdalene*, a ship registered in Nicosia, Cyprus. It listed its cargo as farming equipment.

"The *Magdalene* and a second ship, the *Sophia*, left Beirut yesterday for the port of Constanta in Romania," Baghdadi said. "That farming equipment is actually Soviet-made anti-tank and anti-aircraft missiles, mortars, AK47s, and ammunition."

"How do you know this?"

"Our mutual friend, Janus," Baghdadi said. "As I said, he despised arms traffickers, especially those feeding the Yugoslav Wars. Romania is a natural route for these arms, with a direct border. The last time I saw Janus he alerted me to these two ships."

"Do you know who the middlemen are?"

"I know one, a front company in Nicosia by the name of *P.U.I.U Import/Export*. I believe that our Mr. Mayfield is connected to it."

"Mayfield? Acting alone?"

"That is all I can tell you for now, Mr. Blake. I have already placed my life in grave danger as is. But I believe this information is valuable enough for you to act on it." Baghdadi gingerly sipped his coffee. "Regarding Janus, there is one item that may help you find him. It is rumored that he has an illegitimate son."

The child mentioned in the CIA report. A son!

"What do you know about it?"

"Nothing, other than that the son now lives in America."

Hefflin almost jumped out of his seat. "How do you know this?"

"I caught a glimpse of a picture one time as Janus was going through his wallet. It depicted a young man walking down a path in a park of some sort. Behind him hung a banner on the side of a red brick building. It was maroon in color, with the letter *H* in white. I believe it signified Harvard University."

That was Harvard Yard! What the hell?

"Can you describe the young man?"

"I am afraid I only saw the picture for a moment, and it was old and frayed. I could not even tell you if the boy was dark-haired or blond."

"But how do you know it was his son?"

"I do not, for sure. That he had a son I know from another source. I simply deduced that if he kept a picture of a young man in his wallet, it would be that of his son."

Baghdadi stood. "Have your government stop the ships before they reach Constanta, Mr. Blake, if you are at all interested in saving those poor Muslims. After you verify the contents, you can pay me what you think this information is worth. I trust your judgement. If I see that you act on my intelligence, I will have more in the future. Good day."

Hefflin waited a few minutes after Baghdadi was gone, then left the coffee shop and walked down Calea Victoriei, which, to his surprise, now swarmed with people. Children held tightly onto the strings of colorful balloons; a man dressed as a hen pulled a cart carrying baskets of eggs painted red. He now noticed stores displaying mountains of eggs intricately painted by local artisans.

Easter! Already?

He looked at the date at the top of one of the newspapers he was carrying: Friday, April 16, 1993. Good Friday. Easter Sunday in two days. Where the hell had his mind been? He hadn't noticed the store decorations, which now blared at him.

The truth was that in America he rarely paid much attention to Easter. It was too confusing. Unlike Christmas, which was always on December 25, Easter fell at a different date each year. And in America he had two Easters to keep track of: the Catholic, which followed the Gregorian calendar, and his own Greek Orthodox, which adhered to the Julian. As such, he had decided that Easter was just too mercurial a holiday to follow, so he hadn't bothered.

He felt someone tugging at his sleeve. A small boy, dark-skinned, likely a gypsy, stood beside him.

Where did he come from?

The boy stretched out his hand. It held a folded piece of paper. As Hefflin reached for it, the boy quickly withdrew his hand and held out his other hand, palm open.

"You little beggar," Hefflin said in English. He placed a Romanian coin in the open palm but the boy didn't withdraw it.

"Oh, that's not enough for you?" he said in Romanian. "Who's this note from, anyway?"

"The Owl."

Hefflin removed a dollar bill from his wallet and placed it in the boy's hand, after which the hand with the note reappeared. He opened the note and read.

"Follow the boy. I have what you asked for."

CHAPTER FORTY-TWO

Bucharest
April 1993

THE BOY LED him down a series of side streets for about twenty minutes until Hefflin felt completely lost. At the end of a cul-de-sac the boy stopped before a two-story villa with a stucco exterior and red tile roof. The house was surrounded by a well-tended garden and partly hidden by fir trees. It had been renovated to its pre-war splendor and even had a wrought iron Juliet balcony upon which stood a guard dressed in black. Hefflin now noticed several other men on the property: two sitting in a car, and two others patrolling the perimeter. It reminded him of the Godfather's compound in the film.

He followed the boy through a large, ornate wooden door and into a cavernous living room. The space was adorned with floor-to-ceiling blue drapes laced with gold, colorful Romanian rugs, and red and gold wallpaper. On one wall hung a large icon of the Virgin Mary, on another several black-and-white photographs of what he figured were The Owl's ancestors. On a plush gold couch sat The Owl sipping what looked to be tea.

"Vasili! Welcome to my home. You like? Come sit down." The Owl motioned to him.

"Your home is splendid," Hefflin said, a bit overwhelmed by all the color. He took a seat in a red chair across from The Owl. An elderly woman wearing a colorful gypsy dress appeared holding a silver tray with tea and *cozonac*, the Romanian sweet bread with raisins and crushed walnut.

"This is my wife's sister, Kezia. She inherited me after my wife passed away some years ago." He shook his head in memory of his wife.

The woman placed the tray on the table and left them alone.

"Do not think all Roma are beggars," The Owl said. He raised his arms and looked around the room. "This is nothing. Go up to Moldova where you will find really wealthy Roma living in palaces. But I have done well enough, better than most. Have some tea and *cozonac*."

Hefflin picked up his cup of tea and a slice of his favorite Easter cake, which, along with The Owl's jovial nature, raised his spirits.

"I didn't know you were Christian." Hefflin pointed with his chin at the icon.

"I am Christian Orthodox, like my parents," The Owl said proudly. "We Roma adopt the religion of country we live in, like chameleons." He shook his head. "So, I have success to report. I did not think I would, honestly, since Securitate are pretty tight-lipped. But good thing about Romanians is that there is always someone willing to take bribe." He chuckled, then munched on some *cozonac*.

Hefflin felt his chest start to pound. "So, tell me already. What did you find?"

"Unit U0920 still exists," The Owl declared, "though in different form. After revolution, when new security agencies were formed, unit was placed inside SRI, the new internal security service, under top-secret restrictions. It has no address or budget or personnel, and it is not listed in any official documents. In fact, it does not exist—to any outside eyes, at least."

"Did the man Rodovan Coianu ever work there?"

"He did, until Securitate was disbanded in '89."

So the defector was telling the truth, at least that part of it.

"What is this unit's function now that Ceausescu is dead?"

"That I do not know. Whatever it is, it is very sensitive," The Owl said. "Not even my contact knew."

"I have to find out what that unit is now doing."

"It will not be easy. I had to pay this informant two thousand dollars, and even then I had to squeeze it out of him. He was terrified."

"More reason to find out," Hefflin said. "I have another question, maybe unrelated, I don't know. When I arrived, I saw a policeman on motorcycle stop the traffic so that several black Mercedes could speed by. The taxi driver called them the new oligarchs."

The Owl's expression turned dark. "Yes, those black Mercedes with tinted windows. They drive around like kings, the way Ceausescu used to, stopping traffic, entering garages so that no one sees their faces."

"Do you know who they are?"

"Everyone wonders that, but is afraid to ask. The walls still have ears, even three years after revolution. They try to keep identities secret. They do not want to be marked men. But rumor is they are former Securitate."

"Securitate?"

"Some former Securitate operatives went into private businesses, younger ones, while older continued in new Securitate. Then the story goes that they formed syndicate, to share information. Whoever these men are—and they are all men, no doubt—they have become very wealthy and powerful. They now have fingers in every pie. And they are not satisfied with just legitimate businesses"—the older man's voice rose—"They are now trying to take over what has always been my domain—black market, sex, even drugs. I am being squeezed out of my own world, forced to downsize, as you Americans say." He let out a cynical laugh.

"Is the corruption that bad?" Hefflin asked.

"Corruption has long history in this country, my friend. During Ceausescu's days, Securitate itself started smuggling—guns, heroin, cigarettes, you name it—in order to get hard currency to pay for external operations. Then, after revolution, economy plummeted, almost half of population suddenly unemployed. It was ripe for even more illegal contraband of all sorts, including sex trade. Even common people cross borders with suitcases full of contraband to feed their families. Border guards do not even check. They are all paid off. Oligarchs are so powerful that many consider them as government within government. Iliescu just puppet."

Just as Milan said.

"Their gunrunning is the worst part," The Owl went on. "They feed Yugoslavian war by running arms to Serbs to slaughter Muslims. Blood money is what our Boris called it. He hated them all for that."

"Boris knew about it?"

"Of course. He hated Stanculescu most, who has become multimillionaire running guns."

"Stanculescu? An arms dealer? The man who helped bring down Ceausescu? Who many still consider a hero of the revolution?"

"Same. Stanculescu was defense secretary in new government but left year after it was formed and became arms dealer. But nobody knows much. He is like shadow in cemetery. You think you see it but then it disappears."

"Did Boris know about Stanculescu's gunrunning?"

"In '92, as Boris was dying, he learned Stanculescu was becoming wealthy as arms trafficker to Serbia. He considered assassinating him at one point, but then illness got worse." The Owl's eyes grew moist. "Boris was bleeding heart for Muslims. During '80s, he tried to level playing field by supplying Muslims with arms to defend themselves."

"Boris? But he was Russian, an Orthodox Christian."

"He was good man. He did not care about religion or what his government ordered. He just wanted to avoid slaughter."

"So, how did Boris supply the arms?"

"With me, that is how," The Owl declared proudly.

"You?"

"I have been part of hated and maligned minority all my life. I know what it is like. The Muslims do not stand chance. So, when Boris came to ask for my help, I was only too glad to provide it. We procured arms from Middle East, mostly Kalashnikovs, mortars, and some anti-tank missiles, then shipped them to Albania, which is Muslim country, then into Kosovo and Bosnia and Herzegovina. But what we provided did not compare with what Serbs and Croats were getting. After Boris passed away, I tried to keep it going, but it was losing battle."

"Boris." Hefflin sighed. "A gunrunner."

"He was no gunrunner." The Owl scowled. "He wanted no money out of it. He gave me his share, which was considerable. He just wanted to give those poor souls a chance to live, hoping that by arming them, it would make Serbians hesitate. He was peacemaker. At least he tried to be, God bless him."

Hefflin sank into his chair to reconsider Boris yet again. The man had worked against his own government to be Hefflin's asset, then again to help the Muslims against the Serbs, Russia's natural allies, both religiously and culturally. And the oligarchs were the middlemen for arms to Serbia.

"I had dinner with some wealthy men in a beautiful house in the Popa Soare quarter," Hefflin said. "They identified themselves as The Business Roundtable. Have you heard of it?"

The Owl thought for a moment. "No. What were their names?"

"That's the strange thing, they refused to introduce themselves. The man who seemed in charge called himself Ion Popescu. Some were older, in their sixties and seventies, some younger."

The Owl leered. "How did you meet them?"

"I just received an invitation under my hotel room door. When I arrived, they said they'd heard I was an American businessman who might be interested in investing in Romania."

The Owl cursed in Romanian. "What did these men want from you?"

"They offered me a favorable deal on some company they didn't name that is going to be privatized."

"Just like that? You are unknown American businessman, and they offer you lucrative deal? No, no." The Owl shook his head. "Whoever these men are, they are connected to oligarchs, or maybe they are oligarchs. You may be one of few men who saw their faces. They obviously want to compromise you. You get in bed with them, you never get out. Like Mafia."

Another form of kompromat, *not unlike the communists, only instead of photographs with prostitutes they now use financial deals.*

"Why would they want to compromise *me?*" Hefflin asked. "I just arrived."

"They must consider you dangerous." The Owl clicked his tongue. "I have to watch out for you. You were like son Yuri hoped to have. He chose to spend his last days with you." The Owl's eyes grew moist, then turned hard. "Stay away from these men."

Hefflin stood. "Thank you for your hospitality."

"One more thing," The Owl said. "If you ever find identity of oligarchs, and need—how you say?—leverage, have your NSA find their offshore accounts, if you still have some influence with them. You find those, you have them by their balls."

Hefflin left feeling shaken. The new oligarchs, part of the old Securitate leadership, saw him as a threat and were trying to neutralize him by entangling him in some financial deal. At the dinner he had obviously insulted them with his rhetoric, which he now partly regretted. Still, if they thought he was important enough to try to compromise, they might show their hand in a more direct way now that they knew where he stood. What would they try next? And how did they know so much about him?

A thought lingered behind his reverie, which now surfaced. Gorga was former Securitate. But he had been only a minor apparatchik, at least according to Irina, and was now the owner of two security firms, not the makings of an oligarch. There were thousands of former Securitate men trying to start new businesses.

At least his main objective for coming to Bucharest had produced some results, he told himself. The Owl had verified part of the defector's story.

The boy led him back to the café, then once again stuck out his hand.

"You'll make a good businessman someday," Hefflin said as he dropped another dollar bill.

He took a taxi to the American embassy where he sent a report to Ingram describing what he had learned from The Owl, as well as from Baghdadi. Then, on a whim, he asked Ingram to have the NSA find out if Gorga possessed any offshore accounts. The oligarchs surely did. Though he assumed they would be numbered accounts, and thus difficult to trace, he knew the NSA had powerful new methods, including agents who had access to the names behind the numbered accounts in practically every bank in Europe, the Isle of Mann, Panama, the Philippines, and the Caymans. After having failed to find Ceausescu's money, the NSA had upped its game.

CHAPTER FORTY-THREE

Bucharest
April 1993

THE KGB CHIEF of station in Bucharest, Anatoli Dubrenko, was a rarity in KGB circles. He was tall and lean and possessed the chiseled face of an actor, which he had been in his youth. He had gained his position not because of his security experience—for he had none—but as a result of his being the son-in-law of the mayor of St. Petersburg. His experience was in banking, which provided a clue as to the type of intelligence the KGB sought in the newly created capitalist Romania. Bucharest was already swarming with Western bankers and investors. Dubrenko had just attended a lecture in one of those conference rooms at the InterContinental Hotel where American hedge fund managers had spoken about the investment possibilities that Romania offered.

In one respect, however, Dubrenko was a typical KGB agent. After sitting through the hour-long lecture, during which he salivated over the vast monetary figures the lecturer threw around, he made sure to taste every one of the sumptuous delicacies at the free buffet and down three shots of Swiss vodka at the open bar. Thus fortified, he stopped at the hotel men's room before returning to fill his attaché case with that deliciously decadent Western cuisine.

He entered a stall, placed his black leather briefcase beside him, and let mother nature take its course. He heard another man enter the adjoining stall but didn't take much notice. When his task was completed, he flushed the toilet and was about to take his briefcase when he heard a voice.

"Anatoli, is that you? I thought I saw you duck in here."

When Dubrenko opened the stall door, he saw a businessman from Germany, a man he recognized, a banker from the old East Germany who had now started his own investment firm in the newly unified Germany.

"Franz?"

The East German drew Dubrenko toward him and embraced him. "Anatoli, my friend, are you here, too?"

"Russia needs to modernize," Dubrenko said, letting himself be drawn to the sinks. As he washed his hands he said, "Things are loosening up, you know. Pretty soon the West will be making investments in our country, and we'll be getting fat." He laughed.

As the men began to reminisce about the old days, the man sitting in the adjoining stall dragged the Russian's attaché case under the partition wall, quickly picked the lock, and photographed the few papers inside with his miniature Minox. There was only one of importance. The German had been instructed to keep Dubrenko talking until the operative flushed the toilet. The signal sounded, and Franz invited Anatoli for a drink at the hotel bar, which offered those fascinating American "cocktails." Anatoli returned to his stall, picked up his briefcase, and walked out with his old friend with the hope that Franz was buying. He had never tried a dirty martini. The name, itself, made him quiver.

CHAPTER FORTY-FOUR

Langley
April 1993

As THE DIRECTOR of operations was about to sit down with his first cup of coffee of the day, he was interrupted by a knock on the door. His assistant walked in and handed him a set of papers.

"I think you'll want to see this, sir," the man said.

"What is it?"

"Intel from Hefflin. Just came in. And there is also a piece obtained from the Russian chief of station's briefcase." The assistant left the room as quietly as he had entered.

As Ingram skimmed through the pages, his brow furrowed. Hefflin reported that unit U0920 was still active, but with some other, unknown function.

The second item described an encounter between Hefflin and the Russian Stefan. Hefflin was able to verify that the Russians didn't know the identity of their own mole inside the CIA. They now thought Hefflin might be that mole.

Interesting. Do they actually believe that, or are they just trying to squeeze Hefflin into defecting?

The third item was a report from a man named Baghdadi, along with a copy of a cargo manifest for a ship named the *Magdalene*, describing a suspected arms shipment from Lebanon to the port of Constanta in two ships, the *Magdalene* and the *Sophia*. Hefflin suggested intercepting the ships before they reached Constanta to verify their contents.

Hefflin is getting into issues outside his purview. And who the hell is this Baghdadi?

The last item was intel from the Russian chief of station's briefcase, a translated wire from Moscow:

"CIA closing in on identity of our asset, now in Bucharest. You must convince him to escape to Moscow before he returns home. Top priority."

Ha! Here it is.

Ingram marveled at the stale consistency of the KGB. The same tricks, over and over.

Well, two can play this game.

He wrote something on a pad of paper, then wrote a separate message for Hefflin:

"Focus on your assignment. We will deal with possible arms shipments from here."

He buzzed for his assistant, who entered the room immediately.

"Send this wire to Balzary in Bucharest. And send it exactly in the manner I described."

The assistant looked at the wire message, then the instructions. "Are you sure, sir?"

"Do as I say. Then send this separate wire to Hefflin at Balzary's station."

"Right away, sir." The assistant hurried out of the room.

The wire to Balzary should get the Russians to feel at ease. As for Hefflin, I hope he keeps his fucking nose out of what is none of his business.

CHAPTER FORTY-FIVE

Bucharest
April 1993

HEFFLIN HAD BEEN aware of being shadowed practically since his arrival in Bucharest and had become adept at the game of losing his tails, with or without his ridiculous disguises. But this day he noticed that another figure had joined the game, a woman. Throughout the day he thought he had seen flashes of her on several occasions, but she was better than the others. She always had her face turned away from him and she wore different outfits every time he saw her, sometimes even donning oversized clothing to make herself appear heavier. So how did he know it was the same woman? Her gait, then the way she held her arms on her hips while pondering a mannequin in a store window, the weight on one foot while the other rubbed the ground, like a stallion. The gestures reminded him of Catherine, and so it had made an impression on him.

He recalled a CIA lecture in his training during which the instructor showed countless videos of random individuals that bore similar facial features, expressions, gait, hand gestures, or stances. The instructor's cousin, in fact, had almost identical facial features to the actress Helen Mirren. A classmate's walk resembled the long strides of Sean Connery. The instructor's point was that an agent needed to train himself to recognize these features so he could spot the individuals following him.

There was a second point to the lecture, however: For each individual there existed many variations of a doppelganger. Nature re-
combines the same genes in various permutations, sharing your facial
expressions with one person, your gait with another, the way you
laugh with a third. So how is an agent supposed to distinguish between the same person following him and a stranger with similar
mannerisms? The instructor had no answer.

Maybe the women he had noticed were all different persons who
reminded him of Catherine because he was worried about her and
Jack. He hadn't heard from them and had no way of contacting
them. On several occasions he had contemplated scrapping this entire operation and returning to the States. But then what? She and
Jack could be anywhere. He respected Catherine's abilities enough to
know that he would never find them.

As he now descended the stairs to the lobby of his hotel, he spotted
two large men in poorly fitting suits leaning against the registration
counter, one sharing jokes with the cute receptionist. Hefflin was
about to turn around for a quick exit when the second man called out.

"Mr. Blake, moment, please." The man had a heavy Russian
accent.

The two men sauntered up to him while donning their short-
brimmed black fedoras.

"Our mutual friend would like word with you."

"I'm about to have dinner," Hefflin said, "but a drink at the bar is
not out of the question."

"He prefers more private place, if you do not mind." Both men
unbuttoned their jackets to reveal guns inside shoulder holsters.

"How can I refuse such a gracious invitation? Lead the way."

As they stepped outside, a black Zil parked on the street turned
on its headlights and drove up. In the back seat Hefflin found Stefan
holding a bottle of Stoli in one hand and a shot glass in the other.

"You started without me, Stefan," Hefflin said as he got in.

"What do you expect? I have been waiting for half hour with no one to talk to." Stefan lifted the bottle of Stoli. "Drink?"

Hefflin shook his head. "I'd like to still have a liver by the time I get back home."

"Ah, you boys are always worried about your health. That is nice thing about reaching certain age: you can let go and enjoy life. So, did you consider my offer to join me to find Boris? My retirement fund is crying to be fed."

"I am still considering it."

Stefan leaned back and waived his arm as they drove down Calea Victoriei, as if showing the sights to a tourist. "I love this city. So much intrigue and corruption. Better than any of your American gangster movies."

"What is it you want, Stefan?"

"Always to point. What is hurry? Life is short. Enjoy it while you can. You may find your liver outlasts you."

"Why? Are you going to kill me?"

"Me? No, why would I? Your own people will do that soon enough."

"What are you babbling about?"

"I do not babble. I state facts. You have price on your head now," Stefan said jovially. "Your agency is after you. We just intercepted wire from your director of operations. It says you are to be detained for questioning. I do not know why they have such problems finding you. I do not."

What wire?

"Maybe you're better than they are," Hefflin said, trying to mask his ignorance.

"No doubt. So, did you like our little joke?"

"What joke is that?"

"The one where our chief of station in Bucharest leaves papers in attaché case in bathroom stall for your agent to photograph."

Hefflin remained silent.

"You do not know joke? Well, it continues like this. One paper in briefcase was correspondence from KGB headquarters in Moscow to chief of station in Bucharest. It said CIA is closing in on you and that you must be immediately exfiltrated to Moscow for your own safety. Your director of operations must have had grand party. He finally found his mole."

So that's the game Stefan is playing.

"Where's the punch line?" Hefflin asked.

"What?"

"Every joke has a punch line."

"Oh, yes. Punch line is we have become your only friends. You have only one option: to defect and live happily in Moscow." Stefan's face gleamed with satisfaction. "Is that good enough punch line for you?"

"Why are you telling me this, Stefan? I can easily inform the Agency."

"They will not believe you. They will see it as your pathetic struggle to protect yourself. I am simply telling you so you know that we can easily plant similar information in future to—how you say?—put nail in coffin."

So, Stefan no longer believes I am their mole. He's just trying to squeeze me to defect.

"I think you overlooked another option, Stefan. The one in which I find the real mole."

"It is too late for that." Stefan waved the bottle. "You are what you Americans call 'dead man walking.' If CIA is as good as its reputation, you will either be captured or eliminated within next few days.

It is good thing I found you before they did. So, maybe now you will reconsider my offer?"

But Hefflin did not have a chance to answer. Three black BMWs appeared from side streets to cut off the Zil. A dozen men wearing balaclavas and brandishing pistols with silencers surrounded the car. One of them opened the back door.

"Mr. Blake, this way, please."

"Oh, so this is how you play now, with pistols?" Stefan burst out. "I will not forget this, do not worry. Two can play this game."

As Hefflin exited the car, he heard the masked man say to Stefan: "Mr. Gorga would like you to know that this person is under his protection."

"Oh, really! You think that impresses me?" Stefan shouted. "He is also under protection of Russian state."

The man slammed the door and escorted Hefflin into one of the BMWs.

CHAPTER FORTY-SIX

Bucharest
April 1993

THE BMWs STOPPED before a pre-war building that still glowed with office lights, unlike the buildings surrounding it, which were dark and silent. The men escorted Hefflin into an elegantly decorated lobby, much like the posh pre-war buildings on Central Park West. Three men dressed in blue private security uniforms stood guard. The elevator took them to the top floor, where it opened onto a large room with modern leather seating and an unmanned reception desk. Two more uniformed security men stood in corners like caryatids. Hefflin followed the men down a corridor with several office doors on either side bearing metal plates with names and corporate titles. At the end a door stood open.

The office took up an entire corner of the building, its massive windows offering a view of the sparse lights of Bucharest. Gorga sat before an ornate Louis-the-something desk that Hefflin suspected had been imported from France.

Gorga rose and walked around the desk with hand outstretched. "My dear James, are you all right? Bring some water and a bottle of cognac," he snapped to his man like a doctor ordering medicine.

"I'm fine, thank you," Hefflin said.

"Sit down and have a drink to calm yourself. I see you shaved off your beard."

"I'm quite calm, I assure you," Hefflin said, "but a little cognac can't hurt. And the beard was getting itchy."

A tray appeared carrying a bottle of water and one of Remi Martin with two snifters. The two men sat across from each other with glass in hand, and Gorga asked what had happened.

"The KGB wanted to have a talk with me," Hefflin said, "in their usual heavy-handed manner."

"You've dealt with them before?"

"Once or twice. American businessmen seem to be a target. They wanted to know what business I was involved in, what I was doing here, the usual."

"That's outrageous," Gorga burst out. "I'm going to have a talk with the SRI minister in the morning. We can't have the Russians interfering with our economic development."

He has a direct line to the SRI minister?

"So, how did you know where to find me?" Hefflin asked. "And what's with all the security men in the building?"

Gorga let a smile cross his lips. "My man saw you enter a car with two well-known Russian operatives. He called me for instructions. I ordered him to get you the hell out of there. It's that simple. As far as the security men, well, we are a security company."

"You've been following me?"

"No, nothing like that. I just posted a man outside your hotel. Irina asked me to keep an eye on you. Bucharest is a dangerous place these days, and she was worried."

Hefflin raised his cognac. "I thank you, though I certainly don't want to place you in an awkward position. You have to live with the KGB at your doorstep."

"I hate them, and they hate me, and we both know we hate each other." Gorga chuckled. "The same old men that ran the KGB are now running the new SVR, and they haven't yet accepted the fact that Romania is now a capitalist democracy, even though their own country is also turning into one. So, they try to muck around, spread lies, interfere in business deals, threaten possible investors, just so we know they're still here."

A knock on the door, then a man entered with a tray of delicacies—Kashkaval cheese, Sibiu salami, and taramosalata, accompanied by a plate of sliced bread.

"I thought you might need some nourishment," Gorga said, "but now I realize that I am hungry." He spread some taramosalata on a piece of bread and started munching on it. "You know, the KGB is a nuisance, yes, but it's rare that they actually abduct a Western businessman. And yet, you don't seem that concerned." He took another bite and settled back, chewing silently while watching Hefflin.

Where is this guy going with this?

"They suspect I'm a spy," Hefflin declared, then raised his hands as if to say, "How ridiculous."

"Are you a spy, James?" Gorga asked, his face blank now.

"Of course. Isn't every American?" He tried to brush it off as a joke but saw that Gorga wasn't buying it.

Gorga finished his appetizer, then washed it down with a sip of the bottled water. "You know, we inherited many dishes from the Turks, but taramosalata, or as we call it, *salata de icre,* is one that almost makes those years of Ottoman invasion worth it."

"I always thought taramosalata was a Greek dish," Hefflin said.

"Yes, I know, the Greeks believe that all of civilization started with them." Gorga laughed. "But the word comes from the Turkish *tarama,* fish roe."

Hefflin remembered how his mother would create the delicacy by mixing carp roe, lemon juice, soft bread, and onions, and slowly mix in olive oil. The trick was not to pour the oil in too quickly, thus "cutting it," as his mother would say. She meant that the oil would simply pool and remain separate from the rest of the mixture, spoiling the entire concoction.

"Come, I want to show you something," Gorga said. "We'll take our drinks."

Gorga led Hefflin to the elevator, then down one flight. The door opened onto a large room filled with cubicles where several people sat working before computer screens, even at that late hour. Gorga walked over to one woman and asked her to bring up a file. The screen now displayed images of a face—two faces, in fact. Hefflin felt his pulse rise. One picture showed him at the gala wearing his beard and glasses; the other showed him leaving the American embassy in 1989 with his face clean-shaven. Lines were drawn geometrically to various points from one picture to the next: eyes, nose, cheekbones, chin, and so on.

Facial recognition.

"How long have you known?" Hefflin asked.

"Just got the report yesterday. I wouldn't have needed facial recognition had you shaved sooner and gotten rid of those silly glasses. You were the one face I didn't recognize at the gala, so I had my man take a picture of you. Since you listed yourself as an American businessman, we looked at old photographs of men going in and out of the American embassy to see if you've been here before. The Securitate archives are full of such pictures."

"I'm impressed."

"So, James Blake, aka Bill Hefflin, do you want to tell me what you're doing back in Bucharest?"

CHAPTER FORTY-SEVEN

Bucharest
April 1993

THEY WERE BACK in Gorga's office, their drinks replenished, Hefflin staring at his glass while his mind raced to decide which version of half-truth to deliver.

"In 1989 I was a State Department attaché," he finally said. "I have since resigned and gone into private business, like you."

"Yes, I already know all that. I've read your dossier."

"How do you have access to Securitate dossiers, if I may ask? You're now a civilian, aren't you?"

"Let's just say I have friends," Gorga said, his demeanor now more like that of a Securitate agent. "In '89, you were the cultural attaché of etiquette." He let out a forced laugh. "No doubt you were CIA, here to witness the revolution. If and how you were involved is another question. But that's old news. What is James Blake doing here now?"

"I've come into some money in the past two years—my wife's side of the family. I'm an investor now. Since I know a bit about Romania, I thought I'd see what opportunities existed."

"And how does Irina know you?"

"Like I said before, I'm a friend of her cousin in New York."

"A friend of her cousin," Gorga repeated. "The problem is, I have not been able to find anyone with the last name of Argyris in New York, or anywhere in the United States."

"She married," Hefflin said, prepared for such a question. "She now goes by the name of Anderson."

Why has Gorga gone to all this trouble?

Gorga scowled. "The thing is, William Hefflin is also problematic. Before joining the State Department, you attended Harvard University and Columbia Business School, but that's where the trail stops. My man hasn't yet had time to track it back further."

Hefflin stared at his drink for a long time. He had known way back at Harvard that his "legend" could be easily penetrated if someone really wanted to find his real name. At that time he had not contemplated joining the CIA. It was simply a way for him to fit in with his American classmates, to not feel like an immigrant. After his parents died, his connection to the name Argyris seemed even less important. Little did he know that it would one day come back to haunt him.

There was no point in lying any further to this former Securitate agent. Gorga would eventually find out his original family name from public court records in Massachusetts. Or he would get it out of Irina, one way or another. But how much could he trust this man? Irina's history of lovers had not been exactly stellar. Still, he sensed Gorga cared for his cousin, maybe even loved her.

"Irina is my first cousin. Our fathers were brothers," Hefflin said.

Gorga froze, then sank into his chair and let his gaze drift into the middle distance.

"So, you are the son of the doctor, Spiridon Argyris," Gorga said, shaking his head in amazement. "Why the hell didn't you tell me this before?" He slapped his thigh and burst into laughter. "What an amazing world."

"You know of me?"

"This is beginning to make some sense now. What a good liar Irina is. But she's an actress, after all. That's what they do for a living, tell lies upon lies about a character that doesn't even exist. All spies should take acting lessons."

Gorga continued to laugh while Hefflin sat there pleasantly surprised at Gorga's jovial demeanor.

"You little rascal," Gorga said. "I knew your father!"

Hefflin's chest pounded, his mind in a spin. "How's that possible?"

"I'll tell you, but there's a slight complication, because I'm going to have to tell you about my friend without his permission." Gorga thought for a moment.

"My friend—my best friend, actually—was a good friend of your father," Gorga began. "I was already advancing in the Securitate by the time my friend came to me and said that there was a doctor who got himself into a little trouble. Apparently the government had expelled him from his job at the hospital because he refused to join the Communist Party. The doctor was thus forced to perform illegal abortions to feed his family, which comprised his wife and son, a boy named Vasili. Well, someone informed on him, and the doctor was arrested. So my friend asked me to intervene."

Boris. He's talking about Boris!

"I said to him, 'This man must really be a close friend for you to ask me for such a favor.' He said 'I owe him my life.' He then told me the story of how your father, a soldier in the Romanian Army fighting alongside the Germans, came upon him, a Russian soldier, lying on the ground outside of Stalingrad, bleeding from shrapnel wounds. My friend only hoped for a quick bullet to the head. Instead, your father placed a tourniquet on his bleeding leg and inserted a needle in his chest to relieve a tension pneumothorax, either of which would have killed him in a short while. My friend said he made a promise to himself that, if he survived, he would repay that debt for the rest of his life."

"You are the Securitate agent who ordered the judge to dismiss the case!" Hefflin burst out.

Gorga looked up in surprise. "Your father told you the story?"

"I actually remember when the police came to our house," Hefflin said. "I was five or six at the time. I was terrified. When my father later returned from the court, he told my mother how a man walked into the courtroom and whispered to the judge, then walked back out. The judge then dismissed the case for insufficient evidence."

Gorga laughed. "Yes, I was that man. The Securitate had that power then. Times have changed."

"I guess my parents and I owe you for your help," Hefflin said.

"You don't owe me anything. I was helping my friend. I didn't know your father before then. But it's funny how life creates these connections between people, little links that we don't even know exist. Irina, for example."

"Irina?"

"My friend told me the many things he tried to do to help your family. One of them involved Irina. After high school she applied to the drama school and they rejected her. They didn't like her singing voice, apparently. When he found out he immediately intervened. How, I don't know. But the next year she got accepted. And she became a star." Gorga let out a laugh. "I didn't know her then, of course. I only met her much later, through Gabor. So, you and I are practically family now. And after Irina and I get married, we'll be a real family."

"You're getting married?"

"Of course. What kind of man do you think I am? I love her very much, and I believe she loves me. I am a bit older than her, but I hope that won't be an issue. The wedding will be in July. But she doesn't know it yet, so don't spill the beans."

"You haven't proposed?"

"I planned on doing it at our one-year anniversary dinner . . . but then her cousin showed up." Gorga burst into laughter.

Hefflin sighed. "Sorry to be the spoiler."

"No, no, I'm glad I met you. You added to my future family. And you brought closure to the story with my friend and your father."

"He must have been a good friend to ask for your help," Hefflin said, treading lightly.

"Oh, we go back almost thirty years." Gorga's gaze drifted, unfocused. "I first met him when he was a young KGB agent assigned to Bucharest and I a younger Securitate agent. He showed up one day at our headquarters, a huge man. He was clean-shaven, but every time after that, when I met him in some bar somewhere, he wore a disguise—a beard, a different nose, different color hair. I often didn't recognize him until he spoke to me." Gorga's gaze drifted as he smiled.

"About a year after our first meeting, I was in charge of an operation—my first, actually—to intercept contraband arriving in trucks at a warehouse outside of Bucharest. It involved a man they now call The Owl. In those days he was known as Mr. Magoo because of his thick glasses." He chuckled. "One of the things he smuggled was cartoon magazines from the West. That's how we knew about Mr. Magoo. Later he smuggled contact lenses for himself, so Mr. Magoo no longer fit. Anyway, just as I was about to order my men to move in and make arrests, this tall man appears out of nowhere wearing rags and a white beard. He flashes his KGB identification and orders us to stand down. The KGB was all-powerful at that time. They could send us to some gulag with no questions asked. So, of course, I did as he ordered. As soon as my men were gone he told me to stay, so I could learn something, he said. He then entered the warehouse and returned a moment later with another man who wore a black coat and fedora to hide his face. He placed the man in a parked car and the car drove off. I hadn't even noticed there was a driver inside. He then came back to me and said, 'Let's go have a vodka. It's on me.'

"It was only after we sat down at a bar and began talking that I realized he was the same man I had seen in the headquarters. He told me that a KGB agent had been hidden inside one of the contraband cigarette crates, involved in some operation of his, and that he appreciated my help. That was, as Rick says, 'the beginning of a marvelous friendship.'"

"Close enough."

"He and this man, The Owl, were even older friends," Gorga said. "I think I have always been jealous of The Owl because of that. And because he was making a lot more money than I was, and I wasn't ever able to arrest him. Yes, I was allowed to break up a few of his black market operations, for show. I later learned he was protected by the higher-ups because he helped in certain clandestine operations, and because they were getting a cut of his profits." Gorga chuckled.

"Do you know where your friend is now?" Hefflin asked.

"I haven't heard from him for a couple of years. Either he's back in Moscow or getting rich somewhere, I imagine. But you still haven't told me why you're here."

Should I chance it? This former Securitate agent had helped his father stay out of jail, and had been Boris's best friend. And Gorga obviously still had connections to the Securitate. Hefflin knew he would never have a better chance of finding out about that damned unit.

"Even though I'm now a businessman, I still have friends in the Agency, as you do in the Securitate," Hefflin said. "They asked me to do them a favor."

"Oh?"

"They are still trying to figure out the structure of the new security services in Romania. A particular unit, in fact, called U0920."

Gorga's face grew gaunt, though he tried to hide it by lighting a cigarette. After taking a deep drag, he slowly breathed out the smoke. "I don't know much about that unit, other than that Ceausescu created it to spy on his own people. He was a paranoid son-of-a-bitch. It was disbanded after the revolution."

"I was told it might still exist," Hefflin probed.

"I don't see why it would. Ceausescu is dead. But—"Gorga's face broke into a brilliant stage smile, almost pulling it off as well as Irina would have—"for a future member of the family, I'll make some inquiries."

CHAPTER FORTY-EIGHT

Bucharest
April 1993

THE CHURCH OVERFLOWED with parishioners wearing their best suits and dresses. The crowd spilled outside onto the sidewalk, where hundreds more had gathered to hear the Easter Mass through loudspeakers. After forty years of atheistic communist dogma, the people—some for the first time—rejoiced in the old customs and traditions.

Hefflin had read the reports. Many church priests had publicly admitted after the revolution that they had served as Securitate informants for decades. The Patriarch of the Romanian Orthodox Church had publicly supported Ceausescu up to the very end, even congratulating him after the massacre in Timisoara. He apologized and resigned after the fall of the regime, only to be reinstated a few months later, as had become the practice for the politicians.

Hefflin stood next to Irina and Gorga, who had insisted on going together to midnight Mass.

"We might as well start acting like a family," Gorga had told Hefflin. "Besides, there's nothing like the Easter feast after services."

The entire congregation stood packed shoulder-to-shoulder, for Orthodox churches traditionally contained no pews, only a few chairs lining the walls for the elderly and infirm. Irina had insisted on going to the Greek church, as she had been brought up to do, which had a particular tradition she enjoyed.

It came a minute before midnight. The lights dimmed until the entire church stood in complete darkness, the symbol of ignorance and evil. The crowd grew silent, fearful. Then came the lone voice of the priest, high-pitched, as he exited from behind the enclosed altar holding a lit candle, the holy light of God, and declared, *"Hristos a inviat!"* Christ has risen! The people surged forward to light their own candles from his and spread the light of wisdom.

He knew that the people of Romania had survived those years of communism by believing in a world beyond. The opiate of the masses, Marx had called it. The irony was that it was this opiate that had allowed the communists to hold on to power for as long as they had.

A loud shriek echoed throughout the church—a woman's cry. Then more cries, followed by panicked pushing and shoving by the parishioners behind him. The church lights turned on. A woman behind him kept screaming hysterically. A man lay on the ground. His throat was slit open and blood squirted high in a pulsating rhythm from his severed carotid artery. People scrambled to avoid the blood while more women screamed. Then Hefflin recognized the face, twisted in frozen agony: Baghdadi.

Hefflin shoved his way toward the body and approached it from an angle away from the blood, which had now stopped spurting. *What the hell was Baghdadi doing here? Was he following me?* The thought occurred to him to search the body, then he noticed Baghdadi's hand clutching something. He pried the fingers open and grabbed the object. A watch! He quickly slipped it into his pocket and allowed the crowd to push him toward the exit.

Outside he found Gorga and Irina among the distressed crowd. Sirens howled in the distance.

"How horrible." Irina shuddered. "Murdered in church, on holy ground. Are there no limits anymore?"

"Poor fellow," Gorga said. "It must have happened during the few minutes of darkness. Some dispute among local gangs, no doubt."

Gorga waved to his driver who had been waiting by the black BMW. In a moment they were driving toward the center of the city.

"I can't imagine eating a thing after such a horror, never mind the Easter feast," Irina declared. "Just drop me off at my house."

"Darling . . ." Gorga patted her hand.

"Please, I feel nauseated just thinking about it. I just need sleep."

"You can drop me off anywhere," Hefflin said. "I'll find a taxi."

The car slowed at a taxi stand. As Hefflin got out, Gorga held his arm.

"By the way, the unit you asked me about. I made some inquiries, as I promised. It was disbanded after the revolution, just as I thought. It no longer exists."

The BMW drove off toward Irina's house where, no doubt, Gorga hoped to stay the night, leaving Hefflin to wonder if Gorga had just lied to him.

CHAPTER FORTY-NINE

Bucharest
April 1993

HEFFLIN ARRIVED AT the Hungarian embassy on Easter morning after having called ahead to make sure Balzary had returned. They sat in Balzary's office and Hefflin brought Balzary up to speed about Baghdadi.

"Illegal arms going to Yugoslavia," Balzary mused. "Well, it certainly puts a new wrinkle into the matter. And he said Mayfield is connected to this company in Nicosia?"

"P.U.I.U Import/Export."

"We knew that Mayfield is an arms dealer, so it shouldn't come as a surprise," Balzary said. "And Baghdadi told you that it was Janus who had alerted him to these ships and to Mayfield?"

"He said Janus—our Boris—despised arms dealers. Apparently, Baghdadi and Janus had been exchanging intel for years. And Baghdadi said something interesting: that Janus didn't seem to care where the intel was going, as if he were trying to spread as much secret intel as he could to all sides. To put the military out of business, is what he told Baghdadi."

"Strange fellow, Dovrosky, aka Boris, aka Janus . . . and who knows how many more aliases he used? On the one hand he was an idealist and on the other almost a stoic. He knew and accepted human frailties."

"Baghdadi told me that the intel he gave me placed his life in danger," Hefflin said. "I guess he was right."

"A gruesome murder, and in church, no less." Balzary shook his head. "You alerted Ingram?"

"Yes, before Baghdadi's murder. Let's hope he follows up on those ships." Then Hefflin removed the watch he had grabbed from Baghdadi's dead hand, a Rolex, and showed it to Balzary.

Balzary examined it, turned it over, then handed it back. "Baghdadi died holding this watch? What the hell is special about it?"

"He was standing a few feet behind me," Hefflin said. "I think he intended to give it to me, but I can't figure out why. It reminds me of those expensive watches in Mayfield's drawer. By the way, were you able to get me a meeting with Nicu?"

"I was about to get in touch with you, actually, but your story almost made me forget," Balzary said. "The meeting is on for tonight."

"I guess he doesn't celebrate Easter," Hefflin sneered. "Oh, and I forgot to mention that I had a little encounter with my Russian friend Stefan." Hefflin told Balzary about Stefan's revelation of the trick he had played on the CIA with the fake message from Moscow insinuating that Hefflin was the mole.

"That explains Ingram's message to me. I just got this wire this morning." Balzary handed him a piece of paper.

Hefflin read it aloud. "James Blake is wanted for questioning. Detain if spotted. Avoid the use of lethal force, if possible."

"The strange thing is, it wasn't sent via the most secure lines," Balzary said. "And it was only sent to me. I checked with other allied services. It's as if—"

"—Ingram wanted the Russians to intercept it," Hefflin said. "He wants the Russians to think he fell for their trick, that he decided I'm the mole."

"I guess Ingram knows how to play the game." Balzary smiled.

Hefflin then recounted his meeting with Gorga, who divulged that he was the Securitate agent who had helped Hefflin's father.

"Christ! Can this get any more convoluted?" Balzary shook his head. "Does he know his friend is your Boris?"

"No, I never mentioned Boris to him."

"So, you two are now buddies. You owe him. And he wants you to know that. Does he really intend to marry your cousin?"

"That's what he says. We'll be one happy family."

CHAPTER FIFTY

Bucharest
April 1993

THE HOUSE, A wooden, three-story structure built by the communist elite during their heyday, was located in the outskirts of Bucharest. The relatively new building looked unkempt, the paint already beginning to peel, the large garden abandoned, a jungle of weeds. Obviously Nicu Ceausescu did not live there, but simply used it for this meeting.

Hefflin and Balzary had driven to the rendezvous point in Balzary's limo.

"He's been keeping a low profile since his release," Balzary said. "He's paranoid that some crazed person will take revenge."

Hefflin could understand such fears. Nicu Ceausescu had been accused of ordering troops to fire on civilians in the city of Sibiu, of multiple rapes, and of misappropriation of state funds, among other crimes. Many in Romania did not consider the revolution complete while Nicu was still alive.

The two men guarding the front door signaled for them to raise their arms to be patted down. Satisfied, the men showed them inside, then returned to their outdoor stations.

In the dim parlor Hefflin could make out a worn, gray couch on which Nicu Ceausescu sat smoking. A bottle of vodka and a half-full tumbler stood on the wooden coffee table. As Hefflin's eyes grew accustomed to the low light, he was taken aback by the frailty of the man, the obvious toll the years of heavy drinking and hepatitis had wrought. He couldn't believe this was the same playboy who had scandalized Europe with his notorious parties, fast cars, and faster women. And yet the man was still drinking vodka and smoking. He remembered Boris doing the same after knowing he was dying of lung cancer and declaring, "Why not? You want me to—how you say—close barn gates after horses have escaped?"

Balzary shook Nicu's hand, then introduced Hefflin. Nicu nodded, but made no effort to extend his hand. They sat in chairs across from Nicu, and Balzary began in English with pleasantries and wishes for Nicu's recovery.

The ill man waved off the remarks. "It's nothing that a total body transplant won't cure."

Hefflin was impressed by his good English, but then remembered Nicu had spent years enjoying untold evenings with the sons of nobility in the nightclubs all over Europe, where English was the common language.

"So, is there something I can do for you, gentlemen, or is this a social call?" Nicu asked.

"We're interested in a particular man," Balzary began, then removed the photograph of Mayfield and placed it on the coffee table. "You knew him well."

Nicu glanced at the picture, then reached for the glass of vodka.

"Yes, I've known Harry for years. What do you want to know?"

"As much as you can tell us," Hefflin said.

"He's in Bucharest now, I hear. Why don't you ask him yourself?"

"We were hoping you could fill in some gaps." Hefflin stared at him.

Nicu sipped on his vodka. "You CIA?"

Hefflin hesitated for a moment, then nodded.

"Well, then, since America and Romania are now allies, you can ask the Securitate, or whatever they call it now, to give you all they have on him." Nicu grinned insolently. "But you can't, can you? Iliescu is not to be trusted. The same pigs are in the same sty, and they all need to protect themselves." He lit another cigarette from the one he was smoking and stamped the old one out in the ashtray. Hefflin noticed his hands shook.

"My parents destroyed Romania," Nicu said. "As early as 1972 I told them to relax their grip, to make life more tolerable for the people. But they were paranoid, of the Soviets, especially. My mother fed my father's paranoia as her gluttony grew. You know, she had hundreds of pieces of priceless jewelry that she never wore—just kept them locked in a safe." He chuckled. "Even after decades of being heads of state, they remained peasants. And they eventually got what they deserved." A mirthless smile spread over his lips. Hefflin wondered if Nicu hated his parents for what they had done or for losing it all in the end.

"But they couldn't have pulled it off all alone, could they?" Nicu continued. "They had dozens of sniveling sycophants who did their bidding gladly, even enthusiastically. Did they receive their just punishment? No. Many of them are back in power, especially this snake, Iliescu, who America thinks is an ally." He shifted in his seat, then brushed some ashes off his pants.

"We were talking about Mayfield," Hefflin reminded him.

"He was just another sycophant trying to make himself feel important. I quickly lost interest in him." He waived his cigarette in dismissal.

"He was more than that," Hefflin insisted. "He was an arms dealer. Still is."

"I know nothing about that." Nicu folded his arms, one hand still holding his lit cigarette. The man was obviously lying. But perhaps he was waiting for some inducement, a *baksheesh*, the bribe that oiled the palms for every successful transaction in Romania.

"I am not asking you to provide this information for free," Hefflin said. "I know how valuable your time is. Let's say, fifty thousand U.S.?"

Nicu's eyes lit up. "He must be important to you." His gaze drifted into the distance, an ironic smile slowly spreading over his lips. "You know, there was a time when I would lose that amount in one night at the baccarat table without flinching. Now it seems like a lot. Funny, isn't it?" He let out a groan. "Make it one hundred thousand."

"Fifty is it. I don't haggle. For every minute you delay, it goes down by five thousand."

"All right, all right, I'll tell you all I know about Harry, another snake. Even worse, in fact, because he's an American."

Nicu downed his vodka and poured himself another as a way of collecting his thoughts.

"I met Harry when I was about eighteen or twenty, at a party at the American Embassy," Nicu began. "In those days Western embassy parties were common. My father's paranoia hadn't yet blossomed. Harry introduced himself as an American businessman. He was tall, good-looking, a ladies' man, but older than me, in his thirties, I guessed. Still, we quickly became friends.

"We played tennis together at the Party's private club." He laughed. "Believe it or not, I was pretty good in those days, before the drink got the better of me. Harry told me how he could help in opening up trade with the West, which was minimal in those days. He never missed a chance to brag and insisted he could be a middleman for Romania, not only in business but in diplomatic matters. I never took him seriously. Honestly, I knew very little about state affairs and cared even less. Still, I decided to introduce him to my father, just to shut him up.

"To my surprise, my father and Harry hit it off quite well. He quickly became a regular in my father's office. I didn't know what kind of business they did together—my father never trusted me with state affairs—but Harry began disappearing for weeks at a time. When he returned, he went straight to my father. When I once asked him what kind of business he was conducting, he just laughed it off and said he was sworn to secrecy on penalty of execution. He and my father continued in this relationship for years, maybe even up to the very end."

Hefflin wondered why the CIA didn't know of this relationship between Mayfield and the elder Ceausescu.

"At some point we started drifting apart," Nicu continued. "I got tired of his bragging and his constant hints about some 'very important mission' he had completed for my father. But as my drinking increased, my father sidelined me even further, while seeming to get closer to Harry."

"Did you ever find out what kind of business Mayfield was doing for your father?" Hefflin asked.

"As a matter of fact, I eventually did," Nicu said. "At some point, years later, my father had second thoughts and started grooming me for possible foreign minister. This was after Pacepa defected, and my father was up in arms. He thought he needed to surround himself with family members in key positions, so he brought me closer. As part of my education, he gave me security clearance to delve into files and to receive classified reports of our foreign activities."

Hefflin was well aware of Pacepa, a two-star general in the Securitate and a favorite of Ceausescu, a position that gave him access to all aspects of state secrets as well as to Ceausescu's private life. After Pacepa defected in 1978 and disclosed many of the dirty secrets of Ceausescu's regime, the attitude of the U.S. toward Romania plummeted.

"Funny how Pacepa's defection worked in my favor," Nicu said. "Anyway, that's how I came across the files describing Harry's activities. And they were quite extensive. It was during those days that my father and Arafat became buddies."

Hefflin remembered the intel from Pacepa describing Ceausescu's meetings with Arafat but didn't interrupt.

"They were both fighting for the liberation of their people—the same old propaganda," Nicu said, his words beginning to slur. "My father advised Arafat to become more outwardly moderate, the same way that my father had convinced the West that he was independent of the Soviets. Arafat followed his advice. On the world stage, he looked like a smiling, reasonable uncle willing to find an accommodation with the Israelis, while inside he was still the bloodthirsty revolutionary.

"After that, my father supplied Arafat with small arms and other military equipment—part of our extensive Soviet arsenal. He eventually did the same with Gaddafi, Assad, and others. My father became the secret friend of revolutionaries around the globe. He needed hard currency, you see. Our country was sinking."

"And Mayfield?" Hefflin asked.

"Harry was the man on the ground responsible for making it all happen," Nicu said. "He arranged for the ships, the false markings listing the cargo as construction equipment, the bribes to Middle Eastern officials, everything. He had already been dealing in the arms trade, so he had the connections. Whatever my father couldn't provide, Harry could from other sources. He became a very valuable asset for my father, in many ways."

"How long did that last?" Hefflin asked.

"I don't know. After a while, my interest in foreign affairs waned. The whole thing was interfering with my partying schedule, you see." Nicu laughed, then coughed, bringing up phlegm. He pulled a linen square from his pocket. "It all seemed so petty, so beneath me. Something told me I was destined to have a short life, so I decided to enjoy it to its maximum."

The room remained quiet for a moment. Hefflin wasn't sure if he should ask the question, but then threw caution to the wind. "Mayfield loved expensive watches, I hear. I believe he collected them."

Nicu frowned. "Yeah, during the past couple of years Harry brought back a watch for me every so often from his trips, even while I was in jail—a Patek one time, an Omega another. I think he felt guilty. This is one of them." He extended his arm to show his gold Rolex. "They all suck. None of them keep correct time and a couple of them stopped working altogether. When I complained to him, he said they are supposed to be worn as jewelry, not timepieces." Nicu spit. "You pay thousands of dollars for a trinket with a name on it."

Hefflin removed Baghdadi's Rolex from his pocket and handed it to Nicu. "Is this one of them?"

Nicu examined it, then handed it back. "How the hell should I know? One Rolex looks like any other to me." He looked away, hiding something. "Where did you get this, anyway?"

"A dead man gave it to me."

Nicu's eyes darted to Hefflin's. "What man?"

"His name was Amir Baghdadi. Do you know him?"

"How should I know him? You think I know every low-level gangster in Bucharest?"

No, you know only the high-level ones.

"Was Mayfield ever involved in intelligence work?" Hefflin asked.

"Who the hell knows what he did for my father? They were birds of a feather. But if he bragged to others as much as he did to me, he couldn't have been a very good spy. In fact, with all his gunrunning, I'm surprised he's still alive."

Hefflin tried to assess the man before him, a shadow of his former self who knew he was in his last years of life. He sensed bitterness and a feeling that Nicu felt his life had been stolen from him. But the man was hiding something; Hefflin could sense it.

"You know more about this watch than you're telling me," Hefflin said.

Nicu looked at Hefflin's face, which now bore a fierce determination.

"I offered you the carrot. There is also the stick," Hefflin said. "I can break your neck before you have a chance to scream, and all of Romania will rejoice."

Nicu's rheumy eyes blinked. "All right, I recognize the watch. I gave it to Baghdadi—one of the watches Harry gave me."

"How do you know Baghdadi?"

"He was a guy Harry knew. They used to hang around together."

"No, there's more to it."

"They had something going with these watches, sort of a joke." Nicu raised his voice. "They bragged that the watches made them a lot of money. They said they picked them up from The Watchman."

"Who is this *watchman*?"

"It's not a who but a what—a store in Athens. I figured they were smuggling them into Bucharest to sell on the black market." He shrugged. "What did I care about their petty little games?"

"Why do you hate Mayfield so much?" Hefflin asked.

Nicu's face reddened. "Do you know what it's like to see your father prefer a total stranger over his own son? I know for a fact that Harry whispered all sorts of stories about me into my father's ear. I do not deny that some were true—most, in fact—but what the hell? I was the emperor's son, the inheritor of the throne." Nicu settled back, out of breath. "And then, when he saw that my father's situation was growing hopeless, his heart suddenly bled for those millions of sheep that had never bleated once in forty years. Like all the other vultures, he circled the carcass to pick its remains. Yes," Nicu heaved, "if you can bring him down, you have my blessing."

Two heavy thuds echoed from outside, like sacks of potatoes falling. The conversation stopped and all eyes turned to the front door. Several minutes passed. Then, as they were about to resume, the door opened. A figure entered holding a pistol with silencer. Hefflin sat paralyzed, his brain suddenly mired in molasses.

"Catherine?"

CHAPTER FIFTY-ONE

Bucharest
April 1993

"Catherine, what are you doing here?" Hefflin asked.

"What I should have done a long time ago," Catherine seethed. "Why are you talking to this animal as if he were human? Can't you see he's a lying dog?" She pointed the gun at Nicu. "Here he is, playing the suffering victim, justifying himself, while he's throwing his old buddy under the bus, his pimp."

Nicu focused on Catherine. "What?"

"You heard me. Your pimp. Tell them about Mayfield, how he scoured the streets of Bucharest for young girls to imprison in one of your many houses for you to defile. Tell them!"

Nicu turned to Hefflin. "Does she work for you, or are you just banging her?" A sneer appeared on his face as he turned to Catherine. "There was a time when women like you would beg to fuck me."

A puff, barely a cough, was followed by a hole fluffing the couch cushion next to Nicu's knee.

"I swear I don't know what she's babbling about," Nicu cried, trying to inject honesty into his voice, though his eyes said differently.

"Your knee will go first, then your other one, followed by your ankles, arms, and finally that degenerate appendage between your legs," Catherine said coldly. She took a step closer. "Or maybe I'll start with that."

Nicu's face twitched. Without taking his eyes off the gun, he murmured, "Balzary, do something."

Balzary shrugged. "She's the one holding the gun."

Hefflin focused on Catherine's cold eyes, the tight clenching of her jaw. "What's this about, Catherine?"

A second puff, this one landing between Nicu's legs.

"All right!" Nicu's feeble bronchitic screech seemed almost comical. "Yes, he brought girls. Is that a crime?"

"They were all minors, taken from their homes and orphanages for you to besmirch and then throw away," Catherine said coldly.

"Their parents were well paid!" Nicu cried.

"Many of those children later became alcoholics, drug addicts, and sexual perverts themselves. You stole their childhoods, their souls."

"What lives did they have anyway?" Nicu waved his hand. "At least they got fucked by nobility. For them, that was a memory to cherish for the rest of their lives." He leaned back and smiled dreamily, no doubt replaying the scenes through the haze of alcohol. "What these girls gave me in private they are now selling to tourists on the streets."

"You degraded little pervert. Your matron, God curse her, fed them alcohol and drugs day and night so that they would be compliant. She trained them in perverse games, forcing them to be naked at all times, so they would always be ready in case you showed up."

"How do you know these things? Who told you these lies?"

"No one had to tell me. I was there. I saw it all."

Nicu's eyes shot up at her. "You?"

Hefflin stared at her, numb.

Catherine's body began to shake. "Yes, I was one of those girls. I saw how you beat them, the bruises, the blood that oozed between their legs after you were done with them. Children! Thank God someone saved me before you could put your filthy hands on me."

"Catherine," Hefflin gasped.

"They needed training," Nicu yelled. "If the Arab sheiks could have a harem, why couldn't I?"

"I've imagined this moment for many years, variations of torturing and killing you slowly." Catherine aimed at his groin, her finger touching the trigger, twitching to pull it. A moment of indecision. Her face twisted, fighting the demons. "I've put myself to sleep on countless nights trying to decide whether to maim you for life or just kill you. It's only right that the first bullet should remove that vile organ once and for all."

"No!" Nicu screamed. "Balzary, help me! She's crazy!"

"Catherine, don't," Hefflin said softly. "He's not worth it."

Catherine's chest heaved in turmoil, her muscles tensed in some internal struggle. A moment longer, still battling the demons, then her grip on the pistol relaxed.

"You're right. I can no longer find the hatred, no matter how much I try. Just disgust. And I'm disgusted with myself for wasting all these years on him. I won't soil my spirit anymore. I want him to die a slow, miserable death from his illness."

She lowered her gun. As she walked out the door, she looked like she was gliding—a snake shedding its skin. When Hefflin and Balzary reached her outside, they saw the two security guards lying on the ground, unconscious, their hands tied behind their backs.

"You came prepared with rope?" Hefflin asked, trying to lighten the mood.

"I used the lining of their jackets," Catherine said.

"You ruined their jackets?" Hefflin asked in mock horror. "Thank God they're not Brioni suits."

In the limo Balzary poured vodkas for all. Hefflin made the introductions.

"I remember seeing you two together at Harvard," Balzary said. "I thought then that you made a great couple. It's a distinct pleasure to finally meet you."

"The pleasure is mine," Catherine said. "I've heard a lot about you, most of it good."

Hefflin sat in awe at Catherine's ability to find humor even at moments like these.

"How did you know I was here?" he asked.

"I've been tailing you for a couple of days, *cheri*, while staying at Uncle's old apartment. I figured that sooner or later you'd have to go see that animal to find out what he knows about Mayfield. I was hoping that you hadn't gone to see him yet. It certainly took you long enough."

"I had other things to do, which I'll fill you in on," Hefflin protested. "I thought I spotted someone who resembled you, by the way. But I assumed I was just imagining it, worried over you."

"Good to know that my star pupil still has the stuff." She winked. "So where's Jack?"

"Jacques and Yvette are with Mother at her house in Antibes."

"What house in Antibes?"

"The one nobody knows about, not even you." She smiled. "It used to belong to my grandfather, my adoptive mother's father. At the beginning of World War II, my grandfather sold the house to his banker in Switzerland for one dollar. He thought that would protect it in case the Germans invaded. After the war, his banker sold the house back to him for a dollar in a private contract, but my grandfather kept the house under the banker's name on local records. All taxes were paid by a Swiss offshore account, as they still are today. My grandfather apparently had become obsessed with secrecy after his experiences in the war. In fact, most of his wealth was kept in

Swiss accounts. After my grandparents passed away, the Swiss accounts and the house went to his daughter, my adoptive mother, who never changed the local records to the house. She also likes privacy. So, no one knows it belongs to her. It used to be my secret hideaway during my childhood summers."

"But you left Jack alone? You said you were being followed."

"Why this sudden concern over your son? You are barely able to pick him up without his crying?"

"That doesn't mean I don't love him," Hefflin protested, though he also questioned where this sudden instinct to protect his son came from.

"There are four DGSE men at the house," Catherine said. "And I took steps to hide my destination when I left New York." She turned her face away to hide a smile. "Oh, by the way, I bought a jet."

"You what?"

"It was for security reasons. When I explain, you'll understand."

"All this so you can find that animal?" Hefflin's pulse throbbed in his temples.

"I needed to face him," Catherine said softly. "I didn't know what I would do. I had to find out, about myself."

Hefflin tried to calm his nerves, for he still thought she had foolishly placed their child in danger, as well as his operation. But he had to face the facts as they were. She had just passed through a pivotal event in her life.

"You never told me about him," Hefflin probed, now that Catherine seemed calmer.

"Uncle tried to help me forget about that part of my life, and to protect you from it." She seemed to melt into the seat as a deep look of contentment spread over her face. "I'm all right now. I've met my demon, and conquered him by showing mercy."

CHAPTER FIFTY-TWO

Bucharest
April 1993

HEFFLIN LAY ON the bed fully clothed, his brain on overload with what he had learned that evening. Catherine had gone straight to the shower as soon as they had walked into his hotel room, leaving him alone with his overactive imagination. He knew he had to temper the images now flying through his mind until he heard the story and the agonies she'd had to endure at the hands of that man.

When she reappeared, she was wrapped in a towel, her wet hair trickling over her bare shoulders. She looked fragile and yet even more beautiful in the peace she now displayed.

She sank onto the bed and placed her head on his chest. His heart reached out to her as he imagined the courage she'd have to muster to tell him.

"First of all, it wasn't as bad for me as you imagine, knowing your imagination," she began.

Thank God she can still joke about it.

"He never touched me. I was too young, even for him. Barely nine. But that's how they worked it. They brought young girls—some even younger than me—to become accustomed to their new role, to be trained as his harem. 'Each citizen has to work for the socialist cause in whatever capacity they are capable,' said the old crow, built like a sergeant, who was the head of the place. 'In your case,' she said, 'you are capable of only one thing: to please the prince, our future leader.' I was only forced to stand and watch. It was horrible enough. If I closed my eyes I would later receive a slap from her. Thank God it only lasted a few weeks until Uncle arrived to rescue me."

"Boris?"

"He just walked in one night, showed his KGB badge, and shouted out my name. They immediately dressed me and presented me to him. He was as tall as a poplar and wore a scraggly beard. At first I was scared, but then he dropped down on one knee and smiled at me. 'I'm here to take you to Fili,' he said." Catherine's voice cracked. "When I heard your name, I just broke into tears. He was like an angel who had come to rescue me."

Hefflin's eyes watered. Boris had kept this part of the story from him to protect Catherine. He had been a guardian angel both for him and her. *How many lives can a man save in one lifetime?*

"I cried all the way in the car," Catherine said. "He drove me to an apartment where a woman took care of me for a few days until we left. We passed through communist Hungary with him just showing his KGB identification. To get us into Austria he showed a fake diplomatic passport. I was hiding in the trunk. We were just waved on. When we arrived in Paris, he introduced me to my future parents. You know the rest."

Adopted by a young State Department attaché and his wife, Catherine would pass an enchanted childhood among the wealthy and cultured of Europe.

Then we fell in love again when we met at Harvard. What a world.

"I can't imagine the torment you've been living with all these years," he said gently. "And the scars that it must have left."

"No, no scars. For years I still nurtured some hatred. But as I said to you when we first met, I decided I would not let life create me. I would create myself."

"'I became the center of my own universe,'" he quoted her. "Your words have haunted me to this day."

She laughed. "I must have sounded abhorrent. I could never say that today, now that we have Jacques. He has become the center of my universe."

"At first I didn't quite appreciate it," Hefflin said. "I thought you were a bit too self-centered. But now I think I understand."

"Life introduced me to many experiences—from the marvelous things I saw in the countries to which my father's postings brought me, to the perversions I observed in those few weeks in Nicu's horrible harem. I chose from among them and made them my own. That is what I meant. Except for a desire for revenge. That remained, despite my efforts, until tonight, when I also shed that weight." She sighed with visible satisfaction. "Perhaps if he had molested me, I would have felt differently. Maybe I could not have been able to overcome it. Yes, one could say that I was introduced to sex too early, that I lost part of my childhood. But my childhood had already been lost . . . with losing you when you left for Greece, then with the death of my parents, followed by that horrible orphanage." She gave a small shrug. "The one remnant from the harem exposure is that I've become a bit of a sex addict." She let a smile draw her lips up. "But I enjoy it, and I think so do you, no?"

They remained silent, clutching each other, neither willing to let go.

"Why didn't you tell me you were coming to Bucharest?" he asked.

"I know, and I'm sorry. But I figured your hotel phone may be bugged. I suppose I could have wired you at the American embassy, or at Balzary's, but then I was afraid you'd have me explain myself or try to stop me when I told you. I decided to come on a whim, before I changed my mind. I had to face him. I knew I wouldn't be able to live with myself otherwise."

She sat up, suddenly eager. "So, fill me in on everything."

"You've been following me, so you should know a few things already." For the next hour he recounted all the events since his arrival in Bucharest while Catherine listened without interrupting him. When he was finished, she sat up.

"Show me the watch you took from Baghdadi and the pictures from Mayfield's house."

Hefflin produced the watch and then spread the pictures on the bed. She spent several minutes peering at them closely, turning the photos sideways, then the watch. She finally set them down with a grunt.

"I need a magnifying glass," she said. "But where can we get one at this hour?"

"I'll ask the receptionist downstairs." Hefflin swung out of bed and left the room. A few minutes later he returned bearing two sets of reading glasses.

"Brilliant," she burst out. "Whom did you steal them from?"

"The old bookkeeper in the back room, behind the reception desk. I gave her twenty bucks and told her I'd return them in a half hour."

"You are a great field agent," she purred. She held the two pairs of glasses at various distances on top of each other as she focused on the pictures, then Baghdadi's watch. She did this several times until her face suddenly burst into a smile.

"What?" he cried.

She handed him the glasses. "Look at the watch, then compare it to the pictures of the watches in Mayfield's room."

Hefflin manipulated the glasses to magnify Baghdadi's watch, then the photographs. After a few minutes, he put them back down. "I don't see it."

"Focus on the two position, ten past the hour."

He looked again at the watch, then saw it. "There's a dot missing."

"They're all missing at that same position, every one of Mayfield's watches," Catherine said.

Hefflin peered at the pictures and saw she was right.

"A microdot?"

"Most likely."

"So, Mayfield is receiving some sort of intel via those watches, using The Watchman stores." Hefflin set down the glasses and shook his head. "That's not a bad system."

"According to his planner, Mayfield is due to fly to Athens in a few days," Catherine said. "And that's where The Watchman store is located, according to Nicu. Every month Mayfield flies there, on the same date, to pick up a watch. We have to follow it up." She squeezed into him. "Aren't you glad we now have our own plane? But don't get your hopes up. He's a snake. His slimy dealings may have nothing to do with your mission or Uncle."

"No, no, there's a connection, I can feel it," Hefflin said. "Boris knew him and hated him because of his arms dealings. And there's this dream I had, which I think included Mayfield and Boris, in Harvard Yard, no less. There's something there that I haven't been able to figure out." He kissed her gently on the lips. "I would never have figured out the watches without you. I'm still amazed that you chose me as your lover before you even knew I was your Fili."

"Like I told you: we're kindred spirits—citizens of the world, traveling light." She kissed him gently. "*Cheri*, before we leave Bucharest, I want to see our old neighborhood again, your house, the apple tree."

"We'll go first thing in the morning."

CHAPTER FIFTY-THREE

Bucharest
April 1993

THEY ARRIVED AT their old neighborhood early the next day, excited to visit their former haunt again—the apple tree under which Tanti Bobo would sit and tell them stories, the *maidan* in the back where they used to keep chickens, his old house with all its memories hanging like withered grapes. It was the first time that they were returning together to relive those sacred moments and mourn their abrupt loss the day they were forced to separate.

They approached the house with anticipation, holding hands, almost skipping, as they used to do when small. When they couldn't contain their excitement any longer, they burst into a run.

They came upon it suddenly, almost running past it. They didn't recognize it at first, just stopped and stared, trying to understand what their eyes were seeing. The two-story house, part of his mother's dowry, whose second floor used to be their home, no longer existed. In its stead was a blackened skeleton, its rooftop collapsed over a pile of charred beams. The smell of scorched wood still permeated the air.

They stood silent, as before an ancient ruin, neither able to breathe. Hefflin suddenly doubled over and retched. Catherine placed a hand on his shoulder, her eyes swelling with tears.

"I came here right after I arrived," Hefflin managed to rasp out.

"There was a fire two days ago," a voice said in Romanian.

They turned to see an old woman dressed in black standing on the sidewalk. Hefflin recognized her immediately. She was the same woman who had found Tanti Bobo three years before, beaten by Soryn, the Securitate colonel.

"How did it happen?" Hefflin asked.

"Four armed men came in broad daylight and gave the gypsies one hour to leave. Then they poured gasoline and set fire to the house. They acted like they didn't care who saw them, as if they were untouchable." The woman shook her head. "I hope the doctor and his dear wife never see what happened to their old home."

Hefflin stared at the woman. "You knew the doctor and his wife who used to live here?"

"Of course. I've lived here all my life. They owned all those houses in the courtyard, and used to live alone in that big house until after the war when the communists took over and put another family on the first floor. They were Greeks, but wonderful people just the same. The doctor often treated people for nothing, never even accepted *baksheesh*."

"Do you remember their little boy?" Hefflin asked.

"Of course. Fili. A handsome boy. He used to be friends with a pretty girl named Pusha. Inseparable, they were. The doctor and his family left for Greece. I don't know what happened to the girl after her parents died."

"They are standing here before you," Catherine said.

The old woman stared at them, then her mouth opened wide and she covered it with her hand. "God blessed you and brought you together." She crossed herself three times. "And the doctor?"

"Both my parents have passed away."

She crossed herself once more. "Blessed be their souls. At least they didn't get to see this. I am very sorry for you. The world has gone mad."

The old woman tottered down the street, her head shaking, and entered her house.

Catherine embraced Hefflin. "It's all right, *cheri*. It would have been demolished soon anyway. We have our memories."

"They came in broad daylight. Somebody wanted me to know it wasn't an accident. A warning."

"Who?"

"I don't know for sure, but I have my suspicions. They first beat me up in a staged scene with the gypsies, and now they burn down my house."

"Whoever they are, they must think you're a threat," Catherine said. "Come, let's just say goodbye to our old neighborhood. We've grown beyond it."

"They will pay for this, I swear." He took one last look, then turned and walked away. The house on Strada Sirenelor would always exist in his heart, if nowhere else.

CHAPTER FIFTY-FOUR

Athens
April 1993

THEY LANDED IN Athens in their new jet—which Hefflin had fallen in love with the moment he boarded. He brushed away the guilt about his wealth that always hovered above him and tried to enjoy the opulence of the leather seats and the lush carpeting. The bar was fully stocked and the small refrigerator was supplied with fresh fruit, cheeses, and sandwiches. Plus, not having to wait in line to board a commercial airliner had saved them hours of travel time.

"You chose well," he said as he kissed Catherine.

"Thank you, but I knew that if it hadn't been a security issue, it would have taken a lot to convince you to actually buy it."

"You must forgive my thrifty immigrant mentality," he said, "but I always think of the number of meals this plane could buy."

"No number of meals can equal the safety of our son," she said.

When they exited the airport, they were immediately assaulted by the bright sunlight, which Hefflin remembered from his childhood. They donned their sunglasses, then boarded a cab to the hotel. But as they approached the city, he noticed the driver had taken a circuitous route that had brought them by the Acropolis.

"This isn't the way to our hotel," he said to the driver in fluent Greek.

"Ah, you are Greek!" the driver exclaimed. "Many apologies. I thought you were American."

He was a bronzed fellow, like all Greeks living in the sun-drenched land, and sported a short-brimmed straw hat.

"What if we were American?" Hefflin asked. "You'd still be stealing."

"Well, if I can't steal from Americans, who can I steal from?" The man laughed.

Hefflin remembered the Greek expression he had learned as a child in the refugee camp in Athens. If you wanted to label someone naive, you called him an *Amerikanaki*, a little American.

"Life is not so easy here," the driver went on. "Everyone wants a piece of me—the government, my wife, my lazy relatives, even my dog." He shook his head. "The more I make, the more I give away."

"You can make more in America," Hefflin suggested.

"Oh, don't tell me about America. I have relatives in Astoria. They work like dogs all day and count their pennies at night. What kind of life is that? No thank you. I would rather starve here, in my own country."

There it was again, the question all the immigrants in Worcester repeatedly asked themselves: "Did we make the right decision to emigrate to America? Should we have stayed in our own country, despite the hardships?"

He dropped Catherine off at the hotel—a nondescript, two-star establishment near Syntagma Square chosen to avoid attention—then told the driver, "Kallithea, Skra Street." He needed to see it all again, see if any of the old barracks still remained. And he had to see it alone.

He asked the driver to let him off a block away so he could come upon the site furtively and not scare away the memories. As he approached the corner of Skra Street and Avenue Syngrou on foot, he was shocked to see the new apartment buildings, paved streets, and neatly trimmed green shrubbery. This area of Kallithea had once been a dirt field strewn with run-down wooden barracks and metal Quonset huts—a former military compound turned refugee camp. He and his parents had lived in one of those wooden barracks for a year, along with hundreds of other families escaping the Soviet bloc.

He stood motionless, letting his memories sweep over him, for they insisted on asserting themselves. It hadn't seemed so bad at the time. A child could turn anything into a playground.

The barracks, made of rotting wood and filled with mold, had an outdoor "Turkish" toilet, a hole in the ground surrounded by a wooden stall. It also served as the shower by running a hose from the sink next to it, their kitchen. No hot water, summer or winter. He remembered the CARE packages from the Americans that were filled with essentials—rice, beans, flour, something called SPAM, and, oh yes, Rinso washing machine detergent. The joke among the refugees was that the Americans were so wealthy that they couldn't imagine anyone living without a washing machine, even in a refugee camp. Then the winter, huddling around a gas burner, the wind howling through the rotten beams. His first day in school, shrugging when they spoke to him in Greek, disoriented, alone. But a month later, without knowing how, he was rattling in Greek to his classmates.

"Children absorb a new language like sponges," his mother said.

The final blow, a year later, the worst: Pusha stopped writing. He had assumed she had stopped loving him. He only found out twenty years later that her parents had died and she had been placed in an orphanage.

He knew those days had left their mark on him—the feeling of being homeless, transient, temporary. It wasn't until he had returned from the bloody revolution in Bucharest with his nostalgia cured that he had finally decided to hang paintings on the walls of his New York apartment—his symbol of permanence. Nevertheless, his itinerant childhood constantly reminded him that life was temporary and fragile, and that the final destination may be just around the corner.

It was with this grief for his own humanity that he left Kallithea in a taxi and drove to the hotel where Catherine awaited. She had already donned shorts and sandals and was sitting on the bed, impatient.

"Are you morose after your visit to the barracks?"

"They are no longer, thank God," he answered. "It seems that the remnants of my childhood are being erased one by one. I am left with just memories. In this case, not such happy ones."

"Well, then, we have to create new memories, pleasant ones, to obscure the old."

They had a few hours to kill before the Athens chief of station expected them, so they took a taxi to the base of the Acropolis and started walking the streets toward the marble steps. Although it was early in the day, the area bustled with local people wearing colorful summer clothes, animated, speaking with Mediterranean hand gestures. He realized how much he loved the Mediterranean way of life, which treated the outdoors as an extension of the living room. It was no accident that democracy had flourished in Athens, where the balmy weather allowed its citizens to congregate in the outdoor *agora* to engage in heated political discussions.

He remembered the family dinners in Worcester, after which his father had read the entire *Iliad* and *Odyssey* out loud to him, since Homer's tales were originally oral. Hefflin had also studied the ancient art of espionage in which the Greeks had been ahead of their time. Herodotus recounted spycraft, including dead drops. General Aeneas the Tactician in 357 BC described ciphers, along with eighteen other methods of sending secret messages. Cyprus divided its spy agency into field agents, handlers, and analysts. Ancient leaders understood the need for intelligence services. As Plato observed, whether declared or not, Greek states were in a permanent state of war.

Hefflin suddenly felt proud to be Greek, and his growing suspicion that he might be the son of a gypsy now felt like a betrayal of his parents . . . and his ancestors.

Catherine now took him by the arm and whispered, "Have you spotted our tail?"

"You mean the guy in the tan suit? He's been following us since we got here."

"Actually, since we left the hotel."

The man apparently sensed that they were talking about him, for he now walked up to them.

"Mr. Blake? Greetings from Mr. Papanicolau," the man said. He was referring to the CIA's Athens chief of station whom Hefflin had contacted before leaving Bucharest.

"You were told to follow us?" Hefflin asked.

"To provide you with a car," the man said. "But you left your hotel just as I arrived."

"Had enough culture for the day?" Hefflin asked Catherine.

"Duty calls. But culture continues." She smiled and pulled him along.

CHAPTER FIFTY-FIVE

Athens
April 1993

THE AMERICAN EMBASSY in Athens was located on Vasilissis Sophias Avenue in the heart of the city. Designed by Walter Gropius, it consisted of a classic Bauhaus open structure, with white columns made of Pentelic marble—the same stone used in the Parthenon—surrounding a three-story open-glass façade intended to symbolize the transparency of democracy.

Alexandros Papanicolau—known as Papas among Americans—was a fortyish plump Greek-American who sported a dark mustache and spoke both fluent Greek and English. His corner office with floor-to-ceiling windows overlooked a fountain surrounded by a lawn and, beyond, a high wrought-iron fence.

After Papas finished reading the carte blanche Hefflin had just handed him, he said, "Very impressive. You must be quite an important man."

"Just an important mission," Hefflin said. "I understand that since the Gulf War your Agency personnel has increased substantially."

"Tripled, actually," Papas said. "Athens has become a hub for intelligence agencies from all over the world—Arabs, Palestinians, Israelis, Turks, Europeans, and the ever-present Russians. The hotels are packed with clandestine teams from over two dozen security services. We have our hands full just trying to keep track of them all.

And, since the Gulf War, these guys don't engage in quiet espionage. They kill each other on the street. Two Syrians were murdered in broad daylight just last week. We believe it was Mossad."

"I hate to add to your caseload, but I need a team for a small operation," Hefflin said.

"One more operation won't make a difference," Papas said. "Besides, according to this letter, I have to comply with all your requests."

"It will start with your men keeping an eye on a store called The Watchman. Do you know it?"

"Yes, I think I've passed by it. I believe it's on Avenue Ermou, not far from your hotel. It sells expensive watches and jewelry."

"And I'm going to need a favor from the local police."

CHAPTER FIFTY-SIX

Athens
April 1993

THE SIGN READ THE WATCHMAN in gold letters. Beneath it, in black letters: NEW YORK, LONDON, PARIS, ATHENS, ISTANBUL. A large window displayed luxury watches and numerous bejeweled timepieces cushioned inside satin-lined cases like Fabergé eggs.

He had been eyeing The Watchman store from his rental car since it had opened at ten in the morning. After he handed out Mayfield's picture to the Agency men, they had taken their positions: one dressed as a street sweeper a few yards from the entrance, another sitting at an outdoor café across the street, and another in a parked car.

"No sign yet, sir," Hefflin heard one of the men state in his earpiece.

The Agency reported that Mayfield had landed in Athens the night before and was staying at the Hotel Grande Bretagne, a fifteen-minute walk from the store. Though an Agency man had watched the hotel all day, he hadn't spotted Mayfield exit.

It was now six thirty in the evening and Hefflin figured the men must be getting restless. Could he be wrong about Mayfield? But Baghdadi had lost his life trying to pass on the watch to Hefflin, to inform him of some sort of intelligence operation that Mayfield engaged in. Whatever Mayfield was doing, it had to be important.

The store closed at nine p.m. They had another two and a half hours to go.

There was a crackling in the earpiece. "Subject leaving hotel, approaching on foot from the east."

Hefflin felt his pulse rise. A few minutes later he spotted Mayfield wearing a white suit and white shirt open at the neck, sauntering down the avenue, occasionally stopping to gaze at the store windows, a boulevardier without a care in the world.

"I see him," Hefflin reported. "Give him space."

Mayfield approached The Watchman store at full stride and, for a moment, Hefflin thought he would walk right by it. But then Mayfield stopped and gazed at the display watches in the window, as if something had caught his eye. He then entered the store as if on a whim to ask about some watch he had seen.

He's using spycraft, in case he's being followed.

Five minutes later, Mayfield reemerged and retraced his steps back toward his hotel.

So far, so good.

"Subject approaching entrance to hotel," a voice reported a few minutes later.

"My operative will take it from here," Hefflin said. "Be ready for the next phase."

* * *

The Hotel Grande Bretagne, located steps from Syntagma Square and the parliament building, had a venerable history dating back to 1874. Over the years, it had entertained kings, ministers, artists, and tycoons, and it had served both as the Nazi headquarters during the German occupation and the subsequent British headquarters during the liberation. But even though the grande dame had undergone several expansions and renovations during her hundred years of existence, she was beginning to show signs of fatigue.

Alexander's Bar, the hotel's famed meeting place for Europe's wealthy, oozed luxury and decadence. Its name was derived from the authentic 18th-century tapestry displayed above the marble-topped bar, which depicted in brilliant colors Alexander the Great's entrance into Gaugamela.

A young couple at the bar sipped martinis and talked loudly in Italian. The tables bustled with foreign businessmen enjoying overpriced drinks on company credit cards.

Catherine slid onto the stool at the far end of the bar and ordered a Campari and soda. She wore a tight white dress with spaghetti straps, which featured a slit up the left thigh. Her red lipstick matched her nails, and her blond wig was coiffed in the Parisian style, with one wing of hair curving along her jawline, the same style she had worn the first time she met Hefflin.

She had made sure she arrived before Mayfield. In her training they had called it "following by leading." Was she certain he'd stop at the bar for a drink? No, but she had to play the odds. The man had just successfully completed a pickup and should be ebullient, maybe even a bit reckless, and perhaps want a drink to celebrate. She hoped that a beautiful woman sitting alone in a luxurious bar would be difficult to ignore. She had a backup plan if he went directly to his room.

She removed a silver compact from her opera purse and, in its mirror, observed him enter the bar. He perused the crowd, then his eyes settled on her. She powdered her nose, then replaced the compact in her purse. As she sipped her drink without looking up, she felt his stare burning her figure, branding every part of her. This was the man who had pimped her to Nicu when she was barely nine years old. But she had already chosen to let go of all that—and now considered the man nothing more than a mark to bring down.

He eased into a stool one seat away from her and ordered a vodka martini, dry, with a twist. Catherine finished her drink but did not order another. She wanted to make it easy for him.

As he sipped his drink he glanced at her. Again, she felt the lascivious stare, almost tasted the drooling. She opened her purse as if to settle her tab.

He leaned toward her. "Could I convince you to have another one with me? I've just concluded a business deal, and I need a beautiful woman to help me celebrate."

She turned to stare at him, her eyes demanding why she should talk to a stranger without being properly introduced. *"Pardon?"*

"Ah, you're French. How marvelous. Do you speak English?"

"Along with five other languages," she answered with a heavy French accent.

"Wonderful. The problem with us Americans is that we are an island people. We speak nothing but English. I am an exception. I speak three languages myself, but, alas, French isn't one of them."

"Well, you have some catching up to do." She smiled for the first time.

"Perhaps you can give me some lessons over a drink," he said.

"Perhaps. But I may teach you some naughty words."

"The naughtier the better." He signaled the bartender for another drink for the lady. "What are you having?"

"Campari and soda."

"Campari." He sighed. "That's a drink I never understood."

"You have to grow up with it, like high heels." She showed him her stiletto heels with the black straps hugging her painted toenails.

"I fear they wouldn't look as good on me," he said.

She laughed. "You must shave your legs first. Maybe then."

"Even then. Still, after enough drinks and with the right woman, I would try anything once."

He slid over to the stool next to her. She turned away, allowing a knowing smile to curve her lips.

"So, why is a beautiful woman like you drinking alone?"

"Oh, no, and you were doing so well." Her mouth made an exaggerated *O* like Edvard Munch's *The Scream*.

"You don't like the question?"

"It's so trite"—she flipped her hand—"and dishonest. You don't really want to know anything about me. It would ruin your fantasy."

"You prefer anonymity?"

"No, *you* do. Most men do, if they were honest about it. So, therefore, I do."

"You always do what men prefer?"

"Only if I want to please them."

"Whatever they ask?"

"I haven't found a limit yet," she said, then sipped her fresh drink.

"And what does it take for you to want to please a man?"

"It takes kindness and generosity on his part, to begin with," she said.

"Well, I'm kind and generous to a fault," he said, then gulped his martini and ordered another. "Anything else?"

"A man who is not afraid to let go of his inhibitions." Her eyes bathed his body.

She saw Mayfield stare at her for a long moment as if unsure of how to respond and feared she had gone too far, too fast.

But his face melted into a smile. "Well, with a woman like that, I can be very generous. Stop me if I am insulting you. I don't mean to."

"Not at all. A working woman must remain independent."

"It's a cruel world."

"Only as cruel or as generous as men make it."

"Perhaps we should go up to my room so I can prove how generous I can be," he said.

She glanced at her watch. "I don't know. I am supposed to meet someone in a half hour."

"He will be very disappointed, I'm sure." He touched her hand.

"I don't like to disappoint him," she said. "He is also a very generous man."

Mayfield removed his wallet from his breast pocket, palmed several bills, then slid them beneath her hand.

When she lifted her hand, she saw two five-hundred-dollar bills. "You *are* very generous, *Monsieur.*"

"It's only a down payment," he said. "If, as you say, you haven't yet found your limits."

She looked down demurely, opened her opera purse, removed something, then placed her closed hand on the bar.

"It would be very embarrassing for you, so I suggest we go outside," she said. She opened her hand to show him a Greek police badge.

His face dropped. "You're not serious."

"I'm afraid I am. You are under arrest for solicitation of prostitution. There are two policemen outside to take you to the station. I suggest we walk out quietly, for your sake."

She led the stunned Mayfield out to the street where two men in gray suits stood by a black Opel. They placed Mayfield in the back seat, then both got in the front and drove off.

A moment later a second car pulled up, and Catherine got in next to Hefflin.

CHAPTER FIFTY-SEVEN

Athens
April 1993

HEFFLIN, CATHERINE, AND Papas stood in the empty office of the chief of police in the Athens police headquarters, a sixteen-story concrete-and-glass building on Alexandras Avenue in the Ampelokipi district. They were waiting for the spoils.

"It's nice of the Greek police to be so accommodating," Catherine said.

"We have a very good relationship with their security services," Papas preened. "They've helped us before in all sorts of operations."

The door opened and a plainclothes detective walked in carrying a wooden tray containing various items. "His personal effects, as you requested," he said to Papas in Greek. He placed the tray on the desk and left.

The tray displayed a wallet, a hotel key, a gold sapphire ring, loose Greek coins, and a gold Rolex watch.

"Let's take the watch back to the embassy," Hefflin said.

In the Operations room at the American Embassy, Catherine examined the watch, turned it over, cradled it in her hand, placed it to her ear, then looked at it in the light.

"Do you have a magnifying glass?" she asked.

Papas searched through a drawer in his desk and handed her one. She used it to peer at the face of the watch, then at the back.

"All the dots are there," she said.

"As we expected," Hefflin said.

"But it's a fake," she declared.

"What?" both Hefflin and Papas burst out simultaneously.

"I know real Rolexes," she said. "I grew up with them. My father had three. This isn't a Rolex."

"How can you tell?" Hefflin asked.

"First of all, the weight. This is supposed to be gold. Even if it were just base metal, Rolexes are heavy. Feel this one."

Hefflin weighed the watch in his hand, nodded, then handed it back.

"Second, Rolexes don't make a ticking sound. They're powered by automatic movement, not quartz. You can hear this one ticking without even holding it up to your ear." She turned the watch over. "Third, the back of this watch has the Rolex name engraved in it. They probably thought that would make it look more authentic. The backs of real Rolexes are pristine, without any markings."

"Christ. You sure know your Rolexes," Papas said.

"I grew up with a silver spoon up my ass." She smiled and watched Papas color up.

"Fourth, look at the motion of the second hand," Catherine went on. "It has a jerky movement for every second. The second hand of a real Rolex moves in a fluid, continuous motion. Fifth—"

Hefflin groaned. "Never mind, I believe you. No wonder Mayfield just throws those watches in his drawer. And Nicu complained that the ones Mayfield gifted him broke down. They're probably all fake."

"Have your lab examine that little dot behind the number two on the face of the watch," Catherine said as she handed the watch to Papas.

"The dot?" Papas asked.

"Assume it's microfilm. Treat it gently."

As Papas rushed out the door, Hefflin turned to Catherine. "You are the best operative I know."

"Thank you, *cheri*, but that's a low bar." She winked.

Within a half hour Papas returned with a stack of photographs. "It was microfilm, just as you said."

Hefflin's stomach churned.

Papas spread the photographs on the top of his desk, more than fifty. As Hefflin scanned them, he felt his chest tightening, his anger almost overpowering him. Several photographs contained schematics of a French missile system; others were operational plans for the U.S. Navy fleet in the Mediterranean. Still others displayed NATO deployment plans in Iraq.

"That son-of-a-bitch!" Hefflin said. "He *is* a spy. And this intel is too sensitive to have come from anyone else but . . . "

"But who?" Papas jumped up.

They all stared at the intel in silence. Hefflin's mind was spinning.

"I have to admit, it's quite brilliant," Hefflin said. "The mole goes to The Watchman store in the States with a roll of film, which someone in the store converts into microfilm and places it on a watch. They then mail the watch to their sister store in Athens where Mayfield, an American businessman whom no one suspects, picks it up and delivers it to his masters. No dead drops, no direct meetings, little risk."

"I can't believe that that little pimp is smart enough to run the operation," Catherine said.

"It's all right here," Hefflin said. "We may have underestimated him."

Hefflin continued to riffle through the intelligence until he stopped at the top of the last page. It was titled *Oligarchs of Bucharest*. As Hefflin read, he felt the hairs on the back of his neck rise.

"The oligarchs continue to steal Romania's assets to the point that soon they will wield overwhelming economic and political power. If not stopped, they will eventually run the country, whichever party is in power. Below

is a list of offshore accounts belonging to some of the oligarchs, which can be used as leverage. I have not yet been able to access the names associated with the accounts. This list is not comprehensive. I am sure the Agency is aware of many others."

A list followed with over two dozen numbered bank accounts in Switzerland, Luxembourg, and Lichtenstein. Hefflin felt his anger rise. The Agency knew all about the oligarchs, including their numbered accounts, and Ingram had failed to mention them.

Below the report, almost as an afterthought, were these lines:

"My next package will be my last, the motherlode. The recent KGB defector has caused the Agency to increase its efforts to unearth the mole and it's becoming too hot for me to continue."

Catherine read the report over Hefflin's shoulder. "That certainly puts a new wrinkle in everything," she said. "You have one chance in which to catch him. I think we have the makings of a plan."

Hefflin stared at her.

"You haven't figured it out yet?" She raised her eyebrows. "According to the sign above the door of The Watchman, their list of cities includes only one in the States: New York."

"So we have the location where the mole will drop off his next package," Hefflin said. "And we have the date: a month from now. All we have to do is put a surveillance team on the New York store a few days before he needs to deliver it and see who walks in with a roll of film." He beamed at Catherine. "But suppose the mole drops by days or weeks earlier and the New York store just sits on the intel before sending it out? Or maybe the Athens store receives it early and keeps it until the pickup date? Or the mole pays someone else to deliver the intel?"

"I think this entire operation is very efficient," Catherine said. "I don't think the mole would feel comfortable having someone else deliver the intel or leaving it in the store for days or, God forbid, weeks. He sounds like a man who would deliver his package just in time for it to arrive in Athens by the exact date, allowing a day each way, let's say. And we must assume they don't use regular mail."

"If they use DHL or FedEx, that means a couple of days, at the most, maybe even overnight," Hefflin said. "What do you think, Papas?"

"I think I'm jealous. You not only have a gorgeous operative, but a brilliant one."

Catherine smiled. "Thank you, but aren't we forgetting something? Mayfield needs his watch back, with the microfilm in place. Right now all he knows is that he's being held by the Athens police for soliciting." She let a wry smile curve her lips. "We have to replace the microfilm with one of our own, then let him go."

"How long will that take your people?" Hefflin asked Papas.

"An hour or two at the most. All we have to do is replace it with some old intel we know the Russians already have. But I have to get clearance from Ingram."

"There's no time for that," Hefflin said. "My carte blanche is your clearance."

Papas hesitated. "Sir, this may mean my job."

"Alexandros, if Ingram fires you, I guarantee you a job for life at double your salary."

Papas laughed. "You two make a great team, you know that?"

Catherine squeezed Hefflin's arm. "Yes, we know."

*   *   *

They sat in their rental car on a side street, embracing.

"First you found the microdot on the watches, now you figured out our next move. You've become indispensable in my professional life, as well as in my private one," Hefflin said.

"You always underestimate yourself. You would have figured everything out just in time, like you always do." She kissed him passionately on the lips. "But now I need to return to Jacques. He's not used to me being away for so long."

He had only thought about Jack during the past few days in fleeting stock images of him playing or being fussed over by Yvette and Catherine's mother. Jack had not yet developed enough of a personality to pique Hefflin's interest, or evoke the same attachment as Catherine felt. Perhaps Catherine was right. As long as he remained tethered to that child named Fili, he would have difficulty moving into the role of parent.

"Of course, darling," he said. "Jack needs his mother. You must return to him at once. Your job here is done."

"And you? What are you going to do?"

"I'm going to follow Mayfield back to Bucharest. I think you're right. There has to be someone above him."

"Well, for that, I think you'll need a private plane. I'll take a commercial flight back, using one of my other DGSE passports." She pinched his cheek. "See how handy my purchase has become?" She wrote something on a piece of paper and handed it to him. "The address and phone number to the house in Antibes, in case you need to get in touch."

He embraced her for a long moment, unable to separate now that they'd come together again. "We do make a great team. If only our agencies cooperated this well."

CHAPTER FIFTY-EIGHT

Athens
April 1993

MAYFIELD LEFT THE hotel early the next morning and took a taxi to the Athens airport. Two Agency teams took turns following him in different cars to avoid being spotted. At the airport Mayfield joined the line at the Delta counter.

"Subject bought a ticket and is proceeding to the gate," one of the men reported on Hefflin's earpiece. The return flight to Bucharest was due to take off in an hour.

Hefflin and Papas had followed at a distance and now sat in their car outside the airport, waiting for reports from the teams. Hefflin had already called his pilots to have the jet fueled and ready to take off as soon as Mayfield boarded the flight to Bucharest.

For the next twenty minutes the men reported Mayfield sitting at the gate lounge, reading a newspaper. Then the radio crackled.

"Subject is on the move, leaving gate."

What the hell?

"Subject moving fast, took a turn toward other gates."

"Where is he going?" Hefflin asked Papas.

"Maybe he needs to find a bathroom," Papas said. "This airport is notorious for having few of them."

But this didn't feel like a sudden need for a bathroom break. Mayfield had shown himself to be a cautious operative, behaving as if he were followed. Had he spotted Papas's team, or was he just paranoid?

"Subject at gate for flight to Beirut," the radio crackled. "Plane boarding now."

Beirut! Mayfield bought two tickets and changed flights at the last minute. The fucking guy is a great operative.

"Subject boarded the plane," the radio sputtered.

"Papas, notify Beirut station and have them follow Mayfield when he lands," Hefflin ordered. "I should arrive only a few minutes after him."

If I hurry, I may even arrive before he does.

*　*　*

Hefflin landed at the Beirut Rafic Hariri International Airport a half hour before Mayfield's plane reached the gate. Hefflin used his diplomatic passport to quickly get through passport check and customs, leaving him plenty of time to make contact with the Agency operatives waiting in a blue Ford outside the arrivals terminal.

He spotted Mayfield exiting the airport and getting into a taxi. Hefflin ordered his men to follow at a distance. Twenty minutes later Mayfield arrived at a nondescript hotel close to the famed Commodore Hotel, which had been destroyed during the Lebanese war. One of the Agency men followed him inside. An Agency van with electronic equipment sat parked across the street. A few minutes later the man returned to report that Mayfield had had a reservation and that he went directly to his room, 301.

Hefflin instructed the men to wait and watch. An hour and a half later they spotted Mayfield exit the hotel and turn down a side street. Hefflin ordered the men in his car to follow on foot while he drove the car around the block. He certainly didn't want Mayfield to spot him.

A few minutes later one of the Agency men reported that Mayfield had settled at a table at an outdoor restaurant.

"What's he doing?" Hefflin asked.

"He's ordering lunch, I believe," the agent responded.

Hefflin parked on a side street and waited. The radio crackled.

"A second man just sat down at subject's table. I recognize him—a well-known Iranian operative."

Iranian?

"Bring in the van," Hefflin ordered.

"It'll take a minute to set up the equipment, sir," another voice said in his earpiece.

He waited in the car, sweat pouring down his back. He wasn't used to hundred-degree temperatures. Then he heard Mayfield's voice in his earpiece relayed from the long-distance microphone in the van.

"I have three ships arriving in two days: the *Aghia Maria, Eleni,* and *Aghios Nicholas.*"

"That should be plenty," the man said. "The cargo is in the warehouses, ready to load."

"I'll transfer the rest of the money once the cargo is on board and the ships are in international waters, as usual," Mayfield said. "And I arranged for the Romanian arms to arrive in two months. Consider them a bonus for your help in this matter."

"I appreciate that. When will the ships arrive in the Port of Durrës?"

"In a week, at the latest. And this is the intel I mentioned."

"Subject just passed some papers to his contact," an Agency operative interrupted. "Contact is leaving."

"Stay with the subject," Hefflin ordered. There was no point in following the Iranian operative.

Durrës. That's the main port of Albania. The arms are going to the Muslims in Yugoslavia, not the Serbs.

A half hour later Mayfield walked back to his hotel where he remained for the rest of the day. A little past nine in the evening, the operative sitting in the hotel lounge reading a newspaper reported that an attractive woman dressed in fashionable clothes and high heels arrived at the hotel and was sent up to room 301. At two in the morning, she was spotted leaving barefoot, carrying her heels.

A second shift of Agency men took over for the remainder of the night while Hefflin tried to rest at a nearby hotel where his pilots were staying. He slept badly, the various scenarios swimming in his mind. He had assumed Mayfield spied for the Russians because of his previous ties to the Ceausescu regime—and maybe even to the Russians themselves. But now things looked different. Mayfield had decided to have a layover in Beirut to arrange a shipment of cargo with the Iranian secret service, military equipment, no doubt, going to the Muslims in Yugoslavia. And he had handed over some intel to the Iranian operative.

A little past eleven the next morning, Mayfield got into a taxi and headed toward the airport. Hefflin had already notified his pilots and they were waiting at the airport with a fully fueled plane. But the traffic in Beirut proved to be heavy at that time of day, and by the time Hefflin reached the airport with his Agency team Mayfield had already boarded a Turkish Airlines flight to Bucharest, with a two-hour layover in Istanbul.

Istanbul? Christ.

Hefflin instructed his men to inform the Istanbul CIA station to follow Mayfield after he landed in the event that Mayfield left the airport.

Even though the jet was fueled and ready, it took over an hour before the tower allowed it to take off. By the time Hefflin landed in Istanbul, Mayfield's plane had been on the ground for over an hour. The Agency man from Istanbul station was waiting for Hefflin.

"The subject has left the airport, sir, and was followed to a watch store in downtown Istanbul where he remained for only a few minutes."

The Watchman! That's right, they have a branch in Istanbul.

"The subject had no visible package when he exited the store."

Of course not. He's wearing it.

Hefflin ordered his pilots to be ready to take off within the hour. As soon as the operatives reported that Mayfield had entered the airport, Hefflin joined the pilots on his plane and waited for confirmation that Mayfield boarded his flight to Bucharest before taking off. That confirmation came a half hour later. Hefflin's jet took off thirty minutes before Mayfield's.

*   *   *

He had been waiting outside the arrivals terminal at Otopeni Airport in a rented Dacia for over a half hour before he spotted Mayfield exiting the airport and getting into a taxi. Hefflin followed. It was past seven in the evening and the sun had already set, making it easier to follow the taxi without being spotted but also easier to lose it. Hefflin followed more closely than usual, even finding himself right behind Mayfield's taxi at one point. He pulled back, allowing other cars to enter between them. A few minutes later Hefflin thought he had lost him, but then he spotted the taxi veering off toward an exit.

He's not going back to the InterContinental.

Hefflin turned off his headlights and followed the taxi at a distance through the less-crowded streets, an area of the city he didn't recognize. Then he saw the taxi slow down and take a right turn. Hefflin waited a moment, then slowly drove up to the corner. He spotted the taxi now pulling up to a building he did recognize.

Gorga's offices!

He watched as Mayfield entered the building, the taxi left idling. A few minutes later Mayfield emerged, entered the taxi, and drove off.

Mayfield and Gorga. Christ. They're running an intelligence service. I wonder what is in those computers.

He needed to find out, and there was only one man who could help him.

CHAPTER FIFTY-NINE

Bucharest
April 1993

AT THREE A.M. that same evening, a fire alarm blared throughout Gorga's company building. A dozen personnel working through the night along with several uniformed security men scampered out, then stood across the street, waiting to see if there actually was a fire. Nobody had seen or smelled any smoke, and they joked about another false alarm.

Two minutes later a single fire truck appeared. The people marveled at the rapidity of the response of the usually slow fire department. As several firefighters rushed into the building, two private security guards requested to reenter the building with them but were denied. In the meantime, the driver reported to the local fire station on his two-way radio that he was part of a fire team from the adjoining district and had heard the alarm while driving their truck back from a repair garage. He called to report that the alarm was false. No other fire trucks were needed. The fire station chief expressed relief. They were in the middle of a poker game.

Inside, Hefflin, along with several of Balzary's men, all dressed as firefighters, scoured the offices.

"These are just terminals," said a burly man named Ferco who looked like a grocery clerk but was actually Balzary's IT chief. "There has to be a main computer, probably in the basement."

They took the elevator to the basement floor, a room lit in blue light. At the center of it stood a computer the size of a refrigerator. Ferco approached to examine it.

"It has no alarm system attached to it, and it is an old model from the early '80s." Ferco smirked. "My children could break into this." He and his IT assistant started working on it. It took them seven minutes to hack into the computer and start downloading the files into a black box Ferco produced from his bag. Ten minutes later it was done.

"What do you want me to do with the computer?" Ferco asked.

"Delete all the files, then come here and look at this door."

After Ferco erased all the files in the computer, he approached a metal door at the far end of the basement in front of which Hefflin now stood. The door had a keypad attached to it.

Ferco removed a small device out of his shoulder bag, pressed a button, and scanned the keypad. "It's UV light," Ferco said. "Detects fingerprints." The keypad now revealed four numbers with fingerprints on them. Ferco then unscrewed the keypad, removed a black box from his satchel, and attached two wires to the back of the keypad. "It goes through all the permutations of those four numbers." Ferco chuckled. Within less than a minute, the door unlocked.

A dark staircase led to a floor below. Hefflin found a light switch and descended the stairs. The basement floor consisted of one huge room the size of the entire footprint of the building filled with rows of identical metal shelves stacked with what looked like cardboard file boxes.

"There's another set of stairs going to a floor below," one of the other men reported, then went down to investigate. A moment later he returned to report. "There are two floors beneath this one, with similar stacks of files."

Hefflin pulled out one of the cardboard boxes at random, yellowed and frail, and opened it. Inside he found a thick file with the insignia of the old Securitate above a photograph of a man he didn't recognize. The document was about three hundred pages thick and it contained reports on the activities of the man in the photograph, including multiple incriminating attestations by informants, along with photographs showing the man meeting with various people during the '80s. The report identified the man as a sitting member of parliament who had been threatened with arrest as a result of his homosexual activities if he did not comply with the Securitate dictates. It concluded that the man agreed to all demands and was left in place.

He riffled through other files and found them all to be similar Securitate reports on various individuals who held some positions of power—managers of state companies, mayors, judges, politicians, and members of the government elite. Some documented that the subjects had been official informants for the Securitate, with signed contracts, which the Securitate could later use for blackmail. Others listed offenses, such as skimming money from State agencies, having offshore accounts, being involved in the black market, money laundering, having mistresses or homosexual affairs.

"These are all Securitate dossiers on important people," Hefflin muttered. "We're looking at the Securitate archives."

"That can't be," Ferco said. "The archives are huge, millions of documents. This is only a small fraction of them."

Hefflin then noticed a stamp on the bottom of each file cover: "Transferred to U0920."

This is unit U0920!

Hefflin couldn't believe his luck. He had stumbled into the heart of the oligarchs' intelligence system—thousands of files, which they used to blackmail anyone who stood in their way. This was unit U0920's new function, and Gorga was at the center of it.

"Hey! What are you doing down there?" a male voice called from the top of the stairs. A security guard came down the stairs holding a pistol.

"It's the fire department," Hefflin yelled back. "Just checking for a gas leak."

"How did you get down here? The door was locked." The man stood at the bottom of the stairs now, his gun shaking as he saw five firemen hovering around him.

"The door was ajar, my friend," Hefflin said as he approached the guard. "These files will all go up in flames if we don't make sure there's no gas leak."

"There are no gas pipes down here. Now get out. All of you. Out!"

"You're wrong. There's a gas pipe right there." Hefflin pointed, then grabbed the pistol out of the guard's hands while one of Balzary's men hit the back of the man's head with the butt of his pistol. The security guard collapsed to the floor, unconscious.

"The conversation was getting boring anyway," Hefflin said. He knelt down and searched the pockets of the unconscious guard. In the wallet he found an identity card he recognized.

"This guy is no private guard. He's SRI." *Romania's domestic intelligence service.*

"I thought you said this is a private company," Ferco said.

"It is. But in this case, there appears to be no distinction."

"What do you want to do? We can't just leave these files behind," Ferco said.

"There are too many to carry out."

"Then there's only one option left."

Hefflin hesitated. The intel in these files could be valuable to the Agency, and they provided historical information. Could he just destroy them? But leaving them behind would simply perpetuate the power of the oligarchs.

"You guys go up to the second floor, find a gas pipe, and disconnect it," Hefflin ordered. "In the meantime, I'll start a fire down here. That should give us enough time to get out."

"A gas leak can go up in flames from merely a spark," Ferco said. "You're taking a big chance."

"So are you."

"No, not me. It will be my fastest operative—young Deco over there." Ferco laughed.

Hefflin descended down two floors while the men carried the unconscious guard out of the building. Within a few minutes, Hefflin had created piles of dossiers on each floor and had set them on fire with his lighter. He scrambled up the stairs to the ground floor just as young Deco came running down the stairs from the second floor. They both exited the building at the same time yelling "Gas leak!" in Romanian at the top of their voices. The bystanders scattered for cover.

Hefflin and Deco jumped onto the fire truck as it drove off with all the men, including the still unconscious SRI agent. As the truck turned a corner, a massive explosion blew out the windows on multiple floors of the headquarters, spraying the streets with shards. A fierce blaze that seemed to feed on itself quickly engulfed the building and lit the sky across all of Bucharest. By the time the fire engines arrived, unit U0920 was engulfed in a roaring inferno.

CHAPTER SIXTY

Langley
April 1993

IN HIS LANGLEY office, Ingram studied the report he had just received from Hefflin. It described Hefflin's operation in Athens during which he'd discovered a wide system of intelligence gathering by the American businessman Harold Mayfield using The Watchman stores. And then Ingram came upon a line that forced him to stop and read again. "The intel Mayfield picked up in Athens could only have come from the CIA mole."

Ingram sat back, stunned. *Fucking Mayfield.*

The report did not include any details of how Hefflin had discovered Mayfield's operation or exactly what intel the microdot included. Hefflin then described his planting false intel in a new microdot on the watch, which he returned to Mayfield, who was then allowed to proceed to Beirut, where he met a well-known Iranian operative to finalize an arms delivery to Albania using three ships and to hand over intelligence. Hefflin identified all three ships. Mayfield then flew to Istanbul where he picked up more intel from another Watchman store, then flew to Bucharest where he took a taxi directly to Constantine Gorga's office building. Hefflin said nothing more on the subject.

Ingram stared at the report, trying to fit the pieces together. *Mayfield and Gorga!* He felt Avery's ghost hovering over this operation, this entire sliver of history. Would that infernal man's actions ever stop haunting him? He had to act, before it blew up in the Agency's face, and his.

When he came to the last line of the report, he smiled. A reminder of those offshore accounts Hefflin had requested.

Of course, Bill. Especially now.

He buzzed for his assistant, who entered the room immediately.

"Order the NSA to crash those offshore accounts Hefflin asked about a few days ago. Then wire the account numbers to Balzary to forward to Hefflin and inform Hefflin that they are now empty."

"Balzary, sir?" the assistant asked, perplexed.

"Yes, they're old friends. Do as I say. Then activate our wetworks asset in Bucharest. Here is the target." Ingram scribbled on a piece of paper and handed it to his assistant. "One more thing: prepare a scrub team to fly to Bucharest."

"Yes, sir." The assistant rushed out of the room.

That fucking, ungrateful Securitate colonel, running a mole against the Agency. After all...Well, he will now feel my wrath for crossing me. And I hope he remembers what side his bread is buttered on when Hefflin confronts him.

CHAPTER SIXTY-ONE

Bucharest
April 1993

IT WAS PAST ten in the evening when Hefflin arrived at the exclusive address in the outskirts of Bucharest. He had spent most of the day with Balzary, chewing over his findings at Gorga's office building.

"You stumbled upon the Holy Grail, the Securitate archives, at least a part of them," Balzary said.

"What I saw was only a fraction of the dossiers the Securitate has," Hefflin said. "Probably just those the oligarchs are most interested in."

"You're right, of course. The Securitate archives are vast, spread out over many buildings and warehouses, most of which we don't even know about. In March of 1990 they were transferred to the newly formed Information Service, which reported that the archives totaled 35 kilometers of dossiers, with each meter containing 5,000 documents. As large as that number sounds, it is understated. The Stasi archives totaled 188 kilometers for an East German population of fourteen million. Romania has a population of twenty-three million."

"That must include foreign assets and operations, not just domestic surveillance," Hefflin said. "Too bad most of them will never see the light of day."

"Gorga and the oligarchs won't be happy now that their headquarters has gone up in flames." Balzary smiled, then poured *tsuika* into two shot glasses.

"I owe you yet again," Hefflin said as he raised his glass in a toast.

"Don't think I'm not keeping score." Balzary laughed, then emptied the glass in one swallow. "By the way, Ingram sent this for you." He handed Hefflin a sheet of paper.

Hefflin studied the document for a moment. "Finally. I've been waiting for this for some time." He placed it in his pocket and stood.

"So, where are you off to now?"

"Tonight I'm going to have a little family tête-à-tête."

"Alone?"

"Don't worry. I won't need you for this little event. But I do need an address."

As Hefflin now drove by a tall wrought iron fence, he glimpsed a modern glass and stone structure beyond it, newly built, brightly lit like an opera house. Hefflin hoped Gorga wasn't entertaining. But he wouldn't be in any mood to entertain, would he?

He drove up to the gate and pressed the button on the intercom.

"*Da?*" a male voice said.

"Mr. Blake for Mr. Gorga."

"One moment."

The gates opened and he drove up to the entrance where two security men in plain clothes escorted him into the living room, then left him alone. The heavy wooden doors closed with a thud, as if he were being entombed in a mausoleum. The room was tastefully furnished with modern Italian couches and glass tables. The floor-to-ceiling windows overlooked the dark landscaping surrounding the property.

Irina appeared at the head of the stairs wearing a black silk robe over, apparently, nothing at all. "Is there anything wrong?" she called down, sounding concerned.

"I just wanted a word with him," Hefflin said.

"I just got here myself," she said as she came down the stairs barefoot. "He's been in his office all day. Something happened to his building."

"Oh?"

"A fire, I think. A gas leak." She turned and called out, "Puiu!"

Hefflin's ears pricked up. "What did you just call him?"

"Puiu. That's the name everyone knows him by. It's a common term of endearment. It means 'little bird,' as you know." Irina giggled.

Hefflin tried to remember where he had heard that name before. *Yes, during the gypsy charade.* And then his mind lit up. The front company in Nicosia, Cyprus, that served as the middleman for the arms shipments Baghdadi had mentioned: *P.U.I.U. Import/Export.*

"James. What are you doing here?" Gorga called out as he hurried from his office. He was still wearing his gray suit with his white shirt now open at the collar. He looked frazzled.

"I just needed a drink," Hefflin said, "and a little talk."

"And it couldn't wait until tomorrow? How do you even know where I live? It must be serious. What will you have?"

"A scotch will do," Hefflin said.

Gorga walked over to the ornate bar, poured two glasses, and handed one to Hefflin. "You, darling?"

"You two have your man talk," Irina said as she turned back up the stairs, her robe gaping open to flash a breast. "I'm going to bed." She disappeared up the stairs, the diva in a bit of a huff.

Both men sank with their drinks into opposite chairs.

"Irina said you had a fire," Hefflin said.

Gorga's face twisted. "My building. A gas leak, apparently. A complete disaster. I've been trying all day to have my people try to save something from the ashes." He shook his head, then gulped down the drink.

"I'm sorry to hear that. All those computers."

"Yes, those, too," Gorga muttered, then looked up, sensing he had said too much. "So, what's so important?"

Hefflin removed a photograph from his inside pocket and handed it to Gorga. "Do you know this man?"

Gorga glanced at the picture, then handed it back.

"That's Harold Mayfield, an American businessman. He's been trying to invest in Romania for years. Unsuccessfully, I might add."

"Come, come, you were Securitate. You surely know more than that."

"He's a playboy. Used to run around with that no-good son-of-a-bitch Nicu Ceausescu. We were told to lay off him, so there isn't much more I know."

Gorga's cheek twitched, no doubt annoyed with such trivialities while his building was still smoldering, a tell Hefflin hadn't noticed before.

"He was more than just a playboy, according to Nicu," Hefflin said.

"You went to see that drunk? I'm surprised he's not dead yet. Don't believe anything he says. His brain is always soaked in booze."

"He told me that Mayfield was a good friend of the elder Ceausescu. That he helped Ceausescu sell Soviet-made military equipment to Arafat and Gaddafi."

Gorga hesitated, his annoyance spreading to a twitching of his fingers, then shrugged. "Yes, Mayfield was the middleman. He knew everybody. Neither Ceausescu nor Mayfield cared about the ideology of their clients. If they could pay in hard currency, the sale would go through."

"Mayfield was Ceausescu's gunrunner."

"The entire Ceausescu clan was corrupt as hell." Gorga leered. "Marian and Ilie, Ceausescu's brothers, sold samples of the latest Soviet military equipment to the Americans—not just the plans but the actual equipment for the Americans to study. Ceausescu knew about it, of course. Nothing happened in Romania without his orders. Hundreds of millions went into the family offshore accounts."

Most of it is in my offshore accounts now, my dear Gorga.

"Apparently the same thing went on in Poland, Czechoslovakia, Hungary, and East Germany," Gorga continued. "They were all bankrupt and hungry for hard currency. It saved the Americans billions in planning and development of new military systems." Gorga let out a forced chuckle.

Hefflin could hardly believe what he was hearing. The CIA was so compartmentalized that he had not been privy to any of this intel.

"Was Mayfield involved in this?" Hefflin asked.

"No. These operations were top secret." Gorga hesitated, obviously deciding how much to say. "I later learned that the Securitate dealt with another middleman, a man known as Janus, a mysterious figure whose identity always eluded them."

Janus! Boris! Christ! Boris's fingers were in everything.

Hefflin tried to hide his surprise by changing the subject.

"It's fortunate for Ceausescu that he didn't use Mayfield for those operations, for Mayfield wasn't exactly the loyal type, was he? Mayfield was the Middle Eastern expert. I always wondered about those snipers."

"What snipers?" Gorga's face hardened.

"The snipers from the Middle East who were brought to Timisoara to start the revolution."

"Nobody found any snipers from the Middle East," Gorga said. "I don't know if they even existed. Why are you bringing up all this old history?"

"Oh, they existed all right. One almost killed me. I met two others being treated at Floreasca hospital. They all disappeared right after the revolution."

Beads of sweat rolled down Gorga's temples.

"Tell me about Avery," Hefflin said.

Gorga's head snapped. "Who?"

"Avery, the previous CIA director of operations. He and General Stanculescu brought in the snipers to start the bloody revolution that foiled Gorbachev's quiet coup."

"If you think you know so much, why are you asking me?" Gorga blurted out.

"You were working with Avery, weren't you? And you used Mayfield, the Middle Eastern expert with all the contacts, to supply those snipers and bring them in through Hungary with Balzary's help."

Gorga's coal-dark eyes stared into Hefflin's. "How many people know about this?"

"Not many," Hefflin said. "You can probably count them on one hand. Avery is dead, so that's one less."

Gorga's gaze bored into Hefflin's eyes for a long moment, though his mind was obviously somewhere else. "You are still CIA?"

Hefflin nodded.

"Then you should know who was involved in the revolution."

"General Stanculescu controlled part of the military," Hefflin said, "but he also needed at least part of the Securitate. And you supplied that part."

Gorga nodded. His expression eased slightly. "The country was drowning. We were the only ones left with a communist system. Even Russia was teetering."

"But you and your other Securitate comrades realized that after ridding the country of Ceausescu you were handed a golden opportunity. The men that remained in the newly formed Securitate, as well as those that left it, formed a syndicate that used the Securitate dossiers to blackmail politicians, judges, bankers, and probably

Iliescu, himself, into helping you take over Romania's newly privatized industries and become filthy rich overnight."

"Where did you get all this?"

"Tell me, did Avery have any inkling of what you were planning to do with this new capitalism?"

Gorga let the question hang in the air for a long moment, then let out a soft chuckle. "Avery? He was the one who suggested the whole scheme. That's how he convinced us to join his revolution. He even told us step-by-step how to do it. 'Make a slow, gradual transition to democracy, nothing too fast,' he said. 'During that time, use those Securitate dossiers to blackmail the politicians and judges to help you acquire as much of the country's assets as you can. Become the new Rockefellers and Carnegies of Romania.'" Gorga shrugged, then sipped his drink. "The Americans didn't care that some of us got rich. They just wanted a new NATO member and a new market for their weapons and soaps and deodorants. So he offered to sell the country to us. That's capitalism, Avery said."

Hefflin's stomach turned. He wished Avery dead all over again. But there was more to this story, he reminded himself.

"That explains the new function of unit U0920," Hefflin said. "It was resurrected to become the center of power of your syndicate, with access to the old Securitate archives, and the means and personnel to acquire new intelligence or fabricate it on whomever you needed to blackmail."

Gorga stood, seemingly lighter now that these old skeletons were spread on the table, and poured himself another drink. "They are all corrupt, every single one of them, old communist apparatchiks who have been stealing from government coffers for decades." He waved his hand in disgust. "As the saying goes, behind every great fortune is a great crime. I guess this is mine. But they deserve it."

"How does Stanculescu's gunrunning fit in?"

Gorga's face suddenly grew ashen. "I suggest you not mention that name again, for your own good."

Hefflin leaned back, considering. "Ah, so maybe it isn't you but Stanculescu who is in charge of the syndicate."

"Nobody is in charge!" Gorga snapped. "We are all just businessmen."

"But you don't give yourself enough credit, Puiu," Hefflin said. "Your crimes don't stop at blackmail."

Gorga looked up in surprise. "Only Irina and a few close friends refer to me that way."

"Sorry, I thought we were friends by now. Almost family, you said. It's just that I heard that name used by one of the thugs that attacked me the night I was trying to save a couple of gypsies from being beaten. He told his buddy that Puiu had given strict orders not to kill me, just to frighten me."

"Puiu is a common term of endearment."

"Those gypsies were a setup, weren't they? To scare me into leaving Bucharest so I wouldn't find out about the oligarchs and unit U0920."

Gorga's expression turned dour.

"And when I wasn't scared off, you had your oligarch friends try to compromise me by offering me a sweet business deal."

"It was a good deal," Gorga said. "You should have taken it."

"And when that didn't work, you burned down the house in which I was born."

Gorga scowled. "It was the old ones' doing. I found out about it after the fact. But all they know is brute force."

"In the meantime, you found out Baghdadi had contacted me and offered to sell me information about the oligarchs and their arms shipments. What, did you have his house bugged?"

"His house, his car, everything. The Securitate is alive and well, better than ever, in fact," Gorga said with a touch of defiance. "Only now it's used for profit. Isn't creating wealth what capitalism is all about?"

"You've certainly learned about capitalism quickly," Hefflin said. "But where did you learn about killing?"

Gorga shrugged. "The Securitate taught me that."

"So, you had Baghdadi murdered, in church, no less, to shut him up. But not before Baghdadi told me about the ships full of arms coming in from Beirut by way of Constanta and heading for Serbia by train, all arranged by your Cyprus company, *P.U.I.U. Import/Export.*"

"Yes, some of us do sell arms to our Christian brethren in Yugoslavia—what of it?" Gorga's face burned red. "Do you want those fanatical Muslims to create their own country right next door to us? You live in quiet splendor in that island called America, away from all the bloody wars we have to endure here. Who are you to judge?"

"Just a citizen of the world who hates to see genocide. But let's not veer off my story. There is the object I found in Baghdadi's dead hand as he lay murdered on sacred ground."

Hefflin removed the watch from his pocket. Gorga stared at it, his jaw muscles flexing.

"I didn't understand its significance at first," Hefflin said. "Not until one of my operatives noticed a dot missing—the same dot missing on all of Mayfield's watches in his drawer."

"You broke into Mayfield's house?" Gorga muttered, his look of surprise mixed with respect.

"With Mayfield you had another business going: the selling of intelligence."

"I don't know what you're talking about."

"Mayfield drove to your office building straight from the airport when he returned from his trips to Athens, Beirut, and Istanbul so he could deliver that intel. The mole inside the CIA is not a KGB asset, he's *your* asset. He sends the intel in a microdot placed on a watch face to The Watchman store in Athens, where Mayfield picks it up. It's a great setup and probably quite profitable. You sell the intelligence to the highest bidder."

"You're whistling in the wind, James, or Bill, or whoever the hell you are. You have no proof of these ridiculous assertions."

"I retrieved the microdot, Puiu, and I have that intel."

"You what? But how—?"

"You should ask Mayfield. You'll get a good laugh out of it. As you will over this."

Hefflin pulled a piece of paper out of his pocket and handed it to Gorga. "Do you recognize these numbered accounts in Switzerland and Lichtenstein?"

Gorga glanced at the list, then dropped the paper on the floor.

"I know nothing about them."

"Then you won't care if I tell you that they are now empty."

Gorga's cheek twitched. "Are you telling me that?"

"The NSA has gotten a lot better after the Ceausescu debacle. They were able to track down all your accounts, as well as these, here, which belong to some of the other oligarchs." He removed another piece of paper and dropped it on the table. "I found them on the microdot from the mole. He, no doubt, thought he was giving them to the KGB, which despises you and your oligarch friends. The NSA just needed orders to liquidate them."

"Whose orders? Yours?" Gorga smirked, though his eyes displayed fear.

"Ingram's," Hefflin said.

"He wouldn't dare."

"No? Why not? Will you and your friends claim the money is yours?" Hefflin let out a chuckle.

The two men stared at each other—their eyes locked, unblinking. Gorga's gaze then drifted beyond Hefflin, seeming to consider his options.

"You still don't get it," Gorga said. "The CIA and the NSA have known about these accounts from the beginning. In fact, they set them up for us."

"What?"

"It was their way of controlling us, and through us, the country," Gorga said. "They showed us quite clearly that if we tried to move the money they could make it disappear. Assuming you're telling me the truth, the question is, why have they done that now?"

"Maybe they have a problem with your running a mole inside the CIA."

Gorga's face grew ashen. "You told them that?"

"Who is the mole?"

Gorga stared directly into Hefflin's eyes, as if trying to instill trust. "I honestly don't know."

"This is no time for bullshit, Puiu."

"I don't know, I tell you. I took over The Watchman system from its previous handler."

"Who was this previous handler?"

Gorga hesitated, then spat it out. "My KGB friend, the one who asked me to intervene in your father's court case."

Boris?

CHAPTER SIXTY-TWO

Bucharest
April 1993

"WE MET ONE night at the Athénée bar in early 1990," Gorga began. "He said he had a sentimental tie to that place. He told me he was dying and that he wanted to tie up all the loose ends of his life, as he put it. He said he had a system by which he was receiving intel from his various assets, and that he wanted to hand over his system to me. 'Why let such good system and assets go to waste?' he said. 'What am I supposed to do with them?' I asked him. He told me to share that intel as widely as possible so as to make the world realize it couldn't keep its secrets, that it was useless to waste its money on the military and their stupid games. The intel he was receiving consisted mostly of technical information, he said—specifications of military systems, strategic plans, that sort of thing, not agents or assets." Gorga shook his head. "He was an idealist. I loved him for that."

Boris the idealist again. Christ.

"And you accepted it?"

"It was a dying man's gift to me—my closest friend. Of course I accepted it."

"When did you start using it?"

"Right away, actually. His assets were being paid from offshore accounts he had set up in Switzerland, to which he gave me control. I didn't know the identity of any of the assets. They simply sent their intel via The Watchman system, and I wired the money to their numbered accounts."

"What did you do with the intel?"

"I did as he requested. I passed some of it to the Russians and some to the Americans and the Europeans, all anonymously."

"No, that's not all you did," Hefflin said. "At some point you realized how valuable such intel was, and how much you could profit from it. You started selling it to the highest bidders. That's how you began to acquire your fortune, even before the privatization of this country's industries or the gunrunning. That's how you got to be at the pinnacle of the oligarchs."

Gorga remained silent, his head bowed.

"So, tell me about the CIA mole," Hefflin said.

"I know nothing about any mole, I swear. I told you, I don't know any of the assets. But there is a possible explanation." Gorga considered. "Early in '92, someone made contact with us through The Watchman asking if the system was still operational. I thought it must be one of my friend's assets. This person instructed us to respond if interested by placing an ad in the *International Herald Tribune*. We did so, asking who he is, but he only answered by sending us intel, sensitive intel about American military plans. I realized he must be someone high up in one of the Western intelligence services, but I didn't know which one. This must be the mole you're talking about."

Hefflin thought for a moment. "So, until '92 you weren't getting any intel from this asset?"

"No. I thought this guy learned my friend had died and wanted to know if he could start sending his packages again. I think he assumed he was talking to the KGB, like the other assets. And he didn't demand any money. He just started sending us his intel month after month."

Boris was the mole's handler? I can't believe it.

"What did you do with the intel?"

"I passed some of it to the Russians to stay in their good graces, and sold the rest."

"And how did the Russians react?"

"They suddenly became very excited. They wanted more."

"Which means they hadn't been getting this kind of intel while your friend was alive," Hefflin muttered. "Did the mole pass on any information about a CIA asset named Boris?"

Gorga's cheek twitched. "Yes, later in '92."

"Did you give that information to the Russians?"

Gorga turned his eyes away. "I needed to keep the Russians off my back. I figured that intel was worth a lot to them. What did I care about some CIA asset inside the KGB?"

That asset was your best friend, and mine.

"Did that intel include the identity of Boris's handler?"

"His handler? I don't know. Mayfield was in charge of the details. I never actually saw the intel."

Hefflin shook his head. "A hell of a way to repay your CIA backers, Puiu."

Gorga stood and started pacing. "I have to make it good with them, James. You can tell them I didn't know the intel was coming from a mole in the CIA. Which is true. You have to help me. I saved your father from going to jail, for heaven's sake."

"It's too late for that, even if I wanted to," Hefflin said. "I already reported everything to Ingram. Whatever arrangement you've had with them is now over. A mole inside the Agency is their worst nightmare."

Gorga's face grew somber. "What are you going to do with the money from my accounts?"

"It resides in some CIA stash, adding to their already enormous budget, but that's the least of your worries," Hefflin said. "If you play nice, they may let you live. They may even let you stay in business. But as far as your money goes, I wouldn't count on it."

"What can I do to regain their good graces?" Gorga asked, his voice rising in hope.

Hefflin considered. "We may want you to keep passing intel to the Russians, for one thing, intel we give you." Hefflin realized he used the word *we*.

Gorga nodded, seeming to accept his fate. "And the mole?"

"Don't worry about him. He will no longer be a factor."

Gorga stopped pacing, his body tense, shaking. He rubbed his face with his hands, as if trying to regain some clarity. "You've destroyed my life, you know that? I should just kill you here and now and be done with you." He pressed a button underneath the bar.

"That's no way to talk to a future member of the family, Puiu."

Gorga pressed the button repeatedly, seeming to have lost control over his anger, but there was no response. "Where are my damned men?"

"They're probably unconscious or just tied up. I gave my team orders not to use lethal force, if possible."

"Your team?" Gorga stared at him, confused. "You miserable wretch!" Gorga leaned behind the bar and removed a pistol. "You're not walking out of here alive. You think Ingram will do anything? Ha! He still needs us to keep this country from falling apart. And for his own little gunrunning."

Hefflin looked up. "What are you saying?"

"Nobody has clean hands," Gorga spat. "You're the only stupid Boy Scout around here, just like Avery said." He motioned with his gun. "Down to the basement. I don't want to stain my carpet."

"Put the gun down!" Irina's voice echoed in the stairwell.

They both looked up at the top of the stairs where Irina stood fully dressed, holding a pistol.

"Irina? What are you doing?" Gorga asked, stunned.

"Don't you dare speak to me, you murderer. I heard everything. There are limits even to *my* abhorrent ambitions. Now drop the gun. You know I'm an excellent shot at this distance. You taught me yourself."

Gorga stood frozen, his gun still pointing at Hefflin but his eyes focused on Irina. "So blood is thicker than . . . love, is that it, Irina?"

Hefflin stepped toward Gorga and gently removed the pistol from his hand. Gorga did not resist.

"I am a very wealthy man, Puiu, wealthier than you or your oligarch friends. And I've learned how to use my wealth. If I can bring a team here at a moment's notice to neutralize your men, and if I can destroy your building with all those Securitate files, I can do anything."

Gorga looked up at Hefflin, his mouth agape. "It was you?"

"If you try to assassinate me, or harm Irina after I leave, nothing will remain of your little empire, despite Ingram," Hefflin said. "Not to mention the fact that your family will be killed, then your associates, then you, very slowly. I left instructions."

Irina trotted down the steps in her high heels and swung open the vault doors. "Are you coming, Cousin?"

Hefflin left Gorga sitting on the couch with his head in his hands and accompanied Irina out to his car. Once he started driving, she took out her compact makeup mirror and powdered her face.

"Thank you for your help," Hefflin said, "but I'm sorry you had to hear all of that." He was, in fact, grateful that she had heard everything. He didn't know how he would have told her or whether she would have believed him.

"Once Securitate, always Securitate," Irina said. "I should have known better. It seems that I need you to keep saving me from my bad choices in men. Will I ever learn?"

"Don't be too hard on yourself," Hefflin said. "You didn't know."

"I didn't *want* to know. That's the mindset I learned during the communist days. I just hid from the corruption around me, just focused on my work. I guess I'm still doing the same now. I don't want to face the ugliness of the world." She shook her head. "It's funny. Ugliness exists in the plays I perform in. It's not new to me. But when it appears in my own house, and in myself, I'm always shocked. Stupid, isn't it?"

On the side street after the next block, a truck awaited. Hefflin pulled behind it just as The Owl stepped out. Hefflin left Irina in the car and approached.

"Any problems?"

"No, there were only four guards," The Owl said. "We had ten men in balaclavas. His men just raised their hands when they saw our guns. We tied them up, stuffed their mouths, and locked them in the garage."

Hefflin handed The Owl a bundle of cash. "Thank you."

The old man gazed at the money. "You have it all wrong, my friend. I should pay you. Whatever you did in there, I know Gorga will never be same again."

"Keep it. I may have other jobs for you in the future."

They embraced. Hefflin felt a closeness to the old man that rivaled the love he felt for Boris. "You've taught me how to know who my true friends are," Hefflin said, his eyes growing moist. "I won't ever forget that."

"Good. And I have one last piece of advice: Get out of Bucharest. As of tonight, you have bullseye on your back."

As he drove off with Irina, he knew The Owl had become a loyal friend and ally, as had Balzary. He realized he was creating his own unit outside the Agency's purview.

"Where to?" he asked Irina.

"Home, for a change. I want to destroy every present that man ever gave me."

"Not the Brancusi," Hefflin burst out.

"No, that I will give to you for saving me from that monster. Then I'll sell the rest and donate the money to the poor. No point in wasting it. Is that good enough for you, Cousin?"

"What am I, your conscience?"

"You seem to have taken on the role of my guardian angel," Irina said. "I certainly need one. By the way, is Vulcan's money still available?"

Vulcan was Ceausescu's moneyman and Irina's previous lover. Hefflin couldn't help but smile. "Of course. It's waiting for you to change your mind."

"Well, I have. A girl has to look out for herself in this day and age. I won't have to depend on men like Gorga."

"I'll send you the instructions on how to access it."

"You *are* my guardian angel." Irina blew him a kiss.

Hefflin thought of Boris, his own former guardian angel. Somehow he had inherited that role toward Irina.

*   *   *

Gorga sat on his couch holding his head, shaking. Yesterday he was living on top of the world. Today his entire fortune was at risk, maybe even his life. He needed to regain the good graces of the Americans, that was the first thing. He would call Mayfield and tell him to halt all intelligence operations, at least for the moment. And the syndicate had to be informed. He would be blamed for everything, for letting that infernal man into his midst, for treating him like a friend, a member of the family, even. He let out a bitter laugh. No, they still needed him, as did the Americans. Things would get ironed out. But that man had to pay. No amount of wealth could protect him from the syndicate.

Resolved on his plan of action and feeling a renewed sense of optimism, he picked up the phone and dialed. The phone rang several times and he feared he was disturbing the older man, perhaps even waking him up. It was past eleven at night, after all.

A deep voice answered. *"Da?"*

"The man we spoke about, he was here tonight. He knows everything. He blew up the headquarters and informed his American superiors." Gorga rattled off the events of that evening, feeling like a kid squealing on his classmate. "We need to eliminate him, without leaving any fingerprints."

The man on the other side of the line remained silent for a moment. Then, "Eliminating him goes too far. The Americans won't stand for it."

"But—"

"Quiet, and listen!" The man raised his voice, a military command. "You will do nothing. You have bungled everything from the start. I will take care of him, and our fingerprints won't be on it. Now go to bed."

The phone went dead. Gorga held the receiver for a long time, relieved that such a decisive man was at the helm. Yet his anxiety returned a moment later as he came to realize that his standing in the syndicate had suffered a heavy blow.

He brushed those thoughts aside as he dialed a second number.

CHAPTER SIXTY-THREE

Bucharest
April 1993

HE DIDN'T KNOW how long he'd been lying in bed. After returning
to the hotel from Gorga's house he had taken a long shower to wash
off the deceit and corruption, cursing Gorga in both English and
Romanian until he ran out and started making up new slurs. He
then poured himself a Johnnie Walker Black and lay in bed in his
bathrobe to revisit the most recent events.

The Watchman stores functioned as hubs for intel from various
locations across the globe, part of Boris's legacy. Gorga was the recipient of this intel, but Gorga didn't know that Boris and his best
friend were one and the same, and that he had inadvertently betrayed
him to the Russians.

The fact that Avery had set up the oligarchs and their offshore
accounts was not such a surprise to Hefflin, now that he thought of
it. Avery, and the Agency, would have done anything to ensure that
Romania would not slide back into the arms of the communists.
Creating a wealthy class with political power would guarantee that
a capitalist, free-market system of sorts would endure. But now that
communism had gone out of style, even in Russia, the usefulness of
the oligarchs was no longer obvious. The monster that Avery had
created was now making millions in illegal arms trafficking to the
Serbs and spying against the U.S. Once he had read Hefflin's report,

Ingram must have decided to cut Gorga loose. That would explain why Ingram had suddenly provided Hefflin with the list of Gorga's offshore accounts, now empty.

Still, Hefflin knew he wasn't any closer to finding the identity of the mole. He would have to go through with the original plan of surveilling The Watchman store in Manhattan with the hope that the mole would appear to deliver his last package.

As he was drifting off to sleep, he heard a knock on the door. His watch read a few minutes past midnight. Who the hell could it be at this time of night?

Why don't I just put up a fucking shingle, "Doctor on call, day or night," as my father did in Bucharest?

He took out his Beretta and placed the barrel against the door as he slowly opened it.

Amanda Thayer stood barefoot in a white bathrobe holding a bottle of wine and two glasses. Her hair was down now, still wet, invoking an alluring image of a vulnerable ingénue.

"I'm not just an executive secretary, you know. The Agency sent me to watch over you," she said as she whisked by him.

He slipped the Beretta into the first drawer he found and turned to her.

"The Agency? They thought I needed watching over? Funny Ingram never said anything."

"The method was left up to me." She let out a giggle, then poured the wine and handed a glass to him. "Where have you been? Cavorting with some harlot, no doubt." She eased up to him. "You should be more careful. If you must cavort, you should keep it in the family, for security reasons."

"You know the Agency frowns on cavorting between employees," he said.

"It's all in the name of queen and country."

"I hate to break it to you, but we don't have a queen."

"Duty, then. The point is the same. I am willing to sacrifice my good name for your safety. Not that I have a good name." She giggled again and slumped onto the bed, still holding her glass. "Now, lie down here beside me and sip the very mediocre Merlot I stole from the bar and recount all your wonderful adventures."

Hefflin set his glass on the night table and sat next to her. "And how are you supposed to protect me in your bathrobe?"

"I came prepared." She drew open her robe to reveal a pair of beautiful breasts.

"Did they teach you that in training class?"

"Of course. I've had classes in every art of seduction. I think I should show you, so you'll be able to resist—next time. Tonight, just sit back and enjoy it."

He wondered if the Agency actually had such classes, since he knew the KGB certainly did. Had Ingram really sent this bubbly party girl to watch over him? The thought of Catherine witnessing this scene flashed through his mind. Did this sexual scenario fit into the category of operational necessity?

"The first thing a seductress will do is slowly unfasten your robe, like this," she whispered. "Then, she will softly ask if you have a particular desire or fantasy, which she can fulfill. Everyone has at least one."

He felt himself getting aroused. "What's yours?"

"I'm a pervert at heart. I like to make men squirm." She gently slid her hand down his abdomen.

He grabbed her wrist and pulled it away.

She looked up, her eyes showing surprise. "You're not ready yet? Of course you're not—you haven't even tasted the wine." She picked up his glass and handed it to him.

"But you haven't drunk any either," he said.

"I don't need it. I'm oozing with lust. Besides, I told you wine doesn't do it for me. I've already had three martinis. I brought the wine for you. Now drink like a good boy, then I'll show you the meaning of pleasure." She brought his glass up to his lips.

"Your training should have taught you that you never drink from a glass someone else gave you," he said. He slid her off him and rolled off the bed.

She eyed him, then the glass of wine.

"Nothing bad, honey. Just a little pick-me-up. But I don't think I'll need it." She unfastened her bathrobe and let it drop to the floor. She stood naked before him, one hand gently stroking her breast. He felt disoriented by her beauty.

"You want some of this, sweetie?" She took a step toward him. "It's yours for the asking."

She stretched out her arms, displaying and offering her body to him. She inched closer, her arms now clasped behind her back, a submissive stance. He felt drawn to her, his senses aroused, urging him on.

He saw only a flash, then felt the kick to his groin. He doubled over, the pain shooting up into his chest. Before he could look up, he felt her heel slam the side of his face. He sprawled on the floor, his robe entangled around him, the pain in his groin diminished by the powerful kick that had momentarily numbed his sensations.

"Get up, sweetie. And take off that silly robe. I want to see what you're made of. It's only right we spar *au naturel*, like your Greek ancestors."

As Hefflin's mind cleared, he rolled away from her, untangled himself from his robe, and threw it to the floor.

"That's better." Her eyes bathed his naked body. "My, my, you are impressive. But let's see if the Agency taught you how to use it."

"Who the hell are you?"

"I'm Circe, and you're my Odysseus." She smiled.

He tried to take his eyes off her breasts, the nipples that were now aroused, the curve of the hips. He was still unsure of what to make of this woman. Was she playing a perverted sexual game or was she actually attacking him?

She faked a kick, then delivered a punch to his ribs. He felt the pain shoot through him. As he tried to back away, her foot landed on his chest and thrust him against the wall. The blow took his breath away, and he barely avoided her next kick by sliding to one side.

"There's nowhere to run, sweetie. Tonight you are my slave."

As they circled each other, he tried to resolve the two images before him: the luscious, provocative nude woman and what he was now coming to realize was a deadly enemy. He suddenly remembered Catherine's advice in the event he ever had to battle a beautiful woman: "Treat her as if she were a ruthless, soulless machine."

She jumped onto the bed with one foot, then sprang through the air and clutched his neck between her legs. He felt himself being flipped hard onto the floor.

"You didn't see that coming, did you, sweetie?"

As her legs squeezed his neck, he gazed up into her shaved pubis, his mind still curiously aroused, still trying to resolve the contradictory images. He noticed something below her bikini line—a scar?—in the shape of the letter *N*.

He felt the throbbing in his carotids, the blood and oxygen to his brain slowly being cut off. *It's a soulless machine, goddamn you!* he repeated to himself. The darkness began to close in. He knew he had one last chance before he blacked out. With a final effort, he forced himself to strike a knuckle blow to the side of her knee. She yelped in pain, her legs loosening their grip long enough for him to roll away.

She jumped back on her feet and advanced toward him, her face now tight, angry, a deadly machine in truth. She came at him with multiple blows, which he parried, then he landed a hard punch to her solar plexus. She flew backward onto the bed, struggling for breath. He jumped on top of her, the weight of his body keeping her down, then clutched her wrists and held them above her head.

"Who are you working for?" he demanded.

She responded with a head-bump that momentarily dazed him. As he rolled off her she leaped onto his back, tightened her arms around his neck, and squeezed.

I have to end this—woman or not.

He twisted her fingers to loosen her grip then flipped her over his head. As she landed on the floor, he held on to one arm and came down hard with his other. He heard the crack, then her screams. A blow to her jaw instantly returned the room to silence.

She lay splayed on the floor, unconscious, one arm in an unnatural position, her jaw twisted to one side.

He sat on the bed for a long moment, catching his breath, his thoughts.

A fucking machine. And a killing machine. Two in one. What a bargain.

He phoned Balzary at his apartment and asked him if he could send a team over to collect an assassin.

"Alive or dead?" Balzary asked casually.

"She's alive. Just a few broken bones."

"You're beating up women now?" Balzary chuckled.

"That was my initial weakness, too. Don't ever fall for it."

Hefflin dressed and waited for Balzary, who showed up twenty minutes later with three men. One of the men whistled when he saw the naked woman on the floor, still unconscious.

"I know her," Balzary said. "That's Amanda Thayer—works for Nordam Industries, I believe. She and Mayfield used to be an item a while back."

"Mayfield!" Hefflin's mind suddenly lit up. Why the hell hadn't he remembered before? "That makes sense. Mayfield used to work for Nordam at one point."

"And she's an assassin?" Balzary stared at Hefflin.

"I didn't believe it either, until she almost killed me with her Tae Kwon Do, or whatever the hell she was using on me. You should also analyze that wine. I think it has something in it." He pointed to the glasses sitting on the night table.

Balzary shook his head in disgust. "What do you want me to do with her?"

"Why don't you ask Mayfield?" Hefflin said. "Or, better still, I'll ask him myself."

Balzary's men took the bottle of wine and the glasses to have their contents analyzed. They wrapped Amanda Thayer in a bedsheet intending to carry her out the back door of the hotel and drive her to a hospital.

"I think you need a drink," Balzary said.

"We'll have to postpone that," Hefflin said. "I have one last visit to make. I want to end my business tonight and return home to my family. I miss them."

Balzary patted his back. "Need any help?"

"I think it's better if you're no longer associated with me," Hefflin said. "You still have to live with these characters."

CHAPTER SIXTY-FOUR

Bucharest
April 1993

THE HOUSE WAS still lit even at that late hour, a lone window on the second floor, Mayfield's office. Now that the business conference was over, Mayfield no longer needed to stay at the InterContinental to hobnob with the rich and powerful. Hefflin observed the building for a few minutes to make sure there were no security men stationed outside, then opened the wrought iron gate and made his way down the path to the front door. He found it unlocked. He took out his Beretta and silently entered.

A Chopin piano piece drifted down from the second floor. He held his gun with both hands and examined the living room. Finding it empty, he began climbing the stairs. Halfway up a step creaked, the same damned step he had found before. He froze and listened, then continued to the top floor. The music seemed to emanate from Mayfield's office. He stepped silently down the corridor, swinging his gun toward each dark room, but made a decision not to examine them. The door to the office was ajar, light spilling into the corridor. He reached the open doorway and was about to peer into the room when he heard Mayfield's voice behind him.

"I have a gun pointed at you. Drop the pistol."

Hefflin hesitated, then let the Beretta fall to the floor and raised his arms.

Mayfield pushed Hefflin into the office and motioned for him to sit in a chair. The room was lit by a floor lamp next to Hefflin and another across from him where Mayfield now sat.

"I assume Amanda failed in her duties," Mayfield said. "Is she dead?"

"Only a few broken bones."

"Impressive. No one has ever resisted her. And many have tried."

"I had no trouble resisting her," Hefflin said. "She's been trying to seduce me from the day I arrived. At that pace, she wouldn't be much competition for the whores."

Mayfield winced. "I meant her fighting abilities."

Hefflin shrugged. "That, too. She won't be doing much of either for a while."

"It's a shame. She is dear to my heart." Mayfield scowled. "As for me, I find nothing wrong with whores. I'm friends with several nice ones. They're not hypocrites, like the feminists back home who declare that it's their body to do with as they please and then turn around and brand 'working girls' as victims or drug addicts."

"A compliment from one whore to another."

"Oh, don't play the righteous hero with me," Mayfield snapped. "You're in the dirtiest business there is. At least I deal in money, pure and simple."

"How much money do you need, Harold? You've already made millions with your casinos and gunrunning. And now I hear you're selling arms to the Serbs."

"Not just the Serbs. All sides need arms," Mayfield said. "As far as how much money is enough, you should know that it's never enough. We all want to leave something behind, to be remembered, for good or for ill."

"You'll be remembered not only as a gunrunner, but a traitor who sold secrets to the Russians."

Mayfield brushed the idea away with one hand. "We wouldn't have been as successful in our defense contracts had we not shared some of that intel with our Russian friends. I've been a middleman in many of their arms transactions all over the world, and will be in the future."

Hefflin nodded. "Smart. You and Gorga provide them with intel, and they hire you for their arms deals."

"Ideologies come and go, Mr. Hefflin. Only money remains constant."

"You passed on intel to the Russians that they had a mole inside the KGB, and that I was his handler. So why did you refer me to The Owl when we first met at the conference?"

"I just wanted to steer you on a wild goose chase long enough for my Russian friends to catch up to you," Mayfield said. "I was hoping they would quickly dispose of you. Unfortunately, they proved to be slow and ineffectual."

"My assessment of you has grown over these past few weeks, no doubt about it," Hefflin said. "But even so, you're just one of Gorga's errand boys."

Mayfield scowled. "Yes, he called me after you left his house. He was panicked. He said our intelligence operation is over. He has lost his nerve. That's why I sent Amanda."

"And now she disappointed you, too. Maybe you should read the tea leaves, Harold. Gorga is going down. And you along with him. The way I see it, your only option is to do as Gorga and work for us from now on."

Mayfield looked confused for a moment, then his face lit up. "Oh, I see. You want me to pass false intel to the Russians, is that it?"

Hefflin nodded.

Mayfield shook his head. "I don't think I can live like that, a slave. Besides, at some point the Russians are bound to find out that the intel is false. Then where will I be? No, no, that won't do. I think my best bet is to get rid of you once and for all and tell the Russians their mole is blown. Assets get killed all the time. As do agents. It's not my fault. You won't be around to tell them otherwise."

"The Russians won't be your friends for long when they discover you joined forces with Gorga and Avery to bring in the Middle Eastern snipers to start the revolution, which caused Romania to slip through their fingers."

"Ah, you figured that out, too," Mayfield said. "They wouldn't believe you even if you were alive to tell them. They'd think you're just trying to lay blame on another to save yourself and the CIA."

"Maybe," Hefflin considered. "But they will believe the pictures and recordings of you arranging for an arms deal with an Iranian operative for the Muslims in Yugoslavia, which I already sent to the Agency. The Russians won't like that, not when they're supporting their Christian Orthodox Serbian friends."

Mayfield's face bloomed with a combination of surprise and admiration. "So, that's how you found out—you had me followed. And that woman at the hotel in Athens was your operative? Nice. How did you figure out the watch?"

"Yes, all those watches in your drawer with the same missing dot at the two o'clock position. And then there was your daily planner, all those trips to Athens on the same date each month."

"You broke into my house?" Mayfield frowned. "I swore I would never underestimate you again, but I guess I have."

"Why did Baghdadi betray you? Did he try to go into business by himself? Is that it?"

"Worse than that. He tried to blackmail me. He threatened to spill the beans with that infernal watch Nicu gave him with the missing dot, one of my gifts. There is a lesson there, somewhere, about not regifting." Mayfield shrugged. "Baghdadi was a greedy son-of-a-bitch. He was useful at one time with his Lebanese secret service connections, but he quickly became just a guy to drink with."

Mayfield stood and walked to his desk. "I think it's time for you to disappear, Mr. Hefflin. The CIA will be grateful. You've been nothing but a thorn in everyone's side."

He dialed a number on the phone and said in English, "Come over at once. I have a job for you." He sat back down and waited.

"Where does Stanculescu fit in?" Hefflin asked.

Mayfield tightened his grip on the gun. "How the hell did you find out about him? He's just a businessman, that's all you need to know."

"He's a gunrunner, like you, and your oligarchs."

"I would forget that name if I were you. But come to think of it, you'll soon forget everything."

"Since I'm going to be dead, you might as well tell me. At least I can go to my grave with some understanding."

Mayfield considered for a moment, then seemed to decide. "Stanculescu and Avery were good friends. They planned the revolution, after all. After Avery died, Stanculescu and the Agency remained good friends."

"What are you saying? That the Agency knows about Stanculescu's gunrunning?"

Mayfield let out a chuckle. "They don't only know about it, they are using his services."

"For what?"

"Seeing how the Russians and Romanians are arming the Serbs, the Americans decided to arm the Muslims. Their weak American hearts bleed for those miserable pagans. That Iranian arms deal going to the Muslims is a CIA-funded operation, with Stanculescu, Gorga, and me putting it all together. I had to throw in some Romanian howitzers for the Iranians so they would agree to the deal."

"Which you arranged at the gala, and then reported to those two men. They were Iranian agents."

"The hell you say. You followed me?" Mayfield shook his head. "I'll never live it down. Those Romanian arms were also CIA-funded, by the way. But you're obviously not in the loop."

"Before you kill me, there is one more thing," Hefflin said. "I finally realized who you are, though the idea has been swirling in my mind for some time. A mutual friend of ours once told me that he paid for my education with money he received from a wealthy Asian businessman who made his money in casinos. I believe he meant a wealthy businessman who made his money in Asian casinos. He also said this man was an arms dealer. He was talking about you. I just wanted to thank you."

A look of recognition swept over Mayfield's face. "That money was for you?" He gasped. "That piece of shit blackmailed me into giving it to him, for a good cause, he said. It will help to get me through the Pearly Gates, he said. That bastard."

"It's like the closing of a circle, isn't it, Harold?"

"All for naught. You won't be around to appreciate it. But whatever happened to him? How do you even know him?"

Before Hefflin could answer, a figure appeared in the doorway. He was a tall, gaunt man, in his late fifties or so, and he was holding a gun with silencer.

"Finally, you've arrived," Mayfield said. "I don't want this man's body ever found. Is that clear?"

As the man stepped into the light, Hefflin recognized him. *Pincus's assassin.*

"How do you two know each other?" Hefflin asked. "Of course, you were all in on it with Avery." Hefflin turned to the assassin. "So, who are your masters this time?"

"Same masters," the assassin said. "You are a cat with nine lives."

"It seems I'm on my last one."

"Perhaps. But not by my hand. You moved up my schedule a bit, but once again, I am not here for you."

Four puffs—a baby's cough. Mayfield's chest blossomed with maroon stains, his face full of bemused surprise. He sank to the floor gently, protecting himself with one hand, then settled down with a sigh. The assassin administered the coup de grace, then lowered the gun.

"Why?" Hefflin asked.

The man shrugged. "Orders."

"Whose orders?"

"Does it matter?"

An image burst into Hefflin's mind: his beloved Professor Pincus struggling for breath, awake and aware as his life ebbed from him, the result of a paralyzing agent administered by this same assassin. He felt the rage return stronger than ever, the fury sweep over him, overwhelm him. He couldn't be like Catherine. He couldn't show mercy, not with this man.

"I should have taken care of you a long time ago," Hefflin seethed.

The man turned to him with a faint look of surprise. "I repeat, I am not here for you."

"No. But I *am* here for *you*."

Sudden unease spread over the assassin's face. As he lifted the barrel of his gun, Hefflin lunged forward and delivered a lightning knuckle blow to his trachea. Hefflin heard a puff, then felt the bullet fly past his ear. The assassin dropped the gun and toppled backward onto the floor, his hands to his throat. His chest heaved, his fingers clawed at his throat as if trying to dislodge a bone, but his crushed trachea would never allow him to take another breath. As his face grew ashen, his eyes filled with the horror of knowing that death was imminent. Hefflin did not miss the irony. The assassin was dying in the same manner that Pincus had died, awake and alert, slowly suffocating. The man's eyes gradually lost focus, then turned into doll's eyes.

As he left the house, Hefflin wondered how many notches on his belt the collector of souls had to answer for when he reached the Pearly Gates.

CHAPTER SIXTY-FIVE

Bucharest
April 1993

AFTER USING MAYFIELD's phone to call his pilots to get the plane ready, Hefflin drove back to the Athénée to pack and settle the bill. He wanted to leave Bucharest immediately, before the oligarchs or the police found the bodies. He had spent several minutes wiping down the phone and anything else he might have touched in Mayfield's apartment.

As he entered the hotel lobby, he found Balzary sitting in one of the chairs normally used by the girls to await their next client.

"Changing professions?" Hefflin asked.

"The Russians. They just informed me that I was to produce you within twenty-four hours or they'll start making things nasty for us. They've been looking for you. I guess they missed you while you were in Athens."

"I wonder what the hell happened now?" Hefflin muttered.

"Call your pilots. Get your plane ready. You're leaving."

"I already did. I just have to pack—"

Balzary pulled him by the arm. "Leave your Brioni suits. You can afford new ones. I don't want any shootouts on the streets of Bucharest, and certainly not involving my men."

They got into Balzary's embassy limo idling on a side street. Balzary snapped orders to his driver in Hungarian and the car sped off.

"What happened with Mayfield?" Balzary asked.

Hefflin recounted the events.

"Christ. You remind me of Michael Corleone settling all scores."

"I never intended to kill Mayfield, just to rough him up a bit," Hefflin said.

"Somebody ordered the hit."

"Yes. And I think I know who."

"By the way, that wine you got from Amanda Thayer contained a high dose of a cholinesterase inhibitor, a paralyzing agent. Untraceable."

"To make it look like a natural death." Hefflin shook his head. "She wasn't kidding. When I didn't drink the wine, she decided to go to plan B and just kill me with her martial arts. I guess she thought I was still a Boy Scout, an analyst."

They sped down the dark streets, most unlit, empty, a cemetery in the dead of night. Hefflin wondered how long it would take for his childhood city to become normal again. Perhaps a generation, as Irina had said. But he realized that he had never known this city as anything but a miserable, gray place. His memories had been playing tricks on him, substituting old pictures of Bucharest during the interwar years when it was called "the little Paris of the East." Would those days ever return?

Just as Hefflin finished his thoughts, two black sedans appeared out of a side street and cut them off, forcing the driver to slam the brakes and veer onto the sidewalk. Two more black sedans pulled up from behind to block them. About a dozen figures with semiautomatic rifles rushed out of the cars and surrounded the Mercedes. A moment later a black Zil pulled up alongside. As the rear door opened, the car lights backlit the obese figure of Stefan, who now appeared like a grotesque creature rising from the depths of hell.

Hefflin realized he had never seen Stefan standing before, and the man now appeared much shorter than he had imagined. Instead of Sydney Greenstreet, Stefan now resembled Alfred Hitchcock.

Balzary lowered the window. "What is this outrage? This is an official embassy car. You have no right to stop it."

"We only want your passenger," Stefan said, the light playing sinister tricks, his face no longer that of a buffoon. "We can take him peacefully, or not."

"He is my official guest. You want to start a gunfight on the streets of Bucharest?" Balzary threatened, though he only had the driver on his side, against a dozen Russians.

"I have no quarrel with you, Balzary. But I will not hesitate to shoot."

One of Stefan's men inserted the barrel of his rifle through the open window.

"It's all right, you've done all you can," Hefflin said to Balzary. "He probably just wants to talk."

Hefflin stepped out of the Mercedes and followed Stefan to the back of the Zil. There were two men in the front. The rest of the Russians entered their cars and drove off. As Hefflin settled next to Stefan, the Zil started moving.

"Where are we going?" Hefflin asked.

"To airport."

"But, Stefan, that's exactly where I was going."

"Perhaps. But now you are getting on special Aeroflot flight to Moscow. It will take off as soon as we arrive."

"Moscow?"

"Since you have not voluntarily joined us, we had to revert to other means. Events have changed my plans."

"What events?"

"Events on ground. Antibes, to be exact."

Antibes! My mother-in-law's summer home. How the hell does he know about it?

Hefflin felt a pall of dread descending over him. "What are you saying?"

"Your wife—whom I have not yet met but who I hear is beautiful—thought she could fly your little boy to Nice with caretaker—Yvette, is it?—in your own private jet, no less, to hide in your mother-in-law's dacha in Antibes. Such capitalist decadence." Stefan shook his head. "Our men were waiting for them at airport and followed them. They are holding off on action until they receive my orders."

Hefflin felt the sweat roll down his neck.

"This is my family, Stefan."

"I am sorry I have to resort to such tactics, but you have left me no choice."

"Our activities don't extend to our families."

"Those rules do not apply anymore. I do not know if they ever did." Stefan chuckled. "I suppose I could have just abducted you, but I was afraid you would resist, and I would be forced to kill you. I do not want to risk such valuable CIA asset. Besides, I want you to cooperate fully. So I decided on alternate plan."

"You can't do this, Stefan."

"Your family is safe, for now, unless you refuse to board plane, in which case I will call my men, and you will never see them again."

"Even if I come with you, I'll never see my family again," Hefflin said.

"They can come to Moscow, too," Stefan said cheerily. "We will give you beautiful apartment in center of city, large one, for more children. One is not enough for man like you. I have five, myself."

"I guess you won't be getting your five million dollars," Hefflin said.

"It is unfortunate my retirement fund will have to do without it, but my orders are explicit."

Hefflin clenched his fists, his chest throbbing. Catherine had been right. They had been following his family all this time. It was evident that Stefan no longer believed that he was their mole, if he ever did. Stefan's operation now was to simply blackmail him into defecting and spill everything Boris had given to the Americans and everything he knew about the Agency.

He couldn't let that happen. And he couldn't trust that the Russians would keep their word. He had to warn Catherine. She had said DGSE agents were protecting her and Jack, but a few men could not resist a force like the one Stefan had just used.

"All right, Stefan. You hold all the aces. Let me have some of that Stoli to celebrate our new partnership."

"Now you are being rational." Stefan handed him the bottle and a shot glass. "To our new—"

Stefan did not finish his sentence before the bottle of Stoli crashed into his face and cracked his forehead. Hefflin wielded the bottle once more at the head of the agent in the front passenger seat. The bottle broke this time, wet shards flying inside the cabin. Hefflin then grabbed the head of the driver and twisted it. He felt a crack and the man's head slumped down. The Zil veered onto the sidewalk, decapitated a fire hydrant, and plunged into the side of a building.

Hefflin scrambled out of the car and started running. The streets were dark, eerily empty. He had to find a car to hot-wire and get to the airport, but he was on a highway. Just then he spotted headlights barreling toward him. He ran, but found no side streets or obvious places to hide. The headlights sped toward him and, for an instant, he thought they would run him over. Then the back door flew open and he heard the voice of Balzary.

"Get in. Hurry."

He plunged into the back seat and the car sped off.

"How did you show up so conveniently?" Hefflin asked.

"I've been following to see where they would take you. Lucky that the rest of the Russian team didn't follow. I guess they thought they were no longer needed. How did you escape?"

"Never mind that. Catherine and my family are in danger. The Russians have a team ready to abduct them if I don't go to Moscow and defect." He took out a pen and tore off a piece of paper from his notebook. "Here is the telephone and address of the house in Antibes, my mother-in-law's summer home. Tell Catherine to call the DGSE to get a large team there before the Russians find Stefan and order their men to move in. Then call Ingram to get a local Agency team to the house. I'll take off as soon as I can but I won't get there in time. You got all that?"

"Got it. But I thought Catherine said she already had DGSE men protecting them."

"A few, but they won't be a match for a large Russian operation."

As they reached the departures terminal, Hefflin grabbed Balzary's shoulders. "You've been a great friend, and I owe you my life many times over. I won't forget."

"Don't worry. I won't let you." Balzary laughed. "Now get out of here before I start crying."

Hefflin embraced him then ran into the airport.

Hefflin's private plane took off a half hour later. The flight time to Nice, the closest airport to Antibes, was approximately two hours and forty-five minutes. Adding the half hour before taking off, and the hour it would take him to rent a car at the Nice airport and drive to Antibes, he feared he would not make it in time.

CHAPTER SIXTY-SIX

Antibes, France
May 1993

CATHERINE STILL CLENCHED the telephone even though it was now silent. Balzary's voice had been tense, commanding. A Russian team had been surveilling the house, and they were waiting for the order to move in. Balzary had told her to call the DGSE to get a large team to her, but the DGSE had already removed their men when she had returned from Athens. They could not spend their resources forever, and certainly not on her unsubstantiated fears. And just as Balzary was about to say more, the line went dead. The phone now had no dial tone. The Russian team had already begun their operation.

What to do? As her mind scrambled through possible options, she realized she had none. She was a sitting duck, with no possibility to either escape or resist, not with her family around her.

Then she remembered what one of her DGSE instructors had once said: in every situation, no matter how dire, you can find an advantage. But what advantage could she possibly find stuck in this large old house that dated back to the 1800s? She was in a cocoon, a vault, with no way out.

Then an idea emerged: with no way out, you can only go further in, even deeper. A memory resurfaced, the subconscious working to solve the puzzle. As a child, she had been brought to this house during the summers and had reveled in exploring every corner of it—its seven bedrooms, the maids' quarters in the basement, and the wine cellar below that.

The wine cellar! It stored hundreds of bottles of expensive wines. During the war, the entrance to it had been altered to prevent the advancing German Army from finding it. Instead of a hatch in the floor that one simply pulled open, the wine cellar now could be accessed only through the closet of one of the maids' rooms. The panel behind the closet slid open by pulling down one of the hooks.

Catherine yelled for her mother and Yvette, both of whom hurried out of their bedrooms in their nightgowns as if the house were on fire.

"What is it? Why are you yelling?" her mother asked in French.

"Get Jacques and two bottles of water," Catherine commanded. "I don't have time to explain. And don't waste time changing your clothes."

"Catherine! Have you gone mad?"

"Our lives are in danger, Mother. Now do as I say!"

Her mother had obviously never been spoken to in this way, but Catherine's commanding voice convinced her to obey. Yvette quickly took two bottles of water out of the refrigerator while her mother gathered Jacques. Together they hurried down the steps to the maids' quarters, which hadn't been used in decades, and into the one particular bedroom with the hidden door to the wine cellar.

*   *   *

As soon as the jet took off, Hefflin used the phone in his plane to call the summer house in Antibes. He let it ring for a long time, then hung up. Balzary's call had either caused Catherine and the family to flee, or they had been captured. He then called Ingram's home number and quickly explained the situation. Ingram said he had already received a message from the Agency about a frantic call from Balzary and was about to order Agency and DGSE personnel in Nice to get to the house in Antibes.

That task completed, Hefflin finally allowed his fears to enter his mind, which he had up till then avoided doing. His thoughts immediately focused on his son. His chest suddenly felt hollow, as if part of his soul were being torn out—a completely new feeling for him. For Jack brought both terror and anger. Despite how this turned out in the end, he knew he would forever feel this powerful bond with his boy, a father's bond.

He knelt down to pray. He couldn't remember the last time he had done so, though in the past he had gone through the motions of crossing himself, as his mother had done. He prayed to a God he didn't know. He did not promise to be good or virtuous. He knew that life, especially his life, would not allow him to keep his pledges. He simply appealed to the goodness that priests preached was the essence of God.

He remained prostrate for what felt like a few minutes, but when he opened his eyes, he realized over an hour had passed.

* * *

The wine cellar smelled of dust and mold; cobwebs hung from the ceiling, and a thick layer of dust covered the wine bottles neatly stacked against two walls. Catherine sat on a musty old couch holding Jacques in her lap, while her mother and Yvette sat in chairs across from her. In the old days this area had been a wine-tasting room, but nobody had used it for that purpose for decades.

Little Jacques sat silent, enwrapped in his mother's arms, obviously sensing the tension among the adults. The walls and floors of the old house were constructed of thick oak and rock, making the silence as complete as if they were encased in a tomb. But those same walls would not allow Catherine to hear the men enter the house two floors up. Catherine's nerves were on high alert, her body wet with perspiration, her muscles tight, poised to spring. She carried two Berettas, but she couldn't imagine using them, not with Jacques nearby.

They heard the faint heel of a boot on the floor above them, in the maids' quarters, and they all sat up, expectant. Then more footsteps, even fainter. The men were searching the maids' bedrooms. Catherine placed her hand over Jack's mouth and whispered "Shhh."

Many footsteps now, louder. Apparently, they had decided the house was empty and they no longer needed to be quiet. She heard doors slam, faint voices, some angry. Then the footsteps grew even fainter, and the silence returned.

Catherine exhaled in relief, but she knew this might not signal the end. The predators could be waiting for their prey to come out of hiding.

CHAPTER SIXTY-SEVEN

Antibes, France
May 1993

THE TWO-STORY STONE house perched on the side of a hill in Antibes resembled a small chateau. It was surrounded by several acres of cypress trees, pines, and oaks. To the rear, a large lawn extended to the edge of the cliff, and beyond that lay the azure Mediterranean sparkling with the faint light of dawn.

A dozen or so men dressed in black, wearing balaclavas and brandishing semiautomatic weapons, ran into and out of the house, some searching the grounds. They seemed desperate, perplexed. Their leader, Colonel Ivan Pavlov, barked orders, aware that no neighbors could hear him in that isolated place. At last he received the report that the house was clear. There was no one inside. They had found a loaf of bread on the table, food in the refrigerator, and clothes in the closets. The occupants had left in a hurry, and recently.

Colonel Pavlov stood on the terrace, perplexed. How could they have escaped without his men spotting them? Several of his men had been monitoring the grounds for days. Could they have missed them? Could he have misinterpreted his instructions? He had received his orders to proceed with the operation from an underling in Bucharest, not his immediate superior. Why?

As he was about to lean on the outdoor balustrade to ponder the situation, he heard the distant sound of a helicopter. Then a second one. He could see them now coming from the east, from Nice, as points of light in the dark sky. Where were they heading? As the helicopters approached, he realized they would pass right above him. Wherever they were going, spotting dark figures running around the garden in the middle of the night would certainly alarm them.

He ordered his men to reenter the house and stay away from the windows. He quickly ran inside and closed the door behind him.

The thumping of the helicopters grew louder until they seemed to be right over him, pounding his eardrums. He waited for them to pass, but they remained, thumping even louder, as in a nightmare. He took a chance and glanced out the window and saw the helicopters hovering above the house, spotlights focused down on the house and garden. One of his men ran up to report that several military vehicles and a troop carrier had just burst through the gates of the compound and were approaching down the gravel driveway. In a moment he saw them, accompanied by two black vans, encircling the house, their headlights focused on the building. Men dressed in military uniforms bearing rifles spread out among the trees surrounding the property. He then heard a voice through a megaphone bark orders both in French and English for all the men to come out with their hands raised.

His worst nightmare. If he and his SVR team were caught on foreign soil in the middle of an operation, they would be arrested, tried, and jailed. Their faces would be on the front pages of every newspaper. Even if they were returned to Russia under some sort of deal, he would be considered a failure by his masters, a man who had brought shame to his country. He would be sent to Siberia, or worse, and his men would be posted in some godforsaken outpost. Their lives would be over. He had to make a decision.

He ordered his men to stay where they were, then removed his balaclava and pistol and dropped them to the floor. As he stepped out of the house with his arms raised, the headlights blinded him, making him feel like an actor onstage about to deliver his monologue. He started walking toward the lights. When he reached a point halfway to the vehicles, around which men now stood aiming rifles at him, he stopped and yelled in English.

"I am Colonel Ivan Pavlov of SVR, and I am seeking asylum in West."

Two men dressed in civilian clothes came forward, stepping into the light, their images backlit into ghostly forms. One was the CIA station chief in Nice, Mike Brennan; the other was the DGSE chief of counterintelligence in Nice, Jean Gallant. They walked up to Colonel Pavlov and stood before him.

"How many men do you have inside, Colonel?" Gallant asked in English.

"Ten, sir, armed with semiautomatic rifles and pistols."

"I want them to lay down their arms and come out with their hands behind their heads."

"I am sorry, sir, but I do not think they will do that."

"They are surrounded, Colonel." Gallant raised his voice. "We have overwhelming force and more on the way. There is no escape."

"I am well aware of situation, sir, as are my men."

"Then what are your intentions?"

"If my men surrender, they will face years of jail in France. Even if they are exchanged at some point, they will face disgrace back home and will probably be sent to rot in some frozen outpost. They would rather die." The colonel let a wry smile curl his lips. "This is Côte d'Azure, sir, heart of France's tourism, where privileged from all over world congregate. Think about what bloody firefight would do to your tourism industry. All my men will be dead and many of yours. My men are very good at their job." Pavlov let the image sink in. "A better solution is that I come with you peacefully. I will officially defect and tell you all I know about SVR. As colonel, I have great deal of information. In exchange, you will place my men on charter plane to Moscow, still wearing their balaclavas and thus retaining anonymity. That way maybe they can still remain part of SVR. No harm has been done to anyone yet. Let us not spill blood needlessly."

Gallant glanced at Brennan.

"Wait here," Brennan told Pavlov. "And you can put your hands down."

Brennan and Gallant entered one of the vans, which was filled with communications equipment.

"He said nothing about having hostages," Brennan said. "I wonder where the civilians are."

The two men placed calls to their respective superiors. Within minutes they returned to the colonel.

"We agree to your proposal, Colonel," Gallant said. "Have your men gather their weapons, minus their magazines, and go to their cars. They will be escorted by two of our military vehicles to the airport in Nice where they will board an airplane. As for you, you can go with my friend, here." Gallant motioned to Brennan.

"Thank you, gentlemen. It is good to see rationality win once in while."

The colonel returned to the house. Within minutes his men walked out carrying their weapons, still wearing their balaclavas, and entered their cars. They were escorted by two military vehicles out of the compound onto the road to Nice.

Brennan led Colonel Pavlov to a black car and got inside the back.

"Well, Colonel, let's go to my office where I have a bottle of Stoli in the freezer."

CHAPTER SIXTY-EIGHT

Antibes, France
May 1993

THEY LAY IN bed in the old house, wrapped around each other, watching Jack sleeping peacefully in his small bed next to theirs. Hefflin had arrived just as his mother-in-law, Yvette, then Catherine carrying Jack, walked out of the old house surrounded by the French military, like prisoners freed from decades of incarceration.

"I don't know what would have happened if they had found us," Catherine now said.

"I would have gone to Moscow and they would have let you go," Hefflin said.

"And then what?"

"I would have had to learn a new language. Not so bad."

She elbowed him gently on the ribs.

"The truth is, that for the first time, I felt like a father," he said. "I don't know what I intended to do if I had arrived in time, but my own life no longer mattered."

"It's funny how what looks like a negative actually turns out to be a positive," she said.

"Maybe that's what the spiritualists mean when they say we're on this earth to learn," he said. "I have come to realize that all this time I wasn't just searching for Pusha. I felt cheated out of my childhood.

What I really wanted was to go back in history and live out my childhood as it was supposed to be lived, little Fili loving little Pusha, without it being torn apart. But I now realize life doesn't work that way. Your parents would have still died and you would have still been placed in the orphanage. Or maybe my parents would have adopted you and we would have grown up like brother and sister, which would have dampened any romantic future." Hefflin felt his voice crack. "In a funny way, my parents' decision to leave Romania kept our love alive all these years. And having a child of my own, and facing the possibility that I could lose him, has forced me to become an adult. Little Fili no longer pines for his little Pusha. He has found a new child to love."

"The mind works in mysterious ways."

"You mean God."

"Same thing."

They remained silent, basking in the love that permeated the room.

"You still have an operation to complete," she reminded him.

"You mean *we*."

"No, *cheri*. After today, I am not letting Jacques out of my sight. You'll have to finish this on your own."

"The Russians will never threaten you and Jack again," he said. "The President has already been informed of what happened. According to Ingram, he was livid. Going after an agent's family crosses the line. He will be speaking to President Yeltsin tomorrow."

"Another positive outcome. Maybe we saved another agent's family from going through this." She kissed his cheek softly. "And Stefan said his men had followed us from the airport in Nice? That means our pilot reported our new destination while in flight. And I paid him all that money."

"We'll take care of him later," Hefflin said, "after I finish this damned operation."

Catherine was right. He was the one who had to bring down this mole who had put his family at risk. And there were a few other loose ends he had to tie up.

CHAPTER SIXTY-NINE

New York
May 1993

THE DIAMOND DISTRICT of New York is located on West 47th Street between Fifth and Sixth Avenues. Originally established in 1795 on Maiden Lane, it moved to its present location in 1925. During the 1940s many respected jewelers had fled Europe and established businesses in the Diamond District, which further cemented its reputation. The street is often compared to a Middle Eastern souk or bazaar where deals are struck by handshakes, much of it out on the street between Orthodox Jewish men who have established trust for decades. The relatively few storefronts do not begin to tell the story. Diamond exchanges located inside the buildings represent over 3,000 individual companies, which together bring in more than 90 percent of all the diamonds that enter the U.S. Despite its name, the Diamond District deals in gems of all types, as well as antique jewelry and rare watches.

Squeezed in among the storefronts stood one that dealt mainly in watches: The Watchman. Hefflin sat in a restaurant across the street, peering out the window at the store's entrance. He wondered how many times he had walked past that storefront without noticing it, even as he shopped for Catherine's engagement ring, which he had eventually bought from an old established firm in one of the small offices hidden inside one of those buildings.

His Patek Philippe, which he had also bought from the same firm, now read 5:45 p.m. The FBI team had been surveilling the store for the past three days, and they were getting restless. This was the last day the mole could deliver his intel to The Watchman for it to arrive on time in Athens, and the store was due to close in fifteen minutes.

He had spent the past several weeks planning this sting operation with Ingram and the FBI. Ingram had kept it all so secret that not even his assistant was aware of it. The FBI had relegated the planning and implementation of the operation to an elite anti-terrorist squad, which functioned apart from the normal intelligence-gathering system. Such were the preparations to isolate the operation from any senior members of the CIA, and thus the mole.

A taxi stopped in front of The Watchman and Hefflin's pulse spiked. But then a woman whom he didn't recognize emerged and walked into another store. He told himself to calm down, that the only thing at stake was the Agency, and his life.

Other people entered the store, other taxis stopped to let out passengers, and Hefflin's nerves rattled. After having surveilled the store for three days, he realized how tiring a stakeout could be, especially in a busy city like New York. He wished Catherine were there to help him in this culmination of their operation, but he couldn't tear her away from Jack. He wondered what new twists their marriage would now take.

Many of the storefronts stood dark, having closed at five. It was now nearing six, and The Watchman store was showing its customers out. Through the store window he could see the personnel inside removing the watches from the displays to be locked inside their safe. A moment later, a man came out and pulled down the metal grating over the display window, then the lights turned off one by one until the store stood in complete darkness.

The fucking guy didn't show up!

What had gone wrong? Had they missed the transaction? Had the mole delivered the package using a faceless middleman? Hefflin couldn't imagine the mole trusting anyone else with such intelligence, and certainly not "the motherlode" that the mole had promised for his final delivery.

He heard the orders on his earpiece: "Wrap it up. All units retreat." He saw the telephone repairman, the municipal workers on the street, and several plainclothes agents slowly drift away.

Hefflin remained at his table in the restaurant, still stunned, depression slowly seeping in. They had missed their one chance of finding the mole and avoiding an intelligence catastrophe.

CHAPTER SEVENTY

New York
May 1993

HE SPENT THE evening in a daze. After arriving home, he told Catherine what had happened in just one sentence, "He didn't show up," then retreated to the bedroom and plopped onto the bed fully clothed. She came in a few minutes later and lay beside him.

"He must have gone underground," she said. "He got scared. It's not a surprise. There was nothing you could have done differently."

"It was my operation, and it failed."

"You're always ready to take the blame. You haven't been a field agent long enough to know failure. Operations go wrong all the time, for a variety of reasons."

He knew she was right. He remembered saying something similar to Stanton when they had found out the intel to Ceausescu's offshore accounts that Soryn had provided was outdated.

"I don't know how you guys do it," Hefflin had said. "You go to all this trouble, even risk your lives, and then find out that your contact lied, or got you outdated information, or was just plain wrong."

Stanton's reply: "Welcome to field operations."

"You're right," Hefflin now said as he turned to kiss Catherine. "We have Jack, and we have our lives. Let the Russians have the damned intel. Yeltsin is now a friend."

And yet he knew he didn't quite believe what he was saying. Yeltsin had declared the end of communism in Russia and the beginning of a new friendship with America. But Yeltsin was just a temporary leader who could lose his position at any time, or who could just change his mind. Once Russia got back on its feet, its intelligence services would become an even more formidable force.

He fell into a deep, dreamless sleep. His mind wanted to forget everything that had taken place and start a fresh, new life without the worry of world politics and the KGB, or SVR, or whatever they called it now. When he awoke it was almost noon, and he realized he had slept fully clothed, Catherine having apparently decided to leave him undisturbed.

He showered and shaved, then dressed for breakfast. He was looking forward to a leisurely brunch with Catherine before he would need to fly to Langley to review the failed operation. As he was about to search for Catherine, the phone rang, a male voice.

"Mr. Hefflin, a car will pick you up in two minutes."

They can't wait to drag me over the coals.

Hefflin rushed down to the building entrance without even having had time to find Catherine. A black Ford sat waiting outside. A man in a dark suit and sunglasses opened the back door. Hefflin was surprised to see Ingram sitting in the back seat, his face grim.

"I didn't know you were in New York," Hefflin said as he slid inside. "It looks like we struck out. I'm sorry."

"We miscalculated, underestimated." Ingram scowled. "My fault as much as yours, Bill. I got word from the NSA a half hour ago, just as I was preparing to get back to Langley. It took them two fucking days to find the message."

"What message?"

"While you were gone, the NSA detected a second call from a D.C. pay phone to a number in Bucharest. The second pay phone was a mile away from the first. After that, they tapped all pay phones in a five-mile radius."

"A second call? The mole probably informed the KGB that I was arriving in Bucharest," Hefflin said.

"Two days ago, there was a third call to Bucharest from a pay phone three miles away from the first two. This one the NSA was able to record. Here's the transcript." Ingram handed Hefflin a piece of paper. It read: "Intercepted the following telephone call from D.C. public phone to a number in Bucharest at 8:47 p.m. on May sixteenth: *Berlin to Moscow night train on the eighteenth.*"

"Just the mole's voice? Any response."

"No. That was it."

"Did anyone listen to see if they recognized it?"

"They're doing it as we speak. But I've been told the voice is disguised."

Hefflin stared at the message, his mind racing.

"The last package!" Hefflin exclaimed. "His motherlode. He's not sending it; he's delivering it personally. He's decided to defect!"

Ingram grimaced. "I arrived at the same conclusion."

"But why Berlin?" Hefflin asked. "And why a train?"

"There's a three-day NATO security conference taking place in Berlin right now," Ingram said. "Most of our top people are there. And most of them are on our list of suspects. I didn't go because of this operation. As for the train, it makes sense. It's safer for him. There's no passenger manifest, no passport check, as in an airport. It's anonymous. They only check passports on the train while en route."

"We've got to stop him from getting to Moscow," Hefflin said.

"Today's the eighteenth. It is now almost six in the afternoon in Berlin. The night train to Moscow leaves in an hour. And there are other local trains he could take, depending on the route he chooses."

"No, I think he'll take the most direct route," Hefflin said. "The night train to Moscow, that's what he said. We have to get some of our Berlin men to the train station before that train leaves."

"There are over a dozen top agency officials at the conference who are on the list of suspects, Bill. Our field agents wouldn't recognize them. By the time we send them photographs and get our men to the train station it would be too late."

Hefflin thought for a moment. "I know most of those men."

"What are you thinking?"

"If I fly out within the hour . . ." Hefflin started calculating. "The night train stops in Warsaw, if I'm not mistaken."

"Yes, then goes through Belarus. But that would be cutting it close. And I can't scrounge up a government plane that fast."

"No need, Elliot. I have my private plane. Have an Agency man meet me at the Warsaw train station with the visas I need to get into Belarus, then Russia, if necessary."

"I can't give you any backup. We only have a skeletal crew right now in Warsaw."

"I'm only looking for one man. I don't need backup."

Ingram clutched Hefflin's arm. "You have to get him before the train crosses the Russian border, Bill. If not, God help us."

CHAPTER SEVENTY-ONE

Warsaw, Poland
May 1993

WARSZAWA CENTRALNA, THE Warsaw Central train station, was a modernist structure completed in 1975 under the communist regime. Although it had some innovative features for its time, such as automatic doors and escalators, the train tracks and food stalls were all completely underground, making the entire experience gloomy. By 1993, it had already undergone multiple rounds of repair for poor workmanship and design flaws.

Hefflin had always had mixed feelings about train stations. On the one hand, they represented the starting point of his family's escape from the darkness of communism into the sunny world of Greece. On the other, the memories of Gara de Nord in Bucharest always brought on feelings of apprehension, even terror, that instantly regressed him to a child hanging onto his mother's skirt for dear life. The smell of the tar covering the pebbles on the tracks was enough to harken back to memories of the confusion of track numbers and trains; of the crowds running to board or wildly embrace their loved ones for the last time; of the fear of getting on the wrong train or of missing the train altogether; of the loss of his dear Pusha.

The train from Berlin was scheduled to arrive in a few minutes, but no one from the Warsaw bureau had yet made contact. He needed those damned visas in case his pursuit forced him to enter

Belarus or, God forbid, Russia. Without them, he would be forced to disembark at the border.

As if out of nowhere, the train suddenly appeared and eased into the station. The crowd grew excited. The hurried embraces, the gathering of luggage, the pushing and shoving increased Hefflin's tension. He noticed a man in a gray suit elbowing his way through the crowd, searching, then making eye contact. The man pushed his way toward him, then palmed a small envelope into his hand as he passed by.

Why is it always at the last fucking moment? Is God a writer of thrillers?

The envelope contained an official first-class ticket. Attached were the visas, which the Warsaw bureau had created in their basement. Hefflin allowed the throngs to embark, then as the conductor whistled last call, he climbed onto the train.

A few moments later he felt the jolt, then the slow movement of the train, which brought on a hint of the nausea that accompanied his childhood memories. He quickly realized he was in the wrong car and started making his way toward the first-class car. The narrow corridor was crammed with people, some searching for their compartments, others leaning out the windows yelling their last goodbyes to the friends left behind.

In the first-class car he found his compartment and settled in. At least he wouldn't have to share. He decided to let the bedlam die down before he began his search. He placed his one carry-on on the top shelf and sank into the seat to meditate his nausea away.

CHAPTER SEVENTY-TWO

HEFFLIN STOOD AT the front of the second-class car contemplating his dilemma. He had gone up and down the first-class car knocking on compartment doors, pretending he had lost his traveling companion, searching for a familiar face among the mostly Eastern European ones, and had come up empty. The train ride to Moscow was long and tedious, and he couldn't imagine the mole doing it in anything but first class. But perhaps the mole was ultra-careful, even paranoid. Hefflin now needed to search the second- and third-class cars before the train crossed into Belarus in about an hour. The Republic of Belarus had become an independent country in 1991 after the dissolution of the Soviet Union, but its ties to Russia remained strong, as did its old authoritarian instincts.

There were two second-class cars, with compartments that could be shared, similar to the first class but with four beds in each instead of two. He jostled his way down the corridor between old ladies and tall, solid men who hung out the windows for a smoke and held their ground as he squeezed by. The doors to many of the compartments stood ajar, with people walking in and out, sharing food and gossip in various languages—Polish, German, Belarus, and Russian.

He knocked on the doors that stood shut, excusing himself in Romanian. Sometimes he was met by friendly faces, other times by angry men who tried to block his view of the compartment. Almost an hour passed without his being any closer to finding the mole, and his hopes of success quickly faded.

When he reached the third-class car, his heart sank. It consisted of a narrow corridor lined with rows of bunk beds on both sides. The passengers were mostly Belarusian men traveling to Russia for work. The car stank of body odor, tobacco, and cabbage. Dirty feet hung over the sides of the beds while men smoked or ate homemade meals. A line had formed outside the one bathroom at the back of the car. A baby's cry rang out from one bunk where a lone woman was trying to breastfeed it.

He felt the train slow down, then stop. They had reached the Belarus border. The train doors opened and men in different uniforms boarded. They immediately shouted, "Passports!" then "Narcotics! Contraband!" at the top of their voices. They began pulling down bags and suitcases from the bunks and emptied their contents in the middle of the corridor. One official found a bag of chewing tobacco and confiscated it; another removed a sweater from a valise and stuffed it inside his uniform.

Hefflin returned to his compartment disgusted. The officials in the first-class car acted with less vehemence, but with the same stern demeanor. When they saw Hefflin's American diplomatic passport and visa to enter Belarus, they simply nodded without asking to search his bag. They would have found nothing but a change of clothes, a toothbrush, and toothpaste. He carried his Beretta in an ankle holster, knowing that officials rarely patted down anyone on these trains, especially in first class, and especially diplomats.

Alone in his compartment again, he was at a loss of what to do next. Either the mole had not boarded the train, or he had missed him, which was more likely. He felt the train start to move. As he gazed out the window, he saw they were passing the lights of the border station into Belarus, followed by the looming darkness beyond. They would reach the Russian border in a little over nine hours. As the silence of the night settled over his compartment, the steady tick-tock of the train wheels eased him into a gentle slumber.

*   *   *

He awoke with a start. A knock? He looked around his cabin, and for a moment he didn't know where he was. Then, as the whole scene came back to him, he looked at his watch. He had dozed off for two hours. He heard a second knock, more insistent.

When he pulled open the door, he found a conductor and, behind him, a tall man dressed in work clothes. The workman dismissed the conductor with a few words in Russian, then removed a Makarov pistol from his jacket pocket. He motioned for Hefflin to raise his arms, then closed the door behind him.

"Who are you?" Hefflin asked in English. "What do you want?"

"Turn around," the man demanded in Russian-accented English.

Hefflin did so. The Russian frisked him and found his Beretta in his ankle holster, which he inserted under his belt, then ordered him to sit on the bed.

A moment later the door opened and a man with long white hair and beard stood in the doorway. He was dressed in peasant clothes and wore a *shapka* Russian hat pulled over his eyes.

"Hello, Hefflin," the man said.

Hefflin looked at the man closely, trying to peer under the hat to see the eyes. When he recognized him, his heart sank.

"No! Say it isn't so."

"It is so, dear fellow."

"Tyler?"

CHAPTER SEVENTY-THREE

Train to Moscow
May 1993

TYLER MOTIONED FOR the tall Russian to leave the room, then removed a Sig Sauer from his pocket and sat across from Hefflin.

"He'll be outside, in case I need him, my SVR escort. I thought I saw you enter the third-class car, so I sent him ahead to find you." Tyler looked around the cabin. "This is certainly more civilized than traveling among the unwashed."

"Why did you bother finding me?" Hefflin asked. "I never would have recognized you in that disguise."

"I know how innovative you can be, Hefflin. I didn't want you to do something crazy." Tyler chuckled. "Besides, I feel I owe you an explanation. It's the only chance I'll have."

"So why, Tyler?"

"That's always the question, isn't it?" Tyler said as he leaned back. "Why would you betray your country? I have everything anybody would ever want—wealth, a great education, a loving family." Tyler waved his hand in dismissal. "Yes, my adoptive parents loved me, all right, as one loves a pet. I was the entire family's pet—the kid they saved from a horrible fate, even though none of them actually said it. They're wealthy, bleeding-heart liberals."

"You were adopted? I never knew."

Tyler let his gaze drop to the floor. "That's right. It's not in my files. My adoptive parents did their best to hide it. They even forbade me to refer to them as anything but my parents. Not to spare me, mind you, but to spare their embarrassment. Such hypocrites. And I took it all, even as my hatred of them grew—their exorbitant lifestyle, their constantly scrutinizing the stock market, their petty fear it would all melt away, and their unquenchable thirst for more."

Tyler looked away. "I should have revolted, but I was too much of a coward for that. I needed a good education, so I bided my time, waiting for the opportunity."

"The opportunity for what?"

"To bring down the whole house of cards of this infantile, petty society. But I didn't know how. When I was punched by the Fly Club and Pincus approached me for a possible career in the CIA, I knew I had found my chance."

"For what? Revenge at your adoptive parents?"

"Revenge is too petty. I saw myself as the Archangel Michael leading God's forces against greed and a decadent society."

Tyler stopped, no doubt realizing how insane he sounded.

"No, Hefflin, I'm not delusional. Have you noticed the world around you? The homeless, the lack of healthcare, the generations of the poorly educated that remain mired in the bottom of the cesspool, the half of the country that has nothing for their old age?" Tyler's face grew red, his eyes bulging with anger. "Of course not. We've all been trained to avoid thinking about them, or even seeing them lying in the gutter. The wealthiest country in the history of the world, and half the population lives from paycheck to paycheck, and fifteen percent live in poverty. Who is all this wealth for, Hefflin?"

"So, instead of working to improve it, you decided to try to destroy it?"

"Damn right. I knew I couldn't fix it from within, but I could bring it down from within." Tyler sank back in his chair, deflated. "I know that my efforts alone haven't been enough. But I've surely opened a gash, maybe even hit the carotid. It will take decades for the Agency to figure out everything I've spilled. Some of it they'll never know. Damn them all."

"I could argue that democracy is the best system among poor choices," Hefflin said. "The communists tried and failed."

"Apparatchiks! Poseurs, all of them! Communists in name only. All they cared about was feathering their own nests. Marx would turn in his grave."

"How were you adopted?" Hefflin asked, trying to turn the discussion away from politics.

Tyler smirked. "They wanted to do something good in the world to allay their guilt, so they adopted an orphan, from Romania, no less. How pathetic. Perhaps if they gave away their millions to the poor it would mean something. As it is, it was just a token."

Hefflin's mind froze. "You are Romanian?"

"Not really, as it turns out, but that's another story," Tyler muttered.

Hefflin's pulse bounded in his chest. Was this another of life's coincidences? No, this wasn't ordinary life they were discussing, but the life of a spy in which there were no coincidences.

"Do you know who your biological parents were?"

Tyler stared ahead, settling into a kind of hypnosis. "I didn't know for a long time. Then in late May of my senior year at Harvard a tall man with a goatee just started walking alongside me one afternoon as I was going to Widener Library. At first I thought he was a professor. But then he said he had information about my natural father and that we should go to a bar and talk. My parents had already told me I was adopted, so, naturally, I was intrigued."

Tyler stroked his fake beard, remembering. "For the next few days, we spent long evenings at bars discussing everything under the sun—world politics, communism, capitalism, the military industrial complex, and the poor everywhere that suffer at the hands of corrupt politicians. He kept avoiding talking about my father. On the last day, while we were sitting at a bar, he suddenly removed his beard and wig, which I hadn't even noticed were fake. That's when he told me *he* was my father. He said he wanted me to see his real face. He still refused to tell me his name, however. He said it was for my protection as well as his. He said he was KGB, then even showed me his passport and said he had many, under different aliases, and could travel anywhere in the world. The one he was using at the time had his picture with the goatee and wig and was under the name of Anatoly Popov."

Tyler smiled as he gazed up into the distance. "I guess he thought no pictures of him existed with which I could identify him. But about a year later, when I was working for the Agency, I went through their files on a whim to see if we had a photo of him. By sheer luck I found one of him standing on Lenin's tomb behind Brezhnev. He was identified as Vladimir Dovrosky."

Boris! Tyler is Boris's son? Christ! There are *no coincidences in the life of a spy.*

CHAPTER SEVENTY-FOUR

Train to Moscow
May 1993

Hefflin remained silent, digesting this surprise while trying to decide whether to tell Tyler that his father was Boris, Hefflin's asset. Would it matter to him?

"Did your father convince you to spy for him?" Hefflin asked.

"No, that was my idea later, after I had been in the CIA for a few years. He reappeared when I was in Vienna attending a security conference. He just jumped into my cab one evening as I was about to go back to my hotel. I didn't even recognize him at first. He wore a white beard, a different nose. He said he just wanted to see how I was doing. We got out at some corner and started walking. He began pontificating on how stupid both sides were, the West and the Soviets, how they wasted billions on the military instead of improving the lives of their people. He went on for a long time. Until then I hadn't told him my own feelings on the matter, but his ranting gave me the courage to do so. So, I started on my own diatribe about the many problems in America and how I thought communism, at least in theory, sounded much fairer. All for one and one for all, like *The Three Musketeers*." Tyler grinned. "He told me to forget about it, that communism didn't work either, that it was even more corrupt than capitalism."

"So, what did he believe in?"

"He sounded almost mystical," Tyler said. "He preached personal freedom, yet aimed at the common good, creative minds working for the spiritual oneness of mankind. He spoke of degrading both the East and West until they realized it was pointless to keep wasting their money on the military and on petty squabbles. He was an idealist, I realized, but so was I. After listening for a long time, I suggested that I could help. I remember he gave me one of his looks. 'How do you propose to do that?' he asked. That's when I suggested that I pass on CIA intel to him."

"What did he say to that?"

"He rejected it outright. He said that kind of spying would get me killed, and that he had enough assets, he didn't need another one. But I insisted. I tried to expand on his argument. I said that when both sides realized they couldn't keep their secrets, that they were leaking like a sieve, it would finally bring them to the negotiating table. In addition, sharing intel would prevent stupid mistakes, miscalculations. I bragged that I was good at my job, that it would not be risky. In the end I even threatened that if he refused, I would go to the KGB directly." Tyler grinned. "That shook him up. He finally relented. 'That is crazy idea, but sometimes crazy ideas are best,' he said. That's when he told me about The Watchman system he was using with his assets."

Tyler played with his pistol, his face gaunt. "Our arrangement went on until 1990 when I received a letter from him. He said he was sick, that he didn't have long to live, and that our arrangement had come to an end. I mourned his loss, of course, and didn't do anything for over a year. But then I decided to see if our system was still in place. I figured that someone else in the KGB must have taken over his assets. So, I sent a message via The Watchman to the KGB to see if our arrangement could be revived. I told them I was an asset who wanted to resume our relationship. I intended to maintain my anonymity, so I instructed them to place an ad in the *International Herald Tribune* stating 'Interested in American academic to study the Amazon forests' if the system was still functioning. I saw an ad a few weeks later, but it was altered. It stated, 'Who is academic interested in Amazon forests? No such interest shown before.' I realized then that my father had been fooling me all that time, that he had never passed my intel to the KGB, probably to protect me." Tyler's face grew crimson with anger. "Apparently the KGB was afraid that I might be a CIA plant trying to infiltrate their system. So I sent them intel via The Watchman to establish my credentials, and the system started again, for real this time."

"When was this?"

"Early 1992."

"So, none of your intel before 1992 got to the KGB?"

"Apparently not. During that whole time I was a field agent, relatively low on the totem pole, so the intel I sent my father had been relatively low quality. But then in 1990 the Agency started promoting me into administrative positions until, finally, in '92, I was made deputy director of counterintelligence. It was then that I had access to your file with Boris. One of my packages was that intel, describing a mole inside the KGB, code-named Boris, whom you ran."

Mayfield must have read that intel before passing it on to the Russians. He knew I had been Boris's handler even at our first meeting at the conference. He had told the Russians, but why hadn't he told Gorga? To appear like a big man in the Russians' eyes? To have an ace up his sleeve in case Gorga ever crossed him?

Hefflin listened to Tyler's story, then shook his head. "Your father told you that communism was no better. The Soviet Union has fallen, Tyler. Russia is now a democracy, and Yeltsin has instituted a free market system. So why are you defecting?"

Tyler sighed, his eyes focused on his hands. "All moles are blown in the end, Hefflin, you know that. Sooner or later they would have found me. I'd rather be a hero with the SVR than spend my life in prison. Besides, I think I've delivered enough goods to them to shake up the Agency."

"I'm sorry to have to tell you this, Tyler, but you haven't been sending your packages to the Russians."

Tyler's face turned ashen. "What do you mean?"

"You're an idealist, Tyler. I was, too, once. But I learned to accept that people are flawed. That's why religion and communism are failing. And that's why demagogues fail. Your father taught me that."

Tyler stared at him, his mouth agape. "You knew my father?"

"I knew him well, as Boris."

Tyler's face twisted, his white beard and hair turning his face into a mask of horror. "Boris? But he was your asset. No, no."

"He is buried in a Brooklyn cemetery under a headstone bearing the name Vladimir Kopsin. And the intel you've been sending since his death has gone to a man named Constantin Gorga, a former Romanian Securitate colonel. He has become one of the most powerful men in Romania, partly with the help of your intel."

Tyler stared at Hefflin as if unable to take it all in. "I betrayed my own father? But I don't understand. I never heard of this Gorga."

"Before your father died, he passed on his Watchman system, along with his assets, to his close friend Gorga. You, apparently, were not on that list. That's why, when you started sending your intel again, Gorga didn't know anything about you. But he immediately realized the intelligence you were providing was very valuable, more valuable than what was coming from any of the other assets. He passed some of it to the KGB to keep them happy, including my relationship with Boris, and sold the rest to the highest bidders."

"So, my intel has been spread around, like grain?"

"To our adversaries, it was more like manna from heaven," Hefflin said. "Much of your intel was sent to our Middle Eastern enemies—the PLO, the Syrians, the Libyans, the Iranians, maybe even to al-Qaeda. You have the blood of countless lives on your hands."

"No, no. That's not what I meant to do!" Tyler burst out. "I only meant to degrade the superpowers so they could come to their senses."

Hefflin remained silent, letting Tyler digest the catastrophic consequences of his actions. Finally, Tyler looked up at Hefflin.

"Sorry about all this, Hefflin. None of it was personal."

"But it was personal, Tyler. You placed me and my family in danger. The Russians tried to abduct my wife and son."

Tyler shook his head. "I didn't know. I never meant . . ."

"You notified the KGB about the defector's pickup point."

Tyler nodded. "I knew he was a KGB agent from Bucharest, though I didn't know his identity. Nor did I know it would be you who would meet him. You were no longer even in the Agency. My father had given me a direct number to call in case of emergency. I had never used it before. It was all anonymous. I just left a message on a recording machine."

"That number must have gone directly to the KGB, not to Gorga," Hefflin thought out loud. "While your father was alive, he was probably monitoring it himself. After his death, someone else in the KGB must have received your message."

They sat silent, each unraveling the convoluted events. Then Tyler looked up, his eyes that of a child.

"Tell me how you met my father, Hefflin."

Hefflin recounted his entire history with Boris, including his father's story, in the hope of changing Tyler's plans. He didn't mention Ceausescu's money. Either Boris had already given Tyler part of it or he hadn't. Telling Tyler about it now would only allow Tyler to have something on him. But the thought did cross his mind of giving Tyler enough of that money to help him live out his life in some Third World country under an alias. Despite Tyler's treachery, Hefflin still felt a bond with his old classmate who had helped shape his life by recruiting him into the Agency. And Tyler was Boris's son. He owed it to Boris to try to save him.

Tyler took it all in and remained silent for a long time.

"That's a hell of a story, Hefflin," Tyler finally said. "My father and yours were old and loyal friends. I wish I had known."

"Did your father ever tell you the identity of your mother?" Hefflin asked.

Tyler looked down at his hands. "He refused to tell me when he was with me. But then, early in 1990, he wrote me that letter. You should read it yourself. I don't think I can actually talk about it."

CHAPTER SEVENTY-FIVE

Train to Moscow
May 1993

Tyler removed an envelope from inside his jacket and handed it to Hefflin. Hefflin unfolded the several handwritten pages and began to read.

Dear Son,

This is difficult letter to write for many reasons. I first have to tell you that my days on earth will soon end. I have seen many traitors in my life but never suspected it of my own body. Doctors extended my life for few months, but soon my time will expire. I have been like Russian bear all my life, but now I feel like lamb going to slaughter. So be it. Another alias. I will probably have to break down the Pearly Gates to get in, but maybe Saint Peter has mercy.

At times like this, one usually looks back at life and begins to regret all things he could have done differently. I will not do that. They are just too many. But there are few things that must be set straight.

First, obviously our arrangement has to end. I never thought it was good idea, but I did it to protect you from worse consequences.

Second, I think time has come to tell you about your mother and how you came to bless our lives.

My story goes back many decades, when I first came to Bucharest as KGB agent after War. It was time of youth when passions are highest. At that time, I was accompanying Romanian military unit to clear out illegal gypsy campsites. Gypsies were considered antirevolutionaries by Romanian government because they could never be controlled. That has not changed. Irony is now that communists are gone, I suspect they will be treated even worse.

One evening, as military unit came upon gypsy camp outside Bucharest, I saw most beautiful sight in my life: striking gypsy woman dancing around campfire, with many men and women clapping. She had long, black hair and wore dress made of brilliant colors, with gold bracelets around her wrists and ankles that jangled with every step. Okay, so maybe she did not wear bracelets, and maybe her dress was old and torn, but that is how I like to remember her. Her face was like Cleopatra, her smile was more brilliant than fire around which she danced, her long legs moved like gazelle. What can I tell you, I fell in love then and there. You can say it was lust, and I may agree with you, but it quickly became much more.

I ordered unit to retreat and return to base. Then I sat in forest and watched her dance, mesmerized. More I saw, more in love I fell.

When it was over, they put out fire and everyone went to tents or horse wagons. I watched her enter her tent and saw she slept alone. So, I made decision. It was crazy idea but, you know, sometimes crazy ideas are best.

So, in middle of night, I entered her tent. I woke her up with kiss. I was no brute. She woke up frightened, but did not scream. I have to say that in my youth I was pretty good looking. After she saw me, she kissed me passionately on lips. We talked half of night about her life as gypsy, and I quickly realized how special and misunderstood gypsies were. We made love that first night. Afterward, she said I should come back next night and night after that. Our love affair went on for months. Most of time she came to forest and we made love under stars.

Then one day she told me she was pregnant. But, since I was stupid young man, I did not know what blessing that was, so I said I would arrange for abortion. It could be done secretly, without anyone knowing. I could arrest her entire clan, separate them, then bring her to doctor. But she said no, that she wanted our baby, that she loved me. She knew what that could mean—she could be disowned by her gypsy clan and abandoned. She also knew we could never get married. My superiors would never allow me to marry gypsy. But she did not care. She told me to go, that she would plead with her father and face whatever happened alone.

I did not leave, of course, but watched her from afar. Then one day I caught boy from her clan trying to steal pocket watch from old man. I took him by scruff of neck and told him only way he could stay out of jail was to spy for me. After a few months he told me that her clan discovered her pregnancy and she confessed. She told them that father was young lieutenant in Romanian military and pleaded with them not to banish her. But voivode of clan, who was also her father, had to set example, and not be accused of bending rules for his daughter. So, he told her to leave with what she could carry on her back and they burned everything else she owned. Her name would never be spoken again.

I found her on street after she took entire bottle of sleeping pills she stole. She was so hurt by her father's decision, so crazed out of her mind, that she even forgot about her baby. I immediately brought her to good doctor I knew who pumped her stomach and saved her life and that of baby. Another debt I owed him.

While she was recovering, I came up with another crazy idea. I told her we could provide home for baby in West where he could grow up happier than in Romania. Life under communism was miserable. There was never enough food or clothes or hot water or electricity. Gypsies were hated, as they still are. Baby would have terrible life no matter how much money I provided. At first she did not want to give baby away, but then she realized I was right. Your happiness was what was most important.

In those days, gypsies were allowed to travel to Turkey, so when baby came we gave him to nice gypsy family from another clan to take to Turkey. I gave them money to pay their way from Istanbul to America on ship, and they were only too happy to accept.

I found out later that when they arrived in America they immediately put baby up for adoption. He was too white-skinned, you see, to fit into their family. They advertised him as baby saved from horrible orphanages in Romania. Boy was adopted by wealthy family—another lucky stroke of gypsies. You grew up with silver spoon up your arse but, despite that, you became good student and attended Harvard. I was very proud of you.

At first I never intended to tell you about me. But I suspected that at some point your parents will give you story about Romanian orphanage, and you might go crazy trying to find your real parents. I thought truth was better than lie. So, I came to Harvard to tell you I am your father. At that time I did not know how you would react if you knew your mother was gypsy, so I refused to tell you. Now I decided you should know everything.

I once offered to take your mother out of Bucharest; I would defect so we could live together with you in America, but she refused. She thought it was better that you not know you are half

*gypsy. In addition, she said that I would always be hunted by
KGB. She was right. Besides, we could never provide opportunities
you had with wealthy family. So, she stayed in Bucharest where she
felt loved by kind doctor and his wife who saved her life and yours.
I gave her money, of course, but she did not need much. We were
both happy to hear of good life you were having in America, a life
we could never provide for you. Even though I do not think you
will ever understand way things were in those days, your mother
and I both believed we made right decision for you under difficult
circumstances. I want to let you know how much we both loved you
and how sorry we were that we were not there for you in person. It
broke your mother's heart and mine. We talked about you every
time we saw each other and cried.*

　　*Your mother's name was Isabella, but she was called
Tanti Bobo by doctor's boy, and that is how everyone knew her.
If you ever meet that boy, now a man, you will understand how
magnificent woman your mother was and how much he loved
her. She died in revolution, unfortunately, without seeing her son.
Be kind to your mother's memory, my boy. She loved you very
much.*

With all love in this life and next,
Your father

Hefflin held the letter in his hands for several minutes, unable to
put it down. His chest suddenly felt hollow, as if an evil spirit had
pulled out his soul and was now dangling it before his eyes, ready to
swallow it whole while laughing at his stupidity. He had imagined—
nay, had convinced himself!—that he was the son of that beloved
gypsy at whose breast he had suckled. It would have explained all his
feelings of being itinerant, temporary, an observer of life.

From his pocket Tyler now removed a yellowed photograph and handed it to Hefflin. It showed Boris and Isabella in their youth standing in Hefflin's family courtyard, both smiling as if they were the luckiest people alive.

"You are the doctor's son he refers to, aren't you?" Tyler asked.

"I knew her from the day I was born." Hefflin held back his tears. "She was my mother's best friend, practically my second mother. She was also my part-time wet nurse. I even have a picture of me at her breast. I drank the milk meant for you."

"That must make us brothers in a twisted way," Tyler said.

"She was a most warmhearted and loving woman, full of wisdom and magic. She could tell your fortune in tea leaves, coffee grounds, and palms, and she communicated with a crow, believe it or not." Hefflin smiled. "I loved her very much. And she missed and loved her baby."

"She almost killed me by taking poison," Tyler burst out.

"That was the spontaneous act of a crazed woman, left on the streets by her own father who followed outmoded clan traditions," Hefflin said. "She always regretted that act and was full of guilt."

"I think guilt was the primary motivation for both of them, rather than any love," Tyler said. "My father even offered me money in a second letter, postmarked in New York a few weeks after this one—millions of dollars, apparently. Why would he do that, knowing how much I detested the wealth I grew up with? Guilt. Where he got the money, I don't know. There was a P.O. box return address. I wrote him back and told him to keep it."

So Boris did offer Tyler some of Ceausescu's money.

"Don't be so angry, Tyler. Accept your life and roots. Embrace them. I've had to do the same."

Tyler let out a long breath, as if purging himself of old pain. "Do me a favor, Hefflin. Keep everything you've learned to yourself. The truth is, I'm ashamed to have my background made public—the bastard son of a KGB agent and a gypsy whore. I know that's hypocritical of me, but that's how I feel."

Tyler lit a match and set fire to both the letter and the photograph.

"Haven't you heard anything I've said?" Hefflin burst out.

"I know nothing about those days or that cursed country of yours," Tyler said. "All I know is that I grew up with dreams of my real parents being some deposed Romanian royalty, or a famed scientist whose child was taken away, or at the very least something resembling the family I grew up with. I'm glad you loved her, Hefflin, and I'm sure she was a good woman. I just don't think I'd have anything to say to her."

Hefflin nodded. Tyler had grown up in a world where a gypsy mother would never have been accepted, or understood. And he had adopted those same beliefs, despite the fact that he rejected that world. Another unanchored spirit, now almost destroyed.

"I have one more question to tie up so I can go to my grave with some understanding," Hefflin said.

"Don't be so melodramatic, Hefflin. I have no intention of harming you, just of detaining you until we reach the Russian border."

"You were the one who placed the chalk mark on the tree in Central Park and planted the spike with the message, right?" Hefflin asked.

Tyler looked up, confused. "What chalk mark?"

"C'mon, Tyler, you read about it in my file, the method Boris used to contact me. You thought leaving a message from Boris would rile me, since you didn't know Boris was dead, and you figured I'd tell the Agency because I'm such a Boy Scout. That would cause the Agency to suspect that Boris had been working for the Russians all along, and that I was the mole, which would divert the Agency's attention from the real mole, from you."

"Hefflin, I swear to you I don't know what you're talking about," Tyler said, his voice rising. "Your file says nothing about how Boris contacted you. There's obviously a piece of this puzzle you haven't quite figured out. I suggest you look elsewhere."

Hefflin sat silent, calculating. He had never read his own file. If the details of how Boris had made contact were not in his file, then who would know?

"All right," Hefflin said. "One more thing. What is this final motherlode delivery to the Russians?"

Tyler removed a disk from inside his jacket. "Oh, this? Just a Mac-Guffin, as Hitchcock would say. I can't very well tell you, can I? Then I'd have to kill you." Tyler smiled, then exited the compartment.

CHAPTER SEVENTY-SIX

Train to Moscow
May 1993

THE RUSSIAN RETURNED and sat across from Hefflin as before, brandishing his Makarov.

"How long are you going to keep me here?" Hefflin asked.

"Until I receive orders," the man answered, "in Smolensk."

"But this train doesn't stop in Smolensk," Hefflin said.

"It will for me."

"But what if I don't want to go to Smolensk?"

The Russian grinned. "Then you go to hell. Less trouble for me."

"Well, if that's how you're going to be, I might as well get some shut-eye," Hefflin said, then lay down in the bed and closed his eyes.

The silence returned, even deeper than before. The hypnotic sounds of the train wheels allowed Hefflin to meditate on what he had learned. Tanti Bobo and Boris. Two of the dearest people in his life had loved each other. Tyler's parents. It didn't fit. Tyler was not worthy. Boris must have realized that Tyler would never accept his mother. "Spending my last months on earth with Vasili, true son of mine," Boris had written in his letter to The Owl.

A tinge of hurt passed through him. Tanti Bobo and Boris had both lied to him, or at least had kept information from him. But he understood their reasons. This part of the story was not about him, but about their giving Tyler a better life in America, which Tyler had squandered. It bore a resemblance to his own life, he realized. His parents had come to America to give him a better life. His father had been fifty years old when they left Romania, and his mother forty. They had endured a year in the refugee camp in Athens, then had to learn a new language and create a new life in America. His father had to study medicine all over again in English, then pass the various medical boards, do a residency, and start a new medical career in his late fifties.

His mother worked in a sweatshop to feed the family while his father was studying. He remembered how she would come home every evening, drained from eight hours of sitting behind a sewing machine, then cook and clean until late in the evening. He sometimes heard her weeping in his parents' bedroom, alone, hiding her sorrow from her husband and son.

He doubted that he would have had the courage and strength to start a new life in a strange country at that age. His parents were made of sterner stuff. He suddenly felt a wave of pride at being their son, a Greek, now an American. An honorable heritage.

The Russian's breathing now sounded deep and steady, blending with the tick-tock of the train to form a duet. Hefflin let one eye slide open. The Russian had leaned back in his chair, his eyes partly closed, the gun resting in his lap. Hefflin considered lunging at him but the Russian suddenly coughed and opened his eyes, cleared his throat, then found a pack of cigarettes in his pocket. As he leaned down and used both hands to light the match, Hefflin saw his chance.

He sprang from his bed and reached for the gun in the Russian's lap. As his hand gripped it, he felt a heavy boot stomp his foot, followed by a blow to the side of his head. Hefflin dropped the gun and crumpled back onto the bed. The Russian lifted him up with arms as wide as tree trunks and wrapped them around his chest. Looking directly into his eyes, the Russian chuckled.

"You puny American. You think you are match for Russian bear?"

The Russian tightened his bear hug. Hefflin felt his breath being squeezed out of him. His legs dangled in the air, his arms too close to his assailant to be of any use. He felt like a rag doll, one that giant bear could throw against the wall or tear apart.

A memory, a flash. One of Catherine's Dim Mak blows. Would it work?

What the hell? I'm dead as it is.

He squiggled to free his arms a bit, clenched both fists and protruded the joint of his middle fingers, then struck the man's temples simultaneously as Catherine had taught him. It was not a hard blow, as blows go, but the best he could do. The Russian blinked several times, dropped Hefflin, then fell to the floor like an old oak.

What the hell?

The man's eyes stared blankly. Hefflin felt for a pulse but could not find one. Dead, from simultaneous blows to the temples. He couldn't believe it. According to Catherine's teachings, sensitive points on the body were somehow linked to Chi energy, a concept Hefflin had always doubted.

Whatever this Chi thing is, I have to learn more about it.

He made the sign of the cross three times, then lifted the body onto the bed and retrieved his Beretta, which he placed back in his ankle holster. He then closed the dead man's eyes and covered him up to his chin with a blanket. Just someone sleeping.

Now what?

The sun had already risen, the sky a clear blue. He had to get Tyler off the train before it reached the Russian border. At the very least, he had to grab that disk before it fell into Russian hands. He looked at his watch and calculated. They would be approaching the border in about fifteen minutes. He had to think. Tyler's words rang in his mind. "I didn't want you to do something crazy." Then he heard Boris's voice: "Vasili, sometimes crazy ideas are best."

The idea came as an image, a flash. He removed a shirt from his carry-on and lit it using his lighter. The fire quickly spread to the curtains and bed linen. As he left, the compartment was already filling with smoke.

The corridor stood empty. He ran to the far end of the car to the exit door, waited a few minutes for the smoke to infiltrate the corridor, then pulled the emergency lever on the wall.

He heard the wheels screech, then felt the train jolt, his body thrown against the wall. As the train came to a stop, people bolted out of their compartments. Hefflin cried "*Ogon!*" He hoped it meant fire in Russian. The people started screaming and rushing toward the exit doors. Hefflin pulled open the door and jumped onto the side of the track. He started running toward the back of the train where the third-class car was located. Passengers spilled out of the train cars onto the open field, forming a small crowd. When he stood outside the third-class car, he stopped to search.

An old man with a white beard. How many can there be? But as he perused the crowd, he saw no men with white beards.

Where the hell is he? What would I do in his place?

He dropped to the ground and peered under the train. A moment later he saw a pair of legs run by on the other side of the train. One pair only. He rolled under the train to the other side, then spotted Tyler, still dressed as an old man, running toward the front of the train.

Where the hell is he going?

Then he spotted it: the border, about two hundred feet ahead.

Christ! He's going to cross into Russia on foot!

Hefflin started running, the figure in front of him about fifty feet away. Hefflin felt he was gaining, but his legs began to ache, his breathing to grow heavier. Tyler was now within a hundred feet from the border outposts. The guards on both sides of the barbed wire fence raised their weapons.

Tyler cried out and raised his arms like a crazed man, still in full flight. The Belarusian guards yelled the universal "Halt!" then "Stop!" Tyler glanced behind at Hefflin, then pushed on. A Belarusian guard fired a warning shot in the air and repeated his order to stop. When Tyler was within fifty feet of the border, he reached inside his jacket pocket and removed an object. As he was about to raise his arm to throw it, two shots rang out. A cry, then Tyler fell to the ground. When Hefflin reached him, Tyler's face burst into a smile.

"I thought you'd do something crazy, Hefflin," Tyler rasped, then exhaled his last breath. In Tyler's hand Hefflin found the disk.

He was about to throw it over the border to the Russians.

Hefflin slipped the disk into his pocket and placed his Beretta in Tyler's hand. He touched Tyler's body for the last time and silently commended his spirit to the care of Boris and Tanti Bobo. He then stood and raised his diplomatic passport. "American diplomat!"

The Belarusian soldiers approached, their rifles pointing at him. Hefflin handed over his passport.

"Diplomat, you say?" a soldier asked in English. "You know this man?"

"He's an American. A terrorist. We've been after him for some time."

CHAPTER SEVENTY-SEVEN

Langley
May 1993

INGRAM PEERED AT the computer screen, scrolling through the intel contained on Tyler's disk, his face somber. After arriving back at Langley, Hefflin had spent several hours being debriefed, during which he had left certain parts out, which he intended to tell Ingram privately. At the end of the debriefing, he handed Tyler's disk to Ingram, who took it directly to his office. The more Ingram now read, the darker his face grew. He finally shut off the computer and leaned back in his chair.

"This is certainly a motherlode," Ingram finally said. "Among other things, it contains a list of our agents throughout Eastern Europe and Russia and their assets. It would have been a bonanza for the Russians. Not to mention the termination of some of our people. You're lucky the Belarusians didn't search you."

"They seemed to respect a diplomatic passport."

"The Belarusians are trying to reach out to the West, even though they hold deep ties to Russia. They even released Tyler's body without any red tape. Tyler must have been quite an angry man. Did he tell you his motive?"

"Like Philby and his gang, he was a spoiled, idealistic rich kid who was revolting against his parents' wealth, and that of the West," Hefflin said. He had no intention of telling Ingram that Tyler was

Boris's son, or that Boris was Vladimir Dovrosky. Boris would remain an enigma and, as far as the Agency was concerned, still alive, continuing his charmed life.

"We've rounded up the owners of The Watchman stores and their personnel, and I expect we'll get a great deal of intel from them about those assets." Ingram leaned back in his chair. "I don't have to tell you what this means for you, Bill. You're becoming a legend around here. You not only ran the most valuable Kremlin asset we've ever had, but now single-handedly discovered the mole that threatened to tear our agency apart. As far as I'm concerned, you can write your own ticket in the Agency."

"There are a couple of things I'd like to clear up first, Elliot. The oligarchs, for one. Gorga told me that Avery helped to create them."

"Yes, I was afraid you'd get that out of him." Ingram waved his arm in dismissal. "That was the only way Avery could convince the Securitate to join the revolution. Besides, creating a class of wealthy capitalists is an insurance policy that capitalism will survive."

"They practically own the country, Elliot, while half the population is trying to survive by rummaging in garbage cans and dealing in the black market."

"Unfortunately, that's also part of capitalism," Ingram said. "We have it in this country, too. The wealthy and the poor will always exist."

"And the oligarchs are breaking the Yugoslavian embargo by running guns to Milosevic."

"I'm aware of that."

"Of course you are. You never did anything to stop the ships I informed you about. You're using the oligarchs to supply the Muslims with Iranian arms. That's what Mayfield was doing in Lebanon. Christ. You're breaking your own embargo, Elliot. The oligarchs don't care whom they sell arms to, as long as they make a profit."

"You sleep with dogs you get fleas," Ingram said. "Everybody is breaking the embargo. At least we're trying to give the Muslims a fighting chance."

Boris had done the same, Hefflin reminded himself.

"Why did you have Mayfield killed?" Hefflin asked.

"Yes, Vogel told me you eliminated our wetworks asset. Damn waste of manpower."

"That asset killed Pincus and Stanton, you know that."

"You can't let it get personal, Bill, not in our business," Ingram said wearily. "He was just doing his job, on Avery's orders, which I only found out about later. Yes, I had Mayfield eliminated, but that was purely business. Mayfield had to go. He had his fingers in too many pies, some of which I didn't even know about. After you told me he was involved in running the mole, that was the last straw."

"He was just the errand boy. Gorga was running everything. But you don't want to get rid of Gorga, do you, or the other oligarchs?" Hefflin let out a grunt. "Well, at least I put a dent into their activities."

Ingram's eyes darted to Hefflin's. A look of awareness suddenly blossomed over his face. "What did you do?"

"The oligarchs burned down my childhood home, Elliot. That, too, was personal."

"They what? Christ. And in return, you burned down Gorga's headquarters?" Ingram shook his head. "I was wondering how that happened."

Hefflin removed a computer disc from his pocket and handed it to Ingram.

"This disc contains everything in Gorga's computers," Hefflin said. "And there were three basement floors in Gorga's building full of thousands of Securitate files on prominent Romanians for the oligarchs to use as blackmail. Gorga's building was the heart of the oligarchs, unit U0920. I couldn't let them keep it."

Ingram took the disc and stared at it for a long time.

"I must say, my opinion of you is growing by the minute, Bill." Ingram stood and walked around the room, thinking. "That explains a lot."

"What are you talking about?"

"The operation on your family. My counterpart in Moscow assured me that it was not sanctioned by the SVR, that the man you call Stefan acted on his own, at the request of Stanculescu."

Hefflin felt his chest tighten. "Stanculescu? Are you sure?"

"Stefan, apparently, spilled the beans."

"Stefan is alive?"

Ingram chuckled. "He has a cracked skull, a broken nose, and a hell of a headache, but yes, he's lying in a SVR hospital in Moscow. He wanted to be the hero who brought in Boris's handler."

"And to line his retirement fund, no doubt," Hefflin said.

"That, too. But he's an idiot. The SVR would have sent him to Siberia if he had brought you in. They might still do that."

"Why?"

"Think, Bill. What would happen if all the intelligence agencies started going after the other side's handlers? There would be a bloodbath. No agency would survive."

"But you eliminated Mayfield who was only a handler."

"Mayfield didn't work for any agency. He was a private dealer of intel for profit. I made an example of him. Besides, he had a big mouth. And he knew everything, from the events leading to the revolution to the rise of the oligarchs to the arms for the Muslims. He was a weak link. There's no room for such in our business."

A pall of silence settled over the room, each man replaying the events, the convolutions.

"The last item, Elliot: the defector. The intel he brought in about Boris being a triple agent, working for the Russians all along, was obviously used to incriminate me as the mole. He has to be a KGB plant."

"I wouldn't worry about him," Ingram said, settling back into his chair. "He's in the witness protection program, sunning himself somewhere."

"What? But everything he told us was bullshit."

"I know, Bill. He was just following orders. My orders."

CHAPTER SEVENTY-EIGHT

Langley
May 1993

HEFFLIN'S MIND RACED, trying to review the events that had occurred during the past few weeks, to fit the pieces of the puzzle.

"The defector was part of the molehunt." Hefflin shook his head in disgust.

"And it succeeded, thanks to you."

"So, he was your man?"

"No, he was real enough, a KGB asset we've been doing business with for years. We just convinced him this was the right time to defect."

"You had planned all along to have me interrogate him, to see how I would react. You gave him the false intel about Boris—the intercepted telephone call, the wire from Moscow, everything?"

"Vogel did, to be exact, before sending him out to meet you that night."

"Vogel was in on it?"

"He was only in on that one piece of it. He didn't know the whole story. He has now been moved to Berlin station. A scrub team is in place in Bucharest and a new chief of station will be installed."

"But why did you do all this?"

"Multiple reasons," Ingram said. "First, we already knew we had a mole in our midst, so I needed someone I could trust, someone outside the Agency. You were the obvious candidate. Your actions in Bucharest showed your true mettle. I needed to convince you to return to help us solve this mess. Making you the prime suspect and forcing you to prove your innocence was a powerful motivator. Second, I hoped the mole would try to inform the Russians about the defector, so I allowed some facts about the pickup spot and secondary rendezvous points to circulate among our senior staff. We change them periodically, as you know. It was a bit of a crazy idea, but—"

"—but sometimes the crazy ideas are the best," Hefflin finished the sentence.

"To my amazement, the NSA did pick up a phone call by the mole from a D.C. public phone to inform the Russians in Bucharest."

"That almost got me killed, Elliot."

"Part of our business, Bill. But that served two important purposes: First, it narrowed down the search considerably among the senior staff, to about two dozen or so. And second, it allowed me to see if you still had the stuff. You've been away two years, after all. I must say, you certainly allayed those doubts."

"There was another reason, Elliot. You needed to make sure I wasn't the mole. I still had security clearance, and was getting regular briefings. You wanted to see whether I would actually bring the defector in or eliminate him because I felt threatened by what he had to divulge, like the way Tyler felt threatened."

"Yes, you're right. No one was above suspicion, especially since you later failed to tell me that the defector muffled the listening device during your walk in the garden."

"He told me that Boris's handler was the prime suspect and he should flee if it was still possible," Hefflin muttered out loud. "That was a test?"

"Which you failed," Ingram said.

"I *was* the obvious suspect, Elliot. I didn't want to add to your suspicions."

"Understandable," Ingram said. "And you didn't follow his suggestion to run. Now, since I knew that the Russians had learned about you and Boris from the mole, another reason for setting you up was for the mole to think we suspected you, and thus put him at ease, so he wouldn't flee or go silent on us."

"But why did you send me back to Bucharest?"

"I was at my wit's end, Bill. That mole was a cancer. You were my best hope. I knew how creative you were in Bucharest, how you managed to uncover the underbelly of that rotten revolution, an analyst. If anyone could solve the puzzle, you could. Besides, we wanted to see how the Russians would react to you. We put out the word that we suspected you as the mole. If they knew their own mole's identity, they would welcome our suspicion of you because it would divert our attention from the real mole. If they didn't know his identity, then they might take the bait and try to communicate with you, which Stefan did. He tried to make you admit you were their mole and even tried to get you to help him find Boris, *our* mole inside *their* agency. When you resisted his overtures, he tried to force you into defecting by planting false intel in their Bucharest chief of station's briefcase for our man to find."

Hefflin's head was spinning. "But what if I had been the real mole and had decided to defect?"

"I trusted you by then, Bill. Besides, your family was still in New York. We had our eye on them, at least until Catherine gave us the slip."

Ingram sat back down and leaned back in his chair, stroking his chin. "All things considered, I think it all turned out pretty well, don't you? After your last meeting with Gorga, and your destruction of their headquarters, which they believe was sanctioned by the

Agency—" Ingram chuckled—"the oligarchs have been calling me to beg forgiveness. They will be better allies from now on."

"More like minions," Hefflin said. "But we also know their offshore accounts."

"Yes, we've already cut them by a third, the ones we know about, at least, as a warning," Ingram said. "But we still need the oligarchs to remain in place for now, as an anchor for that still-teetering democracy. When we think the country is stable enough on its democratic path, which will take years, we may provide evidence of their corruption to the Romanian prosecutors, if we find any brave enough to tackle them. That will be a test of their legal and judicial system."

Hefflin's mind was now moving in molasses. "What you're doing is something like terraforming, transforming an alien planet to resemble Earth. Only now you're trying to transform a former communist country to resemble a Western democracy."

"Someone has to, Bill. If not us, who?"

Hefflin marveled at the power and the arrogance of the Agency. Its cynical good intentions had paved the road to the hell that now existed in his old country. And he questioned Ingram's optimism. The corrupt Romanian psyche would take a long time to change.

"There is another factor, Bill. Since you didn't report anything new on Boris, I have to assume that he is still out there, somewhere. He will continue to be hunted down by the Russians, if for no other reason than to find out what he gave us all these years."

"He could be dead for all we know," Hefflin said.

"It even crossed my mind that Boris might have gone into the private intelligence business, like Mayfield, and was the one running the mole," Ingram said. "From the start, it didn't escape my notice that our mole became active just about the time Boris grew silent. But now that you solved the puzzle, I guess it was all a coincidence."

"The world is full of them, Elliot."

But not our world.

Ingram looked up at Hefflin, his eyes sparkling. "Yet another crazy idea that crossed my mind is that Boris might have stumbled onto Ceausescu's offshore accounts and is now enjoying his treasure on some private island somewhere. They never found it, you know."

"I'm amazed at how your imagination works, Elliot, fanciful as it is, and how many layers of thought your operations involve. I must say, my opinion of you has also increased significantly."

"Thank you, Bill. But you do know that at some point you'll need to find out what happened to Boris."

Hefflin stood without bothering to answer and dropped a piece of crumpled paper on Ingram's desk. "That's Stefan's offshore account. I would like it cleaned."

Ingram uncrumpled the paper. "Where did you get this?"

"It was part of Stefan's deal, for me to contribute to his retirement fund."

"His physical torment isn't enough for you?" Ingram chuckled. "You *are* vindictive."

"He went after my family, Elliot. He should be grateful I don't go after his."

"Remind me never to cross you, Bill. Fine. Done. His account is erased. Are we good?"

"Good?"

"With each other. I need to know we're good, Bill." Ingram's eyes bored into Hefflin's.

"We're good, Elliot. I have a lot to learn from you. And, despite all you've had to do, I think your heart is in the right place."

Ingram nodded. As Hefflin moved toward the door, Ingram said, "Oh, by the way, Gorga's body was found floating in the river this morning. I guess the oligarchs are doing their own housecleaning."

CHAPTER SEVENTY-NINE

New York
May 1993

THE FIREPLACE BLAZED in full force at Catherine's insistence, even though the weather had turned warmer. "To make our bodies glisten as if glazed with oil, like the ancient Greek fighters," she said. On the mantlepiece stood Irina's Brancusi, its enigmatic eyes observing the scene unfolding before it. Catherine lay naked on her back upon Boris's mink coat, her Cleopatra eyeliner even more pronounced than usual, with one foot resting in Hefflin's naked lap. He rested his elbow on his knee to steady it and began to carefully paint her toenails in the blood-red color she preferred. It was the first time she had asked him to paint her nails, and it seemed to arouse her. With each stroke of the brush her breathing grew heavier, her eyes drifting upward as if she were entering into a hypnotic state.

"Paint them perfectly," she whispered. "This body is for you."

His excitement rose, even as he felt the pressure of not making a mistake. He willed himself to concentrate, to steady his hand, which wanted nothing more than to touch her. After he finished each nail, he blew on it, causing a soft moan. He proceeded meticulously, Rembrandt creating his masterpiece, one gorgeous nail after another. Why hadn't she asked him to do this before? If he had known it would produce this effect, he would have painted her nails every night.

After more than a half hour, the master craftsman felt he was ready to exhibit his work. Like an artist full of trepidation at his first showing, he held up his masterpiece for inspection.

She opened her eyes, then held her focus on his creation. "Beautiful. But you're not done. In that drawer you'll find what you need." She pointed to the credenza against one wall.

Inside the drawer he found her shaving razor and a needle-shaped clamp that resembled a surgeon's instrument. In its tip it held a metal strip the thinness of a paper clip. He set them down next to her and knelt beside her, his confusion infused with unease.

She guided him to the triangle of hair below her bikini line—her insignia.

"Shave it off," she whispered.

He dared say nothing, just followed her wishes. As he shaved off the triangle of hair, he saw it. A mark.

He started slightly. He had seen it before . . . on Amanda Thayer, a scar in the shape of the letter *N*.

"He branded every girl to mark her as his, even if they were too young for him to molest." Catherine's voice now distant.

Nicu! That demon!

His pulse pounded his chest, his brain, the anger almost suffocating him.

Amanda was one of Nicu's girls! But how . . .

Then it dawned on him.

Did Mayfield fall in love with her in Nicu's harem? Did he adopt her to bring her to the U.S.?

She must have been young, for she had no obvious Romanian accent, only a slight one he hadn't been able to place. Mayfield must have sent her to a Catholic boarding school, followed by a Swiss boarding school, then Vassar, then saw to it that she became the executive secretary to the head of Nordam Industries, Mayfield's previous employer.

Christ. And all that time she was his lover, his concubine, from her early childhood. Was Mayfield even married?

He felt the nausea almost overpower him.

He set his gaze back on Catherine, her breathing deep, her eyes turned upward, almost in a state of meditation.

"It only needs one little line, *cheri*," Catherine whispered, "to make it yours."

At first, he refused to understand what she was asking of him, the image repelling him. Then he let the thought settle.

"I don't think I can," he said.

"You must. Or I will."

He took a deep breath and forced his mind to look at her the way his father, the doctor, must have looked upon the body of a patient, and as Catherine had taught him to look upon an assailant, without regard to their humanity. It was the only way he could do what she was asking.

He rose as if hypnotized and inserted the metal strip held by the clamp into the blazing fire. When the strip glowed red, he returned to her. She opened her eyes, then clasped the hand clutching the clamp, her loving gaze melting into his.

"I will not feel the pain, *cheri*, but only your love."

Could he do it? He must. It was her wish.

Her hand held his as he tried to imbue his love for Catherine into his act, to join her in the bond she was seeking, then advanced the glowing metal toward her skin. When it made contact, she did not scream or flinch, but only sighed deeply, as if feeling his love infusing into her. She clutched his hand tightly even as he tried to pull it back, even as he smelled the burning of her flesh. Finally, she let go, and his hand instantly pulled the instrument away. Before him now appeared an old scar with a new addition, a raw red line, to transform the *N* into a *W*.

"Come inside me now, and let's turn this into a celebration," she whispered.

"Not just yet. Not until I bear *your* mark."

CHAPTER EIGHTY

New York
May 1993

ON A SUNNY, warm May morning, Central Park teemed with the usual suspects, among them Hefflin, Catherine, and Bentley. The birds chirped, of course, and Bentley pulled the leash to try to catch the squirrels that always seemed to be one step ahead of him. Hefflin and Catherine walked arm in arm like two lovebirds along their usual path, enjoying the sunshine while discussing Jack and their plans for him.

"He has to go to Harvard, of course," Hefflin said.

"We have to start earlier than that," Catherine said. "He's got to be proficient in at least French and Romanian by the time he enters preschool."

"Don't overtax him."

"By age ten, I want him to excel in cat burglary, breaking and entering, safe-cracking, codes and secret writing, hand-to-hand combat, and the art of seduction."

"Seduction! At age ten?"

"It's never too early." She kissed him on the cheek.

"What, are you going to make him into a junior spy by the time he graduates grammar school?"

"Certainly not *junior.*" She winked. "I don't want him to be a spy, *cheri,* just to be prepared for life. In other words, to not start out as a Boy Scout, like someone we know."

It was true, he had started out pretty green. But that was in '89, before he witnessed the bloody revolution and before he had been forced to kill. Now he had killed again, and each time he felt the weight of a soul adding to the burden on his conscience. But he told himself that killing was an unfortunate but necessary part of his job. Did he believe in Boris's Pearly Gates? He chose to follow what the New Agers professed, that each person had chosen this life in order to learn.

And he had already learned a great deal: How a parent feels when his child is threatened; how to accept his own heritage—Greek, not Roma—though his peripatetic spirit was closer to that of a gypsy's; and how to accept his new wealth, and the power that it provided. Finally, he now knew that, despite his loving family, the Agency afforded him a home and a purpose that nothing else could match.

On top of it all, he had learned more about Boris, though he couldn't say he now knew the man that much better. Another Greek philosopher, Heraclitus, once said, "character is destiny." If so, Boris's character needed to be assessed by his life, his legacy. What was that legacy? That Boris had been a superb spy and master of disguises was evident. But Boris had also been a father who had sent his boy to America in the hope of a better life. And later, when that boy had revolted against his adoptive parents and had threatened to spy for the KGB, Boris had tried to protect him by reluctantly agreeing to be his KGB handler, while never passing the intel to his masters.

But Boris was also a mystic, believing in world peace and the elevation of the human spirit. He imagined himself as Janus, the god who faced two directions, not past and future, but East and West. He had created a system of worldwide assets that delivered intel through The Watchman system, which he then used to degrade and grind down the two sides toward a breathless détente. The U.S. and Russia had already completed such agreements, and more would come. Perhaps Boris was an idealist, as Tyler had labeled him.

Yet Boris had told Hefflin that man was a flawed creature that always wanted to get the better of his neighbor, that brutal competition was the basis of evolution and capitalism. That was the reason that both communism and religion were failing, Boris, the realist, had said.

So, was Boris an idealist, a realist, or a mystic? What did he really believe in? Did he believe in anything? Who the hell was Boris?

A riddle, wrapped in a mystery, inside an enigma.

His reverie was interrupted by Catherine, who now stopped in midstride, her gaze focused on something in the middle distance. Hefflin followed the direction of her focus until he saw it. His blood froze.

"Am I hallucinating or is it really there?" Catherine asked.

"It's there all right," Hefflin said.

Boris's tree had a chalk mark on it, horizontal this time.

"Fourth tree from the fifth bench," Hefflin said out loud.

They stared at each other, speechless, the beginnings of horror seeping onto their faces.

"What does it mean?" Catherine asked.

He counted the benches and trees and knelt down before an old maple.

"Don't look," Catherine said. "Let's pretend we haven't seen it."

"I have to." He didn't care who saw him; he needed to know. He dug up the earth with his pen until he found the spike. After cleaning it, he pulled off the top. Inside he found a piece of paper. They huddled next to each other as he read aloud:

Dear Vasili,

I hope you do not think you are home free. Ceausescu's money is tainted. At the very least, it should be shared.

Anonymous

AUTHOR'S NOTE

The tragedy of Romania, and of most of the other former Soviet satellite countries that finally escaped communism, is that the transition to democracy was slow, rocky, incomplete, and corrupt. The old communist nomenklatura realized that this transition gave them a unique opportunity to become immensely wealthy. Employing various schemes, including the use of the dossiers in the vast archives of their security services to blackmail politicians, judges, industry managers, bankers, and anyone else who stood in their way, the old nomenklatura acquired newly privatized industries at bargain basement prices.

Corruption is a pervasive aspect of most post-communist countries. During the post-communist era, the wealth of these oligarchs has increased exponentially. The old communist system based on relationships, bribes, bureaucratic powerbrokers, and theft of government funds has flourished in the post-communist era. Bribes are an accepted part of life, from the lowest bureaucratic ranks up to the highest levels of government, and vast fortunes are made from government contracts that go to family and friends. Some leaders even tout these acts of crony capitalism as a positive effort to create a stable upper class that will guarantee the success of democracy.

To this day, the oligarchs of Romania continue to wield vast influence on the government, no matter which political party is in charge. Even though Romania and many other post-communist countries became members of NATO and the European Union, they have consistently been listed as some of the most corrupt nations in Europe. That should not come as a surprise. The old communist regimes were based on secret relationships, bribes, threats, and blackmail. Generations of people grew up on that system. It will take generations to grow out of it.

BOOK CLUB
DISCUSSION QUESTIONS

1. How would you define the oligarchs of Romania? How did they acquire their wealth?

2. Do you think that the oligarchs of Russia and the other countries of the former Soviet Union are similar or dissimilar to those in Romania? If dissimilar, how?

3. Why does Bill Hefflin oppose the oligarchs and why does Elliot Ingram, the director of operations at the CIA, support them?

4. How do the "oligarchs" in the countries of the former Soviet Union differ from the "wealthy" in America?

5. Boris—suspected mole in the CIA—double agent—triple agent—an idealist—a realist—a mystic? What was Boris's aim in sharing intelligence with both the East and West?

6. Who are the gypsies and where do they come from? What is their preferred name? Why does Hefflin think his mother might be the gypsy Tanti Bobo?

7. Why does Hefflin feel rootless, temporary, without a true identity?

8. Did you feel supportive of Catherine when she left her son in Antibes to fly to Bucharest to face her demon, Nicu Ceausescu? Do you think that Catherine was right to keep her past with Nicu Ceausescu secret from Hefflin?

9. What did you think about Hefflin as a father and did that impression change by the conclusion of the novel?

PUBLISHER'S NOTE

We hope that you enjoyed *The Bucharest Legacy: The Rise of the Oligarchs.*

The first in the series is *The Bucharest Dossier*, which introduces Bill Hefflin. The two novels stand on their own and can be read in any order. Here's a brief summary of *The Bucharest Dossier*:

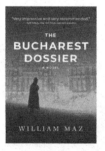

CIA analyst Bill Hefflin becomes embroiled in Romania's bloody revolution of 1989 as he seeks to decipher the identity of his KGB asset and find his lost love. But in the world of Cold War espionage where life is cheap, nothing is as it seems—including Hefflin's own illusory past.

"[*The Bucharest Dossier* is] an accomplished debut—a love story inside an espionage thriller inside a historical record, with all three elements working together to maximum effect. Very impressive and very recommended."   —Lee Child,
New York Times best-selling author

We hope that you will enjoy reading *The Bucharest Dossier,* William Maz's prior novel, and that you will look forward to more to come.

For more information,
please visit William Maz's website:
www.williammaz.com

If you liked *The Bucharest Legacy,* we would be very appreciative if you would consider leaving a review. As you probably already know, book reviews are important to authors and they are very grateful when a reader makes the special effort to write a review, however brief.

Happy Reading,
Oceanview Publishing
Your Home for Mystery, Thriller, and Suspense